. . . BUT TOO LATE SMART

When her men were in place, the captain nodded and the door swung silently inward. The pilgrims were clustered at the porthole, staring out at the raging sea. The captain saw the young man turn, saw his mouth open . . . then she fired the poisoned crossbow bolt.

It took her several heartbeats to realize what had happened next. Her tingling fingers reached up in disbelief to touch the arrow suddenly embedded in her own throat. Imprinted on her shocked brain was the image of the young man catching the poisoned bolt in midair, then hurling it back toward her. The fatal blow had been dealt . . . by a shining silver hand.

She knew them then, but it was too late.

THE ARCANA SERIES:

Silverhand
Silverlight

ALSO BY MORGAN LLYWELYN:

Lion of Ireland
Bard
Druids
Red Branch
The Horse Goddess
The Last Prince of Ireland
Finn Mac Cool

ALSO BY MICHAEL SCOTT:

Tales of the Bard
Banshee
Image
Reflection

EDITOR:
Irish Folk and Fairy Tales, Vol. I-III

MORGAN LLYWELYN

SILVERLIGHT

MICHAEL SCOTT

THE ARCANA, BOOK II

SILVERLIGHT: THE ARCANA, BOOK II

This is a work of fiction. All the characters and events portrayed in this book are fictional, and any resemblance to real people or incidents is purely coincidental.

Copyright © 1996 by Morgan Llywelyn and Michael Scott

A Baen Books Original

Baen Publishing Enterprises
P.O. Box 1403
Riverdale, NY 10471

ISBN: 0-671-87790-9

Cover art by Clyde Caldwell

First paperback printing, July 1997

Distributed by Simon & Schuster
1230 Avenue of the Americas
New York, NY 10020

Library of Congress Catalog Number: 96-7635

Printed in the United States of America

for Brian Daley,
a hero
gone adventuring

What makes a man?

What distinguishes him from the beasts?

And when does a man become more or less than a man? What makes him a god . . . or a demon?

This I have learned: the line that divides man from beast and beast from demon is far finer than the line that separates man from godhood.

From the Journal of Caeled Silverhand

CHAPTER ONE

Perhaps they were pilgrims, but the captain had her doubts. Misha had sailed the Island Sea for twenty cycles, eight of those as captain of her own vessel. She had carried warriors and traders, nobility and slaves, adjusting her prices and manners accordingly, and survived where so many others had failed because she knew how to read people. She could recognize those who would bargain and those who would fight, those who were desperate and those who did not care. She could tell it in their eyes, their voices, the way they moved.

These four so-called pilgrims were full of contradictions. They dressed like priests but walked like warriors; they shunned the company of others but Misha could detect no diffidence in their posture.

The ship's captain gazed with speculative eyes at the mysterious group now huddled on the foredeck. Each morning they spent a brief time there, leaning on the rail and examining sky and sea with an avidity more appropriate to sailors than to pilgrims. The four had taken passage in Sansen, where one young man did all the talking. In educated accents he had claimed they were

1

making their way to the holy well at Tonne, supposedly the site of the lost city of Lowstone.

They were bundled in hooded cloaks, and masked and gloved in the manner of the lepers who sought the well's curative powers. But Misha had observed that their spokesman showed no sign of the disease. In fact none of them *moved* as though diseased, not the grossly fat, green-eyed one who made the deck creak when he walked, nor the burly man with shaggy blond hair escaping from beneath his hood who moved with such animal grace.

The fourth member of the party was undoubtedly female. Misha had glimpsed the outline of high, rounded breasts beneath her cloak, and a tumble of dark curls framed her masked face. She too seemed healthy enough on the brief occasions when she and her companions appeared on deck. Unlike the other passengers, these four seemed to prefer their cramped, stinking cabin and spent most of their time below decks.

On more than one occasion Misha had heard sounds emanating from that cabin which should never have issued from human throats.

The wind shifted. When Misha looked up to check the sails, the long queue of hair depending from the back of her otherwise shaven skull slid across her shoulder like a crimson snake. There was a storm coming out of the north; she could smell ice in the wind. It might be what the Island peoples called a Shipkiller—a sudden gale whipping up huge seas that could take an unwary captain by surprise and dash a vessel to splinters on the serrated shore of one of the islands.

Misha turned to bark an order to Kupp, her first mate, but he was already swinging the wheel, bringing the ship in toward the nearest island. They would ride out the storm in a sheltered bay.

Misha's gaze returned to the pilgrims. Pilgrims indeed! She hawked and spat over the side. They were no more pilgrims than she was. Fugitives, more like. Usually she would not have cared, so long as the passage was paid— in New Coin, in advance. She did not care what paying passengers called themselves, nor what crimes they might have committed.

But these four . . .

The young man, their spokesman, was making his way along the swaying deck toward her. He moved like a trained warrior, carrying all the balance in his hips. Through the slits of his mask his dark, piercing eyes could be seen constantly moving, watching.

"We've changed course," he said, pausing two full paces away from Misha. It was a statement, not a question.

Deliberately nonchalant, the captain canted her body sideways to lean one elbow on the rail. The salt-encrusted leather tunic she wore creaked with the motion. "There's a storm coming up," she said, pitching her voice so low it was barely audible above the snap of the sails and the slap of the sea. It was a tactic she often used to bring people nearer to her. She wanted a closer look at this pilgrim.

As he stepped closer to her, Misha felt a wave of intensity emanating from him that made her catch her breath in surprise. She had lived her life on the waves, attuned to the forces of nature: this man exuded an almost palpable energy.

"Where are we headed?" His voice was level, measured, the diction crisp and precise, but she could not place his accent.

"Straight ahead," she replied, pointing. "See that low island in the distance?"

The young man squinted. "Does it have a name?"

"There are countless islands in this sea, so many that only the Islanders themselves can tell you the names of most of them. I can identify some of the larger ones, but I'm not even sure this island has a name. It may not even be on the chart."

"How long will we need to stay there?"

Misha shrugged. "Until the storm passes over."

"And how long could that be?"

"A day, two, ten." She shrugged again. "Who knows? But which would you prefer: that we sail on and sink, or spend some time at anchor? At least this way you will reach your shrine alive. And which shrine is it again?" she asked abruptly, hoping to catch him off guard.

His voice remained calm. "The holy well at Tonne. Do you know it?"

"By reputation," Misha murmured.

The young man leaned toward her now, reading her as she had been reading him. Again she felt that wave of intensity. In spite of herself, her heart began to thud heavily, though whether with fear or attraction she could not have said. "Have you ever visited the well?" he asked her.

He was so close she could smell him, a mingled scent of cloth and flesh and sweat and . . . and metal? The mystery deepened. Misha tried to keep her voice casual as she replied, "I have never been to the well myself. But I once transported a group of pilgrims who had to be carried on to the island on litters, they were so crippled with disease. When they returned to my ship, they came walking." She made a gesture with her hand, index and thumb forming a circle, then flicking away evil spirits. "At night the sky above the island glows green and blue," she added, unexpectedly dodging to one side, trying to glimpse the man behind the mask. But she only had time to see that he was swarthy and strong-featured before he pulled the hood of his cloak around his face, hiding his broad forehead and thick dark hair. He moved too hastily, like someone with something to hide.

Misha grinned. "Do I frighten you?"

"My religion forbids contact with those not of my caste," the young man replied. He took a step backward, made a sketchy bow, then turned on his heel and hurried away.

His heavy cloak could not conceal the tension in his posture.

The captain ran her hand across her shaved skull, adjusting the long plait of red hair as she watched him gather his companions and disappear below decks. She was stocky, muscular, with a heavy jaw, but she was a woman with a woman's instincts and the young man had disturbed her on many levels. His nervousness reassured her, however. He and his party were probably just another group of the hopeful and credulous, desperate for a cure. They hid some loathsome disease beneath their robes after all; a disfigurement he did not want her to see.

Misha bared her teeth in a humorless smile; putting them out of their misery would be a blessing.

The wide-bodied caravel found shelter in a small bay, where two wings of land protected the vessel like encircling arms. Once they entered the bay the wind dropped immediately, sails on the four masts cracking and snapping. Misha remained on the foredeck until the mainsail and the lateen sails were furled and made secure and the last of the crew went below. Then, after taking a final look around, the captain made her way to the safety of her own cabin.

Even though they were in the shelter of the bay, she knew what could happen to any living thing caught on deck. The Shipkiller drove a solid wall of sleet before it, razor-sharp needles of ice propelled with irresistible force. Such a storm could not only strip paint and tar and shred the sails—it could flay flesh from bone, turning a human being into bloody pulp in a matter of heartbeats. On some of the more primitive islands, criminals tied to stakes were put in the path of a Shipkiller. It was an effective method of execution and savage enough to provide a deterrent. What little remained after the storm passed was tossed into the sea.

The captain pulled a heavy wooden shutter across the polished horn porthole of her cabin just as the first spatters of ice struck the deck above. In moments the hail was drumming on the *Black Pearl* to such an extent it blotted out all other sound.

Misha reached under her bunk and pulled out a small hand-held crossbow, almost a miniature. It was Gallowan work, intricately detailed. She had found it among the possessions of a Gallowan mercenary taking the pilgrim trail in hopes of curing the disease that was slowly eating away his flesh. Misha had put him out of his misery, too. And very profitably.

Bracing the weapon against her broad leather belt, she armed the bow by fitting a tiny bolt into the groove. The pointed head of the crossbow bolt was coated with a mixture of fish oils; death would be swift and agonizing as the lungs froze. When she stepped out into the corridor, Kupp, the first mate, and two of the crew were waiting for her. The mate carried a cutlass; the crewmen had saw-toothed seashell daggers that tore flesh so badly it could never be stitched.

They did not speak to one another. Any sound they made could not be heard above the din of the storm anyway, Misha thought with satisfaction. Moving in easy unison—they had performed this task many times—they positioned themselves outside the door of the pilgrims' cabin. The two sailors stood on either side, the first mate crouched by the latch. Misha placed herself directly opposite the door.

When her men were in place, the captain bared her teeth in a savage grimace and nodded. Kupp lifted the latch with the tip of his cutlass. The door was weighted to swing silently inward. As Misha expected, the pilgrims were clustered at the porthole, staring out at the raging sea. She saw the young man turn, saw his mouth open to question . . . then she fired the poisoned crossbow bolt.

It took Misha several heartbeats to realize what had happened next.

Her tingling fingers reached up in disbelief to touch

the arrow suddenly embedded in her own throat. Imprinted on her shocked brain was the image of the young man catching the poisoned bolt in midair, then sending it spinning back toward her.

Simultaneously the fat man whirled around, tossing his cloak aside. But he was not a fat man. The figure was that of a woman, unnaturally massive.

Kupp drove his knife into the woman's stomach, only to have the weapon shatter to powder against an impervious surface. The woman responded by pulping the first mate's head with one blow of her stony fist.

Meanwhile Misha felt her lungs closing down as the poison did its work. She writhed with pain; her knees buckled and she slid to the floor, clawing at her throat and screaming silently for air.

The two sailors shouldered their way into the cabin, one stepping over her body, but they were also doomed. The burly blond man lashed out with an animal-like agility to claw the face off the first sailor as effortlessly as the Shipkiller would have done.

At the same time, the dark young man who had caught and rethrown the bolt from the crossbow stripped the glove from one of his hands. He chopped the chest of the last sailor, whose eyes rolled back in his head as his heart stopped. He was dead by the time he hit the floor.

Misha's dimming eyes informed her the fatal blow had been dealt . . . by a shining silver hand.

She knew them then, but it was too late.

CHAPTER TWO

"Clever . . . very clever," Gwynne rasped. She lifted the captain's head, turned it from side to side and then allowed it to drop back. "Now this ship has no captain."

"And the rest of the crew will be upset," blond Madran added with a grin that revealed abnormally white incisors and overdeveloped canines. "But do we care?"

Caeled stripped off his cloak and draped it across the dead captain. The gesture revealed a peculiar keepsake he wore on a thong around his neck: an incomplete gold ring, a setting without a stone.

"No one heard anything with all this noise," he assured his companions, raising his trained voice to resonate above the roar of the Shipkiller. "As soon as the storm clears, we should abandon ship." He paused and closed his eyes, trying to visualize this portion of the Seven Nations. "We're right at the edge of the Island Sea. Seamount is the principal island and has a sizeable port; if we can get that far, we should be able to book passage on some other ship without too many questions being asked."

Taking advantage of the fact that Caeled's eyes were closed, Sioraf bent over Misha's body and turned down the edge of the cloak to uncover the dead face. As the slender young woman stared down, faint spots of color crept into her usually pale cheeks. Slowly, with infinite delicacy, she licked her lips.

Meanwhile Gwynne wrapped her own cloak around herself once more, hiding arms and throat with the texture of weathered stone. "Why can't we remain on board this ship?" she wanted to know. "We can force the crew to take us to Tonne."

Madran shook his shaggy head. "Too dangerous. News of our arrival would spread like wildfire, they would never keep quiet about what had happened."

Opening his eyes abruptly, Caeled snapped at Sioraf, "Don't touch her, her blood contains poison!"

Sioraf had already begun enlarging the wound in the captain's throat, but at his command she stood up reluctantly and turned her vivid blue gaze in Caeled's direction. "What about the others?" she wanted to know, indicating the dead men.

Caeled allowed himself a small smile. "I suppose they're harmless."

"They are now," chuckled Madran. "But listen to me, Gwynne. I grant you, we might be able to control the crew on board ship, but once we got to Tonne and they talked to the authorities, we would be arrested as murderers."

Gwynne nudged the broken body of one of the dead crewmen with her foot. As she moved, the wooden planking creaked beneath her weight. Her nickname— the Stone Warrior—was well deserved. "They tried to murder us, we were acting in self-defense."

Sioraf replied, "I'm not sure the inhabitants of Tonne would believe us. When you are a stranger, or . . . strange . . . everyone is against you, in my experience."

Caeled raised his left hand. Light ran molten across the silver metal. "Listen."

"The hail has stopped," said Madran. "And the wind's falling." His moist brown eyes gazed blankly into space as he cocked his head, concentrating on the messages his ears were bringing him.

Caeled nodded. "Let's be gone before the crew reappear on deck." He lifted a cloth-wrapped bundle from the floor and tossed it over his shoulder, affixing it as a pack on his back. Then he picked up Misha's small crossbow and armed it with a bolt from the tubular leather quiver fastened to her belt.

Madran's nostrils flared. "That's a powerful poison. Our captain wasn't taking any chances."

"She took one too many," said Gwynne. Hefting a morningstar, her own weapon of choice, she eased open the door and peered down the corridor. "No one in sight. Let's be gone."

In single file, the four mismatched companions left the cabin. Caeled, who was taking up the rear, pulled the door shut, then squeezed the latch so tightly with his metal hand that it could not be reopened.

The deck looked as if it had been freshly scrubbed. In the wake of the Shipkiller, bare boards gleamed. A few final pellets of hail pattered onto the scoured surface. Beyond the mouth of the bay, the sea was churned to white froth as the storm moved on, dragging curtains of black cloud across a sullen grey sky.

There were red stains on the water where some sea creature swimming too close to the surface had been flayed by the hail.

While Madran and Gwynne lowered the ship's single boat over the side, Sioraf hastily gathered supplies, keeping one eye cocked for the emergence of the crew from belowdecks. But they seemed in no hurry to reappear as she packed dried fruit, wheels of hard cheese, salted meat and biscuits into a barrel. Caeled ran down the deck to a great crossbow mounted in the stern. He was certain the weapon had never been used to harpoon whales. Given Misha's predilections, it must have had a more sinister purpose. He slashed the thick cord with his knife and snapped off the trigger mechanism with his metal hand.

"Why did you do that?" Sioraf asked when he rejoined her to help roll the barrel across the deck.

"I didn't want anyone firing at us."

When the supplies were aboard the small boat, Gwynne waited until Madran and Sioraf had taken up positions in the bow before she slowly lowered herself into the stern. Her weight tilted the bow up out of the water; waves slopped in over the sides. Caeled wrapped a rope around the barrel and lowered it from the deck of the ship. Sioraf and Madran eased it into place, using it to help counterbalance Gwynne.

Caeled was just climbing over the side to join them when the first crewman appeared.

He was a flat-faced Islander, deeply tanned, eyes buried within folds of skin, skull shaven except for a shining blue-black topknot. "You there! What do you think you're doing?"

Caeled glanced over his shoulder. He could leap down into the boat below—and probably capsize it.

"Who are you?" the Islander demanded. There was a shell knife in his hand now.

Caeled realized the crewman had not recognized him without his cloak. "I was just . . ." he began.

"You were just climbing aboard to see what you could steal," the crewman snapped. "Island Trash!" His right hand shot out, blade levelled in a slashing stroke designed to scar. Caeled caught the knife in his left hand and shattered the shell blade. Then with his right hand he struck the Islander in the throat, crushing his windpipe. The man's face turned purplish red as he struggled for breath. Caeled finished him with a single blow to the temple, then tossed him overboard.

He had barely reached the boat when the other crewmen appeared on deck. They ran to the rail and leaned over, shouting.

Gripping the oars, Gwynne pulled, and the laden boat leaped away from the ship.

Furious shouts and curses were hurled after them.
"Island Trash!"

A spear sang through the air, entering the water with
a hiss.

Sioraf tapped Caeled's shoulder and pointed to a couple
of men struggling futilely over the disabled whaling gun.

Propelled by Gwynne's massive strength, the small boat
was rapidly moving out of range even if they got the
weapon working.

"What is Island Trash?" Sioraf asked Caeled.

"Men and women washed ashore on the Islands after
being deliberately set adrift as punishment for some crime,"
he told her. He had a sudden, vivid memory of reading
about such things when he had been in the College at
Baddalaur for three or possibly four cycles, studying in
the Great Library. He had discovered a water-damaged
book of mariners' tales forgotten amid the stacks, and read
with fascination of the Island Sea and the Barbarian Isles.
He had never expected to visit them—then.

But so much had changed.

Once he had been Caeled nam Myriam, a simple
scholar . . . now he was Silverhand, one of the most wanted
men in the Nations, with his description posted in every
town. "A young man of above middle height, dark hair
and eyes, with a left hand of silver metal. The Duet offer
a huge reward for his capture—alive."

Caeled knew why they wanted him alive; no doubt
the twins had prepared an eternity of suffering for the
man who had thwarted them and all but destroyed their
specially-bred army.

Once he believed his life would be spent in the College
as a member of the Order of the Seekers of the Way,
poring over the books he had learned to love. But that
peaceful dream had ended abruptly when the army of
the Bred destroyed the College, together with the resident
Seekers and Scholars. The library was burned, its ancient
wisdom lost forever together with all known history of

the Elder Times. Caeled found that almost harder to bear than the deaths of so many of his friends.

He had a new destiny now: to destroy the twins, who seemed intent on bringing chaos to the world. Once he would have thought it an impossible mission. The Duet were less than gods, perhaps, but more than human.

But weapons of great power had been put into Caeled's hands. He knew the location of two of the Arcana, the ancient symbols which reputedly could restore order to the entropic world.

Now he was travelling with three companions who each had their own reasons to hate the Duet. Sarel and Lares, the incestuous twins who ruled the Seven Nations from their capital at Barrow, had made deadly enemies.

Gwynne had seen her entire family destroyed by a Void, a whirling sphere of appalling destruction generated by the twins. The same Void had snatched her child off her back and blighted her flesh with its bitter force. Her skin was hardening to a granitelike crust, so that men called her the Stone Warrior. There was a possibility the twins might be able to reverse the process, if they chose, but Gwynne no longer cared. Now she lived for revenge. She had sworn to destroy the twins before her affliction rendered her completely immobile.

Madran was of the Madra Allta, one of the were-clans, cursed—or blessed—with the ability to assume the shape of a dog. His only daughter, Pup, had been slain by the Bred army.

Sioraf's father had been the circus master of a small travelling troupe that included Madran and Pup. He too had fallen to the talons and teeth of the Bred. His last thoughts had been for his daughter. Because her mother had been a vampire, Sioraf belonged at least in part to that once-great race which required blood for nourishment.

With the emotional detachment of the vampire, Sioraf felt no desire to avenge herself on the Duet. She stayed with Caeled because he shared his blood with her, and she had grown to depend upon him. But because he hated the Duet they had become her enemies as well; in rare instances, the vampiri exhibited a singular capacity for loyalty.

The four companions in their tiny craft were an odd assortment indeed.

Suddenly Madran pointed to an object in the air above the boat. "Peist!"

The others looked up at a tiny creature with glittering wings, fluttering past them in the wan light of the reemerging sun. "It's a messenger," Gwynne affirmed. "The ship is trying to send word to Noone; word about us, most likely."

"Would they be carrying many peist aboard?" Caeled asked her. He reached for the crossbow he had taken from Misha's body.

"One probably," Madran said. "They're expensive."

Caeled lifted the crossbow and sighted on the flying insect, which was no longer than his hand. A message scroll would be glued to its back carrying news of four passengers who had killed the captain and some of the crew and escaped.

If they were very unlucky, someone would have caught a glimpse of Caeled's silver hand and included that information in the message.

This part of the Island Sea included a main shipping channel, he knew. It would only be a matter of time before the Duet were informed of his whereabouts.

He swiftly calculated wind speed and the insect's flight path, allowed for the rocking of the boat . . . and raised the crossbow.

"You're wasting your time," Gwynne grunted sourly.

Caeled fired.

"You'll never hit it . . ."

The peist disappeared in an explosion of rainbow-hued wings.

". . . at this distance."

CHAPTER THREE

The woman screamed again and again, the sound echoing off the stone walls of the cell. She lay naked and spread-eagled on the metal bed, with her wrists and ankles manacled. When she tossed her head in agony, matted hair clung to her perspiring face.

Hoi was in the final throes of labor.

The pains had come on her quickly, bending her double with both hands clutching at her almost flat belly. She had writhed on the dirty straw of one of the holding pens while acid pain tore through her body and gnawed her vitals. The other women in the pens had moved quickly away, frightened by the savage guttural language of the Steppes in which she called for help. Her cries had brought the guards. They lined the barred walls and waited until the one known as the Breeder appeared. He had regarded the suffering woman impassively, with blank, dead eyes, while his pointed tongue constantly wetted his cracked and swollen lips.

Once he had been a handsome man, but now it was as if his face had caved in on itself. Angular bones were prominent beneath pallid flesh; his eyes were sunken, his cheeks deep hollows. Remnants of once-luxuriant hair clung to his skull in tufts.

Even in her pain, Hoi heard the Breeder's mirthless chuckle. "It is time. Take her."

In the moons since she was taken from the Steppes as a slave, Hoi had never given up hope of escape. She knew that her people would be looking for her. They would never give up until they either had her living body or her corpse. They would take her home no matter what condition they found her in. She was *Shu'steppe*, a child of the Steppes, and the nomads never abandoned one of their own.

When she had heard she was being sold into the palace, she felt a twinge of hope. Surely among so many other servants, it would be easy to slip away? Not immediately, maybe not even soon, but one day—if she was careful never to call attention to herself, and used her position of trust to learn all the passages and exits.

But Hoi had not been sold as a palace servant. Along with a score of young women, she was taken to the dungeons beneath the palace. She found herself in a bizarre chamber with walls, floors and ceilings of metal, the light a diffuse glow that washed color out of everything.

And then the nightmares began.

The man known as the Breeder was at the heart of the nightmares. No expression crossed his dead face as he examined the girls with cold, insensitive fingers, probing, pressing, pinching. Those who resisted were beaten with clinical precision. They received savage blows to the face and limbs, but never to the torso.

Sometimes, in Hoi's dream, a woman came to watch. She had hair the color of amber and eyes of shimmering violet, and Hoi had seen her breasts heave excitedly as she watched the Breeder beating a woman. The *Shu'steppe* knew the type: men and women who took pleasure from the giving and receiving of pain. Among the Steppe tribes such people were called Painlords and considered an abomination.

The amber-haired woman was unfailingly present during the worst of the nightmares, the terrible violations.

The dreams were always the same. It was only later, much later, when Hoi compared her story with some of the other women, that she realized they were more than dreams.

She was tied facedown across a metal bed, her naked flesh pressed against the cold, unyielding surface. A neck brace held her head locked in one position. Out of the corner of her eye, she was aware that something was moving behind her, something dark and monstrous that filled the air with a dry stench like a den of snakes.

The Breeder was there too, and the woman with amber hair.

The dream invariably ended with Hoi breathing in the sickeningly sweet odor of black lotus, from a bowl held close to her face.

Everything faded away, then . . . and she would awake with her groin sore and aching, a feeling like a terrible burn inside her belly.

The last dream was two moons ago . . . and since then she had begun to feel *different*. Her breasts swelled and became painfully sensitive, but her belly did not swell. At the end of the moon cycle the goddess touched her as usual, releasing the cleansing flow, so she knew she could not be with child.

Then one day the unexpected agony ripped through her and she fell to the floor screaming, wracked with labor pains.

"Soon," the Breeder murmured. His fingertips were resting on Hoi's stomach, assessing the convulsions beneath the skin. "Soon." He looked up as the amber-haired woman strode across the chamber toward him.

The crystal heels of her slippers made a clicking sound on the metal floor.

"It is time?" she asked eagerly.

"It is, Majesty. I brought her to term early before the babe could grow too large. I believe that was the problem . . . before."

Sarel, one half of the Duet, rulers of the Seven Nations, watched the woman writhing in pain on the metal bed as she had watched eight women before her. None of those had survived.

With a sudden arcing spasm, the woman threw herself against her restraints so forcibly bone and tendon crackled. A final scream, ear-splitting and insane, was torn from her . . . as her offspring was born.

The Breeder swiftly scooped it up, turning its small head from side to side as he examined the shape and structure, then slid his fingers down the little body to check the alignment of ribs and spine. When he was satisfied, he laid the newborn on its mother's stomach. The infant's mouth opened and closed reflexively,

"A live birth. At last!" the Breeder exclaimed as the newborn began to pull itself up the length of Hoi's body. "Now our new breeding program truly begins."

Sarel's fingers tightened on the Breeder's arm as the babe opened its mouth and sank curving fangs into its mother's throat. Hoi died without ever seeing the monster she had birthed.

"Human and saurian," Sarel said approvingly. "The speed and strength of the carnivorous lizard, the viciousness and intelligence of the human."

The Breeder responded, "Once I bred you a mutant army, but they were hopeless failures compared to what we are developing now. These creatures should mature with astonishing speed as a result of stimulating their growth glands with your miniature Voids. In one cycle of the moon they could be strong enough for war. Of course, you *do* understand that such swift maturation postulates a very short life span?"

Sarel shrugged. "They are expendable."

As she watched with a cold and clinical interest, the tiny lizardlike creature with the human face coiled its tail around its dead mother's breast and began to chew her throat.

course, you do understand that such a task must not be undertaken . . . er, carelessly, or at all."

"I shall undertake it seriously," Paedur replied.

Siena watched Paedur . . . and alchemist limp into the . . . it familiar country with the . . . former associated to fall away and, as the chill . . . a breeze and began to blow, he drew his . . .

CHAPTER FOUR

Gwynne drove her stony fist through the bottom of the boat. For good measure she planted several well-aimed kicks against its sides, then stood back to survey her handiwork with satisfaction. No one would use the boat again.

She turned and struggled up the beach to join the others. "Where are we?" she panted as she reached them. Her weight caused her to sink deep in the sand with every step, and her heart was pounding furiously in her chest. There were times she thought this was how she would die: her heart bursting with the effort of supplying blood to her massive, unnatural body.

Caeled glanced at her as he fastened the little crossbow atop his heavy pack, then settled the pack on his shoulders and adjusted the straps. The long shaft of what appeared to be a spear jutted from the underside of the pack, making carrying it awkward. "This is the Island Sea," he replied, "and there are over seven hundred charted islands. Perhaps twice that many are unexplored. We could be on any of them." He turned to Madran. "What does your nose tell you?"

The muscular blond-haired man lifted his head and

sniffed the wind like an animal. His flaring nostrils quivered. "Not much," he reported. "Nothing of any importance, anyway."

Pointing up the beach with the blade of the sickle he carried—his own favorite weapon—he elaborated, "There's some animal spoor over there. Wildcat, I think. Bit too flat smelling for a marsh lion. Further inland I get the scent of boar, probably pack boar. Animals no bigger than a small canine, but they hunt in packs and can bring a man down and tear him apart before he knows he's killed."

"How jolly," remarked the often-sarcastic Gwynne.

"They're eating," Sioraf said in her whispery voice. "I can smell blood."

Madran nodded agreement. "They won't want to share. Better we go the other direction."

With no further discussion Caeled set off toward a line of steep cliffs rising beyond the last curve of beach. They were deeply indented, comprised of horizontal striations of pale ochre and creamy yellow and greyish mauve that gave way to darker, mysterious shadowings. "Those cliffs look promising," he called over his shoulder to his companions as they set off after him. "We might find some caves among them."

"What do we need with caves?" Gwynne demanded to know as she stumped along reluctantly. "Why slog all the way over there when we could stay right here on the beach and make camp?"

Caeled glanced back with a quick, almost boyish smile. "Shipkillers come in threes, I have read. . . ." He pointed upward.

The Stone Warrior looked up and swore like a sailor. The sky was darkening again; great purple clouds boiled out of the north. She began to trot ponderously toward the cliffs. Even if her toughened skin was able to deflect the hail, her eyes would still be vulnerable, and Gwynne's green eyes were almost her last remaining vestige of physical humanity.

Madran growled, Sioraf gasped. They all began to run.

In spite of the heavy pack on his back, Caeled sped effortlessly over the deep, reddish sand. The training he had received in Baddalaur included such skills as keeping one's balance on a spinning barrel in a pool, or running along a sagging rope suspended between two poles. "Tiny movements," his trainer, the Seeker Armadiel, called from the recesses of memory. "Gross movements upset the balance. Tiny movements always, light and quick but economical."

Glimpsing the yawning mouth of a cave at the base of the cliffs, Caeled veered to his left and ran toward it, trusting his companions to follow. In the last two moons they had allowed him to make the decisions—primarily because of two items he now carried in his pack.

The cavemouth was in shadow, but it looked deep enough to accommodate the four of them. Stones rattled underfoot as Caeled left the last strip of sand and clambered up an incline of loose scree. With his eyes fixed on the treacherous footing, he did not see a dark shape take form within the lesser darkness of the cavemouth.

Sioraf's scream startled him. As he turned back toward her, stones shifted beneath his feet and then the earth seemed to drop out from under him. He fell with a crash onto the scree, quite accidentally avoiding a spear that struck the ground a hand's distance from his head and planted itself there, shaft quivering.

He was scrambling to his feet and tugging the little crossbow free from its straps as the creature from the cave hurtled down upon him. Caeled caught a baffling glimpse of both hair and scales. Then the overwhelming odor of rotten fish washed over him in a sickening wave. He reeled back as webbed hands closed around his head.

The entire weight of the creature was flung against him. With an effort Caeled managed to get his left hand free. Rather than striking at the creature, he grabbed a handful of scaly flesh—and tore it loose from the body. His assailant toppled sideways, bellowing in agony.

In the blink of an eye Madran had thrown himself on it and was slashing at it with his sickle. Flesh parted; the howl became a groan. The creature lay thrashing on the loose scree, which slid beneath its movements so that it slipped farther down from the cavemouth.

Sioraf and Gwynne circled it cautiously, watching the stubby tail lash, the mouth gape as death approached.

"What is it?" Sioraf whispered, extending a hand to help Caeled to his feet.

He started to shake his head, but stopped when strained neck muscles protested with a stab of pain. "I don't know. I never saw anything like it, even in the books in Baddalaur."

The creature was vaguely humanoid, but had short forelimbs, massively developed legs, and a series of hairy crests like a scalloped mane rippling the length of its spine.

Gwynne squinted down at the monstrosity. "Fishman," she dubbed it succinctly. "Local pest, no doubt. Nasty." When the gaping mouth made a last convulsive effort to swallow air, she drew back her foot and kicked the dying creature in the head with all her might. The skull shattered like a clay pot.

Paying the corpse no further attention, she strode forward and peered into the cave. "It seems empty enough now." Her voice boomed hollowly. "It's dry in here . . . but it stinks." So saying, she disappeared into the darkness.

Madran hurried after her, Sioraf following with more reluctance. Caeled lingered at the mouth of the cave to watch the Shipkiller come racing in. Foaming white water formed a pathway for the storm; white-crested waves leaped high in the air as if to embrace the turbulent sky. There was a first flicker of lightning on the far horizon, thin stalks like the legs of giant insects whose bodies were lost in boiling cloud.

The new Shipkiller seemed larger and more savage than its predecessor. Caeled wondered if the ship which had so recently carried them could possibly survive such a storm.

When the hail struck the beach with such force that clouds of sand exploded upward, Caeled drew back inside the cave. He shucked off his pack and let himself slide down into a sitting position, his back against comfortingly solid stone as he continued to watch the storm.

Seen from inside the cavemouth, the horizon vanished. Then the sea was swallowed up. Only the storm remained, a living, malevolent entity, now sweeping the beach with curtains of black rain. Chunks of ice the size of a man's head slammed into the ground, gouging holes in the sand. Twice Caeled saw huge boulders—obviously damaged by previous storms—shatter. When the Shipkiller reached the dead sea creature, it stripped away the flesh and left the major portions of the skeleton clean and gleaming, although some smaller bones were pulverized. Hailstones pounded the spine until what remained of the corpse leaped and twitched in a parody of life.

Unappeased, the storm raced toward the cliffs.

Caeled reached into his pack and took out an object wrapped in cloth.

He could feel the eyes of his companions on him from where they huddled farther inside the cave, but he did not speak to them. There was nothing to say.

Hail hissed like a nest of serpents as the Shipkiller struck the cliff face. The first billow of wind swirled into the cave.

Brushing strands of black hair out of his eyes, Caeled swiftly unwrapped the Stone. A deft movement released the Spear which had been lashed to the underside of his pack, and this he laid beside the Stone.

"Two of the Arcana; worth a king's ransom," Madran commented. Leaving the rear of the cave he came forward to crouch beside Caeled, gazing at the objects with something akin to awe.

Sand was swirling into their eyes now, making them blink, yet Sioraf came forward too and took up a position on the other side of Caeled. She put one hand on his shoulder. One slim, long-fingered hand, with nails like talons. Through this touch he could feel the vampir trembling.

She had told him once that she was afraid of storms, afraid of the dark, and he had laughed. "You? Afraid of the dark?"

She said simply, "I am always cold and the dark is cold."

He recalled having seen her dance for joy in a ray of warm sunlight, and knew she was telling the truth.

Caeled reached up to give her trembling fingers a reassuring pat, then lifted the Stone. "These things look so ordinary," he observed. "One would never guess . . ."
He was holding what appeared to be a small shield of greenish-grey, stonelike material studded with bosses upon which Elder Script was incised. An intricate filigree of metal wire formed a design connecting the bosses with a hole in the center of the Stone.

As Caeled lifted the object there was a rumble of thunder like an angry roar from the Shipkiller, and a moment later a flash of lightning briefly illuminated the interior of the cave.

A cold blue fire played fretfully over the engraving on the Stone.

Caeled felt a tingling surge through his wrists and into the bones of his body. But discipline had been inculcated into him; in spite of the shock he did not lose his hold on the Stone, one of the most powerful and mysterious relics of the Elder Times, part of the quartet of arcane items known collectively as the Arcana. According to legend, when used together the Arcana had the power to make a world . . . or unmake one.

Reverently, carefully, Caeled set the Stone aside and reached for the Spear.

Sioraf squeezed his shoulder. "Don't. You know what it does to you."

The thunder bellowed again, reverberating through the cave. The Shipkiller was a hungry beast demanding to be fed.

"We need information," Caeled told Sioraf, "and we need it now."

The vampir's fingertips brushed the strands of grey that had recently appeared at Caeled's temples. "They take something from you."

"It doesn't matter."

"It matters to me. When you use the Arcana, your blood tastes . . . *old*."

"I've only used them four times, and the first was by accident," he reminded her.

"And each time left you more exhausted. There's no reason to go through that again, now. We're safe enough for the moment."

"We need to know where we are," he insisted. Madran muttered agreement. Before Sioraf could argue further, Caeled inserted the Spear into the hole in the Stone.

Bracing himself, he raised the head of the Spear so the weapon was tilted at an angle which would allow the Stone to slide slowly down the shaft. The first time this happened had been an accident during battle with the Gor Allta. On that occasion, the two Arcana had rewarded him with a jolt of raw power that almost stopped his heart.

When he subsequently used the Stone and Spear, the result had been considerably diminished. Caeled determined that in some way they were responding to his own emotional state. They must be handled calmly, carefully, to mitigate their danger. The Arcana embodied the force of Order; they could be properly controlled only by an orderly mind.

Closing his eyes, he breathed deeply, stilling his thoughts, using the techniques he had been taught in Baddalaur.

When the Stone reached the base of the Spear there was a loud click. A spark rivalling the lightning flashed through the cave, hurling the young man back against the wall.

And in that instant, he knew . . . everything.

CHAPTER FIVE

The white crow soared over a grey and unformed landscape. Occasionally the bird dipped down, pursuing some tiny spark glimpsed in the greyness, a glimmer of color. At this height in the Aethyra only colors interjected by the strongest mind could be detected in the Dreamscape.

The white crow soared still higher, violet eyes gazing unblinkingly over a world Sarel considered hers. When the mood was on her she wore her human form in the Dreamscape, but usually she preferred the image of the white crow, which allowed her spirit to swoop and soar, birdlike. One of her deepest desires, dating back to the dreams of childhood, was to possess wings. She longed for the power of flight; but in a world when she could have anything she desired, where her every word was law, there were some things even one of the Duet could not buy.

She had spoken to the Breeder about creating a winged species of Bred, but when he explained the necessity for hollow bones in a flying creature and pointed out that such a fragile skeletal structure would make them useless as warriors, she abandoned that idea. Still she

28

toyed with variations of it from time to time. There might be some non-military use for winged humans—as messengers perhaps, or silent assassins.

Now the white crow sank lower through the levels of the Aethyra. Sarel was hunting.

Suddenly a starburst of colors shot through the grey mist where dreams were born. Each color represented a strongly felt emotion in the physical world.

Sarel banked toward them, her albino feathers ruffled by the ghost wind upon which she glided. Almost at once the colors began to fade until only the strongest remained. Sarel ignored the radiant blue and gold of joy, the flaming emerald of ecstasy. Her vision selectively focused on harsh red and stabbing onyx, hues of anger and hatred clearly defined against the greyness.

She plummeted down toward a spike of rage and found at its source a tavern keeper in the poorer part of Barrow, savagely beating a young female servant who refused to bed with him.

No sooner had Sarel observed them, than crimson pain drew her dream-presence through the winding streets to a corner where a wealthy merchant was holding off two would-be thieves. A third robber was lying in the gutter, bleeding profusely. The thieves attacked again, swinging cudgels. The merchant dealt one a savage slice with his flame-edged Amorican dagger, then drove his booted foot against the shin of the other. Sarel heard the bone snap. The merchant fell to attacking his disabled assailants with unbridled savagery, releasing his fear upon them.

Sarel was about to move closer when out of the corner of her eye she glimpsed a bolt of sickening purple that drew her irresistibly. She was swept away to a filthy room in the next street, where a young male prostitute was busy castrating a client who had attempted to cheat him.

Interesting . . . yet none of the emotions held the particular fervor she sought. Disappointed, the white crow soared into the Aethyra once more. The passions she had witnessed were ultimately petty and commonplace, they might be encountered in any city, arising from any circumstance or just from the natural brutishness of the people involved.

Sarel was looking for . . . something else.

Aimlessly, the white crow drifted back towards the palace on the hill, where Sarel's physical body waited. As immaterial as a dream, the image of the bird floated through the wall and hovered above a bed where two naked bodies lay entangled on rumpled silk sheets. Her brother's limbs were entwined with hers, their amber-colored hair mingled on the pillow.

They had made love before she had journeyed into the Aethyra, using the generated power of their sexuality to propel her dream-presence ever further. Now their bodies slept exhausted.

Returning, the white crow let her image fade back into human form just as Lares opened his eyes.

He smiled a drowsy greeting.

Sarel opened her eyes and sat up in bed. Her twin was a shadowy shape beside her, but she did not need to see him to know every detail of his body as well as she knew her own. His slender masculinity was not so different from her athletic feminine form; they had the same hair, the same violet eyes, the same fine-drawn, aristocratic features. Each knew the other better than they could ever know anyone else.

"Anything?" Lares asked, putting a hand on Sarel's arm.

She shook her head. "Nothing, I'm sorry to say."

Lares swore and rolled out of bed. Crossing to the window, he pushed open the leaded glass pane and stared out at the stars. "But he's out there. I know; I can almost feel him."

Sarel rose and went to join him, pressing her naked body against her brother's back. "We'll find him," she promised. "Possibly the Arcana are shielding him, but we will find him." Her voice rang with determination.

They were tracking the Silverhand, an erstwhile Scholar and survivor of the holocaust the Duet had unleashed upon Baddalaur. He now possessed two of the ancient Arcana, the Stone and the Spear. Four times the young man had used the artefacts, and four times the twins had felt the backlash of raw energy as a cold silver light flooded the Aethyra.

Ordinarily, any great expenditure of power lingered around the user, invisible to the naked eye but pulsing like a beacon in the Dreamscape, calling forth the curious . . . and the hungry. But after that brilliant silver flood, no residue remained to mark the presence of Silverhand. Only by instantaneous observation of the wave patterns of energy had Lares and Sarel been able to determine that the former Scholar and his companions were moving in a northeasterly direction.

"Next time," Sarel promised. She wrapped her arms around her brother's waist in a gesture of surprising tenderness. "Next time he uses the Arcana, we'll have him." She tugged gently, urging him back toward their bed and the release of sleep, of dreams. . . .

As they turned away from the window the entire Dreamscape momentarily dissolved in a sheet of silver light.

Caeled pressed his hands to his skull, palms against his temples, eyes squeezed shut, mouth open in a silent scream.

The pain! The pain was always intense, a tearing, rending, shattering sensation inside his skull. His limbs twitched, his fingers flexed spasmodically. He was unaware of his spine arching into a bow, or his heels drumming against the floor of the cave. Then his body went limp.

Images blurred and solidified, sounds took on shape.

"This is the Island Sea." The voice that emerged from

Caeled's mouth spoke in a faintly accented monotone. He turned his head as if to look out the cavemouth, but his eyes were still closed. "This isle is without name," the voice said, "without human habitation, though there are bigger islands inhabited by human and Allta a day's journey from here. Once this was an expanse of solid land, a vast continent that straddled the ocean. When the Elder Times ended and the fabric of the world was altered, the continent shook itself apart. Huge areas of land sank beneath roiling waves, islands rose out of new seas, mountains thrust up from the molten bowels of the earth."

The speaker's hands moved blindly across the Arcana, metal and flesh fingers caressing the filigree of wire set into the Stone, tracing the length of the Spear. Sparks crackled between the metal spearshaft and the silver hand, tracing its shape with strands of blue fire.

"We must be wary," the voice continued, as precise and professorial as if addressing an invisible classroom. "These waters are frequented by the Eron, descendants of the humans who survived the Time of Burning. When their meager supplies of food were exhausted, they took nourishment from the sea. But that food was tainted. First it destroyed their minds, reducing them to the level of primitive beasts. Then with the passing of eons they *changed*. They became more adept at living in the sea. They long ago lost the power of human speech, though they can communicate beneath the waves by whistles and cries. Their singing—which is beautiful, ethereal—has lured many mariners to their doom. Be wary of them; they eat flesh raw, and they can mate with human females."

Caeled's voice died to an exhausted whisper. Then his head dropped forward on his chest.

"He was talking about that fishman who attacked us," said the Stone Warrior in an awed voice.

Madran crouched beside him. "Caeled . . . Caeled . . . Silverhand?"

The young man raised his head, turning toward the Madra Allta. His eyes remained closed.

"This city we're seeking, Tonne and its holy well. How many days' journey?" Madran wanted to know.

"Four to Tonne, one more to the place once known as Lowstone . . ." whispered the weary voice. "There was another name, an Elder name . . ." Caeled stopped suddenly. His eyes snapped open. Madran recoiled. The staring eyes were blind and white, without pupil or iris. "Something comes," Caeled hissed.

The white crows raced through the Dreamscape, following the silver light. It retreated with breathtaking speed, flowing away in a liquid wave that washed the grey shadows with a memory of iridescence.

"Faster!" Lares urged. "It's getting away!"

Sarel allowed the ghost wind to carry her upward into the Aethyra where she could move more quickly. The crow shape fell from her as she imagined herself smooth and sleek, offering no resistance to the passage of air. Her arms melded to her body, her legs grew together, the features of her face dissolved into blankness. Her twin appeared beside her, taking on a similar slender, tubelike appearance. As she watched, his skin turned crystalline. Immediately Sarel adopted a crystal texture of her own.

They could still see the silver light ahead of them, so powerful this time that it had not faded as on other occasions. It continued to flow from a single source, a whirling pool of incandescence.

"We have him now!" Sarel cried triumphantly.

The light vanished.

For a few moments the Aethyra shimmered with its residue. In that clean radiance a thousand intelligences were discernible, Then, slowly at first but with ever increasing speed, the shadows returned.

In the world below, nightmares returned to the restless dreamers.

"We've lost him!" Sarel wailed. Her concentration broken by disappointment, she spiralled down through the levels. Her crystal form flickered through a semblance of humanity, then assumed the vague outline of a white crow with a hint of feathers across her shoulders. By the time she reached the lowest levels, the Place of Dreams, she was neither woman nor bird but something caught in between.

"No, sister," Lares breathed. He appeared beside her, his dream-presence now in naked human form, holding out his hand to share his strength with her.

When she touched her brother, Sarel's fragmented image consolidated into a human shape. She allowed herself, for a fraction of a moment, to rest her head against his shoulder.

"We did not lose them after all," he comforted her. "They are in the Island Sea."

"But there are thousands of isles; they could be anywhere."

"They could. But there are less than a handful of ports they can leave from. I'll send peist to our agents immediately. The air-ships will follow." Lares wrapped his arms around his sister, drawing the full length of her body against his. "It's going to be all right. We have them."

On silken sheets, Sarel and Lares awoke in each other's arms.

"We have them," Lares repeated. "It is only a matter of time now."

On the nameless island, Sioraf sat with Caeled's head in her lap. Her long-nailed fingers traced the silver hairs at his temples, the new lines on his forehead. His skin was grey, his eyes rolled back in his head, and when she dropped one hand to his chest his heartbeat was erratic.

Her hunger burned within her, demanding. More than once she bent over him to feed, then stopped. She knew from experience that his blood would be foul and bitter for a time; besides, he could not afford to lose any more strength, and she did not want to do him damage.

To her surprise, the vampir felt *affection* for the Scholar; a feeling she had not experienced even for her father. She realized that Caeled's feelings for her were confused. He was male and she was female; a simmering sexuality, as yet unexpressed, existed between them. But they were not the same species, although vampir and human could breed. Caeled's race had been taught to feel repulsion for vampiri, whereas all her life Sioraf had feared humans, who would totally wipe her kind from the earth if they could.

Yet this young man touched something inside her which she had not known existed. For Caeled, she felt a new kind of desire.

Sioraf's feelings were tempered, however, by the knowledge that she needed Caeled alive to ensure her own survival. The vampir looked back into the cave where Gwynne and Madran were talking quietly together. Madra Allta and accursed freak; she could not use their blood.

There was only Caeled.

CHAPTER SIX

Caeled was sipping brackish water from a leather flask when a huge dog materialized out of the mist and came loping down the beach. Tendrils of fog curled in from the sea to encircle the dog, clinging to his shaggy coat until he sparkled as if etched in crystal.

The dog plunged into a particularly dense bank of fog . . . and a man ran out.

Even though he had seen Madran change a number of times—from man to dog and back to man again—Caeled still found the effect startling. He watched the non-human musculature still rippling beneath Madran's skin as he approached, and observed that the planes of his face remained vaguely canine. Madran was Madra Allta, one of the Clan Allta, those cursed—or blessed—with the ability to assume the shapes of beasts. Some of the Scholars in Baddalaur had believed they were an atavism, a gradual reversion to an earlier, lower form of life. As he got to know Madran, however, Caeled had come to the conclusion that the Allta were a highly developed variant on humankind, combining the keen senses and agility of wild animals with human intellect.

36

If Madran was any example, at least some of them were also more decent and trustworthy than men.

Caeled looked away from Madran and back into the cave where Sioraf lay sleeping, bathed in rosy light reflected from the ochre-colored stone. Hers was a different situation, less straightforward.

She was shifting uneasily in her sleep, and he found himself wondering what nightmares a vampir might have. As her lips drew back from her teeth, tiny pointed fangs were revealed, strangely sinister against the innocence of her sleeping face.

If one did not see her teeth, Sioraf was beautiful.

On the other side of the cave Gwynne was snoring harshly, every inhalation labored. Lately she had taken to sleeping sitting up to accommodate the increasing pressure on her lungs as the slow but inexorable petrification of her body continued.

Freaks and monsters, Caeled sighed. I'm travelling with a vampir, a stone woman and a were-dog.

And then there's me.

He lifted his left arm, letting the wan morning light gleam on the silver hand that extended from his wrist. He no longer remembered what it was like to have a flesh and blood hand on that wrist. He flexed the fingers, the digits moving without effort, without conscious thought. And what am I? Caeled asked himself. Part man, part metal.

We're all freaks.

In some small, private corner of his spirit, Caeled wanted to cry. He was a man, no longer a child, but the boy in him had not died. It still knew fear and despair and terrible, gnawing loneliness. Yet he must not show any of these things. The others were counting on him to lead them. They looked up to him because he had the Arcana.

The weight of leadership was a burden he had never sought, and lay upon him with increasing heaviness. As his responsibilities to others had multiplied, he felt as if he owned less and less of himself. The Caeled he knew was being subsumed into some other being who was marching down an unmarked and dangerous road into the unknown.

Suddenly he felt very, very tired. With all his heart he longed to be back at Baddalaur, safe in the familiar College among the brothers who had taught him and protected him.

But they were gone. Baddalaur was destroyed, and nothing—even the two Arcana—could roll back time.

Caeled wished he could simply curl into a tight little ball and make the world go away.

"You look sad, my friend." Unself-consciously naked, Madran crouched in the mouth of the cave. Reaching out a big hand that still looked somewhat like a wolfhound's paw, he stroked Caeled's hair. The Allta's touch was surprisingly gentle. "Your pelt is turning grey," he commented. "Is that what using the Arcana does to you?"

Caeled sighed. "In those moments when the Arcana works through me I gain so much knowledge—many cycles' worth of knowledge—that a few grey hairs are a small price to pay, I suppose."

"You are worrying about the Duet?" Withdrawing his hand from Caeled's head, Madran flexed his fingers deliberately. The bones popped, the knuckles cracked before settling into a totally human configuration.

"They came close to me last night. I could feel them in the Aethyra, watching, waiting for me to use the Arcana. They know roughly where we are."

"They won't rest until they have us," Madran warned. He stood up and pressed his hands to the small of his back, rubbing the realigned muscles. "I had better get dressed."

"What's going to happen to us?" Caeled wondered aloud.

Madran raised one shaggy eyebrow. "I thought you knew."

"So did I."

"But now you don't?" Cocking his head quizzically, Madran crouched beside Caeled again.

"Perhaps I am just beginning to appreciate our situation," the young man replied. "We are four, against the might of the Duet."

Madran stared at him, huge brown eyes fixed on Caeled's face.

"When I activate the Arcana, I think very logically and comprehend many things," Caeled murmured, gazing past his friend into some gloomy inner landscape. "For example, I'm beginning to see the futility of what we're trying to do. We can't hope to defeat the twins, Madran. They not only control the army of the Bred, but also have the resources of the Seven Nations at their disposal. And we are only four."

"Logically, four cannot stand against the Empire of the Duet," replied the big Allta. "But logic makes no allowances for passion. I passionately desire to punish the twins because their Bred killed my daughter. Gwynne hates them because they destroyed her family. The twins earned Sioraf's enmity when they caused the death of her father and destroyed his circus, which protected her and her way of life.

"Then there is you. Why do you want to wage war on the Duet, Caeled?"

The young man gestured to the Stone and the Spear. "Because it is my destiny to find the Arcana," he replied in the tones of someone repeating a lesson learned by rote. "If I am able to bring all four of the artefacts together, I can repair the damage the twins are doing and restore order to the world. The Duet have sown the seeds of chaos that are causing its disintegration, you know. Have you not observed the deterioration of animal life, the failure of crops, even the disruption of the seasons. . . ." He stopped. Madran was shaking his head.

"Why have you set yourself against the Duet?" the blond man repeated.

"I just told you."

"You told me a lot of things, but not your *real* reason."

Caeled frowned. "I don't know what you mean."

"All that talk about destiny. It sounds very impressive, but it doesn't mean anything. Can you hear a destiny, taste it, smell it? It is simply a way of justifying what you really want to do, in here." He extended a forefinger to touch the center of Caeled's chest. "You want revenge on those who destroyed Baddalaur and killed your friends."

"There's a lot more to it than that!"

"Do you think so? I don't. You hate the twins; everything else is incidental. All of us hate them and want to see them destroyed for personal reasons. If some greater good results, that's a bonus."

Slowly, Caeled rose to his feet. "But hatred is such an . . . unworthy motivation."

Madran smiled, and in that smile was the grim determination of the born predator. "I assure you," he said, "revenge is the best of reasons."

They stopped at noon so Sioraf could feed. As they made their way around the perimeter of the island they had found no game and only a little vegetation. The place was practically barren, with the exception of a few stunted trees and some giant palmlike ferns that proved to be inedible.

However, Caeled and his companions would be able to live on the plentiful fish that the sea provided. But the vampir had grown progressively weaker. She stumbled and fell twice, the second time tearing a long gash in her thigh from which a colorless liquid oozed sluggishly. Caeled helped Sioraf to her feet. "I thought vampiri bled."

"We do—when we have blood to spare," she said. The shadowed flesh around her eyes was taut with pain.

Wordlessly, Caeled pushed up his sleeve and pressed his right wrist to Sioraf's mouth. The vampir pushed his hand away. "Later, when you are stronger and your blood is clear. I'll take a little then."

"Take it now!"

Sioraf gave him a searching look, her face as pallid as a sheet of kenaf. Then she nodded. Her tiny fangs nipped the flesh of his wrist, perforating the skin. Next her pointed tongue rasped across his flesh, laving the wound with saliva to numb the pain.

Her eyes met his once more. "Go ahead," he grated.

Gripping his arm tightly with both hands, she bent her head and suckled on his wrist.

A great shudder ran through him. As Sioraf drank from his veins, Caeled's blood surged at her summons. His own weakened physical state made the sensation more intense than ever before. His body had no defenses. Waves of pleasure that were perilously close to pain vibrated along his nerves, setting his heart thundering, his lungs heaving, arousing him almost to orgasm.

Abruptly, Sioraf broke off and lifted her head to look at him with knowing eyes. "Enough," she whispered. Her grip on his arm grew gentle. With her tongue she gave one last, deliberately lascivious lick to his wrist, then flashed a sweetly wicked smile. "For the moment."

Already color was flooding back into her cheeks.

Caeled looked at his wrist. As he watched, the puncture wounds closed, fading rapidly to mere bruises. But his skin still tingled from the touch of her tongue.

He was obscurely embarrassed to discover the other two had watched the performance. When Madran met Caeled's eyes he quickly looked away.

But Gwynne was not so tactful. "Be careful, boy," she warned. "One of these days she'll drink you dry, leave you a husk."

Caeled grinned shakily. "Does that mean I will become a vampir too?"

Gwynne's stiffening facial muscles prevented her from smiling, but there was something akin to a harsh laugh in her voice. "'No, it means you will be dead."

Sated, Sioraf drifted away. After feeding she seemed to become dreamy, langorous. She wandered down a stretch of beach, aimlessly following the curvature of the island.

Madran glanced at Caeled. "Do you want me to go after her?"

"Please. I don't want her to be alone; anything might be out there. Don't bother her, just stay close. I would go myself, but I feel a little light-headed."

When Madran and Sioraf were out of earshot, Gwynne said to Caeled, "Be wary of her, boy. Her race is not human, not even Allta. When the blood lust takes them, they become monsters."

Caeled could not prevent the sudden smile that curved his lips.

Gwynne noticed. Not for the first time, she told herself the young man was fair to look upon. "Beneath this stone surface," she said aloud, "I am still a woman. Beneath her soft skin, Sioraf is something else. Remember that when she's tearing your heart out."

"She's half human, her father . . ."

"Half human is not good enough. The human part is subsumed in the vampir. I'm warning you for your own good."

"I'll remember."

"No you won't," Gwynne said quietly. "Because when she sticks those fangs in you, you'll think of only one thing."

Before he could reply, they heard Madran shout in angry surprise. Like an echo, Sioraf screamed. Then they both disappeared.

CHAPTER SEVEN

As always, it was drawn by its sense of smell.

Edible flesh not far away. Rich fat whose scent awakened the salivary glands as the luscious smell settled thickly on the back of the throat.

Another odor was borne on the damp sea wind, however. It detected a whiff like rotten fish, the unmistakable smell of one of its own kind, but with an added element. The creature recognized the acrid tang of death.

Low in its throat, it growled.

Riding the tide in toward shore, it concealed itself in a dense mat of floating purple seaweed torn up from the seabed by the recent storm. To anything watching from the land it would have appeared nothing more than a massive bit of flotsam trapped in the long, oily strands of the weed. But once it reached the shallows, the creature moved.

Oily hair clung to its rounded skull as it thrust its head up through the seaweed for a closer look.

Bones were strewn on the reddish sand. A broken spine gleamed, stripped of flesh by the Great Roarer. The skull

43

had been shattered by a massive blow. That was not the work of the Great Roarer.

The Eron sank lower in the seaweed, absorbing what it had seen.

Then it began to sing. The song was without words. Low and plaintive, it·ululated through the water, calling, calling, calling. Grieving for the one who could not answer. The song was as dark as the sea and as old as time, and every living thing that heard it understood its bitter message.

When the song was ended, the creature surfaced again and gazed toward the land where lay all that remained of she who had been its mate. The rising tide rattled the bare bones, dislodging the skull and rolling it over and over in crescents of foam.

A tiny scatter of much smaller bones, soft as cartilage, was briefly revealed by the shifting of the skeleton. The dead Eron had been carrying unborn young. She had made a nest for herself in a cave on the land while she awaited the birth. There the single infant would have been tenderly nurtured until it was strong enough to be led to the sea. Her kind mated once and for life, producing a solitary offspring each birthing season from a single coupling at the beginning of their long relationship.

In spite of their hideous form, the Eron had a certain primitive intelligence and a great capacity for devotion. They bred but once, yet they remained hunting partners for as long as they lived, scouring the seas as a skilled predatory team. The loss of a mate meant the loss of a partner as well as a companion and diminished the entire Eron community.

The male sank beneath the waves once more, listening. The water was beginning to hum with a myriad of songs as other Eron gathered, drawn by a powerful instinct to avenge their dead sister.

CHAPTER EIGHT

Lamar knew the new girl was cheating him. He even had a good idea just how much. He had run a wharfside tavern and brothel in Rock, the capital of Seamount, for most of his adult life and had seen hundreds—perhaps thousands—of whores in his time. Many of them were Steppe women or Island women who indentured themselves for a cycle or two to make New Coin to send back to impoverished families at home. Others were southern women, professionals from Galloway or Shemmat, or Marocan beauties who came north to the islands because the pickings were richer than at home. Occasionally they were even paid in precious Old Metal. If they survived the weather, the disease and the customers, they could amass a modest fortune.

There were tales of women who had come to Seamount with nothing but the ragged clothes they wore, and left a few cycles later as luxuriously attired as princesses, dripping jewelry and possessing a retinue of slaves.

Lamar made certain his new recruits heard such stories. He neglected to mention, however, that he had never met those specially fortunate women.

The particular new girl who was causing him trouble was Lili, one of the Island peoples. Short and dark like most of her race, she was also tattooed with the most extraordinary designs Lamar had ever seen. Many of his customers were tattooed, but Island men generally had themselves ornamented with simple geometric patterns in colored inks. Lili was inscribed with gilt and silver that glittered beguilingly whenever she moved.

Curiosity had been her initial selling point. Subsequent word-of-mouth as to the skill of her performance insured ongoing success. Lili was a virtuoso. She could put more excitement into one heavy-lidded glance than Lamar's other girls could bring to an hour's sweaty work beneath a man. And she loved her job, there was no doubt about it. She was tirelessly inventive, and genuinely avid for sexual embraces. No man repelled her as long as he was male.

She was, in short, a treasure. And a cheat.

Sitting behind a worn wooden table, Lamar compared his figures with the sums the girls had returned to him. It was his afternoon for doing his accounts. He knew exactly how many men each girl had taken and how long they had spent. Because most of his customers were regulars, he also knew how they paid. As he sucked on a pipe long since gone cold, the innkeeper's tiny, almost feminine fingers etched columns of figures onto a sheet of kenaf. Then he sat back with a grunt of annoyance.

Two of the girls had come up short: Bleu and Lili. Bleu he could dismiss; the girl's mind was almost gone anyway, befuddled by cycles of hard drinking and, more recently, an addiction to Eron scales. He reckoned she had a season—two at the most—before the narcotic scales destroyed the rest of her mind. Undoubtedly that was where she was spending coin that was rightfully Lamar's—giving it to some scale dealer in a dark alley. She would not be a loss.

But Lili . . . the innkeeper drew a careful line under

her name at the top of a column. She was holding back a third of her earnings. Probably laughing at him as well, thinking herself cleverer than he was. They all did, at first. He was small and slight and not in any way prepossessing. His vision was poor and his voice was high and women tended to take him for a bit of a fool.

They were wrong.

"Anadyr," he called.

An enormous man lumbered into the room. Anadyr was a second-generation Islander, one of the dregs who belonged to no clan of their own but wandered around the fringes of the Island Sea. Others scornfully called such undesirables Island Trash. They referred to themselves simply as the People. Born and bred and left an orphan on one of the unnamed islands, Anadyr had reached adulthood by living as a savage. Like a wild beast he had survived by killing without hesitation or conscience. He ate his meat raw; he demolished anything that stood in his path.

Rescue from this life had come when Anadyr was discovered on a dismasted fishing vessel floating aimlessly in the Island Sea. He was the sole survivor, though from bits of flesh and hair littering the deck, he was suspected of having fed off the bodies of the missing fishermen. The charge could not be proved, however.

In all probability, the fishermen had captured him on some nameless atoll and were taking him back to Seamount to sell on the slave block when he broke out of his restraints and attacked the crew. No one would ever know—and Anadyr never told.

While aboard the boat, he had been cruelly tortured by his captors for their own amusement. Much of the skin had been peeled off his face and skull. His sufferings had engendered enough pity among the people of Seamount to keep him from being imprisoned or executed. He was ultimately auctioned off as a curiosity much as the fishermen may have intended in the first place.

Lamar had bought him on a whim. Few had been willing to bid on such a hideous piece of Island Trash, especially one who was feverish and weak from his injuries, and looked as if he might die at any moment.

But Anadyr had not died. Lamar had personally nursed him back to health, hand-feeding him raw meat and patiently teaching him to drink milk from a cup. Within ten days, Anadyr was back on his feet . . . and Lamar had gained the most devoted of servants. In the cycles since, Anadyr had become even more than a servant. Immensely powerful, totally without scruples except where Lamar was concerned, he was the innkeeper's devoted henchman.

Now he took a seat across the table from Lamar, habitually turning his face away so as not to inflict the sight of his worst scars on his master. The top of Anadyr's head and the right side of his face were covered by a web of painfully tight white scar tissue. His left eye was a slatey blue; his right was a milky globe.

Fixing his one-eyed stare on Lamar, the massive man growled, "That Lili maggot? Is she causing you trouble?"

The innkeeper nodded. "When will they ever learn, eh?"

"She thinks you're stupid, but she's the fool."

"Teach her a lesson, my friend. Don't break any bones, leave no scars, no damage to the merchandise. Just . . . give her an education."

The scarred giant nodded.

"After her first lesson," Lamar went on, "give her ten days to think it over, then send in someone to check up on her, someone she won't recognize. Give him a large amount of New Coin. If she steals it from him, then you may scar her. If she lies to me about the amount he paid, then break her legs."

"She will do both," Anadyr predicted.

"I fear you're right, which is unfortunate. I hate to have such a valuable property put out of service. But if you must scar her and break her, do it publicly, at least let it serve as a warning to the other girls." Lamar gave a long-suffering sigh. "Why do they do this? I don't cheat them, I keep them physicked, well fed; I protect them, I don't allow anyone to hurt them . . . and I only take three quarters of their earnings. That Kathan whore-mistress on the docks takes nine tenths of her girls' earnings and she insists they lie with everyone." He stopped suddenly, realizing that Anadyr's attention had wandered.

The big man was no longer looking at Lamar, but staring toward the nearest window.

"Something's spying on us," he warned. "I feel it." Crossing to the window, he flung the shutter open.

At first glance the street outside seemed deserted. A row of peddlers' stalls was at one end, beside the wharves; at the other stood the pressing plant, with a mountain of oyster shells piled up in front awaiting disposal. From the giant orange molluscs, tough as leather and as large as a man's hand, enough oil was expressed to supply all the lanterns in Rock.

But no lanterns were needed now. Though the day was overcast, Anadyr could clearly see the tiny rainbow hovering in the air outside the window.

With a movement almost too quick for the eye to follow, he snatched the brilliantly colored peist. Holding it between thumb and forefinger, he carried the insect back to Lamar.

As the innkeeper gazed at the peist he felt ice form in his stomach. A message received in this way invariably meant trouble.

Anadyr, reacting to the expression on his master's face, crushed the peist between thumb and forefinger. He tossed the ruined body onto the table in front of Lamar. "It never arrived," he said.

The innkeeper replied gloomily, "The people who sent this message will know it got through." With the point of his knife, he unrolled a strip of kenaf that had been wound around the creature's abdomen. He pressed it flat on the table and squinted at the minute script. Then he grinned; for once it was not bad news after all.

"The Silverhand is headed this way! Not only that, but he is accompanied by a woman with skin like stone, a Madra Allta, and a vampir. He travels in strange company indeed, Anadyr. The reward on him has been doubled again, this says. That means a fortune to the man who finds him."

"What is he doing this far north?" Anadyr wondered. Picking up the dead messenger, he ripped the wings from the peist, held the crushed body to his mouth and began sucking out the juices.

"Fleeing the Duet, of course. Examine the registers of all ships coming in to port. You're looking for four strangers, any four strangers. They may attempt to disguise themselves, though given their basic descriptions, that won't be easy. Let me know if any vessels are late, or if there were any disturbances aboard ship. Go into the other taverns around the town; investigate all newcomers yourself. Put together a small team of men—use only men you trust, mind—and pay them well to hold themselves in readiness."

Anadyr wiped his lips with the back of a meaty wrist. "Those four might not come through here at all."

"It depends where they're going. If they are simply fleeing to the safety of the islands, they could go in any direction. On some of the more remote isles they might escape detection for many cycles—if they did not run afoul of Island Trash, or the Eron. However, if they are making for one of the northern or eastern cities, they undoubtedly will have to come here first for supplies."

Lamar tapped the kenaf with the tip of his knife. "The Duet must be fairly certain they're coming here, because they are dispatching an air-ship to Seamount. They don't say who will be in command, but I'll wager it will be

Kichal, who led the army of the Bred. He will need careful handling; we don't want any reports going back to the capital claiming we failed to do everything in our power to capture the Silverhand."

"You fear this Silverhand?"

"I fear the Duet. And anyone they trust enough to make Commander of the Bred."

"You need not be afraid of them because I will let nothing hurt you," Anadyr insisted. "Nothing and no one. I do not fear the Duet, nor their servants either."

"You will," Lamar said softly. "You will."

CHAPTER NINE

Caeled leaned over the edge of the gaping hole in the ground and peered down. Madran and Sioraf lay at the bottom of a deep pit, almost invisible beneath the coating of sand that had rained down on top of them. Madran sat up and ran his hands through his shaggy hair, clawing out ochre-colored sand and grit.

"Are you hurt?" Caeled called anxiously. "How's Sioraf?"

Coughing and spitting, the vampir emerged from the sand at Madran's feet.

"We're fine," Madran said.

"Speak for yourself," Sioraf told him. "It was dark under that sand." Her voice was shaky and her face was even more pallid than usual.

Gwynne came lumbering up, her breath wheezing in her lungs. "Are they hurt? Is it an animal trap?"

Caeled shook his head. "I don't think so. There are no spikes. But it's very deep, I can't reach them."

Balancing her weight precariously, Gwynne leaned over the edge of the pit and peered down. "Looks like a mine shaft . . ." she began. Just then the edges of the pit crumbled away and she pitched forward. Caeled grabbed for her belt, but the leather was torn from his hands as she fell forward. The Stone Warrior crashed to the bottom of the pit in an enormous explosion of sand.

When Caeled looked around, seeking something to help him get his companions from the pit, he noticed what appeared to be a round head bobbing on the surface of the sea some distance from the beach. A second head appeared; then a third. Caeled squinted, trying to make out details, but his eyesight had been diminished by too many evenings spent reading by dim light in the library at Baddalaur.

As he stared seaward the heads disappeared one by one, as magically as they had appeared.

Caeled turned back to the pit. Lying flat on the ground to distribute his weight so he would not cause another sandslide, he peered over the edge. "Is everyone all right down there?"

The Stone Warrior was sitting on the ground, coated with brown sand and looking as indignant as her stiffened facial muscles would allow. Madran and Sioraf were on either side, having thrown themselves out of the way when she fell. If she had landed atop either of them, her weight could have proved fatal. "We're all right," she snapped. "Just get us out of here."

Madran climbed to his feet and dusted himself off again. Digging his fingers into the wall of the pit, he tried to lever himself up, but the wall crumbled away beneath him. He went to the other side of the pit and tried again only to have whole sections of the wall dissolve into fine sand. At last he looked up at Caeled and called, "Throw down the rope!"

"Which rope . . . the one you're carrying?"

Madran's bark of laughter was rewarded by a cold glare from Gwynne.

"If you were to stand on Gwynne's shoulders and then you, Sioraf, were to stand on Madran's, I could haul you up," Caeled suggested. "Then together we could pull

Madran up. But . . . but I'm not sure if all three of us together could pull you out," he told Gwynne.

With a sigh, the big woman laboriously got to her feet. She unslung her morningstar and prodded at the wall until she broke free a slab of hardened sand. "When I rode with the Snowscalds," she said, "we made our camp in the Spine and controlled trade through the high passes. Occasionally we performed certain services for the scattered mountain communities, trading our skills for wool or leather or weapons." She hammered out another section of wall. "Once we were called to Minehaven, a community close to the edge of the Spine. They mine some copper ore there, and a tiny bit of silver."

She jabbed at the wall again. More sand broke away. "There was an earthquake, not uncommon in that part of the Spine. Part of the mine collapsed, killing many men and women, and the cages that carried the miners to the lower levels were completely destroyed. Twenty miners were trapped at the bottom of a pit, far, far deeper than this."

"What did you do?" Caeled asked.

"Raised the level of the floor." Standing back, she slammed her morningstar into the wall until sand and grit cascaded around her. Then she called up to Caeled, "Bring water, we'll mix it with the loose material to make it firm."

Caeled's head disappeared from the opening.

"We will work on this side only," Gwynne told Madran and Sioraf. "When he brings water we can start mixing it. You, Sioraf, pack the material in close to the base of the wall, and gradually we'll be able to build up a ramp."

"But what about the tide?" Sioraf wanted to know. "What if it comes in while we're all still down here? Would it not pour in upon us and drown us?"

Madran assured her, "The tide doesn't come this far up the beach."

"And if it does, you two can float to the top of the

pit," Gwynne added sarcastically. "Don't spare a thought for me."

Madran hit the wall a mighty blow and a huge section of sand and grit fell away. He started to say, "I wonder what this place was . . ." then caught his breath in astonishment.

A gleam of grey-white metal was visible beneath a patina of red sand.

Gwynne ran her hand across the surface, brushing it clear. With a sideways glance at her companions, she began tracing the edges of a framework with her hardened fingers.

"It's a door!" Sioraf breathed, reaching past the Stone Warrior to touch the panel. "Old Metal. A fortune in Old Metal!" She traced the arcane hieroglyphs of Elder Script etched into the surface of the door. "I wonder where it leads? Could we use it to find our way out?"

Gwynne muttered, "Probably rusted solid." She rapped on the door with her knuckles and was rewarded with a hollow boom. Dropping her mace, she planted both feet solidly, pressed the palms of her hands against the door and pushed.

Nothing happened.

She stepped back. "Rusted solid, as I thought."

"Do it again," urged Madran. "Only this time don't push in, push across. Here, I'll help you." He took up a position in front of the door beside Gwynne. At his nod, together they pushed the door to the right.

Nothing happened.

"Other way," Madran said. Veins appeared on his forehead and his massive neck and shoulder muscles bulged. "Push!"

The door shifted.

Sand cascaded down around them, but they ignored it as they heaved the door to the left, metal screeching, to force a tiny opening on the right-hand side. Sioraf grabbed Gwynne's morningstar and slid the bulbous head into the opening, then leaned back on the haft, using her weight to lever the door. It began to move, grinding open, but stuck halfway. Musty, foul air washed over the trio. Sioraf scrambled back, hissing like a cat.

Forcing himself to ignore the smell, Madran thrust his head through the opening. White lights flickered, abruptly illuminating the interior with a shadowless glare.

Madran withdrew his head and stepped back. Turning his face toward the sky, he called, "Caeled. Get back here. Now!"

He had no vessel that would carry a substantial amount of water back to the pit. Filling and refilling his water bottle would take an age, his cloak was porous, and there was nothing on the beach from which to fashion a bucket.

So Caeled sat down on a smooth stone to think. Stretching his legs in front of him, he gazed around, awaiting inspiration. "No problem is insurmountable," Scholar Nanri had once told him. The young man's jet-black eyes located the high water mark on the beach, then measured the distance to the pit. Too far; even at high tide the sea would not reach the pit. But . . . he smiled fleetingly, and for an instant, despite the grey hair and the lines on his forehead, he looked young again.

"Yes!" he exclaimed softly, pleased with his idea. He saw where he could trace a zigzag channel in the sand from the high water point to the pit. The incoming tide could then be controlled simply by blocking the flow with a stone. Caeled trotted down the beach, looking for a suitably shaped stone with which to dig the channel.

It knew something of the inhabitants of the World Above. They could be deadly, but they were also weak and soft-skinned. They could not survive in the Real World; they could not tolerate the salty atmosphere, nor fly on the currents.

Yet they could breathe the thin, burning air of the

World Above, and move swiftly across unyielding surfaces on their fleshy feet. Their voices were sharp, harsh noises that dried into nothing as soon as they left their mouths, unlike the song of the Eron that reverberated through the Real World in waves of poignant beauty.

The softskins of the World Above were savages. Their deadly nets trawled through the Real World, snatching the little brothers and the dark sisters, occasionally even taking one of the Eron in a tangled embrace. They fouled the atmosphere of the Real World with their waste, sickening the Eron, driving them further and further from the Bitter Places where the inhabitants of the World Above gathered. They killed without need, without reason; they did not even kill for food. Like the Sleepless One from the dark depths of the Real World, they killed for pleasure and left their victims to rot.

So had they left its mate.

And what was her crime? To defend her nest, to secure the resting place of the pup she would soon bear.

Lidless eyes broke the surface of the water. Translucent membranes promptly slid across the exposed orbs to shield them from the dry atmosphere of the World Above. On the beach, the Eron saw the softskin who had been there when its mate was killed.

The Eron's sharp eyesight detected her blood still on the softskin. If it killed and ate the softskin, then it would be absorbing a little of her back into itself, making her part of the Eron again.

The creature's webbed feet paddled gently, guiding it into the current it sought. Silently it drifted closer to the beach.

The softskin was bent over, seeking something, its back to the Real World.

The Eron slithered out of the water. Its oily scales made no sound as it glided across the sand. Coming up behind the preoccupied softskin, it lifted its upper body and reached into the seaweed pouch around its neck to

produce a flat, polished bone. The curved edge of the
bone was honed to razor sharpness, its tapering end
sharpened to a deadly point.

Pausing, the Eron held the bone to its lipless mouth
and breathed upon it. This was one of the God-bones,
the remnants of the God-shapes, the vast beings who
sang the most beautiful of the Eron songs. A God-bone
was a talisman of great power.

Clutching the bone, the Eron crept closer to the
softskin. The wind was blowing toward it from the softskin,
and blowing its own odor away, back to the sea. It would
get very close before the softskin was aware of its presence.

When only the length of its shadow lay between them,
the Eron drew back its weapon for the killing stroke.

"Caeled! Get back here. Now!"

Caeled jerked upright. At that moment a movement
was reflected on the back of his silver hand. Alerted just
in time, he threw himself forward and heard behind him
the hiss of air parting before a blade.

He hit the sand rolling and was instantly on his feet
again, turning in one smooth motion.

He found himself facing a monster.

Similar to the beast that had attacked him earlier, when
it rose on its thickly muscled hind legs it was almost as
tall as a man. The skin of the belly was a mottled white;
otherwise the creature was covered in scales of leprous
green speckled with black. Flaps of skin depended from
upraised forelimbs that ended in hands with webbed
fingers. A stubby tail lashed back and forth in anger. The
head presented a mocking parody of a human face. Both
sides appeared to have been pushed together, elongating
the nose, mouth and lower jaw into a single point. The
eyes were offset on either side of a bony ridge that bisected
the face. There was no chin and no neck, but a mane of
coarse black hair erupted from the top of the skull and
rippled down the scaly back.

Caeled glanced toward the crossbow lying on his pack farther up the beach. He wondered how fast the creature could move. Would he have time to race to the crossbow, load it and fire before the thing was upon him? Unlikely.

Even as he stared at the monstrosity from the sea, a dozen more surfaced and came wading through the surf. In the instant when they distracted Caeled's attention, the first creature leapt.

Caeled spun to one side, slashing at the creature with his metal hand. He caught a handful of the scalloped mane and tore it free from the body. With a howl of pain the creature staggered sideways. Now that the air was drying its scales they exuded a decidedly fishy odor.

"Caeled? Where are you? What's happening?" Gwynne's voice roared from the pit. Startled by the unexpected call, the creature tried to turn; but awkward on land and already off-balance, it fell instead.

Caeled seized the opportunity and ran.

Madran, Gwynne and Sioraf were looking up toward the top of the pit when they heard pounding footsteps approaching. Suddenly, shockingly, Caeled flew through the air above them, leaping over the pit in one huge bound. "Look out below!" he shouted. A moment later a second figure appeared at the brink of the pit, stopped suddenly, then toppled as the edge gave way. It crashed to the ground at Gwynne's feet. Faster than thought, the Stone Warrior crushed its skull to pulp.

Caeled reappeared above them. "There's plenty more coming," he called down. "Too many for me to fight alone."

Madran gestured to the door in the pit wall. "Then you had better come down here; we may have found a way out."

Caeled disappeared, returning almost at once with his pack. He tossed it down to Madran, then eased himself over the edge and dropped into Gwynne's arms.

✧   ✧   ✧

By the time the other Eron gathered around the mouth of the pit, the softskin and his companions had disappeared. One of their own lay crushed and dead below them, but none were tempted to go down to retrieve the body. In the wall of the pit was an opening into the Deadly Places. Experience had taught the Eron that if the softskin had gone in there, he would not be coming out.

CHAPTER TEN

They found themselves within what appeared to be a long tunnel lined with some metallic substance. Madran's nostrils flared. "What do you smell?" he asked Caeled.

Caeled drew a careful, assessing breath. "Dust, decay. Stale air. And a scent like rotten eggs."

"Magic," murmured Sioraf. "Elder Magic." Wrapping her arms around her slender body, she rubbed briskly at the flesh of her forearms. "My skin tingles."

"I can feel it too," Gwynne said, sounding surprised. She brushed at the flesh of her left arm with her right hand. Flakes of a hard but paper-thin substance spiralled to the metal floor. When she continued to rub, the grey-brown crust that covered her skin broke away in chunks, exposing granular-looking tissues that leaked a pale pink fluid.

The Stone Warrior began backing toward the doorway through which they had just come. "Something's wrong with this place," she said hoarsely. She stepped back out into the pit, but no sooner had she emerged than a boulder crashed at her feet. More stones and boulders rained down from above. Their pursuers were waiting.

Gwynne hurriedly returned to the tunnel. "We can't get out that way . . ." she started to say. Then she hesitated. Her eyes met Caeled's. In their grey depths he saw an unfamiliar expression—fear. Staring at him, the Stone Warrior whispered, "I feel . . ."

"What?"

"My skin crawls as if there are insects beneath the surface." She rubbed at her bald head. "I feel lice on my scalp, my ears ring, my mouth is dry." She stuck out her pink tongue. "Is my tongue swollen? It seems huge. What's happening to me?"

Caeled lifted his left hand—and a bright spark leaped from his silvery fingers to Gwynne's stony breasts.

"Poisoned!" Sioraf hissed. "We're being poisoned!" Her pupils dilated. The skin on her face drew taut, throwing cheekbones and forehead into stark relief until she looked almost skeletal.

"The vampir's right," growled Madran. His voice sounded harsh even to himself. Lifting his hands to his face, he stared at them in dismay. The muscles and tendons were flexing and knotting; the configuration of the veins was visibly changing. Impossibly, the were-change was coming on him.

"It's that purple glow!" Sioraf cried, shrinking back and pointing toward the nearest metal-sheathed wall.

Caeled followed her gesture. "I see no purple glow."

"On either side of us, pulsing," Sioraf insisted, looking anxiously from left to right. "Poisoning us!"

Caeled still saw nothing, but the intensity of her conviction persuaded him. "We had better get out of here," he said. "Now." He put his right hand on Gwynne's arm and was startled to feel her petrified flesh crackle beneath his grip. Shoving the Stone Warrior farther along the tunnel, he urged Sioraf after her.

He turned to find the Madra Allta desperately fighting to control the were-change that was transforming him. His facial planes had already altered and his nose and mouth were thrusting forward preparatory to becoming a muzzle. His large brown eyes looked at Caeled with an expression of bafflement.

"This can't be!" Madran protested. "If the change takes place spontaneously, it's permanent. There will be no going back. What can I do?"

Caeled felt a wave of sympathy. To lose control of one's body . . . forever . . . would be worse than losing a hand. "Run," he commanded. "Run! Away from here!" He gestured in the direction the others had taken . . . then realized that blood was seeping from his left hand where the silver metal joined the fleshly wrist.

He flexed his fingers. Pain stabbed along his arm, burning through the muscles. The little finger refused to respond but remained rigid. The hand seemed to be coming loose.

He fled after the others.

They raced down a corridor lined with metal that made their footsteps echo eerily. Milky white bars set in the curved ceiling matched their pace, illuminating each section of corridor ahead of them, then fading away behind.

The Elder Magic was affecting all of them now. When he caught up with Sioraf, Caeled was horrified to discover that her beautiful features had become more than skeletal. She looked almost ratlike, with fangs protruding from a lipless mouth and eyes narrowed to cruel slits.

Gwynne was shedding stone skin with every ponderous step she took, her entire body seeping pale fluid and dark blood. She emitted a constant low moan of agony. Madran was caught in a terrifying amalgam of man and beast, a nightmare creature with the furry hide of a dog covering a partially human frame. Caeled felt as if his left hand, his silver hand, was about to tear loose from his wrist. The pain was excruciating, and blood had begun to seep out around the joining of flesh and metal.

Then he became aware that the Arcana in the pack on his back were growing warm; hot; vibrating.

With his eyes on the floor in front of them, watching for obstacles in their path, Caeled saw the red line running from one wall to the other but it meant nothing to him. As soon as he crossed it, however, the pain in his arm eased.

Simultaneously Sioraf gasped, "Purple glow. Gone." She collapsed onto the ground a few paces beyond the red line. Beside her, Gwynne leaned back against the metal wall. Her knees gave way and she slowly slid down, smearing the wall behind her with ichor. Madran dropped to all fours. Then his body convulsed in a curious parody of copulation as bone and muscle reformed into a human structure.

Caeled tried to stay on his feet, but he felt weak, light-headed. Glancing around, he could see nothing threatening, so he sank to the floor and sat cradling his left arm. The bleeding had stopped. All his fingers now flexed smoothly at his command.

The phenomenon, he decided, must have something to do with the purple glow only Sioraf had seen. He did not doubt her; she was a vampir, but she did not lie. And whatever it was had stopped when they crossed the red line. The Elders obviously had left some magical guardian in the corridor, some enchantment which warped living creatures, causing them to revert to . . . to what? Their true selves?

In Caeled's case it had changed nothing of his physical self, but had tried to remove his artificial hand. As he pondered on this he recalled that the magic had affected the Arcana, too. Magic fighting magic?

A high-pitched warbling song—clear as crystal— echoed down the corridor. Moments later a figure appeared some distance behind the four companions. Singing its song of unearthly beauty, one of the sea creatures advanced toward them. The milky lights illumined its path and allowed them a good look at the monster.

It was neither fish nor man, Caeled thought, but something in between, as Madran had been caught between man and dog. Was this one of the fabled Mere? But the Mere were only a myth, a wild tale spun to amuse children and beguile the credulous. Besides, they were described as beautiful and this creature was hideous.

Mere legends were common to most races; Caeled had read them at Baddalaur. In the realms of fantasy the Mere had once ruled the world, not as one of the Elder Races but older still, from a time before the before. The world was mostly ocean then, the stories claimed, though surely that was impossible. Then melting mountains under the sea supposedly gave birth to islands, and the Mere learned to walk on land.

After eons the Elder Races had appeared and occupied the land until the Time of Burning. The old tales claimed brutal Elders had driven the Mere back into the sea, where they built palaces beneath the waves. Fable, of course. The Elders, so revered by the Order of the Way at Baddalaur, were benevolent. Everyone knew that. They . . .

Caeled's thoughts snapped back to the present danger. The creature's song had changed. No longer was it beautiful; the melody shrilled with pain.

The young man narrowed his eyes and braced himself, ready to leap to his feet. The creature had stopped advancing. It began swaying to and fro. Shadows crawled across its skin. Then Caeled realized they were not shadows, but muscles beneath the flesh, warping in the same way the change had rippled through Madran.

No sooner did Caeled think of Madran than the Madra Allta stood beside him. He had reverted to his human form, but was still panting nervously.

"Allta?" Caeled inquired, gesturing toward the creature.

Madran shook his great head. "No. We of the Clan Allta know our own. That is not our kind."

The song stopped. The creature, which had not reached the red line in the floor, collapsed, crumpling very slowly as if its bones were dissolving. It fell between two sections of corridor, so that the lights overhead kept flickering off and on in an attempt to match its position. The creature spasmed; there came a sound of snapping and tearing, then the body shivered and seemed to fall in upon itself.

"It's dead," Caeled pronounced when all movement ceased. As if in confirmation, the lights above the creature went out.

Madran's hand carved the complicated blessing of his kind on the air. "What in the name of all the gods happened?"

"I think the purple glow Sioraf saw was some sort of magical ward," Caeled told him, "designed to strip us of magic. My silver hand, your human shape, Sioraf's human form, Gwynne's stone skin: all magical manifestations. The Arcana responded too, by the way."

Just then, the lights above the dead creature came on again.

The creature stirred, rose.

Standing erect and proud in the milky light was a naked woman: tall, elegant, her body gleaming with a soft pearlescence. She bore the faintest trace of scales on her shoulders and belly, rainbow-colored scales that only added to her beauty. This radiant vision took a step forward, stretched out her hand as if in entreaty . . . then began to wither with frightening speed. Her flesh shrivelled on her bones and fell away. As she collapsed a second time the lights mercifully went out once more.

"So they *were* Mere," Caeled whispered, awestruck. If the so-called legends of the Mere were true . . .

Before he could pursue the thought any further, Madran bent to help him to his feet. The huge brown eyes of the Madra Allta regarded the young man sympathetically. "You are troubled by what we just saw."

"Yes. No. I don't know." Recalling the rat-faced creature, Caeled darted a surreptitious glance at Sioraf. Was that her true face?

"I've found another door," Gwynne said, interrupting his thoughts yet again. She was the most visibly changed by their recent experience. The fluids that had seeped from her tissues when part of her crust was torn away had now hardened on the remaining surface, leaving her scabrous. Deep new lines were etched around her eyes. Whatever had happened to her had been agonizing.

With a terrible effort, she had fought back the pain, however. Now her interest was focused on her discovery. Reaching out, she started to put her hand on a panel set in the wall.

"Don't touch . . ." Caeled began warningly.

But the door had already hissed open.

CHAPTER ELEVEN

Throughout his long life, men had called Shantay a genius. In his latter years a sect had grown up which worshipped the venerable old man, and in the larger cities, schools of philosophy were founded on his teachings. He was accepted as being the oldest man alive, and he did not deny rumors that he was the last survivor of the Elder Days and the son of an emperor in a distant land.

In the days following his death, Justin, his secretary and closest friend, discovered a hoard of manuscripts secreted in a hidden vault beneath Shantay's house. Most were from the Elder Times, and included plans and drawings that Shantay had claimed were his own invention. Also among the papers were documents proving that Shantay was no emperor's son, but the illegitimate offspring of a grain importer and a wharf whore.

When Justin recovered from the shock of his discovery, he attempted to bring his knowledge to the attention of Shantay's followers. But he was torn apart by the crowd and branded Justin the Apostate. Thereafter, no one dared question Shantay's origins or teachings.

Wherever he came from, the old man's genius was never in doubt. Shantay had managed to steer a path through the increasingly dangerous political situation in the latter days of the reign of Los-Lorcan, when the Duet were fighting their way to power. By his fourth decade even he believed the legends that had grown up around him. Indeed, his life assumed legendary proportions: he was imprisoned several times, survived three assassination attempts and two kidnappings, had seven wives and fathered forty children, made and lost several fortunes. When he died at the age of eleven decades, he had only recently taken his eighth wife, a woman young enough to be his granddaughter.

The Duet decreed a ten-day of mourning in his honor. Shantay's body was laid out in the cathedral in Barrow, a tribute denied the dead Los-Lorcan. However, his corpse was barely cold before the twins had his laboratories closed, enslaved the assistants working there and seized his estate, which they claimed in the name of their subjects "for the good of mankind."

Shantay left behind a legacy of remarkable inventions, the greatest being the air-ship. Once he had dreamed of making such vessels available to everyone, opening up the Seven Nations to free trade and enabling travellers to get from Thusal to the Southlands in a single day.

But following the demonstration of the first air-ship and Shantay's impassioned speech about freedom to travel, the Mariners Guild had staged a militant public protest. At the same time, a disastrous fire broke out in Shantay's laboratories. Rumor had it the two events were not unconnected.

The Guild then petitioned the Duet, who agreed to ban the sale of air-ships to the public. Any sales which took place must be authorized by the palace, they announced. Shantay knew better than to argue, but he complained privately to his disciples that his greatest invention was being taken out of his hands.

Soon a story began circulating Barrow that Shantay was building an enormous air-ship to transport his entire family far away from Barrow. Abruptly, Shantay's favorite wives and six of his daughters were given rooms in the palace and made ladies-in-waiting to Sarel. A few days later the charred remains of a huge construction of wood and leather were found in the sea south of Barrow.

After that Shantay worked exclusively for the Duet, laboring in an elaborately equipped complex of laboratories behind high walls.

The earliest air-ships, which resembled nothing more than giant inflated leather bladders, had been unreliable and unstable. But once he was working for them, the twins provided Shantay with an unlimited supply of prisoners and slaves for experimental flights. Many perished in crashes, or died in explosions of the various highly flammable gasses being tested in the thin leather balloons. Those who managed to survive a flight were put to death by the Duet to preserve secrecy.

In time, Shantay had perfected the system, using a mixture of hot air and a gas distilled from human and animal ordure. He experimented with various fabrics, eventually substituting a type of treated silk stretched across a flexible frame for the original leather. He changed the wooden baskets for carrying passengers to strongly woven wicker. Shantay's assistants continued his work after his death, creating bigger and bigger air-ships, which by then were commonly known as shanti.

The Duet used shanti in battle on at least three occasions. The first time was against the Imperial Rebels who had supported their father, Los-Lorcan. The shanti played a decisive part in the victory. As the scouts floated high over the battlefield, they were able to report troop movements which enabled the Duet's army to encircle the rebels.

On the second occasion shanti were used, however, a lucky shot from a fire arrow ruptured the silk bag and the vessel exploded, raining fire down on the Duet's army beneath. Despite this setback, the twins were ultimately victorious. But the third time they put a shanti into the air—carrying twenty warriors—in the ill-fated attempt to take Camarg Castle on the south coast, a single man wiped out the entire force with a red-hot slingshot.

The Duet resolved never to use shanti in battle again until the flammable gas could be neutralized. Thereafter, shanti were employed only for non-combat situations such as transporting small numbers of troops and supplies across country. Even the powerful Mariners Guild did not protest, mindful of the saying that the twins had few enemies in Barrow—few living, that was.

Sarel, wearing a suit of shimmering white mail over black silk, stood on the dock watching the loading of a sky-blue shanti. The woman held a perfume-soaked cloth across her nose and mouth in an attempt to counteract the appalling smell of burning faeces emanating from the air-ship. Lines of naked slaves were loading the shanti with food, armor and weapons, while technicians double-checked every detail of the craft.

Two seasons previously, a slave had managed to sabotage a shanti by ripping a tiny hole in the leather and plugging it with clay. As the shanti ascended the clay dried, cracked and fell out. The balloon collapsed and crashed onto the City of the Dead, the cemetery beyond Barrow. The place was home to thousands of the city's destitute. None of the twenty human warriors in the craft had survived, and thrice that number of cemetery dwellers were killed in the crash and explosion that followed.

The slave responsible was kept alive for twenty-two days of torture before he finally succeeded in dying.

Holding her mask snugly across her lower face, Sarel strolled down the line of slaves. Her violet eyes swept over each face and form. None dared meet her gaze. It was whispered that the last man who had the temerity to stare at the female half of the Duet had been terribly punished by Sarel herself, who burned out his eyes with hot coals.

The icy, inhuman perfection of her features made such a story believable.

She walked up the gangplank into the interior of the spacious basket beneath the swelling balloon. Inside, the faecal stench created an overpowering miasma. In spite of her perfumed mask, Sarel's eyes began streaming and she coughed.

At the sound Kichal whirled, hand automatically dropping to his sword hilt. Then he fell to his knees before Sarel. "My lady, forgive me, I did not know you were coming down here!"

"A whim," she said lightly. "A mere whim. Stand, Kichal. The Commander of my Bred need not grovel before me. What will the men think?"

"My men respect me. They know I respect you. What should they think?" The powerfully-built warrior rose to his feet, blood-red eyes watering.

"Can you smell the odor of the gas?" Sarel inquired.

"Yes, my lady."

"Strongly?"

"No. But I am aware of it."

"But you could not always smell it?"

"No, my lady."

Sarel nodded thoughtfully. Two cycles ago, she had introduced a tiny Void into Kichal's head, destroying portions of his brain, burning away memory and emotion, negating free will. As an unintentional side effect, the process also burned out his sense of smell and taste. At the time she had speculated as to whether his senses might someday regenerate naturally. Now it looked as if they had.

Would the regeneration of brain tissue make him less susceptible to her? Sarel wondered. She resolved to reintroduce the Void when he returned from this mission.

"When are you leaving?" she asked as she drifted around the cabin, taking care to touch nothing. All surfaces were coated with a malodorous grime.

"Within the day."

"You understand the importance of this mission?"

"Yes, my lady."

"I want the Silverhand. I want his companions too, dead or alive, it matters little to me. But I need the Silverhand *alive*. And when you capture him, be sure to break his legs so he cannot run."

"I will bring him back," Kichal promised. As Sarel turned away, his red eyes fixed on her back, watching the play of shadows on the shimmering mail as she moved. Somewhere in his damaged mind thoughts stirred, but when he attempted to concentrate on them they slithered away.

"It would be easier if I could have some of the Bred with me," he called to her as she started to leave the shanti.

Sarel half-turned back toward him, shaking her head. "I cannot give them to you, the beasts refuse to approach shanti. Perhaps it is because of the odor, or possibly the saurians are simply terrified of heights. No matter." She lowered the cloth she was holding and very deliberately smiled; that famous smile which made her beautiful beyond all women. Once again Kichal felt himself enthralled. "It is of no consequence," she was saying. "The Saurian Bred are finished as a species. The Breeder is developing a new strain for us: New Bred, grown from humans crossed with saurian stock. They are faster than the original Bred. These creatures are far more intelligent, capable of thought and speech. He assures us they will be unswervingly loyal. He has also given them an astonishingly accelerated growth rate by manipulating some gland in the throat. By the time you return, we should have some ready for your inspection."

Kichal looked up, and Sarel's smile widened. "Oh yes,

they will still be yours to command. But this time you will have an army worthy of you . . . of us.

"The New Bred will have no fear of heights and the smell of the gas will not bother them. Furthermore, Shantay's former apprentices have now developed shanti that are safe for use in combat areas. The basket is lacquered, the balloon coated with a skin that should make it impervious to weaponry. And each vessel can carry a hundred warriors.

"We have been using the prototype for our imperial craft while workers labored tirelessly to produce more. A score are completed now; within days we shall have a hundred." Smiling, Sarel stepped closer to Kichal, pressing herself against his body. "Think of it," she breathed. Her violet eyes grew dreamy as if with lust. "With the new shanti and the New Bred we will be invincible. Bring me back the Silverhand, Kichal, and then prepare for war. You will lead the New Bred in a campaign that will dazzle the world!"

For one fevered moment, Sarel pressed her mouth to Kichal's. Then she spun away.

He stood staring after her until her slim figure disappeared from sight. Then he slowly lifted his fingers and pressed them to his lips, where Sarel's kiss had burned. On her lips there had been a faint flavour of excrement. It had been a long time since he was aware of taste.

The sun was dipping below the horizon when the shanti took off. Red-gold light washed across the condensation on the silken balloon, setting a score of rainbows a-shimmer. Brilliant against a darkening sky, the air-ship presented a vision of ethereal beauty.

From the palace roof the twins watched its departure. The faintest hiss of foul gas wafted to them. "Will Kichal succeed?" Lares asked his sister in a tired voice. He had spent the day wandering the grey Aethyra landscape searching for the Silverhand. There was no sign of him, no aura, no telltale spark. Only the faintest of suspect ripples glimmered above the Island Sea, but not enough to pinpoint his location.

"Of course he'll succeed," Sarel replied reassuringly. She hated the weariness she heard in him. Her brother must be strong. Whatever he was, she was; they were inseparable in the true sense of the word. "We've never come so close before," she added, "and this time we shall get the Silverhand, I promise. He will no longer be a threat to us."

Standing behind Lares, she wrapped her arms around his chest and pressed her cheek lovingly against his back. "I've sent Kichal and forty of our personal guard to capture him. Kichal will do anything for me, undertake any sacrifice. He will gladly die rather than lose his quarry. The Silverhand stands no chance against such fanaticism. The game ends."

CHAPTER TWELVE

The opening door revealed a second tunnel. From the doorway, twenty broad metal steps led down to the metal floor of this new section. Strips of light were embedded in the ceiling, some sputtering fitfully but others dead, leaving areas submerged in pools of shadow. This second corridor seemed to slope downward, but it was hard to get any real idea of its configuration as it vanished in darkness. The walls were sheathed in panels of a form of Old Metal, with gleaming greyish-white surfaces untarnished by time.

Caeled caught Sioraf by the shoulder and pulled her forward to look through the doorway. "Can you see any purple glow in there?"

While the vampir beside him peered down the new tunnel, Caeled noticed the protective transparent membrane that slid across the surface of her eyes when confronted with a new situation. Sometimes he forgot what Sioraf was. But sooner or later, something always reminded him.

"No purple," she reported in a whisper. "But I am growing weak with hunger, Caeled."

He moved an infinitesimal distance away from her. The image of the rat-faced creature was still vivid in his mind. "Not yet. We need to move on."

"I hunger!" Sioraf insisted. Her fingers plucked at his arm but he pretended not to notice, turning his attention instead to the Stone Warrior.

She stood beside them, absentmindedly brushing at the hardened excrescences of her skin. "What do you make of this tunnel?" Caeled asked her.

"The whole place reminds me of the city of Gor. I think we should be ready for anything." Gwynne started to lift her morningstar, then lowered it again. "I'm as weak as a babe!" she complained, sounding surprised. "I don't like this place, I don't like it at all. The pain I experienced back there was terrible enough, but being weak frightens me. I had rather anything than feel vulnerable." She gave a bitter laugh. "Perhaps I am beginning to prefer being a woman of stone."

"Can you explain any of this?" Caeled asked her. "You have had experiences we have not."

"The strange glow Sioraf saw seems to have been some form of magic—or reverse magic," Gwynne replied. "It only affected certain of our attributes, parts of each of us that are . . . different. What some might call enchanted, I suppose. Or abnormal, depending on your point of view. I have heard of such violet light before.

"There are standing stones in the Spine that are shaped like doors. When thunder and lightning roll through the mountains, these 'doors' blaze with color and become actual gateways. It is claimed that if anyone with a certain sort of disease passes through at that time they will be cured. I have never seen the phenomenon myself, but those who have say the stones glow with a purple light. The Light of the Gods, they call it."

"Are such tales true?" Caeled wondered.

"Who knows? The stones are guarded by a fanatical

sect that has allowed no one to pass through the gateways in fifty cycles."

"If it were possible for you to go through such a gateway, could it cure you of your affliction?"

Gwynne considered the question, then said slowly, "Even if I thought so, I don't believe I could make myself do it, any more than I could return to that tunnel we just left. The agony . . . the sense of helplessness . . ."

Sniffing loudly, Madran loomed up behind them. "The air ahead is more stale than in the other tunnel," he commented. "But I smell nothing else. I think it's deserted."

"Well . . . since we can't go back . . ." Caeled pulled the small crossbow from his pack. Cocking the weapon, he inserted a bolt and then thrust a second bolt into his belt for easy access. "I'll go first. Madran behind me, then Sioraf. Gwynne, you take up the rear."

With a dismissive grunt, the Stone Warrior pushed past Caeled. "Don't be stupid. If there is an attack it will come from the front, and I am least vulnerable." She tapped her chest, stone on stone. "You're too valuable to lose," she added.

Her weight made the metal ring as she trundled down the steps and out onto the sloping metal floor of the corridor.

In the distance there was another metallic, clanging sound. Then a ghostly wind moaned along the tunnel.

Gwynne retreated back up the steps.

The sound stopped.

She rounded on Madran. "I thought you said it was deserted?"

Holding his sickle at the ready, the big Allta edged past her down the steps, constantly turning his head from side to side and sniffing. The hair at the nape of his neck bristled. When he reached the bottom step he paused with head cocked for several moments, then looked back at Caeled. "Nothing," he stated flatly. "There is nothing living down here."

"Anything dead?" whispered Sioraf.

"Nothing that smells," he told her. He took a cautious step onto the corridor floor.

Metal clanged again and the ghost wind moaned.

"Something's coming," warned Caeled, lifting the crossbow.

Madran backed up.

The sound stopped.

"It must be," Caeled said, "a relic of Elder Times." Less frightened than curious, he scampered nimbly down the steps. The moment his foot touched the corridor floor the sound came again, vibrating through the tunnel.

Madran made a snuffling noise. "The air is clearing!"

Caeled drew a deep breath. "Let's go," he told the others. "Stay close together."

The four companions gathered at the foot of the steps, then cautiously set off along the corridor. As they advanced the tunnel increasingly angled downward, taking them ever deeper into the earth and forcing them to brace themselves against the incline. A thick layer of dust carpeted the floor. Disturbed by their passage, it billowed up around them yet did not settle again but, curiously, kept on rising . . . spiralling upward to disappear close to the ceiling.

Sioraf sneezed once or twice, as delicately as a cat.

On they went; and down, down.

What would Scholar Nanri have given to see this place? Caeled asked himself. A part of Elder Times preserved as if the Elders had only left yesterday!

There was—had been—a chamber in Baddalaur that served as a small museum for displaying artefacts from the Elder Times. A few of the objects were identifiable, but many had purposes too obscure to even guess.

Opulence had been a habit with the Elders. These tunnels were, Caeled thought, a perfect example of their extravagance. With a single Old Metal panel off the walls, a man might live as a king today.

Caeled recalled a heated debate between Scholar Nanri and Brother Daniel, the Senior Librarian, about Old Metal in the Elder Times. Nanri was convinced the Elders actually manufactured various forms of the metal rather than working raw ore taken from the earth. Brother Daniel had conceded that Old Metal was not now found in a natural state, but insisted its manufacture was impossible. Too much heat would have been required, and there was no conceivable technology that would have allowed for the working of such a hard material in quantity. A case in point was Caeled's silver hand, made of reforged Old Metal by the craftsmen of Baddalaur. Even such a small item had taxed their capabilities to the utmost.

"Old Metal was an instantaneous creation of the gods," Daniel had pontificated. "A miracle, if you will. There is no other explanation."

Caeled smiled, remembering. What would Brother Daniel have said if he found himself in this metal-lined corridor? No doubt he would argue that this too was a creation of the gods. Caeled, however, was beginning to believe Nanri had been right. Inconceivable as it might seem, the Elders had manufactured great quantities of Old Metal; the proof was all around them.

But did possession of such skills not make them gods?

His speculations were interrupted by a sharp curve in the steadily descending tunnel. "Be careful here," Gwynne warned. They advanced cautiously . . . to find themselves facing an enormous fan set into the wall in front of them. The Old Metal blades were taller than Madran and broader than Gwynne.

Madran's nostrils flared again. "This is the source of the clean air and the ghost wind."

Caeled nodded. When he took a few steps toward the slowly revolving blades he could feel some force pull at him, but he continued to advance. He wanted to get a look between the blades. On the other side there seemed to be interesting shapes . . .

With a loud bang, the fan suddenly speeded up. A mighty rush of air pulled Caeled off his feet and sent him sliding down the floor towards the whirling blades. His silver hand scrabbled for purchase, but the suction was irresistible.

Madran lunged for him and caught the hem of his cloak, jerking him back just as his feet touched the edge of the framework housing the mechanism. Gwynne hastily rammed her morningstar between the blades. They ground to a halt and the fan stopped, though deep in its core there was a sound like angry insects buzzing.

As Caeled climbed shakily to his feet, realizing how close he had come to a horrible death, the fan gave off a sinister hiss and sparks exploded from its center. Caeled and the others hastily scrabbled backward. They heard something fall to the floor, then acrid grey smoke billowed around them. When it cleared they found Gwynne's morningstar lying at the base of the smouldering fan.

"A thousand, maybe fifteen hundred cycles old and still working, until you appear," Caeled said to Gwynne.

"I should have let it eat you," she replied as she examined the head of her morningstar. Though still usable, the weapon was badly damaged.

Caeled reached a cautious left hand toward the fan. A blue spark leaped from its center to his silvery fingers. Then it was quiet.

"It's dead," said Gwynne.

Caeled squatted to peer between the stilled blades.

"Nanri!" he breathed. "How you would have loved this!"

There was a grill behind the blades. Through the metal mesh, he could see an entire Elder city.

CHAPTER THIRTEEN

There were many legends of the Elders, and many artefacts from the past to lend the legends credence. Across the Seven Nations, from icy Thusal to the bitter Southlands, through the barren Steppes to the World's Edge, tales were told and retold, and in the telling, changed and altered, until there was not one history of the Elder Times, but many. During his cycles as a Scholar at Baddalaur Caeled had become familiar with most of them.

Some facts were generally accepted: before the Time of Burning, beings known as the Elders ruled the earth, arrogant and proud, capable of controlling every aspect of existence. Beings who were surely gods. Even the elements bowed before them. And then, as is common among the powerful, the gods warred.

There followed the Time of Burning. The Elders fled the world they had destroyed, leaving only blurred and broken remnants of their culture behind them.

Ages passed. Religions eventually arose to worship the vanished Elders, and philosophers built careers by attempting to explain both the gods and their disappearance. Some insisted that the current era held the final days of human and Allta alike, with the world a debased mockery of the paradise the gods had created.

There were those who contended that the Elders left the world because common folk ceased to revere them, devoting themselves instead to the mundane and trivial. By denying the need for gods, humankind drove them away. At least, that was one opinion.

The followers of Duetism believed the twins were a latter-day version of the gods, returned to the world to benefit humankind. This was, of course, a credo encouraged by the Duet themselves.

Other sects—heretical and forbidden—preached that the term gods was erroneous, and the powerful beings so labelled were really demons. They worshipped those ancient demons and dreamed of restoring them to their former glory with themselves as privileged acolytes.

Still others claimed the Elder gods were little more than men, but men with extraordinary powers. They spoke of an Elder culture which was in effect a highly advanced civilization composed of humans and Allta.

So what am I seeing? Caeled asked himself. A city of the gods? Or of men?

After prying off the grill behind the fan, he and the others had found themselves in a vast underground cavern which contained an intact Elder city, lit by thousands of miniature suns set atop slender, highly ornamented Old Metal poles. The lights were as artificial as those in the tunnels. Shantay the inventor had proved that such lighting was theoretically possible, but even his genius had been unable to turn theory into reality.

Caeled stared in wonder at the lights. How long had they been burning, how much longer would they continue to burn?

Footsteps echoing eerily, he wandered along deserted streets and shadowy laneways lined with what appeared to be empty shops. How old was the city? Was it one of the truly ancient towns, old even in the Elder Times, or was it one of those the gods had built in the last days before the Time of Burning?

Caeled smiled, suddenly reminded of one of the few times Nanri and Brother Daniel had agreed on anything. They had spent an entire season arguing about Elder architecture. Each bolstered his own argument by citing examples of surviving ruins. Finally they came to the joint conclusion that a wide variety of buildings had been erected to suit a wide variety of purposes. What some of those purposes might have been, neither man would speculate.

It was obvious, however, that the Elders built with permanence in mind. Buildings had been occupied for many generations. From surviving foundations, Scholar Nanri hypothesized that the Elders were able to construct astonishingly tall buildings by using a metal framework to allow them to stack floor upon floor.

Perhaps a different clan had occupied each storey? Sadly, no one would ever know. But many of the buildings past which Caeled now walked rose to a greater height than he had ever seen. The College of Baddalaur had been higher, but it was carved out of an extinct volcano, not built with cut stones. These were precisely fitted together so cleverly it was hard to see the join. Only a hairline of mortar showed, if one looked very hard. Some of the buildings were of grey stone flecked with tiny sparkles, while others had a creamy golden hue. But all were beautiful.

Nanri and Daniel had debated at length about the details of Elder construction. Their most heated arguments concerned the use of Old Metal as a building material. The secret of its source, whether natural or manufactured, had vanished with the Elders, leaving only remnants of silvery or dark blue metal that was almost as strong as stone and seemed impervious to the passage of time.

The metal commonly used in the Seven Nations was much softer, incapable of holding an edge and far too weak to sustain the weight of construction. The most skilled smiths could not make it more durable. Nanri and Daniel had agreed, reluctantly, that until their own age discovered—or rediscovered—the secret of forging and working hard metal, humankind would never advance.

Caeled thought again of the corridors through which they had just passed, with their wealth of Old Metal.

On a whim he turned to the right, following a street just wide enough to accommodate three chariots abreast. Defending this place would be impossible, he thought to himself. There was no natural cover. The tall buildings that lined the street on both sides had enormous glass windows, and doors also of glass, so the interiors were clearly visible. To his eyes they looked cold, forbidding.

Perhaps this was not a city at all, he thought, but a conglomeration of temples. Some whispered that the Elders had worshipped strange idols. Yet why was it built below ground? Was the place devoted to the worship of underground gods, creatures who dwelt in darkness?

If so, why offend them with artificial light?

And if the Elders were themselves gods, why would they build temples to other gods?

Each new step seemed to add to the mystery.

Caeled had never before heard of an Elder city built beneath the earth, though on the Steppes underground habitations were commonplace. There they served as protection from the freezing winds and abrupt falls in temperature that could turn a man into icy meat in a matter of heartbeats.

He stopped in the middle of the street and tilted his head back, his eyes following the multistoried buildings as they climbed into the dim upper recesses of the cavern. Perhaps the city had not always been under the ground. In the seasons following the Time of Burning, all the legends agreed that the earth had shifted, the seas rising and falling, land becoming sea, islands appearing where there had been none before, whole continents slipping below the waves.

Could the earth have swallowed this city during that ancient cataclysm?

Brushing his hair from his eyes with his metal hand, Caeled shook his head. No. The burning globes and strips would never have survived such violent upheaval, he reasoned. So this city must have been built underground deliberately.

But who occupied it, and what happened to them? Madran's inhumanly sensitive nose told them the city was long-deserted. The place was quite without odors, other than the mustiness of antiquity: no rot, no putrefaction, no smell of flesh or vegetation. Anything living was less than a memory.

Caeled felt a pang of disappointment. The little boy buried inside the man longed, just once, to see one of the Elders materialize before him.

He wandered down a sidestreet where the paving was as smooth and featureless as if molten rock had flowed and then solidified in the street shape. Many-storied towers lined the street, fabulous creations that appeared to be mostly glass. Crossing to a structure sheathed in some dark, smoky crystal, he tapped the surface with his metal fingers.

The material rang like a bell.

Almost at once Caeled heard running footsteps. Soon the others appeared from the various areas they had been exploring. Gwynne, as always, was the last to arrive. Her grim visage was grimmer still with the effort it cost her to hurry.

"What's wrong?" she demanded to know. "Why did you make that noise?"

Caeled smiled. "Just my curiosity," he said, tapping the glass again. "I've never seen anything like this before."

"There is a window in the palace in Barrow . . ." Madran

began. He paused in astonishment as a tiny crack appeared in the heart of the enormous window. With appalling speed the crack spread, radiating outward until the whole window disintegrated into a cloud of sparkling particles.

Caeled stared at the heap of crystal powder in horror. To have survived so long . . .

"There is a window in the Duet's palace in Barrow," Madran continued, drawing Caeled's attention from the glass. "I saw it once from the outside when the circus played there. It's in the shape of an enormous rose, composed of thousands of pieces of glass from the Elder Times. Los-Lorcan commissioned it in the first year of his reign, we were told. It was finally completed six seasons before the Duet seized power."

"People claim that the faces of his treacherous twin children are worked into the design of that window," Sioraf added. "The Duet are depicted as serpents with human faces."

Madran grinned wolfishly. "I doubt they would have left it intact if that were so."

"We should move on," Gwynne suggested. She looked toward Caeled, but he had resumed staring at the shattered glass. Madran draped an arm around the young man's shoulder. "This is an ancient place," the big Allta said gently. "It is as fragile as a spider's web, delicate and perfect, but destroyed with a touch. Don't reproach yourself; a sneeze would probably have broken the glass."

"Did you know," Caeled said abruptly, "that the Elders had glass plates and pitchers? I saw drawings of them in the library at Baddalaur. They must have been worth a king's ransom." He slowly turned around, his eyes roving over the city. "Look, my friends, here we are surrounded by a fortune in rare glass. Scholars and princes would kill to gaze upon this place. A whole family could live on the proceeds of selling just one sheet of this crystal."

The others were watching him intently. Caeled realized he was talking too fast, the words spilling out.

He placed the splayed fingers of his metal hand against another window, and gently—gently—pressed inwards. The glass shattered as before. "So here we are surrounded by this great wealth," he said, "and we can do nothing with it. Our touch destroys it.

"Once the Elders were surrounded by such wealth. Moreover, they had skills and magics we cannot imagine . . . yet they are gone. All this lost to them. Lost to us!" His voice rose in a wail of pain.

Gwynne's words cut through the sound. "You're not making sense," she snapped. "Pull yourself together."

"This place doesn't make sense!" he replied bitterly. "And yet I've been trained and schooled to believe that everything makes sense, that there is a reason for everything, an order underlying all that is."

"There doesn't have to be a meaning."

"There does!"

"Why?" Gwynne asked. She waved a hand at the city. "This is an Elder city. In the mountains of the Spine there are scores of similar examples, not so well preserved, I'll grant you, but they are there all the same. In one sits part of a boat. A boat in the middle of a city in the mountains! Where is the meaning in that? Either it fell out of the sky . . . or the seas rose and washed it far inland. I've watched men duel to the death to defend one opinion or the other. And do you know what? It doesn't matter!

"This *place* doesn't matter, Caeled, and whatever Elder mysteries you find here have no relevance. Their world ended with the Time of Burning. The Elders vanished, leaving behind these remains to confuse us. Instead of looking back, we should be looking forward. Instead of seeking to understand the past, we should concentrate on the problems of the present and the future."

"But what are we to believe in?" Caeled asked in a hoarse voice.

"Believe in yourself. And believe this: if we do not stop the Duet, then they will wreak destruction on the world we have now and perhaps plunge us into another Time of Burning." She tapped the bag on his back. "If you need something from the past to believe in, put your faith in the Arcana.

"At least we know they work."

"What is he so upset about?" Gwynne asked Madran later as the two watched Caeled, with Sioraf close by his side, again wander off down the street.

Madran growled, "Have you totally turned to stone? Can't you understand? He was taught to believe that the Elders were gods, and the ancient times were a paradise. Despite the tales that come down to us from that terrible age, the people who taught Caeled filled him with a reverence for the Elders and all their works. Now he is questioning those beliefs."

"Do you question them?"

"My upbringing was quite different from Caeled's," the Allta replied. "I did not study ancient books; what I know I learned through my travels with the circus. That sort of life teaches you to question everything. Personally, I doubt if the Elders were gods, but the possibility doesn't worry me much one way or the other. It has nothing to do with us."

"So you think he fears the truth. Or what you believe is the truth."

"I think he knows the truth. Admitting it is the problem."

Meanwhile Caeled went down one street and then another, drawn by an insatiable curiosity. Sioraf continued to cling to his arm; he knew what she wanted, though she said nothing. As they walked, he found himself making comparisons to the city of Gor in the Forest of Taesir, the refuge of the terrifying Treeselves-Cityselves. The avenues of Gor were broad and spacious, unlike the narrow streets of this city, and Gor's buildings were much less high. Gor seemed in retrospect to be a horizontal city, whereas this one was vertical, as if its towering structures were holding up the earth above.

Abruptly Caeled tugged free of Sioraf and struck off down a laneway. At the far end, a building of mellow golden stone caught his eye, its very architecture setting it apart. A wide panel set above the entrance bore traces of an Elder script that had once been picked out with some bright color, now too faded to decipher. But when he peered through the glass doors he gave a cry of delight that brought Sioraf running after him.

The building housed a library.

The interior arrangement bore little resemblance to the one Caeled had known so well in Baddalaur, however. Here row upon row of books lined the walls on open shelves that appeared to be made of metal. More free-standing metal shelves filled the center spaces, reaching almost to the ceiling and crammed with books. Still other volumes were stacked on tables or piled in bins.

Only for a heartbeat did Caeled hesitate. Then he put his shoulder to the door and pushed. A lock held briefly, then gave, and the door slammed open with a shattering of glass.

When Sioraf came running back in search of Gwynne and Madran, she could not make them understand what was wrong. But they followed her, to find Caeled kneeling on the floor in the center of the library, his face buried in hands of flesh and metal. He was weeping bitterly.

"Are you hurt?" Gwynne wanted to know. She shoved Caeled's hands aside and turned his face up to hers. "Are you hurt?"

He managed to shake his head.

The Stone Warrior looked around. "I would have thought you'd be delirious with joy to find a place like this."

Caeled's sobs intensified.

Sioraf caught Gwynne's eye. Slowly, meaningfully, she

reached out and touched one of the nearest books with the tip of her finger.

The volume crumbled to dust.

"So much knowledge," Madran muttered, his moist brown eyes sweeping across the tightly packed shelves.

"And none of it accessible," Gwynne added. "How ironic!"

CHAPTER FOURTEEN

Caeled was no longer sure when night had ceased to be dark for him. His vision had been excellent until he damaged it with so much reading in poor light, but fortunately, at Baddalaur he had been taught to heighten his other senses by way of compensation. Impressions had begun to cross sensory boundaries, so that at times he could hear color and taste shapes. Then after his first use of the Arcana, something remarkable had happened.

At first it was no more than a slight improvement in his night vision. What had been a formless blackness became a dim landscape of purple and dark green. His eyesight grew steadily sharper, however, until by now a moonless, overcast night was as clear to him as early twilight. In such a setting the contrast of even a small fire could burn painfully into his hypersensitive eyes.

Caeled's perceived twilight lent the Elder city a special beauty. Empty glass windows reflected a panoply of shadows ranging from the exquisite to the grotesque, and the textures of stone shopfronts took on a richness not apparent by daylight.

The four companions had been crossing what appeared

to be a main thoroughfare when the lights abruptly died, plunging the city into darkness. Madran, growling, clutched his sickle. Gwynne swore as she waved her morningstar blindly in the air. "I can't see anything!" she protested.

Caeled swiftly gathered them into a knot facing outward, weapons at the ready. But no menace appeared.

"There must be something that makes the lights go on and off on their own," Caeled said at last, lowering his loaded crossbow. At his words, Sioraf slipped her ripple-edged dagger back into its scabbard. "The old writings agree," he went on, "that the Elders could order the world around them to function according to their will. Obviously some of their spells are still working."

"Perhaps the lights here are somehow attuned to natural light in the outside world," Gwynne suggested.

"That's it!" exclaimed Madran. "You're a clever, ah, woman. Night has fallen in the world above, I can feel it in my bones." He smiled. The smile widened into a grin that left his red tongue lolling from the side of his mouth. A shudder ran through the big Allta, then with a joyful grunt he threw off his human form, summoning the were-change.

When only a huge shaggy wolfhound stood where a man had been, the grin remained.

"He prefers this image," Sioraf told the others. "He has always said it is more comfortable to go on four legs than two, and his senses are much sharper. Female dogs," she added mischievously, "find him irresistible."

Caeled lifted the sickle Madran had dropped and strapped it to his pack. "Perhaps we should get off the street for a while anyway, just in case there is some danger," he said. "It might be unwise to keep wandering around a strange city in the dark."

No one argued.

He led the way to the nearest building and forced open a door. Sioraf guided Gwynne. Madran padded along beside them, ears pricked and nose atwitch.

They found themselves in a low-ceilinged shop whose walls were lined with empty cabinets. A cursory search failed to find anything remotely edible. Cobwebs sagged with the weight of dust.

Stomachs rumbling with hunger, the four companions settled themselves to wait for the coming of the dawn in the world outside, in hopes it would mean a return of the lights in the underground city.

Gwynne propped herself against a wall in a sitting position. Soon she was snoring hoarsely. Her labored breathing made Caeled wonder how long it would be before the weight of her stony flesh crushed her lungs.

After a time, Madran got up and trotted from the shop, going off in response to some canine instinct. Caeled made no effort to call him back. The Allta's were-life was his own.

The night seemed endless. Caeled tried to sleep, but hunger kept him awake. The whisper of cloth told him Sioraf was also restless. He heard her creeping closer to him—in search of comfort?—but a memory of her rat-faced visage in the first tunnel flashed across his mind and he shivered in spite of himself.

"I'm awake," he warned.

Sioraf stopped and lifted her head. Even with his improved vision he could not make out her features; her blue eyes were lost in pools of shadow. "I didn't mean to disturb you," she said. "I just wanted to get close; I'm cold."

"I couldn't sleep."

"Nor could I."

Caeled glanced out through the dusty glass shopfront at the lifeless city beyond. "What do you suppose it was like in the Elder Days?" he wondered aloud. "Would there have been lights burning in every window, and people walking up and down the streets? Music from open doorways, perhaps—but what sort of music? Or maybe the Elders never went out at night, maybe they just slept.

On second thought, maybe they never slept, didn't need to sleep. They accomplished so much, maybe . . ."

"That's too many maybes," Sioraf told him.

"I know. Or rather, I do not know; that's the problem. I want to know. Everything we see only reminds me how ignorant I really am."

She snuggled close to him. "Even with all your education?"

" 'Education teaches us how much remains to be learned,' " Caeled replied, quoting Nanri his tutor. "The books I read at Baddalaur turned the Elders into beings of mythic proportion. Their creations were mightier, their inventions more complex—everything was greater than we could ever aspire to. They had bridges of the thinnest wire and towers of gossamer webwork. Fragments of Elder lore mentioned shanti capable of carrying hundreds of passengers into the sky, and metal ships—an impossibility, I realize now, because metal does not float—that could transport thousands across the seas.

"But seeing the reality of Elder cities . . . I'm not so certain. Oh, the wonders they wrought with metal and glass are very impressive. But somehow none of it is as . . . as *godlike* as I expected. I can imagine beings not too different from myself living in these cities.

"What about those beings? The Elders were very powerful, that much is indisputable—but why does so little remain of all they must have created? And what were they actually like, Sioraf? It is presumed that they resembled modern folk, but we've found no images we could be certain were those of Elders. There are some ancient statues of Allta-like creatures, immense carvings preserved in dry places like the desert. Surely those weren't the Elders? They weren't half animal, were they?"

Beside him, Sioraf shifted her weight and stretched. "I am half-vampire and half-human," she reminded Caeled.

"That's different," he said impatiently. His mind went racing on, throwing up one question after another. Aside from a vague awareness of the cold radiating from Sioraf, he hardly noticed her. "Another thing—why were there so many different ancient languages? I have studied some of them, but their number only makes me wonder why the Elders needed so many. If they were as wise as we assume, would not one language suffice?"

Sioraf gave a sleepy murmur he could interpret any way he liked.

But he did not need her to listen; he did not need to speak aloud at all. The questions went on inside him.

This deserted city—this extraordinary, ordinary town—raised questions which struck at the very heart of his beliefs. Having explored its streets and laneways, he was forced to the conclusion that it was built for ordinary men and women. Although the buildings towered to the distant roof of the cavern, everything was in human proportions. The doors were designed to accommodate human height, the benches were shaped to suit the human buttocks and angle of leg. Nothing here was designed for giants.

But was it not written that in the Elder Days there were giants?

This city offered no proof of the existence of giants—or of gods. Only of human builders with skills far beyond those known in Caeled's era.

So—were there no gods? Had there never been gods? Were the Elders simply mortal?

If that could be true, then what of the Duet, who claimed kinship with the gods? On that claim they had founded a religion devoted to themselves which approved of everything they did, no matter how extreme.

Were the twins mortal too? Or . . . were they something else?

With a chill, Caeled realized he was thinking thoughts that his education in Baddalaur had never prepared him for, thoughts that could lead . . . where?

"I'm hungry," Sioraf said suddenly. She rested a long-fingered hand on his bare arm.

Glancing down, for a moment Caeled thought he saw the hand twist into a taloned claw.

"I need to eat."

"So do I," he replied.

"But you can feed me, Caeled."

He peered into her face. In spite of the darkness, his enhanced vision allowed him to see her very clearly now: the fine bone structure, the huge eyes, the soft mouth. "What would happen if I were to drink vampir blood?" he asked with a humorless grin.

"You would sicken. But if you drank enough over an extended period of time you would become one with us."

"Us?"

"The vampir."

"Are there any advantages?"

Sioraf curled close against his body, drawing heat from his flesh. He could smell her scent, that of ivory and moonlight. Lying down, she rested her cheek against his thigh and he felt a pulse begin to pound in his body.

"You would be very long-lived," she told him, "impervious to all but the most devastating injuries. In some ways you would be stronger, swifter, more agile . . ." her voice trailed away.

"None of those are sufficient reason for me to become a blood drinker," Caeled said. His left hand began absently stroking her hair. There was the soft hiss of metal against silk. "I once read that only females become true vampiri," he remarked.

Sioraf was suddenly conscious of his cold metal fingers at the back of her neck. The sensation was not unpleasant; a tiny thrill ran down her spine. "I have seen male vampiri," she said, "but they are rare." With an effort, she laughed. "Not so rare as a half-vampir like me. Caeled, did you ever long to be . . . ordinary?"

"I was ordinary, once," he told her. "Just a little boy like any other."

Her voice was wistful. "Was it wonderful?"

He looked down in surprise. "Wonderful? I never thought of it that way. We were poor and we had a lot of problems. In those days I longed to be anything but ordinary. I wanted to be a famous hero or a mighty king; anything that would make my mother proud of me and give her an easier life."

"My father wanted an easier life for me," Sioraf related. "He always hoped the human part of me would grow stronger and outweigh the vampir until I could be like anyone else. 'When things get better,' he used to say."

"My mother was always saying that too!"

"And did things get better, Caeled?"

"No. She died. Horribly."

Sioraf buried her face against his body. "Like my father," she murmured.

A wave of pity swept over the young man. He started to gather her into his arms until a memory stopped him. "In that first tunnel," he whispered, "I saw something."

"What?" Sioraf's voice was still muffled.

He hesitated. Then the words came tumbling out. "I looked at you and saw a rat-faced creature, terrible, vile."

Sioraf sat up abruptly. "Are you frightened of me? You must not be. Listen to me. Just now you were questioning the legends about the Elders. There are legends that the vampiri are shape-shifters, that we transform ourselves into rats or bats or curls of smoke in order to sneak up on our prey. Those tales aren't true, I assure you. They are cruel, though, and they hurt; they cause people to hunt us more savagely than we ever hunt.

"What is true is that humans, looking at us, sometimes see the image of their own hidden fears. Or their deepest desires. Some men perceive me as a beautiful goddess, you know. I'm sorry if . . . Are you very afraid of rats?"

The question caught him off guard. For a moment he recalled the rats of his childhood, the scourge of the long succession of filthy tenements he and his mother lived in, creatures so bold they would climb into a child's bed at night and gnaw his face. How many nights had he awakened screaming, just in time . . .

Sioraf twisted her head to look up at him. "Is that what you think of me? Am I a horror to you?"

He thought he heard pain in her voice. "No," he replied gently.

"Yet you saw me as a beast."

"I saw a beast," he agreed, "but you're telling me it was something from inside myself." He attempted a smile. "I have no control over my buried fears."

Sioraf gazed up at him for a long time, while he wondered how well a vampir could see in the dark. Could she read the expression on his face?

At last she said, "What *do* you think of me?"

"I think . . ." he paused, uncertain of the answer.

"If I were a human female would you like me better?"

Caeled said nothing.

"Do you hesitate because I am vampir? Does my blood drinking repel you so?"

Caeled wanted to deny it, but he could not speak.

Sioraf rose to her knees, bringing her face so close to his he could smell her breath. It did not smell of blood, but reminded him of bitter herbs and sweet flowers. And summer rain. "I was born this way," she said. "I had no control over it. If you must condemn me, condemn me for what I do, not for what I am."

Caeled reached out and placed his hands of flesh and metal on the vampir's shoulders. "I won't condemn you," he promised. "You are different, that's all. Well, I am different too, I'm not ordinary any more. Not with a silver hand.

"You drink blood, and that does bother me. But so long as you take sustenance only from my veins and no one else suffers, it's all right.

"But when I saw that . . . that *thing*, in the tunnel, suddenly I wondered if I was seeing the real you. And I couldn't bear it!" His fingers tightened on her shoulders. "If this body you wear is nothing more than a lovely shell meant to disguise and deceive . . . to hide something ugly . . ."

"If that were so," Sioraf said wryly, "I would have chosen a more comely form."

"Forgive me."

"There is nothing to forgive. But you still haven't told me what you really think of me."

"I think I love you," he said slowly.

She drew in a sharp breath. Then, "Have you ever loved before?"

"My mother. Nanri, my teacher."

"Have you ever loved a woman?"

"No," he admitted. "Have you ever loved a man?"

"Yes," she said. "But they could not forget that I was vampir."

Caeled noted the use of the word "they" and asked no more questions. He did not want to hear the answers. Without a word, he rolled up his sleeve and pressed his wrist to Sioraf's mouth.

She did not bite, merely touched her lips to his skin. "It has been a long time since a man said he loved me," she murmured. Her words were warm on his flesh. "And then it was a lie. I was only desired for the gift of near immortality I could bestow."

"I don't want that."

"I know. I know now."

Her touch was a kiss. Caeled sat quietly, eyes closed, revelling in sensual delight. Then he remembered. He cupped the back of her skull and pressed her face hard against his arm. "Feed," he said tenderly. "Let me feed you."

Her bite was ecstasy.

When Madran returned later, his were-dog senses caught the bitter odor of blood on the dry air long before he reached the shop. He loped forward with a growl in his throat.

When he got to the doorway he paused, hackles raised, and scanned the interior for some sign of enemies. He detected none but dropped to his belly anyway, creeping with cunning stealth. Once he was inside he saw Gwynne sleeping propped against the far wall, her mouth slightly ajar. And in one corner, Caeled and Sioraf were asleep in a tangle of limbs.

They were both naked. The vampir's skin was as white as bone in the gloom, but her lips were red and her cheeks bore a rosy flush. As Madran went nearer he saw puncture wounds on Caeled's arm—and bare throat.

They reminded the Madra Allta of rat bites.

CHAPTER FIFTEEN

Without warning, Anadyr wrapped his huge hand around the back of the drunk's head and slammed it facedown on the wooden bar. A shocked silence descended on the crowded tavern. Most of the customers were bleak-faced men who worked on the wharves.

The drunk was Bocht, who in addition to being the son of a prominent wine merchant was catamite to the local magistrate.

Anadyr turned a menacing glare on Bocht's drinking companions and deliberately unwound a length of chain from around his waist. He gave it a lazy swing. The metal was inferior and soft, bearing no resemblance to the great alloy known as Old Metal. Only the most debased material was available to anyone below the rank of emperor and even this would have been beyond Anadyr's reach if it had not been for the influence of his employer.

The chain was not intended for hard usage. But the threat was obvious. When he was sure no one dared interfere, Anadyr plucked the stunned young man's purse from his belt and shook out the contents onto the bar.

Shimmering Eron scales scattered like jewels across the dark and polished wood.

Anadyr gave a triumphant shout.

Pushing aside a leather curtain, Lamar appeared from a room in the back. The little man glanced first at his hideously scarred servant, then at the flakes on the bar. His round face registered disappointment. "You all know me," he addressed the room at large. "I deal honorably with you, and I expect treatment in kind. There are no short measures here; integrity is my watchword."

No one said anything.

"And you know I have the best girls!" he went on, raising his voice. "I keep them clean, well fed, and disease free, for which you should be grateful. Or at least your wives should," the innkeeper added with a grin.

There was a pause, then a ripple of hesitant laughter.

Lamar had won; he had them on his side now. He said, "And you all know Bleu. Some of you have known Bleu quite often, in fact."

The laughter swelled appreciatively. A stocky man with a red, bushy beard whistled and stamped his feet.

"Well, Bleu is now addicted to Eron scales. I don't need to tell you what that means for the poor girl."

Heads nodded sympathetically. Addiction to the scales was fatal and the last stages were agonizing. The entire musculature of the body warped, tying the unfortunate sufferer almost literally into knots. Webbing appeared between the fingers and toes. The epidermis changed, coarsened, began leaking a foul-smelling oily substance that was toxic to any normal person who might touch it, preventing anyone from nursing the dying individual. By the time the addict drew a final breath, little remained that looked human.

It was a fate no one in the tavern would wish on a friend.

Lamar wrapped his free hand in Bocht's perfumed hair and lifted his head off the counter. The young man's elegantly shaped nose was elegant no longer. It was badly broken and streaming blood, and the eyes on either side were already swelling.

Bocht tried to speak, but Lamar promptly slammed his face down, destroying the nose past any hope of restoring. He screamed with pain.

"We have laws down here on the wharf," Lamar said dispassionately. Continuing to hold his victim by the hair with one hand, with the other he reached under the bar and produced a shell knife. The honed edges of the blade were as sharp as razors, glinting with menace in the light of the oyster-oil lanterns. "Not many laws, it is true, but those few we observe are important. One of them prohibits anyone peddling Eron scales, because we know how addictive they are. The dreams they bring are irresistible. Once a man or woman has sucked on the scales, they will do anything to get more.

"This wretched Bocht was supplying Bleu with the drug. She sold her possessions to buy more scales, then began stealing from her customers—and from me. I don't like that. I don't like it at all. It makes me very, very angry." To emphasize his words, Lamar jerked Bocht's head forward. While his audience stared, he abruptly sliced off the man's ear with his knife.

This time, Bocht's shriek of agony made strong men flinch.

"But that's not all," the innkeeper continued. "My servant has discovered that Bocht embeds Eron scales in sweetmeats and sells them to the children of folk who work on the wharves."

Men leaped to their feet with cries of rage. Knives and cargo hooks appeared out of nowhere.

"Wait," Lamar ordered sternly. Several men had rushed forward already, but he fixed them with a cold stare that made them hesitate long enough for Anadyr to bear down upon them, chain-wrapped fist very much in evidence.

They waited.

"We also have evidence," continued Lamar, "that this disgusting individual introduced Eron scales into his father's wine—with the old man's approval." He calmly sliced off the young man's other ear. "I disapprove of using good wine to create more addicts."

Bocht sagged in his grip. Blood was pouring from his wounds and he appeared to have fainted from the pain.

With a shove, Lamar thrust him away from the bar. He fell sprawling on the sawdust-covered floor.

No one moved to help him.

"You will note I have marked him in the approved manner of the wharves," the innkeeper drawled as he wiped his knife blade on the bar towel. "Let all who look on Bocht know him for what he is. An outlaw. Outside the law. Henceforth no law protects him." He turned away and disappeared behind the leather curtain.

No sooner was he out of sight, than it began. Lamar paused just behind the curtain, listening with satisfaction as Anadyr flung back the door to the street and the crowd rushed outside, carrying Bocht somewhere in their midst. Through the open doorway came grunts and shouts, and the sound of blows striking flesh.

If Bocht's mangled body was ever fished from the bay, the sea creatures would have obliterated any clue as to who or what killed him. His lover the magistrate would have an insoluble mystery on his hands.

By the time Lamar reemerged, Anadyr had mopped the blood off the bar. Smiling was impossible for the huge man because of the scar tissue on his face, but his single blue eye was twinkling. "How much of that was true?" he asked his employer.

"Enough. A seed upon which the tale grew. Bocht was a scale user, and he did give Bleu some scales in return for a piece of jewelry a sea captain had given her. He was greedy. He had the magistrate eating out of his hand; he could have remained with him for cycles, living well and easily, but he always wanted more, more of everything.

Remember when you beat Lili for holding back on me? She blurted out that she was going to run away with Bocht, he was going to take her south, make her rich. Probably by pimping her," he added bitterly. "Well, I could not allow that, could I? And, being a practical man, I saw a way to take two fish in one net. Now I've not only eliminated Bocht from Lili's plans, but I've begun the ruin of his father's wine trade as well. The old man was increasing his prices to me beyond all reason. No one will purchase any more wine from him once they hear a rumor his stock is contaminated with Eron scales."

"Is it?"

Lamar laughed unpleasantly. "Not that I know of."

One by one the drinkers reappeared. None spoke of what had happened in the street outside, but all applied themselves with energy to the task of drinking.

The inn enjoyed a most profitable night.

As the evening wore on, the crowd thinned out, then swelled again, and the rooms upstairs did a brisk business. Lamar was amused to note that the unfortunate Bleu got more than her share of the custom. He speculated on the profitability of travelling south with the night's proceeds, visiting Barrow in hopes of acquiring some new women. Under the influence of the Duet, the females of Barrow had become famous for their skill in the more exotic erotic arts.

Lamar's colleague Dudley, who ran a brothel on the other side of Rock, had once possessed a pair of identical twins from Barrow. Their services had been in much demand in that city, where all twins were admired, but he had lured them away with promises of a fortune to be made. When they reached Seamount, however, they realized they would see little of the fortune. The coin they earned disappeared into Dudley's capacious pockets. In his establishment they proved an extraordinary draw . . . until one died of accidental poisoning.

A terrible loss; Lamar had comforted his friend at the

funeral. He subsequently used the same poison on a female Madra Allta whore Dudley imported. The Allta took the form of an elegant racing hound at the height of passion, and the demand for her was so strong that she was booked days in advance—until her unfortunate demise.

Anadyr promptly spread a rumor that the cook who worked for Dudley had a hidden record as a wife-poisoner.

Business, Lamar reflected, demanded that one keep on his toes and not let the competition get ahead of him.

Lamar and Anadyr stopped serving at midnight and began clearing the bar. This far north taverns closed early, then reopened shortly after dawn to accommodate those who preferred to drink their breakfast.

When the bar was empty Anadyr patrolled the dimly lit upstairs corridors of the inn, tapping on certain closed doors with a cudgel. The evening's last clients—half a dozen men and one lone woman—dutifully appeared and made their way out into the night.

No one was in the mood for a dispute with Lamar or his henchman.

It was the innkeeper's habit to rake up the coals and sit before the fire for a while after closing, allowing the tensions of the day to drain away as he smoked his favorite pipe. Meanwhile, Anadyr cleared the tables, carrying dishes and beakers into the back for the women to wash in the morning.

"Join me," Lamar invited as Anadyr walked past him with a loaded tray.

The Islander grunted grateful assent. He found two clean beakers and filled them with spicy southern mead, then joined his master before the fire. From a pouch affixed to his belt Anadyr took a lump of butter wrapped in oiled cloth, and began rubbing it over his damaged skin. "Will there be trouble about Bocht?" he asked Lamar.

The innkeeper considered the question. "Unlikely. You kept the scales and Bocht's purse?"

"I did. And added more scales, as you suggested."

"So there is the evidence. We had plenty of witnesses here tonight. Neither you nor I killed him, although I was perfectly within my rights to do so. The community should be in my debt, removing such a menace from the wharves." He drank deeply and licked his lips. "I think everything will be fine. We'll hear no more talk from Lili of running away, and I daresay there will be no more stealing from me, either. And Bleu—how is she?"

"Exhausted," Anadyr grinned.

"Give her a couple of Eron scales, that will invigorate her." Just then Lamar noticed Anadyr stiffen. Without a word, the innkeeper rose and made his way to the bar. From underneath he produced a cut-down whaling crossbow, designed to fire two arm-length barbed bolts simultaneously.

"Visitors, Anadyr?"

"Someone's coming," the servant affirmed. He unwrapped his chain from around his waist and held it two-handed, ready.

Lamar whispered, "I don't hear anything outside. Are you sure?"

"Positive. Just wait. Can't you smell it?"

"What?"

"Waste. Human waste."

Lamar started to laugh even as the door shuddered beneath a pounding blow, then sprang open. "We have important guests, Anadyr! Fetch more mead."

Kichal wafted in on a stench of human excrement. It clung to his flesh and to the crimson and ebony leathers he wore.

After welcoming him effusively, Lamar put away the crossbow and ushered Kichal to the most comfortable chair. With his own hands the innkeeper poured a brimming measure of mead and urged it on his visitor, holding out the beaker at arm's length. Kichal fixed his red eyes on the innkeeper, watching with amusement as the small man attempted to conceal his revulsion at the appalling odor.

"I understand the shanti still use human gas," Lamar remarked. He was trying to breathe only through his mouth. He avoided meeting the commander's eyes; they looked like weeping wounds.

Kichal ignored the remark. "You got our message." It was a statement, not a question.

"Indeed we did. We were overjoyed, to learn that you would be paying us a personal . . ."

"The message peist that was sent to you did not return."

"The journey proved too strenuous," Lamar replied, dry-mouthed. "It's such a long flight from Barrow."

Kichal wondered if the man was lying. Would it be worth hitting him? He cast a measuring glance at the servant. Island Trash, obviously, but powerfully built, much more of a danger than his master.

The man's solitary eye made him vulnerable, however. Although Kichal had not bothered to bring any bodyguards in with him, he was confident he could overpower Anadyr. The erstwhile Commander of the Bred had one great advantage: he could feel no pain.

But no sooner had he congratulated himself on his invulnerability than he became aware of the chill of the stone wall at his back. Worse—he could smell the stink he carried. He could even taste the sweetness of the mead in his mouth, which for so long had tasted nothing.

Sensation was returning.

Disconcerted, he tried to get back to the business at hand. "Make your report, Lamar," he snapped.

Lamar raised his hand and beckoned Anadyr forward. The servant had disliked the red-eyed Kichal on sight, but he respected anything more dangerous than himself. Kichal was very dangerous.

"This news is fresh," said Anadyr. "On the midday tide today, a free trader called the *Black Pearl* arrived in the harbor. They barely made port. The captain was dead, and her ship had been caught in a Shipkiller."

"A particularly deadly ice storm," Lamar explained before Kichal could ask.

"A surviving crewman said the ship was carrying pilgrims." Anadyr continued. "They boarded at Sansen and claimed they were going to the holy well at Tonne."

"The site of the lost city of Lowstone," Lamar added, "in case it's relevant."

"I will decide what is relevant." Kichal sipped his mead thoughtfully. The thick, sweet liquor reminded him of summer, of hot sun on meadow grass and the taste of honeycomb . . .

He pushed the unbidden memories aside. They made him feel sad and it was a very long time since he had felt sad. The emotion was disconcerting. "Go on, what about these pilgrims? I assume you have some reason for mentioning them?"

"There were four of them. They disguised their appearance as best they could, but one was young and female, another young and male. There was also a very heavy man or woman—my informant could not be sure which—and a tall man with shaggy hair."

Kichal's crimson eyes stared unblinkingly at Anadyr. The servant felt a trickle of fear along his spine. "They killed the captain and some of the crew," he continued.

Lamar had never heard the giant sound nervous before. "Allow me to interject," he said to rescue Anadyr. "Misha, the captain of the *Black Pearl*, was a capable officer and a friend of mine, but she made the most of whatever opportunities came her way. . . ."

"She robbed and murdered passengers?" Kichal asked blandly.

"Murder is such an ugly word."

"So is what happened here today," replied Kichal.

With a sinking feeling, Lamar realized he knew about Bocht; perhaps knew far too much for the innkeeper's good. This man represented the Duet and they had eyes everywhere. Terrible red eyes . . .

It was Anadyr's turn to try to rescue his master. "As the pilgrims escaped, a member of the crew noticed that the young man had a silver hand," he offered as a distraction.

Kichal leaned forward and caught the servant by the front of his robe, hauling him forward and forcing him to his knees. His strength was unlike any Anadyr had ever encountered. His eyes were blazing. "This is truth?"

Anadyr attempted to pull away, but the commander's grip was unbreakable. The stench was sickening. "Truth! I swear it! I questioned him myself, and he would be afraid to lie to me."

"You say they escaped? Where?"

"Near an unnamed island, a shunned, haunted place," Anadyr said hoarsely.

"How much of a lead have they got?"

"A day. No more."

"Is there any way off the island?"

"None."

Kichal shoved Anadyr away from him and stood up. "We will leave immediately. And you are coming with us."

Anadyr turned a stricken face toward his master, but before Lamar could protest on his behalf, Kichal produced a whip made of fine metal wire no thicker than a finger. With a flick of his wrist he sent it curling through the air. The tip of the lash snaked into a lantern, extinguished the flame with a hiss. Lamar recalled hearing that the twins insisted their officers hone their skills on live targets. An expert with a whip could send the metal tip of the weapon deep into his victim's body and shred a beating heart.

Lamar swallowed hard. "Anadyr will be pleased to accompany you," he promised.

CHAPTER SIXTEEN

There were times when Sarel desperately longed for a child. She had discussed it with her brother and Lares was more than willing for her to conceive. But something always held her back. The fear of what she and her brother might produce, perhaps; the niggling doubt that instead of the beautiful genius she envisioned, an offspring of their mating might be deformed and mad.

Given their family background, such a fear was not unfounded.

When the Breeder began to work for them, conducting his experiments, she spoke with him and expressed her fears. He explained the dangers of sibling matings. "The risk would be heightened a hundredfold in your case," he told Sarel, "because your father, Los-Lorcan, sired you and Lares on his own younger sister, Anuna. Already there is a dangerous degree of inbreeding. You two are fortunate indeed that you are not, ah, damaged in some way."

Damaged, indeed! Sarel's temper had flared at the mere suggestion, until the Breeder cowered before the fire in her eyes. "You are both perfect, perfect!" he cried hastily.

To mollify her, he had suggested that once his experiments were perfected, Sarel and Lares could safely conceive a child together. He would be able, he claimed, to manipulate the embryo, shaping it to their design. "Your child will be perfection itself!" the Breeder assured Sarel.

But the longed-for conception had not yet taken place. Sarel still hesitated. Waiting for the right time, perhaps . . .

Now, as she wandered among the breeding pits that had replaced the dungeons of Barrow, she thought of them as hatching her children. Or at least an acceptable substitute. It was a pity they would have such short lives.

Each tiny sunken cubicle held a single bed to which a naked woman lay strapped. Some of the women were beautiful. All were healthy, the finest breeding stock from the Seven Nations.

Those kept in the underground pits were in an advanced state of pregnancy. Once successfully inseminated, they were isolated from any outside contact and their pregnancy strictly monitored. A powerful narcotic was added to the artificial compound on which they were fed, to keep them almost comatose. It was imperative that they remain quiet; the greatly accelerated maturation process of the foetuses they carried could be upset by any violent movement or emotional outburst.

The pregnancies progressed to full term in less than sixty days. If a woman survived the first birth, she was promptly reimpregnated. The record was three live births; no woman had survived a fourth.

During the initial experiments, Sarel had introduced a tiny Void into the front of the women's skulls, destroying much of their higher consciousness. The process not only robbed them of human intellect, but left their offspring dull and mindless, ruining them for Sarel's purpose but establishing a curious link the Breeder wanted to pursue later.

"We have such an opportunity to learn about the way

the mind works!" he enthused to Sarel. But her greatest excitement came from watching these creations develop and knowing they were completely in her power.

She often spent days wandering among them, as now.

Occasionally a moan echoed through the underground chambers as a woman came to term. Then the Breeder's red-coated servants came scurrying, pulling on armored gloves and breastplates.

After one particularly anguished cry grated on her ears, Sarel headed for the converted chapel. It was a relic of the Elder Days, the last remnant of the original city upon which Barrow was built, and as a child she had been terrified of the ghosts and wraiths said to haunt its precincts. Lares once told her that originally the chapel crowned the brow of a hill, but now it lay underground, incorporated into the substructure of the palace.

She had vague memories of her mother praying there before a circular window of colored glass. If she concentrated, Sarel could still see Anuna kneeling on the stone floor with her hands clasped over her heart and an expression of entreaty on her face.

On their seventh birthday the twins had found their mother dead in that position, with not a mark on her body. But in place of the look of entreaty there had been one of release and ecstasy. As children at the time of her death, the twins believed she had been taken by her god.

Later, they suspected she had been poisoned by their father, who was infatuated with a Kathan sorceress. The woman was kind to Lares and Sarel and introduced them to various magics, but then Los-Lorcan tired of her and she disappeared. Palace rumor claimed she had gone back to her own tribe.

Only the twins knew it had taken the Kathan ten days to die.

Now the ancient chapel was converted into a nursery. Sarel had chosen it for that purpose herself, to replace the old, bitter memories with something totally new. Something she could control. Padded cages lined the walls. Each one held a youngling, and instead of the milky smell of newborn humanity, there was an oily stench. They had to be removed from their mothers—Sarel smiled at the word—immediately following birth . . . otherwise they fed on the bodies that had just borne them.

In this room, no youngling was older than ten days; beyond that they were released into training pens.

The creatures hissed and squalled as Sarel walked down the center aisle. Sleek hairless heads turned to follow her, leathery tails rasped across bedding straw, claws scratched at unyielding bars. Although less than ten days old, the occupants of the cages were already as big as human adolescents.

These were Sarel's "children."

From the moment of their birth, they were indoctrinated. Portraits of the twins covered the chapel walls, the names of Blessed Sarel and Blessed Lares were continually chanted within the nursery, and fabric saturated with their body smells was used for swaddling the newborn. Sarel was determined that these creatures, these New Bred, would be totally loyal, having no sense of themselves apart from the Duet. She had learned a valuable lesson from her father's paid mercenaries, who had no personal loyalty and had been willing to betray him to anyone who offered a higher price.

Sarel and Lares had offered them a higher price.

Now she stopped before the cage of one of the recently born; four days old and as tall as a human child of ten. The youngling crouched in the back of the cage, staring unblinkingly at her. Each of the New Bred was slightly different. This one was male, human in appearance except for a faint patina of scales on its chest and upper arms. The low forehead was vaguely reptilian, but the eyes were almost the color of Sarel's and bright with intelligence.

The creature grew uneasy under Sarel's scrutiny and

half turned away. She could then see the band of scales that ran down his spine and melted into a long, muscular tail. As the youngling moved, clawed human feet shuffled through the straw.

In the next cage its sister paced endlessly in a tiny circle. This body was more lizard than human except for budding mammalian breasts, and a shock of white hair framing a face any human girl would have been proud of . . . until she opened her mouth. The interior of the mouth was that of a serpent, complete with fangs and forked tongue.

Sarel had a special fondness for these two; they were the first New Bred twins to be born. The mother had not survived. In the final days of her pregnancy her offspring had begun gnawing their way to freedom.

Standing back, Sarel looked from one to the other. She wondered if they felt the same sense of connection she and Lares possessed, as if they were alone against the world. Perhaps she would keep these two; she would have the Breeder train them as her personal guards. Twins for the Twins.

She smiled. The male growled, the female hissed.

"My loving family," murmured Sarel.

She walked into the next chamber. Here the cages were larger, the New Bred they contained were almost fully grown. Some had speech. And they all knew their mistress, Blessed Sarel. One by one they knelt as she passed, pressing their heads to the floor, averting their gaze.

Sarel moved slowly along the line of cages, examining each naked body with critical eyes. What would it be like, she wondered, to mate with one of these creatures? Would their animal lust be lessened by their fear of her? That big male—the one with the bony protuberances on either side of his forehead. His body was extremely powerful, his sexual organs massive and fully developed. What would he be like in a state of rut?

Sarel smiled to herself, imagining.

Aware of her gaze, the male flattened himself on the floor of his cage. Muscles rippled across his broad back as his tail lashed rhythmically, threatening to smash the bars.

Sarel's smile widened. Soon the entire world would bow to her as the New Bred did now. Nothing would be able to stand against them.

But as she rounded a corner, she had a sudden terrifying glimpse of a silver hand protruding through the bars of a cage.

Her heart thudded painfully until she realized it was only a trick of light, a stray beam from a lamp illuminating the scaly hand of one of the New Bred.

Sarel drew a shaky breath and turned her back on her children. Heels tapping briskly on the floor, she hurried from the chamber. In her wake a swirl of bittersweet perfume lingered, causing the New Bred to sniff the air and roll their eyes adoringly.

Where was Kichal, she wanted to know as she hurried into the upper regions of the palace. He should be back by now, she must have his report.

Nothing must be allowed to stand in her way . . . especially not the Silverhand.

CHAPTER SEVENTEEN

"I discovered this last night during my wanderings," Madran explained, splashing through a puddle of water to squeeze through the crack that angled across a burnished metal wall. At some time in the past the earth had shifted and a seam in the metal had twisted open. "I believe it's a way out of the city; I can smell sea salt and fresh air. Be careful, those edges are sharp," he added as Sioraf followed him with a graceful wriggle.

"Hope I fit," muttered Gwynne. Turning sideways, the Stone Warrior inserted her bulky frame into the opening. Her unyielding flesh scraped and rasped. "I'm stuck!" she complained. Madran took her arm and pulled, Caeled pushed from behind, and together they finally managed to get her through. Her stone skin grated against the torn edges of the metal.

Caeled prepared to join the others, but first he looked back one final time at the Elder city. The artificial lights on their tall poles cast a glow that made the place look new: this was how the city must have looked the day it was completed, he thought to himself.

Stone buildings stood out cleanly, streets gleamed in

the sharp light. The reflections that sparkled on glass windows and doors gave the illusion of life inside. Caeled had seen architectural wonders in his short life—the City of the Dead beyond Barrow, incredible Baddalaur built within an extinct volcano, the city of Gor with its many domes—but they all paled beside this fabulous creation.

How much manpower had been required to erect such a place, he wondered. Had the vast cavern in which it stood already existed, or was that too an Elder creation, an artificial cave scooped out of the bowels of the earth by Elder lore? And who paid for it all, for the design and the materials and the labor? In the Seven Nations combined there was not enough wealth to pay for the Old Metal and glass this one city contained.

But what impressed him most was the prosaic practicality of the place. Humans and Allta could move in tomorrow and be perfectly at home, every convenience ready to hand. The city raised more questions than it answered. Had it once been lived in, used? Its pristine condition argued otherwise. But if there had been no inhabitants, why were there shops? And why was it built underground?

Constantly aware of the two Arcana in the pack on his back, for a single instant Caeled was tempted to use the ancient artefacts to see if they would enlighten him. In that cyclonic moment when their power ran through him and knowledge rang like a bell, he might find the answers he sought. But he knew he had neither the time nor the energy to make the attempt. In the previous instances when he used the Arcana, he had received a plethora of images that overwhelmed him, most of them little more than confusing fragments that he could not sort out in his mind. Asking a direct question usually resulted in broken pieces of the complete answer, and usually the answers themselves raised even more questions. Brother Daniel, the Chief Librarian in Baddalaur, once told him that knowledge begged more knowledge. He was beginning to realize what the old man had meant. Moreover, the knowledge the Arcana imparted was like the wisdom acquired in a dream, shockingly clear at the time, but tending to fade away quickly.

Maybe it would be different if he could acquire the other two artefacts: the Cup and the Sword.

"Caeled?" Madran's voice echoed in the tunnel which lay beyond the crack in the metal wall.

"Coming," replied the young man, reluctantly turning his back on the Elder city. He spared a last thought for the lights behind him burning as they had burned for countless cycles; as they might well continue to burn . . . for how long? How long was eternity?

That was the sort of question the Scholars used to debate in Baddalaur.

Gas escaping from the shanti roared as the craft descended. The stench was appalling. Even Anadyr, who was accustomed to the wharfside odors of rotting fish and slime, leaned over the edge of the huge basket which served as a cabin and vomited into the sea below.

Kichal turned his head so that the silent red-eyed crew lining the cabin would not see him pinch his nostrils shut. Blood-colored tears leaked from his own crimson eyes, which, like theirs, had been permanently damaged by the small Voids Sarel had implanted in their heads.

Working the chains, Kichal closed the vents, cutting off the escaping gas. The shanti began to rock in the air currents rising from the islands below.

Anadyr wiped his face on his cloak and staggered over to Kichal. Avoiding eye contact with the Bred commander, he said, "This is the place. The ship the fugitives were on took shelter in the bay below us. According to witnesses, that's when they escaped to one of the islands . . . the one just ahead."

"Is there any way off that island?"

"Not without a boat. There are a vast number of islands in the area, but the currents are too dangerous for anyone to swim from one to another, and the seas are inhabited by Eron, who do not allow intruders into their world," he added. "No, they would need a boat."

"Look out one of the forward windows," Kichal remarked dryly.

Anadyr went forward, wiped the steamy window with his sleeve, peered down at the island they were fast approaching. On the beach lay the splintered remains of a wooden boat.

Squinting, Anadyr could just make out the impressions of webbed feet in the sand around the boat. "Eron!" he nodded. Glancing over his shoulder, he met Kichal's unnerving red stare. "The Eron are sea creatures, common enough in these waters. They give birth to their young on land, however, and there is a heresy that they once were human. But whatever their origins, they are savage now, and extremely dangerous. Though their meat is poisonous to us, they delight in eating human flesh." The scarred man smiled savagely and jerked a blunt thumb at the island below. "You can forget about capturing those fugitives. Without a boat, they were trapped on the island . . . and from the number of tracks, I'd say the Eron got them."

Without warning, Kichal vented the gas, flooding the cabin once more with the smell of excreta. Anadyr gagged violently. The commander's lips curved in a rare smile as he said, "We're not going back, we're going down. I need evidence for my mistress."

"You'll find none," warned Anadyr, choking and red in the face.

"If the four we seek were attacked on that beach I have no doubt we'll find something, even if it's only some dead Eron. I've encountered those renegades before, and I assure you they will not have given up their lives easily."

"The Eron will have left nothing, I tell you," Anadyr insisted. "They are appalling creatures, they devour their own dead!"

"Shanti!" Madran hawked and spat, trying to clear the smell from his airways. He pointed north across the island. "That way."

"The Duet's army," Caeled replied with certainty. "They've found us, then; no one else has shanti." He paused in the mouth of the cave and looked around, trying to fix the location in his mind. A tunnel at the back of the cave led down through the earth for a long, twisting course—and eventually to the crack in the metal wall, and the Elder city. Perhaps if he had a future, he would come back and explore the city at leisure. But even as he entertained the thought, he knew it was an idle dream. Life was hard and getting harder; he would probably never return, but at least he had seen it, and he would content himself with that.

"Stay here," Madran snapped, jerking him back to reality. The Allta was swiftly warping into his canine shape. Leaving a puddle of clothes behind, a huge shaggy dog loped away from the cave and across the beach toward sand dunes which hid the sea beyond. As Sioraf crouched to look between them, Caeled and Gwynne stood watching the dog run almost to the top of the nearest dune. Sinking to his belly, ears flat against his head, Madran peered warily over the crest of the sand hill.

Meanwhile the stench in the air was growing stronger every moment.

"What in the name of the Nations is that?" Gwynne asked in disgust. "Stinks worse than any latrine I ever smelled."

"Shanti," replied Caeled. "Air-ships powered by a gas produced from human waste. Only the Duet use them, they have a monopoly. I read about them in the library at Baddalaur."

"Shanti! Yes, I too have heard of them, though I've never seen one." Gwynne was making a conscious effort to breathe through her mouth, her lungs laboring under her granite skin.

Caeled dropped his human hand onto Sioraf's head. Her hair was silky beneath his touch. "Are you all right?"

The crouching vampir nodded. "I'm just tired," her soft voice whispered. Her nostrils were drawn tightly shut and a translucent membrane had slid across her blue eyes. He could hear the faint hiss of her breath as she inhaled through barely parted lips.

On the sand dune, Madran flowed back into his human shape. Keeping the hill between himself and the sea, he turned to beckon to Caeled.

The young man shrugged out of his backpack, unshipped and loaded his crossbow, tucked Madran's sickle under his arm, and darted out of the cave. Bending low, he ran toward the dune. "Keep your head down," Madran growled as Caeled joined him.

Lying flat on his stomach, Caeled wriggled up the dune and peered over the crest. He gasped in astonishment.

A large shanti was descending onto an island separated from theirs by a stretch of water. The body of the airship, a huge balloon, was the pure azure blue of a summer sky, its beauty as breathtaking as the foul gas it exuded was revolting. Caeled watched it maneuver with ponderous grace toward the shattered remains of a boat.

"That's the island we *were* on!" Caeled exclaimed, grabbing Madran's arm so tightly with his silver hand that the big Allta winced. "We must have come under the seabed to get to this one. So the city must be beneath both these islands. I didn't realize it was so big!"

"I suspected as much," said Madran. "While you were sleeping, I went exploring." He smiled, showing a mouthful of white teeth. "Makes you wonder what else lies below the Seven Nations."

❖   ❖   ❖

Four multiclawed anchors were tossed overboard, biting deep into the beach to hold the shanti grounded. One of the crew threw a rope ladder over the side and clambered down. Immediately, another man tossed a heavy crossbow down to him, then followed him down the ladder. In the basket above, marksmen continually scanned the ground below and kept watch as the warriors left the air-ship.

Kichal climbed easily down the swaying ladder, conscious of the fresh wind blowing off the sea. Its salty tang cleansed the foulness from his nostrils. He could not remember when he had last enjoyed the smell of sea air more—*images of a woman and child on a beach like this, on a day like this, but long ago, so long ago*—he could not remember when he had last been able to smell like this.

Anadyr followed him. The Islander held a coral knife clenched between his teeth. He dropped lightly onto the reddish sand beside Kichal, landing in a crouch with the knife suddenly in his hand.

"Read me what happened here," Kichal ordered, pointing to the disturbed sand around the wrecked boat.

Anadyr examined the area, then backtracked to the water's edge, where icy water frothed and foamed over his misshapen toes. He had not stood on an island beach in a long time, and the experience abruptly brought back his appalling childhood. His overwhelming memory of that time was of constant hunger, constant fear, and the chill of salt water around his feet when he ran into the sea to escape the creatures who had hunted him for food or for the pleasure they took in killing. Loneliness, cold, terror . . . He stared out to sea for a moment, lost in a world no one else could know.

"Anadyr!" Kichal's voice cut through the air, and the scarred man's reverie. He fell to his task, looking for the telltale dome of an Eron head, or some unnatural rippling of the water. But he found nothing. He was not reassured, however. If the Eron attacked they would do so with shocking speed, and perhaps in great numbers. Those they did not kill at once they would drag into the sea and drown, then store in their coral larders.

Anadyr had been only a boy when he found evidence of an Eron larder following a violent storm. Scores of bodies, some of them recognizable as having once been human, had washed up on the beach in various stages of decomposition. Each was impaled on a pointed stake driven through the body from rectum to mouth. The choice fleshy organs were invariably missing.

That memory returned to Anadyr now, and he took a hasty step back from the lapping waves.

"They came ashore here," he said, pointing to a long groove in the sand, "and dragged the boat up there." He walked back and forth along the beach for a time, following traces invisible to Kichal's eyes. At last he approached a cavemouth. "There was a fight here . . ." Stepping around an invisible circle on the ground he moved cautiously closer to the cave and peered inside, knife at the ready. After a brief hesitation, he ducked inside.

Kichal waited.

Anadyr reappeared long moments later. "It looks like they spent the night in here," he reported, "and then set off in that direction . . ." But just as he raised his arm to point, his scarred face turned ashen and he screamed a wordless warning.

CHAPTER EIGHTEEN

A war song had been sung. A death song had been whistled.

And the Eron had gathered.

From the seas of the Seven Nations the clans of Eron had come north to the Island Sea to mourn their dead sister. All the Eron were related by blood and mating ties, and though the clans had spread far and wide to inhabit the waters of the world, they retained close contact with their kin. The element that nourished and sustained them carried their voices clearly across great distances.

When they arrived, they had discovered that yet another of their number had been slain by the softskins. An entire branch of the clan was destroyed by pitiless savages from the World Above, the tragedy compounded because the female had been in pup. Offspring were rare among the Eron. Indeed, the Seniors speculated that in a triad of generations, the race would be no more.

The Eron clans had assembled at the coral caverns to sing the Great Songs relating the history of the Water Folk, part of their ritual of mourning. The females, the

Keepers of Tales, wove weed tapestries as they sang, and the males circled them in stately procession.

Abruptly, the singing stopped.

The Eron, as one, had detected a revolting gaseous odor seeping through their liquid environment. Mingled with the stench, part and yet apart from it, was the unmistakable, mouth-watering smell of the softskins.

Without a sound—for there was no need of speech among the clans—the Water Folk had collected their weapons. While some went to avenge their dead brother and sister, others began making eager preparations for a feast.

CHAPTER NINETEEN

"Eron," Caeled whispered, as the sea offshore roiled with scaled and furred creatures.

Even as the first warning shout was echoing across the waves, the Eron were scuttling out of the water with terrifying speed. They were armed with spears and curved coral throwing sticks. One of the red-eyed shanti crewmen raised his crossbow and fired at a creature bearing down on him. The bolt struck the Eron high in the chest, staggering it momentarily, but it shook off its pain and kept coming. As the crewman struggled to reload his crossbow the Eron lunged, talons slashing, jaws gaping, and ripped off the top of the man's skull.

The coppery odor of blood enflamed the creature. Throwing itself onto the dead body, it began gnawing at the ruined head like a child devouring a sweet.

It did not drop its prize and fall dead until four more bolts thundered into its body.

The Eron swarmed over the beach, raining spears and sticks on the outnumbered crewmen. The shanti soon bristled with their spears, and a throwing stick opened a long tear in the azure fabric of the balloon. The airship lurched unsteadily like a wounded animal.

The Eron drew back, whistling and warbling—beautiful, ethereal sounds—and then reformed their attack.

They had realized that the throwing sticks did more harm than the spears, and now they hurled the coral weapons in earnest, with deadly accuracy. Huge flaps of material were torn away like flesh. Cables supporting the superstructure were severed; one parted with such force that its backlash tore open the basket beneath the balloon. With a long, hissing sigh the shanti revolved slowly in midair, then crashed to the beach with a certain ponderous grace. Its destroyed beauty was accompanied by a last sickening exudation of excremental gasses.

The Eron threw themselves onto the wreck, ripping and tearing at it, employing the tactics they used when they fought one of the finned hunters of the deep. By the time they realized that the shanti was not responding like the wounded beast they had assumed it to be, ten Eron had fallen to the crewmen's crossbows. Double that number were badly injured.

A silent message passed among the creatures. As if guided by a single mind, they turned in unison to concentrate their attack on the crewmen instead.

Kichal impaled the nearest Eron on his two-handed sword, then leaned back, trying to lift the surprisingly heavy creature off the ground. It lurched down the blade, webbed fingers clawing. With a thrill of horror, Kichal realized that the creature was not attempting to push the blade out of its body—it was *pulling* itself along the blade to get at him. Twisting the sword back and forth, he finally succeeded in freeing it from the Eron's body, then drove the weapon deep into its throat.

This time the wound was fatal.

Another Eron launched itself at him. It features were finer than the first, with an almost human appearance.

The commander freed his reeking sword and dodged to one side, staring.

Matted weed-green fur had become silken hair, scaled flesh had turned smooth and pliable, the graceful hands reaching for him ended in long, supple fingers. The beautiful young woman—*so familiar, so familiar*—opened her mouth and smiled, showing tiny white teeth . . . then the tip of a knife erupted through her throat.

The light died from the woman's eyes. Kichal's own eyes were strangely misted. He detected a sudden, acrid odor.

Blinking away tears, he saw Anadyr crouching over the body of an Eron, pulling his knife from her throat. "Beware these creatures," he growled. "They possess a powerful magic. Their sweat causes visions, making their prey see what they most desire. Their dried scales are a drug that is traded like coin in some parts of the Island Sea."

Kichal looked at the body on the ground. Now he saw only a scaled and furred monstrosity, but he remembered with painful clarity the image he had glimpsed. A lovely woman, familiar . . . and dear.

Was that what he most desired?

And if so, who was she?

Battle-honed instinct made him spin around, drop to one knee, and in the same fluid motion brace his sword hilt against the ground, blade pointing up at an angle. A charging Eron was impaled. Kichal freed the blade and ripped the creature open from groin to sternum, spilling its innards onto the stony beach.

"If we stay here we die!" Anadyr exclaimed, his voice rising in panic as more and more of the Eron appeared out of the sea.

Kichal looked down the beach. Only three of his men were still standing. The rest lay scattered in various stages of dismemberment, while Eron tore at their flesh with talons and teeth. His men had given good account of themselves before dying; a number of Eron lay beside them. But not enough, not nearly enough.

As Kichal watched, one of the surviving crewmen dropped his sword and spread his arms wide, with a blissful smile on his face. A voracious Eron flung itself into his arms and promptly bit off his face.

"Get down!" Anadyr cried at that moment. Kichal dropped to the ground. He caught a glimpse of Anadyr spinning a length of metal chain. It buzzed over Kichal's head and hit something with a sickening crunch. He rolled aside as the blinded Eron collapsed to the ground, mouth open, howling silently. Kichal drew his sword across its throat.

"This way," said Anadyr through gritted teeth.

"Are you injured?"

The scarred man shook his head. But tears of pain glistened in his muddy eyes. "Can't you hear them?" he asked.

The commander shook his head. "Wind, waves . . ." he began, and then stopped. At the very edge of his consciousness, he felt rather than heard the faintest susurration. A delicate whisper, no more than a hint of sound, yet intoxicating, compelling . . . and deadly. He found himself thinking of Sarel.

She was humming the tune until she caught herself and stopped. Abruptly, she realized that she had been replicating sounds she was actually *hearing*—haunting, terribly wounded—and suddenly knew where they were coming from: the Aethyra.

Sarel turned and fled down long banner-lined corridors toward the royal apartments. A door opened as she approached. Lares appeared in the doorway, brow creased with concern. He had felt his sister's anguish as she approached. Wrapping his arms around her, he pulled her into the room and slammed the door. Magical wards sizzled into place, sealing the chamber.

They never left it unguarded now.

"Give me your strength," Sarel pleaded, pressing her lips to her brother's. Through her open mouth she inhaled his breath, his energy. As she felt his male power flood through her body she relaxed against him.

Closing her eyes, Sarel allowed herself to follow the thread of sound toward its source.

They had killed twelve of the creatures and mortally injured another fourteen. The sword was almost an extension of Kichal's arm by now, cutting clinically, moving economically but with devastating effect. He was hoarding as much energy as he could. His enhanced warrior's reflexes were keeping him alive, so far, against ever-increasing odds. Anadyr stood with him back to back, chain humming in the air, biting through scaly flesh, doing horrendous damage.

But Kichal could tell that the Island Trash was tiring. Once he fell, they would both be overwhelmed. There was a time in the recent past when Kichal would not have cared; he had lived only to serve the Duet. Death in Sarel's name would have been an honor.

But now . . . something inside himself had changed. Now he wanted to live. Not for Lares or Sarel, but for himself. *He wanted to live*.

"I'll try to cut us an escape path through these monsters," he told Anadyr breathlessly. "Follow me."

Anadyr grunted. His chest and arms were badly clawed by Eron talons. If he did not clean the wounds very soon, they would suppurate. If he survived to sundown he could be a very sick man. "Go on," he told the commander grimly. "I'll be right behind you."

It was Kichal.

Sarel realized she was hearing the sounds through Kichal's ears. From the Aethyra, she looked down on two exhausted men surrounded by dead and dying creatures of some sort, monstrosities that looked more fish than animal.

What had happened here?

The shanti was down and torn into almost unrecognizable shreds. Lumps of bloody meat on the beach were all that remained of the crew. What force could have defeated a war shanti crewed by her own hand-picked warriors? Surely not those grotesque sea creatures.

Ignoring the struggle taking place on the beach, Sarel expanded her consciousness, attempting to locate herself in relation to the Nations. She was floating above an island-studded sea. Clusters of primitive hamlets dotted the larger islands. To the north lay a mainland of snow and ice. She knew where she was now—the Island Sea, to which the Silverhand and his companions had fled.

But had Kichal found them? Had these creatures attacked before or after he caught up with the fugitives? Before, probably. Kichal would have contacted her immediately if he had his quarry in custody.

Allowing herself to drop lower toward the beach, Sarel hovered over one of the sea creatures and studied it curiously. Was this one of the fabled Eron? Even in death it was impressively lethal-looking. She made a mental note to discuss her discovery with the Breeder; perhaps these creatures possessed qualities that could be incorporated into the New Bred.

Meanwhile Kichal and an ugly, scarred giant of a man had broken free of the creatures and were running down the beach, pursued by more Eron. One came perilously close to the scarred man, but Kichal decapitated it without breaking stride. Sarel was wondering whether she should expend energy to assist the commander, when he and the scarred man suddenly disappeared into a gaping hole in the ground. Four of the Eron tumbled in after them.

Hovering over the pit, Sarel watched impassively as Kichal and his ugly companion killed the four. Savage talons had succeeded in ripping three deep, parallel grooves in Kichal's face, however, and one of the Eron had bitten a chunk out of the scarred man's thigh.

The remainder of the Eron gathered on the lip of the pit and started to hurl down spears and stones upon the two humans at the bottom.

Although her powers in the physical world were limited, Sarel began gathering her energy to distract the creatures . . . when Kichal and the scarred man vanished again.

Peering more deeply into the pit, she expected to find their spear-impaled bodies. But the hole was empty. The two men were gone. Focusing her concentration, Sarel tried to trace them, but it was as if they had ceased to exist.

And then, faintly, like the merest gossamer thread of spiderweb brushing across her face, she felt the tiny tingle of power.

A power as recognizable as a signature.

The Arcana.

With a triumphant cry, Sarel soared into the Aethyra. Her form flowed through myriad permutations until resolving itself into a crystalline entity. Looking down from a height, she saw him then, saw his pulsing silver-light aura against the pastel hues of an island.

Dismissing Kichal from her consciousness, Sarel sped toward Caeled.

She located him crouching behind a sand dune on a neighboring isle. The woman's scream of hatred tore through the Aethyra, but was inaudible in the physical world . . . except to the Eron. As one they turned and fled to the safety of the World Below.

CHAPTER TWENTY

"Something's wrong," growled Madran. The shaggy blond hair on the back of his neck rose like hackles.

As Caeled watched the Eron fleeing into the sea, leaving barely a ripple in their wake, he knew the Allta was right. The Eron had won, they had proven the vulnerability of the shanti and the Duet's elite red-eyed troops. Yet now, at the height of their victory, they had turned and fled.

Something must be very wrong indeed.

At that precise moment he heard Sioraf's high-pitched scream.

Ignoring Madran's shouted warning to wait, Caeled turned and ran. He plunged headlong down the sand dune, shading his eyes against the bright sunlight with his human hand. But even so he could not make out the details of the shadowy cavemouth where he had left Gwynne and Sioraf.

The vampir screamed again, a cry that stabbed into his skull and set his teeth on edge. Her voice was shrill, inhuman. He knew she would not have wanted him to hear her make such a sound—unless she were too terrified to control herself.

Then, as he raced across the beach, he felt it: a prickling of the skin on his shoulders, an icy hollowness in his spine, and the sudden overwhelming conviction that something was racing up behind him.

He tried to tell himself it was only Madran running after him, still bearing the residue of the were-change.

But it was not Madran.

Caeled had almost reached the mouth of the cave when suddenly his silver hand pulsed white-hot. A stab of agony lanced the length of his arm to the shoulder, so intense and unexpected that he lost his balance. He staggered; a stone turned under his foot. Quite distinctly, he felt the air *twisting* behind his left shoulder as he fell. Thanks to his Baddalaur-trained reflexes he hit the ground rolling, already bringing up his crossbow . . . but nothing was there.

Sarel laughed in triumph.

Although her Aethyra presence could not interact with characters in the physical world, she could influence them. The Silverhand could not see her, but she realized he had some sense of her on an intuitive level. That was enough; she could use it to incapacitate him.

Summoning her energies, she changed the density of her Aethyra form, allowing its crystalline surface to reflect the wan northern light.

The air rippled, pulsing in rhythm with the agony of Caeled's hand. The atmosphere was distorted as if with a heat haze—then for an instant Sarel appeared. Her naked flesh was carved of crystal, threads of amber formed her hair. Only her violet eyes were human—and terrifying. Caeled aimed the crossbow.

Sarel winked out of existence.

The crossbow bolt hissed through the air—and buried itself in Sioraf's chest as she stood in the mouth of the cave.

The vampire was hurled backward by the blow. She fell to the floor of the cave with her hands clawing ineffectively at the shaft protruding from between her breasts.

Caeled staggered to his feet. "I saw . . . I saw . . ."

Madran had come up behind him, panting. "I know, I felt it too," he said. He rested a comforting hand on Caeled's shoulder for a moment, then hurried past him to kneel beside Sioraf.

Her eyes were wide and staring. There was surprisingly little blood on her chest.

Gwynne came forward from the back of the cave, carrying Caeled's pack. She set it down carefully before lowering herself, with great difficulty, to a sitting position beside Sioraf. "She warned me that something was approaching," the Stone Warrior said. "Then the Arcana grew hot. Your pack glowed as if it held live coals, Caeled."

"Sioraf may have seen what I saw: one of the Duet. Sarel. She was standing between me and the cave. I fired at her but she disappeared and I hit Sioraf instead." His features contorted with grief. "I didn't mean to! I would never hurt her!"

"She knows that," Madran told him. He was examining the vampir's wound with tentative fingers. "Sarel must have been what frightened the Eron away." When he touched the crossbow bolt, Sioraf groaned. "I'm not sure if there's anything I can do," Madran concluded sadly. "This looks like a mortal wound."

"There is something I can do." Caeled tore at his pack, freeing the Stone and the Spear.

"Too dangerous to you," Gwynne warned. "We can spare the vampir, but not you."

Caeled ignored her. Holding the Stone in his metal hand, he drove the Spear through the opening, then tilted it upward to allow the Stone to slide down the shaft and click into place.

A powerful convulsion ripped through his body. Spine arched, muscles spasmed. He fought to hold onto his consciousness in spite of feeling as if he were about to explode.

Knowledge, when it came, was like a wash of white light pouring over him.

At once he understood that the pain he was feeling was the result of having the Arcana in close proximity to Sioraf's pain. The Arcana were amplifying and transmitting her distress for him to experience.

But with the experience came a total understanding of Sioraf's body. He knew how to save her.

Gritting his teeth, Caeled straightened. Every breath hurt; air seared into his lungs like fire. His limbs were cold, yet tingling as if there were pins and needles in his hands and feet. A great pressure on his chest threatened to stop his heart.

He was feeling Sioraf's dying moments.

"We don't have much time," he gasped. "One of you—open my vein." The words sounded slurred. Through dimming eyes, he could no longer see Gwynne and Madran. "Drench her wound in my blood," he instructed, "and then pull out the bolt. Give her more blood to drink afterward. It is her only chance."

"You could not survive the loss of so much blood," argued Madran.

"Do as I say," Caeled grated, fighting to keep his thoughts clear. Grey shadows were closing around him. Somewhere within them, death circled him like a hungry predator.

His vision briefly cleared enough to see that it was the Stone Warrior who lifted his right arm and dispassionately sliced open a vein with her knife.

Blood spurted, dappling Sioraf's pale skin. Holding Caeled's arm, Gwynne pressed the severed vein to the vampir's chest, letting the blood flow until it obscured the entrance wound.

Then Madran took hold of the crossbow bolt and drew it out, grunting with the effort.

Sioraf's flesh gave up the weapon with a sickening squelch.

The Madra Allta then held the wound open while Gwynne filled it with more of Caeled's blood. The damaged tissues bubbled and seethed, then, perceptibly, began to heal, sealing themselves until nothing remained but a puckered white scar.

Caeled's head was swimming. He was icy cold all over now.

When Gwynne pressed his arm to Sioraf's mouth, the vampir's lips parted of their own accord and she drank thirstily.

Caeled's pain and weakness were replaced by a feeling of euphoria. He could taste the salty copper of his own blood in his mouth. Warmth flowed through his limbs, lending him strength. The feeling was incredibly sensual and arousing.

He saw the Stone Warrior's green eyes glance down at his body in its thin tunic.

Riven by the force of the Arcana, weakened by loss of blood, sexually aroused, his spirit was in turmoil. Without conscious volition it slipped from his body . . . and soared into the Aethyra.

From this vantage point Caeled surveyed his surroundings. Eron consciousness bubbled at the corner of his vision. His brain was clear now; he felt strong and able. He turned his concentration upon the Eron and easily traced them to their lair beneath the island.

In one of the underground caverns that seemed common to the region, scores of the creatures were milling in confusion. The cavern floor and seabed beyond were littered with Eron bodies. Some bore evidence of terrible injuries, but others had no mark on them except for a pale ichor that leaked from ears and eyes.

Then Caeled became aware of the singing, cascading

trills that formed an inhuman but achingly beautiful music. As he strained to listen, phrases seemed almost familiar, words almost intelligible.

　. . . *a song* . . .
　. . . *a song of pain* . . .
　. . . *a song of death* . . .

Something had sung a death song, a very particular combination of sounds that stabbed into the hypersensitive ears of the Eron and tore through their very brains. Frantic with pain, they had tried to escape into the deep sea. There the song was taken up by the waves, echoing endlessly, spreading in vast concentric circles that reached out and out to the next body of water, and the next. No matter where they were, when the song reached them, Eron died.

Caeled tried to draw away from the deadly music by moving more deeply into the Aethyra. But he heard the song change into a shriek of triumph, of savage victory.

The sea caught the scream and amplified it and, in less than a score of heartbeats, the last surviving Eron in the cavern below the island were writhing in their death agonies. Before the final echoes had vanished, the first waves of the death song were reaching Eron clans in the most distant oceans. The weak and the young succumbed immediately as their delicate inner membranes ruptured. They floated helplessly to the surface, easy prey for predators.

The strongest survived for a time, but the majority of them were either blinded or struck deaf. Maddened by shock and pain, they turned on one another, completing what generations of enemies had failed to do: the annihilation of the Eron.

Caeled drifted through the Aethyra. For a time he seemed to lose all sense of direction. Then he was above the island again, looking down. Within the mouth of the cave he could see Madran and Gwynne holding his body close to that of Sioraf.

The vampir was clutching his arm with both hands and pressing it greedily to her lips.

As he started to drop down toward his companions, Caeled detected a whiff of musk blowing through the Aethyra, strangely mingled with the smell of dry rot. He glanced up.

Two white crows plummeted toward him, claws extended, beaks gaping, violet eyes aflame.

CHAPTER TWENTY-ONE

Blood, the essence of life, forged the link.

Sioraf opened her eyes and gazed into the Aethyra.

White crows circled a small dark-haired boy who beat at them with puny fists. The huge birds darted in, savaging him with beak and claw. Bright red blood splashed their albino feathers as they tore open his face above the eyes and scored cruel furrows along his arms.

Lying slumped across Sioraf, Caeled moaned. Ugly wounds appeared on his forehead and arms.

One of the white crow images flickered and changed into a jackal-headed man. His muscular arms caught hold of the terrified boy and bent him backward while the canine muzzle slavered over his exposed throat. Meanwhile, the second crow circled the pair, cawing triumphantly. Then it too changed.

Every movement was an effort. Sioraf felt cold, so cold; there was ice in her veins. In the instant before Caeled fired she had seen the brief sparkling appearance of the crystal woman, and realized what he was trying to shoot with his crossbow.

She could still feel pain in her chest, a terrible pressure between her breasts, but Caeled's blood was a warm unguent on her skin, soothing her. The taste of his blood in her mouth was the most restorative of meals. She ran her pointed tongue over her red lips, savoring.

With numb fingertips she reached out to touch the Stone as it lay locked on the shaft of the Spear. Sudden heat flowed up her arm. Dark spots appeared around the perimeter of her vision. The images of the boy and the jackal-headed being—and a strange, androgynous figure who seemed to have joined them—were fading, fading . . .

The vampir lunged forward. The effort tore open the new scar tissue between her breasts, parting the skin like a sheet of wet kenaf. With an outflung arm she struck the joined Arcana and sent them rolling back against Caeled's metal hand.

Frightened boy became confident youth. Youth became man. Flesh became metal.

A silver hand inserted itself between the closing jackal jaws. The hand expanded, stretching the jaws to breaking point. Simultaneously the hermaphrodite twisted, changed, acquired reptilian features. The creature attempted to bite the young man's head but its curving fangs slid harmlessly down a metal skull.

Lares the jackal fell back, struggling to reconstitute an Aethyra image. He became a marsh lion with the head of a man, while Sarel flowed into the regal shape of a cat-headed female. They glanced at each other with two pairs of startled violet eyes. "He's good!" Sarel hissed angrily.

As Caeled drew himself to his full height, silver light ran like water along his new metal form. In the Aethyra, word became flesh . . . or stone . . . or metal, or any combination the imagination could envision.

Recovering from their surprise, the twins attacked again with teeth and claws that lengthened into pointed spikes.

Sarel's nails pierced Caeled's metal chest, Lares' fangs punctured his metal shoulder.

The pain was like fire.

Caeled imagined his flesh turning to liquid flame.

The heat given off by his metal body seared his attackers. Twisting away from them, he flung himself higher into the Aethrya and hurled down a fiery rain upon the writhing Duet. There were screams of pain before they too assumed shapes of flame and sped upward to wrap themselves around Caeled's body.

Madran whispered a prayer as he saw the terrible wounds opening on Caeled's skin, the deep punctures sinking through his clothing into his body. The Madra Allta braced himself, summoning his own reserves of strength, and pressed the heels of both hands against his young friend's temples. With a total concentration of will Madran poured the power of an Allta into a suffering human.

Caeled's fire grew briefly brighter as twinned flames lapped around him, then it was extinguished by a pall of black smoke. Within the blinding smoke the nature of the attack upon him changed, becoming a series of hammer blows from an unseen opponent. He tried to alter his Aethrya form to one more resistant, but his strength was fading. Pain was making concentration difficult.

Looking down, he could still see his physical body lying across that of the vampir. Sioraf's eyes were open. She was gazing right at him.

Then Madran pressed both hands against his face.

At once Caeled felt an infusion of new strength. Raw, elemental energy flowed through him. He swiftly warped through a score of changes, trying on one form after another, but the twins met him change for change. They became water to his fire, metal to his glass, fire to his ice.

Whatever he attempted, they countered.

Gwynne placed the two Arcana in Caeled's hands and

closed his limp fingers around them, hoping they would help him. But as she handled them her own petrified flesh began to seethe, causing almost unbearable pain. The granitic skin on her arms rippled as if something alive were wriggling beneath the surface. She looked down . . . and briefly found herself staring in shocked disbelief at normal flesh.

Forms flickered.

Sarel became crystal, Lares jet.

Caeled became light.

Silver light blazed through the crystal and shattered it into hundreds of sparkling, whirling shards. Within each fragment, Sarel screamed. The jet that was Lares melted into tarry black globules.

Silver light blossomed in the heavens and flowed downward, washing over the small group huddled at the cavemouth. Caeled's physical wounds healed at the touch of the light. Stones blossomed into beach flowers. Madran once more became a huge, white-blond wolfhound with limpid brown eyes, while Gwynne reverted to a handsome woman in her middle years. She managed one glad exclamation before the light faded and the flowers withered and died.

The warrior turned back to stone; her cry of joy ended in a sob of despair.

Because Sioraf was hidden beneath Caeled, none witnessed any alteration to the vampir's features.

In the great palace in distant Barrow, courtiers and servants listened, trembling, as agonized howls echoed and reechoed through the corridors. But no one dared approached the locked doors of the royal apartments.

No one went to help.

Few were genuinely upset to know the Duet were suffering.

CHAPTER TWENTY-TWO

Fifteen men had died that their blood might fill the stone bowl.

First they had been tortured to heighten their emotions, cruelly abused by men who had spent a lifetime perfecting the skills of feet and fists, fingers and elbows to defend themselves. Now these specialists used their skills to inflict pain. Some of the victims, young men who had fallen asleep in what they thought was a primitive monastic guesthouse and awakened in a prison cell, had fought back. But they were the sons of farmers and laborers. They stood no chance against the highly-developed martial skills of the Seekers Reborn.

Their torturers took great care to avoid spilling one drop of the virgin boys' precious blood.

When the first blows fell some of the youths pled for mercy. Confused and disoriented, they feared they had committed some crime. As neophytes they might have broken a rule of the Order unwittingly.

Others responded with anger. They had given up their families and all that was safe and familiar to join the mysterious new teaching order that had appeared out of the west, promising wisdom and wealth, and they were furious at being assaulted without reason. But bonecracking blows quickly silenced even the most belligerent.

One by one the young men—none of them older then fifteen summers—were dragged out of the cell and down a long corridor. At the end of the corridor, the cowled and hooded high priest waited.

None of the youths had ever met the Hieromonach of the Seekers Reborn, and he deliberately knew nothing about them. He did not want to think of them as people; to him they were merely a source of energy. Vital, essential energy. If there was another available source he would have used it, but only human essence possessed the qualities he needed. And if a few peasant boys—little better than savages really—had to die for the greater good of the Nations, then so be it.

The unconscious youths were dropped facedown on the floor with their necks on the rim of the sunken bowl. Then the Hieromonach dispassionately drove the sharpened tip of his staff of office through their throats, opening the jugular vein. Hot blood hissed as it spattered into the cold bowl. For a moment the crimson fluid turned black; then it was absorbed into the stone and disappeared. When the stone was satiated, the remaining blood began to pool in the bottom of the basin.

As life after life ended, the stone bowl filled to the brim.

Leaning on his staff, the Hieromonach—he of the narrow head and narrow eyes and narrow, bitter lips— peered down into the pool of blood. His sharp features were accentuated by crimson shadows, while around him a shimmering red-black aura twisted in invisible currents. The stench of blood and death and suddenly emptied bowels filled the chamber.

The high priest drank in the combination of smell and emotion. Pain was intoxicating to him. As he flung aside his staff, his spirit soared.

Upward through the mountain that squatted atop a warren of ancient caverns his consciousness whirled, through passageways of polished stone and gleaming metal, past glassy ceilings and doors encrusted with intricate ornamentation. Fuelled by pain and death, his spirit passed through the curiously flattened mountaintop where the rusted ribs of a metal craft lay like the bones of a decaying giant. Up, up it flew, climbing ever higher.

Once—how long ago it seemed!—he had clothed his spirit in the image of an owl for such journeying. Now he travelled the Aethyra in the guise of a black-taloned eagle. Once he had been Rasriel, Hieromonach of the Order of the Seekers of the Way, head of the largest and most respected teaching order in the Seven Nations. Now he was high priest to a dozen ragged, frightened men who called themselves the Seekers Reborn. He possessed little more than his staff of office and the clothes he had been wearing when he escaped from Baddalaur. He was constantly in fear of the Duet's Bred army, knowing they must be hunting any survivors.

During a desperate trek through hostile lands, Rasriel had contemplated the reason for his troubles. Though it would be easy to blame the twins for everything, he had always favored negotiating with the Duet. The Seekers and Scholars of Baddalaur had possessed many skills which the twins might have found useful. In time the Order could have become invaluable to the Duet and worked its way into their confidence. Then it would have been simplicity itself to topple the twins and replace their chaotic reign with the rule of order.

But those careful plans of Rasriel's were overthrown. The Duet had attacked and destroyed Baddalaur.

He was convinced he knew why.

Rasriel had been at Baddalaur when Armadiel the Seeker first brought Caeled to the College. Caeled was a child then, a scrawny, dark-haired little urchin with the stump of his left arm wrapped in bloody cloth.

Maseriel, the former Hieromonach—blind old fool—had insisted the wretched child was the Spoken One of legend, a uniquely gifted being who would overthrow the tyrants and restore order to a chaotic world. Maseriel had gone to his grave claiming he found the savior. He had not lived long enough to realize he had instead sewn the seeds of Baddalaur's destruction.

From the beginning, Rasriel had found it hard to accept Caeled as the Spoken One. He was of humble origins, an unprepossessing boy. Surely the Spoken One would radiate power and majesty, his nobility plain for all to see. But Caeled brought nothing but trouble. He was, Rasriel began to suspect, a fraud.

Maseriel had sent Armadiel on a quest for the Spoken One because he wanted to go down in history as the Hieromonach who discovered the savior. In time the Seeker had returned to Baddalaur with a boy who superficially fulfilled the prophecies, including such details as his dreadful injury. Armadiel admitted, however, that he had removed the boy's hand himself. That was enough to make Caeled suspect.

So Rasriel had waited and watched, and finally concluded the boy had been planted by Maseriel for his own aggrandizement. How like him, Rasriel thought bitterly.

When Maseriel died, he did so in Caeled's room. Had he quarrelled with his protégé? Had Caeled refused to do something the Hieromonach wanted, then threatened to expose the fraud, thus causing the old man to collapse?

Perhaps Caeled had murdered Maseriel for some selfish motive of his own. It could never be proved, and Rasriel did not really care. Maseriel's death had cleared the way for himself.

But then the Duet had vented their fury on Baddalaur. Rasriel had no doubt they were seeking Caeled, supposedly the Spoken One who was destined to overthrow them. Caeled was to blame for everything, for horrors Rasriel relived every night in his tormented sleep.

Before the Bred army stormed Baddalaur, the twins had unleashed Voids into the very heart of the College. How many had died in those first few moments, sucked into whirling centers of nothingness while the White Scream rang through the air? How much priceless knowledge was lost forever with the slain Scholars and Seekers in the ruined Great Library?

Those who survived the Voids had faced the monstrous army of the Bred. They had escaped a malign elemental force only to fall victim to the warped creations of nature gone mad.

Rasriel had led nineteen other members of the Order through a maze of passages tunnelled out of the extinct volcano that was Baddalaur. As they fled, for a while they could still hear the screams of the dying and the howls of the Bred.

In the days that followed, two of the older brothers had died in their sleep, perhaps speeded on their way by the shocks they had undergone. Another two had succumbed to a creeping slime that infected their wounds, driving them mad with terrifying dreams. Mountain bandits had killed another, and one man simply walked uncaring over the edge of a cliff, disappearing without a sound into a raging torrent below.

The thirteen survivors had continued eastward, following Rasriel because they believed he had a specific destination in mind. They had not known that for the first time in his adult life, their leader was without a plan.

Now, as he soared through the Aethyra using skills mastered long ago in the College, Rasriel looked down at the earth below. He could trace their erratic route through mountains, across rivers; could see the barren wilderness that almost claimed all their lives, the poisoned wadi where walking away from the crystal-clear water was the hardest thing they had ever done.

Every step they had taken was fraught with danger. They were close to death from hunger and exhaustion when they found the flat-topped mountain.

From the Aethyra it was easy to see the shape of the mountain and realize it had once been something else, something far more impressive than a geologic formation. From his first glimpse in the light of a setting sun, Rasriel had known the angled planes were too regular to be natural. Hoping against hope, he speculated that they had found a relic of the Elder Times.

The first time he soared into the Aethyra and surveyed the mountain from above, he knew he was right.

His exhausted band had spent the first few days camped in shallow caves close to the base of the mountain. They lived off fruits and berries, their bellies constantly cramping, and drank brackish water that flowed from openings in the mountainside. Openings that were perfect, unnatural circles carved in stone.

Seeking to learn more about their sanctuary, Rasriel and two of the stronger Seekers had projected their spirits into the Aethyra. From that vantage point they discovered numerous caverns under the mountain, successive layers that extended far below the level of the surrounding countryside. In some ways the place bore a remarkable similarity to Baddalaur, lending credence to the belief that the College was constructed on the plan of an Elder city.

Observing from the Aethyra, it was easy to imagine what such a city must have looked like in the distant past. It appeared to have been one enormous building, floor stacked upon floor, each storey the size of a country estate. Some prehistoric cataclysm had caused the storeys to collapse into one another and the entire structure to sink into the earth, settling at a much lower depth. Or perhaps the ground had risen around the building.

Much of the interior of the building—or mountain— was still a mystery. Enormous portions were physically

inaccessible, and some of the chambers were invisible
even from the Aethyra. From experience, Rasriel
suspected this was because of metal sheathing on the
walls.

Some of his band had begun calling the mountain
New Baddalaur. The name was inappropriate, even
blasphemous in a way. Baddalaur had been a college
dedicated to learning and healing. This grim, truncated
peak was a dark temple where thirteen fugitives huddled
in fear, bolstering their fading powers with blood and
pain.

But they must, they would, survive.

Rasriel turned his back on the mountain and sped
westward, allowing the Ghost Winds in the Aethyra to
carry him into the higher reaches.

Discovering that his powers were fading had been a
terrifying shock. Sending his spirit into the Aethyra had
become harder and harder, and he was no longer able
to sustain its existence there for any great length of time.
Initially he credited his weakness to the sock of Baddalaur's
destruction and the rigors of the journey afterward. He
expected to recover with time and rest.

Instead he and his band grew weaker, even in the
sanctuary they had found. Rasriel took the first steps to
reverse the problem when he found a mountain lion
trapped in a gully. He meant to kill the animal for meat,
but a sort of madness overtook him. He tortured the
creature first, seeking some sort of retribution for the
pain and fear he had himself undergone.

The frenzied explosion of animal emotion had sent
an unexpected burst of energy into Rasriel's own spirit.
His dazed mind began to think more clearly, recalling
certain studies in the histories of Baddalaur. He knew
what to do next.

The practice had been strictly prohibited by the Order
of the Seekers of the Way, but there was some evidence
that the earliest adherents of the Order were familiar

with blood sacrifice. Their skills had been attained through many techniques, not all of them passive.

Rasriel returned to his band and told them what they must do. Finding a shepherd boy alone in the hills, they seized him, abused him cruelly, then killed him . . . and felt their spirits expand with power.

Subsequently, it was a simple matter to convince the ignorant peasantry of the region that Rasriel and his followers represented a new teaching order, one which could make princes out of pigkeepers. They soon had an adequate supply of eager young acolytes. Virgins; Rasriel always stipulated virgins. Their blood sizzled the hottest.

None of the boys would ever return to their villages.

The Seekers Reborn could not exist like this indefinitely, Rasriel knew. Sooner or later the locals would begin asking questions. Even peasants were not totally stupid. Thirteen men, even such as his, could not stand against an enraged mob.

So now he travelled the Aethyra in search of the Silverhand, the false savior.

When Rasriel found him, he would give him to the Duet . . . in return for amnesty.

CHAPTER TWENTY-THREE

"So you're alive." The relief in the Madra Allta's voice was obvious.

Caeled struggled to sit up, groaning aloud as aching muscles protested. "I feel terrible," he mumbled. The lining of his mouth was thick and his tongue was too big.

"You look terrible," Madran agreed. He smiled, revealing gleaming canine teeth. "Do you remember what happened?" he asked as he pressed a solicitous if hairy palm to the young man's forehead.

Caeled appeared doubtful for a moment; then his eyes widened. "The twins!"

"The twins," his companion echoed. Flopping down beside Caeled, Madran propped himself on his elbows. A glance down the beach revealed Gwynne and Sioraf hurrying toward them. "You did battle with the Duet in the Aethyra, my friend. And you nearly lost."

Fragments of memories whirled like windblown leaves; settled. "I remember now," said Caeled ruefully. Running his hands over his body, he searched for the wounds he knew he had received.

"They're gone," Madran assured him. "The Arcana's

silver light healed them, I suppose. Washed them away."
His voice dropped. "It changed all of us. The light made
Gwynne a normal woman for a heartbeat or two. Better
if it hadn't. Now she must come to terms with her
disfigurement all over again. She's very bitter, Caeled."

Sioraf darted up to crouch by Caeled's side. Her vividly
blue eyes were filled with concern. The vampir's long
fingers danced delicately over his flesh, tracing the thin
white lines of scars already healed, then brushing the
new silver hairs at his temples.

Sioraf made a tiny mewing sound of sympathy. Then
with lips firmly closed, she pressed her mouth to Caeled's
in a gesture of welcome. Her breath was moist on his
face, a fragrance of ivory and moonlight. "I saw them,"
she whispered. "White crows, a jackal-headed man, a
cat-headed woman; I saw them all."

"They are but aspects of the twins," Caeled replied.

Gwynne's bulky shadow fell over them. With the sun
behind her it would have been impossible to make out
her expression even if her stony face had been capable
of one. But Caeled could feel the anger emanating from
her. Slowly, with her stiffening joints grinding in a way
that was painful to hear, she knelt beside him. She also
examined his healed scars, but she gave no evidence of
sympathy. "Sioraf said you were fighting the Duet."

Caeled nodded.

"And when it seemed they were about to overwhelm
you, you unleashed a silver light that destroyed them."

"The light of the Arcana repulsed them," Caeled told
her, "but I am afraid it did not destroy them."

Extending one hand, Gwynne held it over his head.
She closed it to a fist, then opened it again. The movement
caused particles of flesh like tiny flakes of mica to fall
onto Caeled's upturned face. "For a moment I was human.
The light wiped away this abomination and gave me my
flesh back. It was incredibly painful but . . . do it again!"

Even through her damaged vocal cords, Caeled could

detect the anguish in the woman's voice. What must it be like, he wondered, to be trapped in a petrifying shell? To be capable of movement yet insensitive to touch; the only sensitivity that of the tormented spirit.

He thought of his metal hand. What would it be like if his entire body were metal, like the shape he wore in the Aethyra?

Reaching up with fingers of flesh, Caeled caught and held Gwynne's hand. Her granitic flesh was rough even to his callused palm. "I cannot do as you ask," he said regretfully.

Gwynne loomed immobile over him, giving no sign of emotion. Then, very slowly, she pulled her hand free of his and turned away from him. Folding her arms across her breasts, she stared down the beach to where the incoming surf foamed pink with blood. Long-billed gulls were gathering at the water's edge, swooping down to snatch fragments of Eron flesh from the water.

"Cannot or will not, Caeled?" she asked in a toneless voice. "You were able to use the silver light to save yourself from the Duet."

Caeled struggled to his feet and started to reach out to the Stone Warrior again, but drew back at the last moment. He had made a mistake, taking her hand. They all knew she hated to be touched.

"The Arcana directed the light, not I," he tried to explain. "I had no control over it. If we can find the other two Arcana and bring the four together, perhaps it will be possible to guide the whole. I hope so."

Even as he spoke, words and concepts were gathering in his mind. Some were familiar, like the mathematical formulae Brother Daniel had tried to teach him in Baddalaur, but others were totally alien. Like creatures he had never imagined they stalked through his brain, making suggestions he could not decipher.

He was certain they had not been in his head before the silver light washed over him.

Caeled circled the Stone Warrior until he was standing directly before her but she refused to meet his eyes. Staring over his head, she said, "I was human again. You cannot imagine what that meant to me. I wish I had not lost the ability to weep; tears might wash away some of the pain. But for just a moment I could feel the breeze on my face and the stones beneath my feet. I felt the touch of my clothing against my skin. My *skin* . . . Oh, Caeled . . . !"

Suddenly she gripped his shoulders with hands capable of crushing them. "This is a living death!" she cried. "Do something!"

Without thinking, Caeled stepped forward and wrapped his arms around her.

She was so surprised she did not push him away. She could not remember when a man last held her. . . . *Silan!* Silently she called the name of her dead husband, and a fresh grief tore through her.

"When I lost my hand," Caeled was saying gently, "I felt a little of what you must be feeling. Part of me was gone forever. It was a sort of death. I can only guess how much worse it is to lose your entire body. I promise you this, Gwynne. The day I learn to control the silver light, I will make you a woman again."

He stood holding her, and she let him. Her body was like a pillar of stone in his embrace, yet strangely enough he could feel a steady thudding deep within. After a while he realized it was her heart.

The causeway appeared as the tide retreated, a narrow strip of sand and shale separating the island from a larger isle which, like the one they now occupied, appeared to be mostly sand and rock, with cliffs rising precipitously in the distance. There were, however, a few shadowy patches which could be vegetation. "At least we might find something to eat over there," Gwynne said.

Madran examined the newly emerged surface of the

causeway doubtfully. "I'm not sure I'd trust the footing."

"If we stay in the center we should be all right," hazarded Caeled. Shading his eyes, he scanned the causeway. In a few places it was no wider than the length of his forearm. A loss of balance by someone as cumbersome as Gwynne could mean a tumble into the sea.

Madran pointed. "See those darker patches of sand? There's water under them, maybe even quicksand. In the Southlands there are sand eels and mud scorpions in quicksand; I'd rather not fall into something like that."

"At the moment, it seems to be our only way off this island," Gwynne reminded him. "We can wait here until the twins return, or we can take the chance." Shoving past Caeled and Madran, she strode out onto the causeway.

Stones shifted beneath her weight. Shells crackled; sand slipped. Water quickly filled the deep footprints she left behind. But the surface seemed capable of supporting her weight.

"Caeled, you go next but stay several paces behind," Madran directed, "so if she does go into the water, she'll go in by herself. That way you'll still be able to help her."

After carefully adjusting the backpack that held the two Arcana, Caeled stepped out onto the causeway. Madran's suggestion was sensible, but they all knew if the Stone Warrior fell the three of them together would not be strong enough to lift her back onto land.

Madran pushed a reluctant Sioraf after Caeled. "Go ahead," he urged. "I'll bring up the rear." The Madra Allta waited until his three companions were strung out along the causeway before he set foot on the surface. His dark eyes continually scanned the sea to the left and the right. He had not mentioned the dark, finned shapes he had noticed in the water. Fear could cause one of his friends to make a mistake and he did not want them seized by the predators which had been devouring the bodies of the dead Eron.

The water was still stained with Eron blood.

Caeled had said Sarel killed the Eron accidentally, but a whole species had been wiped out whether it was intentional or not. Madran shuddered. It was but a short step from snuffing out the lives of beasts to having no regard for life itself. He was dismayed to realize the twins, the most powerful rulers the Seven Nations had ever known, were so lacking in feeling. As a carnivore he could accept blood and death, but he could not understand indifference.

Gwynne had not looked at herself in a mirror for a long time. Not since she was first afflicted by contact with one of the twins' Voids—the same Void that snatched her living baby off her back and swallowed the rest of her family. Following that fateful day she had fled to the Snowscalds' camp high in the mountains. Before marrying Silan she had spent the early years of her womanhood among the female outlaws known as Snowscalds, and after her disfigurement they seemed the only family left to her. So she had returned to them and they had cared for her. Women who had seen and endured much pain themselves, they were gentle with Gwynne.

They had never given her a mirror so she could see what the Void had done to her.

She had suffered indescribably for a time, and there were occasions when the Scalds chained her to a rock to keep her from hurling herself from the mountain. Once the initial petrification had taken place, however, the pain lessened. Though much of her skin had hardened to a crust, there were still some patches of pale flesh. The inside of her mouth and her green eyes seemed unaffected by the process, and for a time one breast and nipple had been undamaged.

Lately, however, even these were beginning to harden. The flesh was not true stone but closer to a grey rigid bark, flaking on occasion. When broken it leaked a pale ichor that quickly hardened over the wound.

When it had seemed as if the worst might be over, Gwynne had left the Snowscalds and gone in search of healing. She had set out for Baddalaur in hopes of being cured by the Seekers of the Way, whose Healing College was renowned throughout the Nations. But she arrived too late; the Bred had attacked and the college was a smoking ruin.

Gwynne had met Caeled as he was fleeing from Baddalaur, a young Scholar who had just seen the only home he knew destroyed. From the first their fates had seemed curiously entwined. He intended to challenge the Duet, who were responsible for the destruction of Baddalaur. With the loss of the Healing College, Gwynne's own destination had become the twins' palace in Barrow. She was determined to confront them and force them to reverse the disfigurement caused by their Void.

So the shocked young Scholar and the bitter Stone Warrior had set out together on their quest—and along the way found Sioraf and Madran as well.

From Caeled the others had learned of four ancient artefacts said to be capable of reversing chaos and changing the world. They had already located the first two, the Spear and the Stone, whose power was incomprehensible but potent. But it was only today, when she felt the hardened crust melt away and her own flesh briefly return, that Gwynne fully appreciated the potential of the Arcana.

Forgetting for the moment where she was, the Stone Warrior stamped her foot in frustration . . . to have come so close to normalcy and then lose it again!

Her foot sank halfway to her knee. She pulled it free with a hideous sucking sound to find a thin black worm coiled around her ankle, banging its blind head against her stony skin. Balancing precariously on one leg, Gwynne reached down to pull off the worm. The creature immediately twisted itself around her wrist instead. "Sand eel," she muttered in disgust as she tried to shake off the serpent. But it clung tenaciously. Meanwhile a second eel and then a third were slithering around her feet. By smashing her left heel against her right ankle Gwynne crushed one of the creatures. But when she set her foot down again the unstable earth collapsed inward, exposing a seething nest of sand eels. They erupted in an oily wave. She barely had time to shout a warning before they were swarming up her legs.

CHAPTER TWENTY-FOUR

The pain was excruciating . . . yet strangely welcome.

Ice stabbed through his veins, acid devoured his muscles, red-hot lava blistered his skin.

Kichal attempted to scream, but his throat was choked with sand and salt. When he blinked, bloody tears poured from his eyes, carving furrows of agony down his cheeks. Every part of him hurt, from the hair on his head to the toenails on his feet. The total pain was indescribable and inescapable.

When he swiped an arm across his face to try and clear his brimming eyes, the touch of his sleeve was like stripping off skin. Purple light flooded the passage where he stood, an almost tangible light that sank into his flesh and flickered along his nerve endings. The light was not of itself painful, yet it summoned pain; pain that welled up from deep inside him as if some powerful corrosive were replacing the marrow in his bones.

He ran a trembling hand across his throbbing head. The lightest touch of his palm so abraded his scalp that his close-cropped hair was pulled out by its roots. He felt the separate pain of each follicle as the individual hairs tore loose and showered down around him.

Breathing *hurt*, heartbeats *hurt*. The simple act of sustaining bodily life had become torture.

Yet he could feel. That was the wonder, the amazement of it. He could *feel*.

A figure loomed before him, hideous in the violet glow, a mountain walking on two legs. Kichal struck out automatically, but the effort made him shriek with pain. Then as the shape came closer the commander recognized Anadyr's scarred features.

Gripping the front of Kichal's tunic, the Islander hauled him forward. Anadyr appeared to be saying something but, through the roaring of blood in his ears, Kichal could only make out fragments of words. Hearing *hurt*. With a final whimper, he surrendered himself to Anadyr and the pain.

When he ceased resisting, the torment lessened fractionally. He was able to think clearly enough to understand that pain meant the return of sensation, and be thankful.

In the beginning, when Sarel first claimed his body and mind, she had rendered him totally numb. Even his memories were wiped clean. He could move and speak but nothing more. The spectrum of sensation was lost to him.

One intensely focused emotion had returned when Sarel flooded him with a wild and artificial rapture. The ecstasy immediately became addictive. Since he was otherwise insensitive he had lived for those moments. He neither knew nor cared that she was controlling him through them. He devoted himself to her and her brother, doing whatever they asked in return for his few moments of bliss.

After Kichal had spent some time in the Duet's service, he dimly came to understand that he was devoid of normal feelings. The emotions others felt—the joy of lovers, the grief of the bereaved, the terror of victims, the despair of the condemned—these held no meaning for him. He wondered if he was dead, a corpse reanimated by the twins' mysterious powers. Not that it mattered. Nothing mattered.

But as he watched Sarel work her evil magic on others, he gradually realized what she had done to him. She had taken a man and turned him into an unfeeling *thing*.

Recently, and for reasons he did not know, her influence over him had begun to fade. As his true self emerged, Kichal could appreciate how much he had lost. The advantages—strength, endurance, the strange intimate communion with Sarel, freedom from pain or hunger or weariness—were far outweighed by the disadvantages.

He had been stripped of his humanity. He was no longer a man.

As he stood in the tunnel of purple light, wracked by unaccustomed pain, a great black wave of anguish rose up and swamped him. His knees buckled and he moaned like a soul in torment.

Anadyr promptly hoisted Kichal onto his broad shoulders. The commander fought against oblivion, but it was no use. He was sinking into a sea of tantalizing half-memories: faces that were almost familiar, places he almost recognized. Were these memories from his life as a man? Or were they things he had only witnessed while Sarel's puppet?

In a clear blaze of recollection he watched a woman burst from a crowd, clutch at him, saw himself strike her down. He felt nothing; it was like looking at a picture painted on a wall. Then he saw a child crouch over the fallen woman and turn to look at him with eyes that blazed with hate . . . eyes he knew . . . Kichal screamed aloud.

He knew them both, the dead woman and her child. Knew them all too well!

Startled by the scream, Anadyr heaved Kichal off his shoulders. The pain as his back and head struck the metal wall of the tunnel was excruciating, but it was nothing compared to the agony of memory. The bloodied face of his wife. The accusing eyes of his child. They were worse than the most savage pain of the body, and to escape them Kichal plunged gratefully into the darkness.

CHAPTER TWENTY-FIVE

The odor of the sand eels was a bitter stench that turned the stomach. It was the first smell members of the People learned to identify, for it warned of death.

Lying flat on his belly, Mock parted the razor-edged marram grass and peered down onto the beach. When the acrid stink drifted to him on the wind from the sea, the boy knew a sand eel nest had been breached. The invader was undoubtedly dead by now. A large nest of the creatures would deliver a swift and almost painless end, unlike the days of lingering fever and nightmares that came from a single bite.

Mock saw four figures on the strip of reddish, stony beach that formed a causeway connecting the two islands. He squinted hard against the glare from the sea as he sought to make out details. Three men and a woman. One of the men, a thick ugly brute, was coated from the feet almost to the hips by sand eels. Cupping his pointed chin in his hands, Mock settled down to enjoy the entertainment.

"Filthy things!" Gwynne scraped a handful of the reptiles off her thighs, crushed them to pulp in her fists and tossed them into the water. More eels swiftly wriggled out of the nest and plunged into the water to devour the remains of their dead fellows. As she struggled to free herself of the creatures the Stone Warrior staggered backwards. She tried to regain safe footing, but the ground kept collapsing under her weight.

Sand eels invariably chose pockets of unstable soil for their egg laying. Quicksand protected the newly hatched young from predators, but could prove a deadly trap for the unwary who stumbled into them. As had happened often in the past, the very earth was delivering a meal to the nest of eels.

Floundering, Gwynne sank deeper. Eels flowed up her body, twisting around her knees, her thighs, coming perilously close to her groin. She gave a cry of revulsion. Grabbing one, she tore it from her and held it up so she could see its tiny eyeless head, its circular mouth filled with needle teeth. The mouth kept opening and closing, trying to bite. The eel was a fully grown adult the length of her forearm, though as thin as her finger, with an oily, muscular body that defied her grasp. In spite of all she could do it threatened to wriggle free. With a sinuous twist, the creature lowered its sightless head and attempted to fasten its teeth in her arm. The teeth scraped harmlessly against her hardened flesh.

In a single swift motion, the Stone Warrior cracked the eel like a whip and snapped off its head.

"Give me your hand," Madran called to her. Balanced on the crumbling edge of the pit of eels, he stretched out his right hand to Gwynne. With the left he stabbed with his sickle at the writhing creatures, trying to force them back. In their blindness they were unaware of the weapon until it sliced into them.

Gwynne strained as best she could and tried to take his hand, but at that moment a sand eel wriggled up her back and over her shoulder, coiling around her forearm. As its head weaved toward the Madra Allta he gave a yelp of surprise and drew back. Swiftly recovering, he uttered a savage oath and cut the reptile in half with his sickle. Then he braced himself and reached out once more.

The Stone Warrior's fingers closed on Madran's wrist. He gave a great heave and tried to haul her out of the pit, but she was sinking deeper with every move she made. She could not keep still; she could not help trying to fight off the poisonous eels before they could bite those portions of her skin that were not petrified.

They were now trying to attack her groin, one of the few places on her body that was still vulnerable. Instinct guided the blind creatures to helpless flesh. "Help me!" she cried piteously.

"I'm trying . . ." Madran panted, straining.

Caeled appeared at the Madra Allta's shoulder. In one lightning move, he caught Gwynne's arm with his silver hand. He hurled his weight backward, pulling. Metal screeched on stone. The strength of the hand actually succeeded in cracking the petrified flesh. But Gwynne's weight was working against her. Although Madran caught Caeled around the waist and added his own strength to the effort, she continued to sink lower into the seemingly bottomless nest of eels.

The writhing mass swarmed up her body. One wrapped itself around her throat and butted its head against her stony cheek before locking its teeth onto her ear. There it dangled for a moment until the tiny teeth shattered against the unyielding surface. The eel fell back into the ooze.

"Do something!" cried Gwynne. She heard panic in her own voice but she did not care; she was past the need for courage. Buried hip-deep in voracious eels, she was moments away from death when the first one broke through to a vital part.

"Use the Arcana," Madran demanded of Caeled.

"There's no time!"

"And no need," whispered Sioraf as she joined them.

✧   ✧   ✧

Mock wriggled forward for a better look. This was getting interesting!

The four obviously had been crossing from the Eron Isle—but how had they escaped the Water Folk?—when the thick ugly man stepped into the sand eel nest. From this distance it looked to Mock as if he were sinking into a pool of roiling black water. But why was he not already dead? The eels were biting furiously, their heads slamming again and again into the ugly man.

Men who slipped into dangerous madness, mothers who birthed the more extreme abominations, infants who were born too crippled to survive, all such were given to the eel nests by the People. Death was instantaneous. Mock himself, having been born undersized and puny, his left leg withered and twisted, was destined to be given to the eels. Fortunately his father had fought for him. He argued that others with worse afflictions had become assets to the People. According to legend even Tenjiku, the warrior-priest who had united many of the island tribes, had been horribly mutilated. Yet consider the heights he had achieved!

Why was the eels' poison not working on the man with grey skin, Mock wondered as he watched the scene on the causeway. The other two men, one wild-haired with a long nose and jaw, the other dark and slender and wearing some sort of silver glove on one hand, kept trying to pull the grey man out. Though the eels continued attacking, their victim still lived and moved.

It was only a matter of time, though. Even Mock knew that.

And then the woman stepped forward.

With a graceful gesture, Sioraf threw off her cloak and flung it aside. Then she pulled her simple, undyed shirt over her head, rumpling her dark curls and baring herself to the waist. Standing first on one leg and then the other, she slipped her feet out of her soft leather boots, then stepped out of her leather trousers.

Totally naked, she deliberately walked straight into the eel nest.

Mock stifled a startled exclamation. Madwoman!

But when the eels touched Sioraf's pale flesh, they withered. Her companions watched in disbelief as the vicious serpents writhed and collapsed, turning into brittle strips. One launched itself from Gwynne's shoulder and landed on Sioraf's breast . . . only to convulse, then fall dead. Its body slithered down across the scar between her breasts.

Reaching out with long-fingered hands, Sioraf had only to touch the eels still clinging to Gwynne, and they dropped away like burnt sticks.

Several eels attempted to crawl up Sioraf's legs, but they were dead before they reached her knees. She moved forward calmly, wading through the nest. The reptilian mass became a pool of death. Alerted now to her presence, the surviving eels recoiled from her and spilled out onto the narrow causeway, making for the sea.

Sioraf knelt in what was left of the nest, which now resembled a bed of blackened cinders. The bodies of the dead eels at last provided a firm surface, a bottom for the quicksand. She ran her hands along Gwynne's legs, clearing the last of the eels from her. When none remained on the Stone Warrior, Sioraf stood up. She sprang out of the destroyed nest without letting either man help her, then walked past them along the causeway. Her back was straight and very white; her hips were more rounded than they appeared when clothed.

After she had gone several paces toward the next island she turned and looked back. Caeled was gazing in obvious admiration at her naked body.

She gave him a half-shy smile of invitation. "Aren't you coming?"

He roused himself with a start. "How did you kill those eels?"

It was the Madra Allta who replied. "The vampir's touch is anathema to many serpents."

Sioraf nodded. "Never forget—mine is vampir flesh. I am only half-human. Never fully human," she added in a voice almost too low to hear. Then she forced herself to smile again; lazily, mockingly. "Bring my clothes, will you? Even a vampir can catch cold."

Breathless with excitement, Mock slid out of the long grass and limped hurriedly away to tell the others what he had seen.

CHAPTER TWENTY-SIX

The things on the bloody bed had once been beautiful. They had possessed delicate, unblemished skin, violet eyes, amber hair. Now they were so much burnt meat. Their staring eye sockets were crusted with blackened blood; their hair lay in crisped strands across the silk pillows.

In the Aethyra Lares turned to look at his sister's spirit, floating as insubstantial as gossamer beside him. By destroying their artificially-constructed Aethyra images the silver light had robbed them of much of their strength. Lares could still vividly *feel* the light washing through his jet form, turning polished stone to liquid. When his twin's crystal form was shattered, glass shards had ripped into his liquid center and let it bleed away, completing the destruction. Abruptly disembodied, he and Sarel had been driven to seek shelter in their flesh.

But when they awoke in their chamber at Barrow they discovered that the destruction of their Aethyra forms had also affected their physical bodies. Bloodied and burnt, they were stripped of the outer layer of skin. The pain was unbearable. They had no choice but to hurl their naked and vulnerable spirits out into the Aethyra once more. Their rapidly fading strength would not long sustain them there, however, nor was it sufficient to construct new forms.

Eventually they must sink back into their ruined bodies, and that would be the end of them.

"Sister . . . ?" Lares whispered fearfully.

"I don't know," Sarel replied, answering his unasked question. She was appalled by the creatures on the bed, the woman who had been herself, the man who was her mirror image. She had no idea what they might do next.

Allowing herself to drift lower, she floated horizontally, face to face with her body. She tried to divorce her emotions from the mass of suppurating flesh and objectively assess the damage. The charred flesh was hanging in blackened shreds, but only the outer layer of skin was involved. The exposed muscle beneath, though bloody, seemed intact. But the eyes were puffed closed and the lips were split and cracked as a result of being exposed to concentrated flame.

If the bodies lived, the skin might heal in time, but she and her twin would be hideously scarred. Furthermore, they would spend many moons in constant pain, unable to bear the touch of clothing or blankets—unable to touch one another. And when it healed their flesh might permanently be numb, devoid of sensation.

The pull of her body was growing stronger, calling her spirit back. She could feel the intimations of terrible pain at the edges of her consciousness. If agony overwhelmed her she would no longer be able to think. She had to make a decision now.

Sarel's mind was racing. As so often now, her thoughts turned to the Voids, those twin engines of rampant growth and chaotic destruction.

She could introduce a tiny Void into their—her!—skull, to destroy that portion of the brain which felt pain. But the same area also responded to pleasure. To destroy one would ruin the other. And she could not imagine a life without the rapture she knew in Lares' arms, without the touch of her twin, her lover.

Even death would be preferable to that.

"Sarel . . ." Her brother's voice was hoarse with pain. Poor Lares; he had always been the weaker of the pair, the sickly child, too sensitive to hot and cold, often struck down with chills and fevers. How could he survive in a ruined body?

"Sarel . . . do something."

She made a lightning decision. "Give me your essence, my brother," she commanded. "Give me all of it; everything you are." Sarel reached for Lares. She clamped upon his spirit with fierce concentration, bringing all her will to bear. For a moment she thought they would be torn apart by the power she felt surging through her, the raw force of her determination.

Then they flowed together into ultimate union. Now they were no longer two, but one; no longer halves, but whole. It was a technique they had used before, though rarely, for it was exhausting. But those moments had been uniquely exhilarating, when their powers were intensified a hundredfold and sense of Self was replaced with sense of Us.

"We need more strength." Sarel's voice sounded masculine and authoritative in her head, while Lares heard words he had not uttered tumble inside his skull. One mind, one voice, one being. Their single shape, almost but not quite palpable, shimmered like a phantasm in the warm air of the bedchamber. Then it flowed toward the locked metal door—and through to the other side.

Records would subsequently show that twenty-two guards and fifteen servants had died as some mysterious and deadly curse spread through the Imperial Palace. Eyewitnesses spoke of the victims convulsing in agony. As their bodies surrendered their energy, their limbs thrashed with enough force to snap bones and tear muscles. When the spasms passed all life had drained from them. Only corpses remained.

"Now!" Sarel exulted. When she flung her arms wide, ripples of surplus energy radiated through the Aethyra. She could feel the stolen life forces surging through her, the thoughts and fears and memories of the dead entangling with hers. She was them, she was Lares, she was herself. She was simultaneously less and more than all of these.

Keeping her brother's spirit entwined with hers, she looked down at the two bodies on the bed. Pitiful ruined creatures, she thought. But that was also Lares lying there, the fleshly Lares who had shared her mother's womb. Lares, whose body had been more precious to her than her own. She must do what she could to help him.

Sarel folded in upon herself, concentrating her reenergized will into an intense, minuscule probe. Originally she had used this probe to develop creatures like Kichal by introducing tiny Voids into the skulls of her victims. The Voids destroyed selected portions of their brains in order to turn them into mindless slaves responsive only to her. Countless men and women had died in her experiments before Sarel had perfected the technique, however.

But her experiments had yielded other results as well. She had discovered how to control not only the emotions, but how to use the mind to affect the physical shell. It had worked on others. Why should it not work on the fleshly bodies of the Duet?

She reached out.

"Be careful, sister," Lares warned.

She felt a flicker of annoyance. Sarel knew, even better than Lares, just how dangerous this procedure was. The portion of the brain she wished to work upon was buried deep in the skull. A slip, a tiny moment of imprecision would doom Lares to permanent mindlessness.

As her consciousness probed deep, touching the seat of pleasure, her brother's damaged body shuddered in ecstasy. A fraction of an instant later the same touch on his pain center caused him to scream. Sarel fought off pity and kept going. The pain must be endured, to get to the . . .

There.

The most infinitesimal pressure on her target flooded the tiny grey area with heat. The body of Lares started violently. The sudden movement flung Sarel out.

The twins watched from the Aethyra . . . and waited. They were both aware that they could be witnessing the end of their earthly life together.

A random trembling began, only tiny movements at first, but soon Lares' body was shaking like an old man with ague. Then deeper shudders wracked his form. A soft continuous moaning issued from the gaping mouth.

"Is it working?" his voice whispered to Sarel.

"I don't know."

"I feel . . ."

"What? You feel what?"

In the Aethyra, Lares' spirit suddenly vanished.

Sarel ran her hands down her naked body, cupping her breasts, teasing the taut pink nipples. She spun so that her amber hair swung around her shoulders in a silken veil.

Lares reached out and caught her wrist. His fingers closed where a puckered cicatrix—evidence of an old snake bite—had been. But the flesh was whole and smooth.

Sarel turned to her brother and ran her fingertips down over his ribcage. Then, dancing lightly around him, she trailed them across his buttocks, feeling for the scar left when he fell out of a tree as a child and tore himself open on a branch. The scar was gone.

The healing process she had initiated, first in Lares and then for herself, had caused their bodies to slough off old tissue. Skin and hair had been replaced; scars and blemishes had vanished. The twins had lost weight because the vast amount of energy the process required burned up body fat, leaving them sleek and taut.

They were themselves again, but perfected.

Lares turned and drew his sister into his arms. Her breasts flattened against his hairless chest. Her skin—her new skin—smelled of attar of roses. "Do you know what this means?" he asked.

Sarel pressed her lips against his throat, delighting in the feel of his strong pulse. "We can renew our flesh . . ."

"For ever and ever. We will never grow old, never age," he said in wonder.

Sarel laughed softly. "We should thank the Silverhand when we next encounter him."

"The next time will be the last time," Lares promised, but his words were swallowed as Sarel pushed him back on the bed. There, amid soiled sheets and flakes of burnt skin, they celebrated their new bodies.

CHAPTER TWENTY-SEVEN

He remembered a woman, a woman who cried and howled and screamed as this man was doing; cries which had haunted Anadyr's childhood, filling his nights with nightmares that lingered long after he was awake. Was the woman his mother? He was unsure. The event was long ago, when he was a very small boy. So much had happened since, so many dreadful memories swirled through his mind that one tended to blur another.

He remembered her, though, retained a vivid image of her being seized by a band of marauding Island Trash who had spent a long night abusing while her screams tore the air. The child Anadyr had once been buried his head in his hands and tried not to listen. Later, when the cries faded to whimpers and later still, when even the whimpers had faded, he had known the woman's suffering was over. He wept then, alone in the dark.

Over the years that followed he had become very familiar with the sounds of pain. He knew the tone of terror and of agony, not only the agony of the flesh but that of the spirit, which went much deeper. But never had Anadyr heard cries that echoed the screams of his childhood . . .

Until now.

Crouched on his massive haunches, the scarred man watched Kichal writhing on the ground. The warrior was curled into a tight ball with his arms encircling his head and his fingers hooked like talons over his eyes. There was blood on his hands, but from what Anadyr could see he had not torn out his own eyes—yet.

Anadyr was astonished at the intensity of his screams. They were not the usual howls of pain, nor were they the shrieks of a coward.

Kichal sounded as if his soul were being torn out by the roots.

The Islander reached toward the suffering man. With powerful fingers he dug into the side of Kichal's neck, pinching hard enough to cause him to shudder, then fall silent.

Without the screams echoing through his skull, Anadyr could think again.

He knew where they were. This was one of the Dead Places; the Island Sea was littered with these relics of a lost age. They were supposed to be haunted, but as a boy Anadyr occasionally had been forced to take shelter from predators or other Island Trash in metal tunnels very like these, and had never seen a ghost.

The Dead Places had wards and guards, of course. There were stories of Islanders who had attempted to live in some of the metal rooms opening off the corridors. Within a season they were mad. Even worse, their skin sloughed off their bones.

Was this what was happening to Kichal?

Anadyr reached out a tentative finger and stroked the nearest pale wall. It was slick and cold . . . and dead. When he was still a boy he had learned to tell the difference between a *live* wall—its metal sheets thrumming with a distant energy—and a dead one. Still, it would not be wise to remain here. The Eron feared these ruins as much as the Islanders and rarely ventured inside, but they had been known to fill a tunnel mouth with noxious seaweed and wait for the fumes to drive their prey out into their waiting talons.

Anadyr got to his feet with an agility that belied his massive bulk. With a sigh, he heaved Kichal over his shoulder. He only briefly wondered why he should bother with the man. Self-interest was the most obvious reason. Kichal was close to the Duet and an important person in his own right. If Anadyr looked after him, he might be well rewarded. He might even get to visit the court at Barrow, long a secret dream of his.

Anadyr had never been ambitious in the usual sense. Content to be Lamar's bodyguard, he had devoted himself to the man who had once rescued him. But . . . but now there was Kichal.

Yes. Kichal. Anadyr plodded off down the tunnel, carrying the inert weight of the unconscious commander and thinking slowly, carefully. His mind was not quick but it was thorough.

All Islanders shared an innate belief in destiny. Life among the islands could be short and brutal, and they had long since learned to grasp any opportunity that came along. *Never ignore driftwood* was a basic tenet of island life. Snatch every opportunity, let none slip away.

Islanders believed there were points in a man's life when he had control over his destiny—times when a single action, or inaction, would dictate the course of the rest of his life. Kichal represented such an opportunity for Anadyr.

But he had another, deeper reason for helping the Bred commander. Anadyr remembered, with anguish, the screaming woman of his childhood. As a small boy he had been useless, her screams an indictment of his impotence.

But he was a man now. And the cries of the suffering Kichal touched something very deep inside him.

❖   ❖   ❖

"Where are we?"

Anadyr looked toward the distant metal ceiling. "In a Dead Place," he responded. He knew Kichal had been awake for some time, though the other man had not spoken. He had continued to lie as if unconscious while peering at his surroundings through slitted eyes, surreptitiously assessing his situation. At last curiosity had forced him to ask the question.

"We are in a ruined . . . town, or something like a town," Anadyr went on, "deep below one of the islands."

Kichal struggled to sit up. The Islander made no move to help him. Kichal must surely realize that Anadyr had carried him through the tunnels, but to offer further assistance to a warrior might be taken as an insult.

Anadyr contented himself with asking, "How are you?"

"Hungry." Kichal sounded surprised. He had not experienced the sensation of hunger—real hunger, mouth-watering, stomach-rumbling hunger—for a long time.

"You have slept most of the day," Anadyr told him. "If you are as hungry now as I am, we should try to find something to eat. Then you'll want to think about getting back to Barrow . . ." As he spoke his gaze fell on Kichal's face. The Islander's mouth gaped; the pupil of his one functioning eye dilated with surprise.

"What's wrong?" Kichal asked in alarm. His hands flew to his face, exploring. He did not recall being wounded; did not recall much of anything very clearly.

He only knew he felt very strange.

Anadyr reached over and slid Kichal's knife with its highly polished blade from the sheath at his waist, then tilted the weapon so its owner could see his reflection.

Sudden tears welled in Kichal's eyes . . . his normal, human eyes: warm grey with flecks of brown around the pupil, but no trace of crimson at all.

"These old places, Dead Places, still have ancient magic in them," Anadyr said. "We passed through some sort of enchantment in that tunnel. To me it felt like a swarm of insects crawling over my skin, but it had a terrible effect on you. It seemed to burn away part of you. Or tear away part of you. I brought you here to get you out of it."

Kichal's eyes took on a strange, inward-looking expression. "She's gone," he whispered to himself. Then, louder, "She's gone!". He threw back his head and gave a great shout of triumph. "I am rid of you, Sarel! Your magic is gone from me!" The words echoed and reechoed off the metal walls and came singing back to him, multiplied and distorted but still ringing with joy.

He was cold and hungry, aching in every muscle, aware of bruised shoulders and abraded flesh, but he relished the discomfort. He could *feel*.

He shuddered as he recalled standing at attention behind Sarel while she carried out her hideous experiments on victim after victim. He had watched impassively—unfeelingly!—as she robbed others of everything that made them human and reshaped them to her purposes.

As she had done with him.

In order to turn him into an inhuman fighting machine she had . . . she had . . . he squeezed his eyes shut, but the terrible realization surfaced anyway, stark and clear in his brain. She had taken him from his family. His wife, lost to him. *A dead woman lying in the street while he walked away, uncaring?* And his boy, where was his boy now? Was he still alive? How long ago had it been?

Time had ceased to have any meaning. He had been in thrall to Sarel. But now he could see that he had been merely a tool, something she could easily discard when its usefulness was at an end.

No one could stop her. No one could stand against her and her twin brother; their power was total.

No one . . . except . . . she had known fear, he remembered now! That fear had prompted this mission. He was to find one called . . . the Silverhand, who possessed ancient artefacts known as . . . the Arcana.

Kichal's brain, restored to his own sovereignty, was racing.

If Sarel and Lares feared the Silverhand and his companions enough to send a Bred commander and an elite troop against them, they must represent a very real threat to the Duet. Kichal had been a soldier all his life. One of the first rules he had been taught by his own warrior father was "Respect your enemy but never fear him, for in that fear you will sow the seeds of your own destruction." He remembered those words now. He remembered everything.

Kichal smiled grimly.

Sarel had taken everything from him and he had not been able to fight her, but Sarel was afraid of the Silverhand.

Kichal meant to ensure that those seeds of fear would blossom into a deadly fruit.

"I'm not going back to the capital," he announced abruptly.

Anadyr tried to hide his disappointment. "You aren't going to Barrow?" He had already begun anticipating life in the great city. The music, the drink, the women who might be available for a price even for a hideously scarred man . . .

"No, I have another mission. But you saved my life and for that I am grateful—more grateful than you will ever know. You kept me alive long enough to appreciate what living means. I am sorry I have nothing to give you in return. If I don't go back to Barrow I have only the clothes on my back and a few coins of New Metal in my pocket, and I shall be needing those myself."

"I do not want your clothes or your coin. I did not look after you for their sake."

"Why then?"

"In memory of a woman's screams," the Islander replied cryptically.

Kichal turned to look across their strange, metallic

surroundings. "What the twins would give to see this place," he murmured, shaking his close-cropped head. "Though they might only think of it as a new source of metal. That which is not useful to them personally does not interest them, I'm afraid."

Glancing sidelong at Anadyr, he said, "It is difficult to explain, but the Duet did something to me. They made me a puppet, jerked and pulled at their command. Especially *hers*." His mouth twisted into a bitter shape. "But now I am free of their control, and I don't mean to lose myself to them again. There are others like me, so many others. I cannot undo the past, but perhaps I can make up for it, a little. I am going to set myself against the Duet, and I will not rest until I have brought them down."

Anadyr drew a sharp breath.

"You consider me a fool?" Kichal asked him.

"I . . . I do not know what to think of you."

"Think of me as someone who is grateful to you, and be glad of it. I can be a dangerous enemy."

The big man nodded. "Of that I have no doubt."

"Then listen to me. We were sent to capture the one being the twins fear. They do not want anyone to think an ordinary human can successfully defy them. If people were to suspect, it would destroy the myth of their omnipotence.

"I cannot make the Duet fear me as they do Caeled Silverhand, but I can travel the Nations telling of him. I can weaken their influence in that way, and perhaps inspire others to stand against them."

"Why are you telling me this?"

"Because one should tell a friend what one is about to do," Kichal replied quietly.

A friend. Anadyr rolled the word around in his mouth. In his life he had been called many things, but never friend. Imitating Kichal's accent, he asked slyly, "Is one allowed to tell a friend that he is mad?"

Kichal smiled. "One is."

"And is one allowed to accompany a friend?"

"Yes, if that is what you wish. I would be glad of your company."

Anadyr gazed thoughtfully at the former Bred commander. With the blood color gone from his eyes Kichal no longer seemed so terrifying. Set deep in a rugged face, his grey eyes were almost . . . kind. And desperately sad.

"You will find that you can rely on me," the scarred giant promised. "I am one of the People and proud of it, though some would say I am only Island Trash."

"And I am Kichal," the warrior replied, reaching out to take his extended hand. "Human again."

CHAPTER TWENTY-EIGHT

Madran sniffed repeatedly, feeling a vague apprehension. The stench of sand eel that still hung in the air was masking some other disturbing odor.

"What is it?" Although Gwynne was preoccupied with picking bits of sand eel off her skin, her warrior's reflexes responded to Madran's sudden tenseness.

"I'm not sure. Something . . . a smell . . ."

"These?" She flung a charred scrap of sand eel from her in disgust.

"No, something else. Warm, living . . . a mixture of sweat and . . . fish . . ."

The Stone Warrior straightened and hefted her morningstar onto her shoulder. She had come to respect Madran's instincts. "What else lives here?" she asked as she surveyed this larger island through narrowed eyes. Beyond the beach the land swept upward into a palisade of steep, rugged cliffs. The stone of which they were formed was horizontally striated in bands of ochre, pale cream, and deep lavender. A few straggling vines seemed to cling to them here and there; otherwise they were barren.

On the beach itself, the reddish, boulder-strewn sand was deserted except for Caeled and Sioraf some twenty paces ahead, heads bent as they walked and talked together. Between the beach and the cliffs lay a strip of rolling dunes where tufts of some coarse, greyish grass waved in the breeze from the sea. Otherwise nothing moved.

Madran replied, "I don't know if anything lives on this particular island. But you can never tell who we might encounter. There are the Islanders who tend to stay around the towns, and then there is a breed commonly known as Island Trash: descendants of escaped criminals and the outcasts of the Seven Nations, the diseased and the dispossessed. They live in the more remote places. I've learned a bit about them because most circuses have at least one or more of the People, as they call themselves. They are frequently deformed and spectacularly tattooed."

"And do you know *why* we are tattooed, Madra Allta?" asked a voice behind them.

Madran swore and spun around, raising his sickle defensively. Gwynne turned in unison with her morningstar at the ready. In an instant they found themselves ringed by barbed spears. At least thirty people appeared around them as if they had risen out of the sand. Dressed in ragged clothing and even fabric woven of seaweed, all were armed. They carried spears, clubs, or shells broken and honed into knives.

"No!" Madran cried to Gwynne as she gathered herself to fight. The spears could do her little harm, she knew, but at his command she made herself relax.

"You are wise as well as knowledgeable," said the person who had spoken to them.

Madran looked toward Caeled and Sioraf, only to see them surrounded by a small mob of similarly ill-clad people. They were being driven back at spear point to join himself and Gwynne.

The speaker continued, "It is unlikely that we will harm you if you make no attempt to harm us."

Madran turned back to face a short, slender woman of indeterminate age. She might have been beautiful or grotesque, it was impossible to tell which, for all her visible skin was tattooed with swirling, twisting, coiling blue patterns.

"Do you know why we are tattooed?" she repeated. Her voice was quite lovely, mellow and low.

"No," Madran replied. "And I don't know how you identified me as Madra Allta, either."

"You do not shrink from the sight of us," the woman commented without directly answering his question. When she turned her head slightly, he could see flat, tattooed flesh where her ear should have been. She had been born earless; only a small hole indicated the aural aperture.

A glance at the others in the surrounding circle revealed a number of deformities. A tall man stood on clubbed feet; a very young woman appeared to have no bones in her arms, but brandished her spear in sinuous tentacles. An oldster bent and twisted by the years had no nose, mere nostril slits.

All were tattooed. Each met Madran's gaze with lifted chin and defiant eyes.

Madran looked calmly back at them. "I am Madra Allta," he acknowledged. "We are monsters in the eyes of many of humankind. I know how it hurts to be condemned for what I cannot help, so I do not judge others by their appearance. But I would like to know why you are tattooed. I have never heard the explanation."

"Few of us are born without disfigurement," the woman who appeared to be leader of the group replied. Her eyes were the same color as the sea, Madran noticed. "So we use our flesh as blank canvas to draw attention away from our imperfections." She lifted her arms and spread them wide. The coarse fabric of her sleeves slid down, revealing more blue tattoos. "Amongst our people it is the originality of the tattoos, the intricacy of design, the delicacy of the workmanship which is admired. Having no physical beauty to begin with, we create it upon ourselves."

Madran nodded in understanding. Without taking his eyes off the woman's face, he tucked the handle of his sickle into his belt. "I once travelled with a man from the Island Sea. Moi—he told me that was his name—claimed to be one of the People. He had spent four seasons just tattooing the image of an eagle onto the palm of his hand. You could see every feather, every pinion. It was a remarkable sight."

"But he did not tell you why he was tattooed?" Gwynne interjected.

"Perhaps he did not trust me."

"He must have trusted you if he told you his name," said the tattooed woman. "The People have little of material worth, so we place great value on our names and guard them jealously, sharing them only with our closest friends. The same is true not only here on Home Isle, but wherever the People live in the Island Sea. We have several colonies, a necessity as the resources of Home Isle are limited. Your friend Moi would have come from one of the southern islands, I think. The bird is a favorite design of theirs. It signifies that they have travelled far."

Unexpectedly, she reached out and pressed the palm of her hand against Madran's chest. He did not flinch. His face remained impassive as she brought her hand back toward her nose and sniffed it thoroughly. "What happened to Moi?" she enquired when she had familiarized herself with Madran's scent.

"He fell to one of the Duet's foul creatures when they attacked our circus caravan. He died bravely, a hero."

The woman made a small, soft sound of approval or grief, he could not tell which. Then stepping past Madran, she stared into Gwynne's face. Slowly, deliberately, she stroked the Stone Warrior's arm. "You are ashamed of your shape, this crusted skin you wear."

Gwynne was startled by her perception. "This crusted skin is slowly killing me. I am not ashamed of it . . . I am terrified of it," she added, surprising herself.

"A warrior should always be honest." The tattooed woman turned then and faced Sioraf, who had been brought up behind her.

"And you are the vampir," the woman murmured.

Their eyes were almost identical in color, Sioraf's being a vivid blue only slightly darker than those of her interrogator. But the tattooed woman for all her scars seemed more human than the icily beautiful vampir.

"I was always told," the woman said, "that the touch of a vampir's flesh was deadly to serpents. I didn't believe it until today, when one of our lads came to tell us how you destroyed a nest of sand eels. I'm not sure I even believed in vampiri. We've never seen one on our island. Yet now here you are." She reached out to touch Sioraf's alabaster flesh, but the vampir drew back with a hiss.

"You need have no fear of me, little one," the woman said gently. "But I will consider it a courtesy if you refrain from touching those of the People who have scales." She smiled. Sioraf could not tell if she was joking or not.

"And you," the woman addressed Caeled last. "What are you?"

He met her gaze squarely. "Just a man."

"Just?" This time her tattooed fingers sought and found his silver hand and trailed across the metal. Then she licked her fingertips. Caeled was briefly repelled to observe that even her tongue was tattooed. "You are more than a man, I feel. You taste not only of Old Metal, but of ancient power."

"Do you always touch and taste your captives?"

"Always. I can tell the truth in your heart by the flavor of your flesh, the trembling in your muscles, the tension in your bones. And you are not my captives," she added. "Come." Turning away, she set off up the beach. The crowd lowered their spears and parted to let her pass, then almost immediately melted away, disappearing behind roseate rocks or slipping into lavender-shadowed hollows among the dunes.

Within moments only Caeled and his friends, and the tattooed woman who was rapidly striding away, remained visible.

Caeled raced after the woman. "Wait! If we are not your captives . . . what are we to you?"

The woman paused, waiting as he came up to her. She blinked tattooed eyelids. "These are the islands, and we are the People. Now you are on the island, you too are part of the People."

"We do not intend to remain here . . ."

"No one does," she said sadly. "But no one leaves."

The People occupied a warren of caves connected by tunnels that honeycombed the cliffs high above the beach. The lowest level of caves was accessible by an inclined trackway carved into the cliff face and barely wide enough for one person, reminding Caeled of a similar arrangement connecting the cells at Baddalaur. In places the track had been deliberately cut away and a narrow wooden walkway thrown across the divide. The crude bridge could easily be withdrawn, leaving an intruder stranded.

A series of pulleys depended from horizontal timbers above the higher cavemouths. Groups of the People operated the pulleys in order to crank up wooden baskets, thus lifting catches of fish and other heavy objects from beach level.

"You could hold off an army here," Gwynne remarked as the tattooed woman led the four companions up a trackway, then onto a long flight of well-worn stone steps leading toward the second level of caves.

"And we have," came the low-voiced reply. "In the first Island Wars four hundred cycles ago, the warrior-priest Tenjiku masterminded the defeat of the Kathan when they came out of the east slaughtering all before them. History records that the Kathan were defeated at the Ford of Black Rain on the mainland, but in truth the cream of their army died here at the foot of these cliffs. Much more recently, my father died defending this place against the yellow-haired Ice People from the Frozen Lands."

"I think I read something about Tenjiku once," Caeled commented absently. He was concentrating on climbing the slippery steps and holding onto Sioraf, who was beginning to tremble violently.

"Tenjiku was the savior of our people," said the tattooed woman. "Blessed be his name. We were nothing before him. He united Island Trash into the People. He showed us the meaning of strength in numbers, and encouraged us to respect our deformities as evidence of our individuality. It was he who taught us that there are no strangers; the only true strangeness is that within. Now we welcome any friendly visitors. We share our fish, our seabirds' eggs, our fresh water with them. We will even extend our hospitality to vampir and Madra Allta," she added, "providing you do us no harm."

Sioraf was trembling more than ever. She pressed against Caeled, crowding him on the narrow steps.

"But you still have your defenses," Gwynne called from her position at the rear. "So obviously you do not welcome everyone."

"We have welcomed you," she replied stiffly.

"Yet you know nothing about us."

The tattooed woman turned to look back at the Stone Warrior. "We know more than you think. We know you fled the privateer that sought shelter from the Shipkiller a few days ago. We know you blundered into an Eron nest and slew one of the mothers, and we know the Eron came for you. We also know about the shanti that was searching for you. We watched unobserved as the Eron did battle with the red-eyes. We saw the Water Folk triumph, then mysteriously die in a cataclysm. The same event sent many of our people mad with pain and dreams. We also know that you are feared and loathed by the Duet . . ." she paused to spit over the edge, "and that is reason enough to welcome you." Beckoning them to follow, she resumed climbing.

"You claim to welcome strangers," said Madran, trying to look past the tattooed woman to ascertain how many steps remained. He did not share Sioraf's fear of heights, but even he was beginning to feel slightly queasy. The steps were increasingly steep and it was a long way down. He began to wish they had made the ascent in a basket. "What happens to those strangers you do not like?"

"We kill them," the woman calmly replied over her shoulder. "And eat them."

"You're joking!"

"Of course I am." The woman laughed. "We don't eat them. We feed them to the Eron."

They continued in uncomfortable silence until the steps ended at another carved trackway. As they gratefully stepped onto the level surface, Caeled noticed a curious little lizard keeping pace with them, scurrying over the stone cliff wall almost at shoulder level. Its body was almost transparent, as if made of glass, but each time it crossed one of the horizontal bands of color that marked the cliffs it changed hue to match. In turn it was ochre, lavender, creamy buff. He would have liked to pause for a closer look at the delicate frills that encircled its throat, but when he fixed his gaze on the creature it promptly darted into a fissure and disappeared.

The cliff face, he observed, was deeply scored with many fissures, the surface folded back upon itself until it was impossible to get an idea of its basic shape. He could only tell that the cliffs were high and wide, jutting against the sky like sentinels protecting the island.

"We are almost there," the tattooed woman announced, drawing his attention.

They had begun passing circular openings in the stone

wall. Each cavemouth was ornamented with a different set of sticklike figures carved into the surrounding rock. Caeled's flesh fingers trailed across the carvings, finding their tactile language *almost* familiar. "What do these symbols mean?" he asked the woman.

"No one knows. These caves were here long before Tenjiku encouraged us to make our homes in them. Some of the older ones even lead down into the Dead Places. But *this* one . . ." She stopped before a relatively small cavemouth and ducked inside without warning, her voice echoing. "Come this way. There is something you must see."

"I'll wait here," said Gwynne, eyeing the dark hole dubiously.

"And I," Sioraf whispered. "That woman frightens me."

Madran drew a deep breath. "I smell something old . . . and long dead. I will remain here."

"I smell it too," said Caeled, "but one of us should go. We've come this far." Shrugging off his backpack containing the Arcana, he gave it to Madran. "Guard this with your life." Then he ducked into the cave after the woman. "Wait for me!"

A moment later he was slipping and sliding down a slope that ended in a bank of red sand which erupted in a cloud, obscuring his vision.

"I'm waiting," said a voice.

Caeled gave a start. The sand shifted under him and he had to fight to keep his balance. The place, wherever it was, was very dim; he could hardly see anything. The voice had come from in front of him . . . yet he was aware of the tattooed woman *beside* him. Someone else had spoken.

"I've been waiting for you for a long time." The voice was high, thin, sexless. "You are Caeled Silverhand, Keeper of the Arcana. Slayer of Worlds."

Caeled straightened. "You know me, but who are you?"

Light flared, sulphurous and blinding. For a moment

Caeled thought his eyes were burned and screwed them tightly shut. When he opened them again the area in front of him was lit by the glow of fish-oil lamps. He was standing in a small chamber hewn out of solid rock, either by nature or by the agency of humans, it was impossible to tell which. The walls had a curiously shaped smoothness, however. Sheets of what appeared to be parchment were stuck to them in a random pattern. There was some form of writing on the parchment pages but Caeled could not read it; the script was both oddly familiar and illegible.

Yet it was not the strangest sight in the chamber.

Caeled found himself confronted by an incredibly wizened man contained within a wooden cage. At first he thought the man's skin was blue, until he realized the wrinkled flesh had been tattooed so totally that the repeated injections of dye had run into one another.

"Who are you?" Caeled repeated, rubbing his eyes to get the sand out of them.

"I am Tenjiku."

"But Tenjiku is legend, and long dead!"

The old man smiled. "Not all legends are dead, Scholar."

CHAPTER TWENTY-NINE

Wood creaked as the old man approached, moving stiffly on rigid limbs. In the yellow light cast by the fish-oil lamps, Caeled observed that what he had first thought was a wooden cage was in actuality a frame fitted to his body like an artificial skeleton, supporting his flesh from the outside. Cleverly arranged timber laths made it possible for atrophied muscles to walk, even though one foot was amputated at the ankle.

The sight sent a pang of sympathy through Caeled.

What at first appeared to be a broad leather headband around the oldster's forehead was revealed as a fitting holding his skull against a back support that ran the length of his spine. The scrawny neck was too feeble to support the head any longer without such help.

"What do you see, Caeled Silverhand?" asked the man in the wooden frame.

"An old man," was the truthful reply, "who is obviously much loved and cared for by this community."

The blue ancient grunted, drawing his thin lips back into a toothless smile. "And how does your scholar's training lead you to that conclusion?"

Caeled spread his hands. "You live here in some comfort, strapped into a cleverly designed contrivance that enables you to walk. I would imagine simply getting into the device each day is difficult, so you must have assistance. These people must love you deeply to keep you fed and cared for in such circumstances."

"We are not savages who abandon our old people," said the tattooed woman, who had been standing beside him unspeaking until now.

"No, only our most deformed infants," replied Tenjiku cryptically. Then he raised his voice into a cracked command. "Leave us, woman!"

"But . . ."

"Leave us, I say. Go to the central chamber and tend to your other duties. The Silverhand will not harm me." Tenjiku clattered across the floor, his movements reminding Caeled of a crab scuttling sideways.

With a scowl on her face, the woman turned away and disappeared into a narrow tunnel at the back of the chamber.

"She means well," said Tenjiku as he made his way to a blackened pot suspended over a tiny fire in a niche in the wall. Stirring the liquid simmering on this makeshift stove, he added, "If I were willing, she would be my wife." He looked up and turned his head, forced to move his entire body to do so. Only then did Caeled realize that he had only one eye. Instead of a functioning left eye Tenjiku had the image of an eye tattooed onto a withered lid in a sunken socket.

"My twenty-second . . . or would she be my twenty-third wife? I don't remember. I think I married one of them twice," he mused, turning back to dip a long-handled spoon into the pot. "You will take tisane with me, a pleasant drink made from local herbs and . . . other things. Quite restorative." Without waiting for a response, he ladled two scoops of a pale greenish liquid into clamshell cups. "Come over here, boy, I will not eat you. We have much to talk about, much to say to one another, but precious little time to say it in."

Caeled crossed the room and took the proffered cup with his metal fingers. Tenjiku's single eye lingered on the workmanship of the hand. "Remarkable! Such skill, such a combination of ancient craft and modern technique. Plus a little of what you would call magic."

Caeled transferred the cup to his other hand and flexed his silvery fingers in front of his face, trying to see what the old man saw. "Why—what would you call it?"

"In my time that skill went by another name, but there is no place for the word in your vocabulary. Perhaps in five hundred cycles it will have come back into fashion." Carrying his cup, the shrivelled blue man walked stiffly to a large wooden open-sided basket that depended from the ceiling and maneuvered himself into it. When he was in place his feet did not quite touch the floor. The basket seat swung for a moment, then settled into a gentle rocking motion. "Sit," he told his guest.

Since there was no other seating available, Caeled dropped cross-legged to the floor and propped his back against the cave wall. Clutching the cup of tisane in hands of flesh and metal he brought the rim to his lips. The liquid exuded a spicy aroma. He sipped cautiously. The brew tasted of grain and herbs and something vaguely medicinal, and spread a warm glow through his body.

"You know quite a lot about me, it seems," he remarked, taking a second drink, "yet I only know a name for you. A name that could not possibly be yours."

"You think not?" The old man rocked gently, keeping his single eye fixed on the wall above Caeled's head. "Why do you question?"

"I have several questions. How do you know so much about me, what will happen to myself and my friends, and why do you call yourself Tenjiku when he lived four hundred cycles ago?"

"Let us discuss the last question first. How old do you think I am?"

Caeled gazed at the man. His blue-dyed skin was such a mass of wrinkles it gave no clue to his age, nor did the single greenish eye in its yellowing eyeball. "Old," he concluded. "Very old, but surely not four hundred cycles."

"No," agreed his host. "I am much, much older than that."

Caeled gaped at him. *"Older?"*

"You are surprised, in spite of all your studies in the Great Library at Baddalaur? I tell you there is a tribe in the Frozen Lands whose members sleep through the entire Cold Season, awakening only for the few short days of summer when they eat and breed. The least of them lives two hundred cycles, and some a great deal longer. Few know of them, of course. Only someone who has achieved a great age has heard all the tales . . . I ask you again, Caeled Silverhand. How old do you think I am?" He suddenly fixed his single eye in burning command on Caeled's face.

"I . . . I honestly don't know."

The wizened creature in the basket chair said, "I am far older than the oldest of that race in the Frozen Lands."

Keeping his face impassive, Caeled replied, "I see."

Tenjiku managed a tiny nod in spite of the binding that held his head to the spine support. "A lesser man than you would have laughed, or mocked."

"I was taught to observe and think before drawing any conclusions. Once—and not so long ago either—I would have argued with you, saying what you claim is impossible. Since I left Baddalaur, however, I have seen . . . *wonders*. So I'll accept what you say." He sipped more of the tisane. "And I shall not insult you by asking for proof."

"What proof . . . and why would you need any? You either trust me, or think me a liar and untrustworthy. The choice is yours."

"I trust you," said Caeled promptly. Intuition warned him that more depended on his answer than he knew.

"Good. I will repay that trust."

"But you have not told me how you know so much about me."

Tenjiku's laughter was a phlegm-choked wheeze. "My dear boy, the Aethyra is positively aquiver with you and your activities. The imprint of you is clearly readable to the gifted eye. Plus, every time you use the Arcana you send shock waves through the Aethyra. Some of the more fragile layers are beginning to disintegrate. Every being with a screed of power is following your progress. Not all are friendly . . . but neither are they enemies."

Caeled shook his head. "I'm not sure I understand."

"If you do not understand, you do not know how to use the Arcana," Tenjiku snapped.

"I don't," Caeled said simply.

It was Tenjiku's turn to be incredulous. "But surely you were trained for that very purpose!"

"Not really. I was still a Scholar when Baddalaur was destroyed, I had not yet been initiated into the ranks of the Seekers. Only those who had taken their final oath were trained in the most esoteric mysteries. I was not taught the secrets of the Arcana; I use them by instinct."

"Yet with only your native powers to guide you, you have shaken the Aethyra." The old man swore softly. "Truly you are the Spoken One."

Caeled got to his feet. Standing before the old man, he gripped the thick cords that held the basket chair in place and stared into Tenjiku's single eye. "You can help me, can't you? You can teach me. You can tell me what to do."

The breath that wheezed out of ancient lungs smelled of eternity. "There are things I can tell you, but I cannot teach you what you ask. No one can, you will have to discover for yourself."

Caeled stepped back, turning quickly so that Tenjiku

would not see the anguish on his face. He concentrated on the flames of the small fire, imagining his tension spiralling up and away with the smoke. "Every time I use the Arcana," he told Tenjiku, "I seem to grow older with abnormal speed. Can I do anything about this?"

"Do not use the Arcana," Tenjiku replied. "It's as simple as that. The Arcana draw their power from you, but they are out of balance because you only have two of them. Therefore they leech your youth and strength. In the past it was not uncommon for one of the Arcana—either the Sword or the Spear—to be plunged into the body of a slave. The weapon took the essence of the slave for its energy and did not feed off its user.

"I can help you to this extent, Caeled Silverhand. To minimize the aging effect, you should use the Arcana from the Aethyra and direct the energy back to this world."

"But how?"

"With the force of your will. The Arcana work by enhancing one's own will, amplifying it, allowing thoughts to be made tangible, putting flesh on ideas." The old man sounded wistful. "Think what you could do with such power. Imagine what others could do with it." Tenjiku shook his head.

"Three hundred cycles ago, Caeled, the entire Sond Tribe—two thousand or more—vanished. One of their adepts had discovered the location of the Cup, the most dangerous and powerful of the Arcana. Be mindful now that he was not in physical contact with the object, he simply saw it by looking through the Aethyra. But the merest touch of his excitement, linking with the power of the Cup, caused the Arcana to pulse with incredible energy. The adept disappeared in a stupendous explosion of light and sound that spread out from the man's hut in a vast, perfect circle. Everything for a great distance was laid waste. Even now, three hundred cycles later, the land is uninhabitable. Any who attempt to live in that region are soon disease-riddled and mad."

The young man shuddered. He had used the Arcana so naturally, so unthinkingly.

Tenjiku smiled at Caeled's discomfiture. "Rest easy, you seem to have escaped that fate."

"So far. But how can I know it won't happen the next time?"

"Because yours is the bloodline of the original creators of the Arcana. Each of the four encoded something of themselves into the objects . . ."

Caeled pressed his hands of metal and flesh against the sides of his head. "Stop! Enough! I don't understand. I am not uneducated, yet you are using concepts beyond my comprehension. Speak to me in words I know."

Tenjiku sighed. "In the Elder Days, before the Time of Burning, before the Fall of the World, four . . . magicians . . . created four magical . . . objects. They invested each object with the sum total of their wisdom. Such complete knowledge gave the objects sentience. By that I mean, bringing them to life, though not in ways you or I would call life.

"Their name, Arcana, refers to the hidden knowledge, the mysteries they contain. But before the Arcana could be used as a unit the last great magics destroyed the Elder world. Since then one or another of the Arcana has been found from time to time, though very few have been able to extract even a fragment of their power. And always at a heavy price.

"The Arcana have ravaged this world, Caeled. Every one of them is bathed in the blood of innocents, of whole nations. Within the Arcana resides all the might of the Elder World. With the four of them, and your abilities, you could recreate the Elder Days.

"But to do that would mean destroying this world," Tenjiku added.

"You sound as if you would not care to see a return to the wonders of the Elder Days."

"There were no wonders," snapped the old man.

"How do you know? I personally have studied the Elder Days quite extensively," Caeled said with a pardonable pride. "They have long been a fascination of mine and I have made every effort to learn all there is to know about them. To this end I have read countless books and manuscripts, pored over maps and charts . . ."

"But I was there," Tenjiku said softly.

CHAPTER THIRTY

At first I tried to keep up my daily journal, for that is how we were trained in the College at Baddalaur. Both Seekers and Scholars wrote down their various personal observations, notes on their travels or their intellectual explorations, tales they had heard, comments about the people they met and the times in which they lived, and stored all this information in the archives of the Great Library. Over many hundred cycles these journals formed the base of the most complete compendium of knowledge available about the Nations and surrounding lands.

Once I thought I too would spend my life as a Scholar. Someday my notes would be added to the archives so that all I had learned would survive me, and perhaps be of some small benefit to generations yet unborn.

But that was before the College was destroyed; before the brothers in the Order of the Way were butchered by the Bred.

Now I keep notes only irregularly, when I can snatch a few moments, and mainly as a tribute to the College and the precepts it taught a lonely, frightened boy.

As I scratch these words onto a sheet of kenaf, I can

feel the presence of the two Arcana beside me. They are in my pack on the ground, close by my left hand. It seems such a short time that they have been real to me. Before that I knew them only as legend, though I was aware the entire resources of the College had been directed towards finding them. Scholars had dedicated their lives to recovering the Arcana, reputations had been made upon the discovery of a single clue that might lead to their whereabouts. Every Seeker and Scholar dreamed of being the man who would at last unravel the mystery.

As a boy I shared those dreams. Then boyish daydreams became vivid and disquieting nightdreams, experiences so real it took me days to shake off the effect. I thought I had outgrown those dreams, but they returned to me while I slept following my meeting with the man called Tenjiku.

The experience was the same as ever. I rode to the edge of the world and discovered a towering palace of crystal and silver on an island surrounded by a lake of fire. A swaying metal bridge led from the mainland to the palace doors. As I made my way across, flakes of rust were dislodged and drifted down into the molten lake below. How clearly I saw them!

Then I was walking through corridors of glass, my reflection distorted beyond recognition; past towering columns of Old Metal worth an unimaginable fortune, until on an altar in the center of a sunken circular chamber I found the four Arcana. The Sword and the Stone, the Spear and the Cup. In my dream, I saw myself claiming them and returning to Baddalaur a hero.

But reality has proved to be nothing like that dream. I actually found two of the Arcana in the possession of the cannibal Gor Allta in the Forest of Taesir. They had been used in sacrificial rituals to feed the beastfolk.

When I touched them I knew what they were. Cycles of training in willpower and concentration came to the fore, allowing me to use them. But I am still unsure just how it is done . . . or if they use me instead. Certainly they take a little from me each time I employ them. They steal my youth; they drain my life.

Perhaps Tenjiku speaks the truth, and it is simply because the Arcana are not in balance. Four were created in the Elder Days, one for each of the elements. The four need to be together to function properly.

With the two I have I can already work wonders. With all four I could reshape the world. I could restore order. In Baddalaur they told me that was my destiny.

But lately, I am beginning to wonder—what *is* order?

Tenjiku tells me I could recreate the Elder Times, yet would that be for the best? I believe it to have been an age of wonders, but also of great terror and appalling danger. Is it the destiny of every great race to fall into savagery and begin the long climb to civilization again? How often does this happen?

When I was a boy, I knew the answers to everything. Life was so simple then. Now, I am a man, educated, literate, trained in many disciplines—and I find I know nothing.

Once I wanted the Arcana to destroy the twins and bring order to a chaotic world. Now I am not so sure.

Paradoxically, the Duet's despotic rule in Barrow has brought great prosperity to that region. Barrow was nothing more than a small town with a good harbor and an enormous cemetery before the twins chose to live there. When they overthrew their father, Los-Lorcan, and established a new court, the surviving nobles fled the old capital and joined them. The town became a city. Builders made fortunes creating new palaces and mansions for the nobility. Merchants grew rich supplying the ever-increasing population and the expanding army. Carpenters, farmers, armorers and shopkeepers all benefited; taverns and brothels flourished. Thousands of people live better lives than they ever had before. They have plans, dreams, futures . . .

If I destroy the Duet, do I destroy all that?

And what of these Islanders who call themselves the People?

The products of the lost and the outcast, they live primitive, brutal lives. I have yet to see one who is not deformed in some way. The *civilized* Islanders hunt them for sport, putting a bounty on their ears. I have heard that they keep the most misshapen heads for trophies to mount on their walls.

And yet I have found the People a far more noble race than the other Islanders. They have a highly organized society. They venerate the aged for their wisdom, care for their sick and mercifully slay those it would be cruel to keep alive. They do not attempt the conquest of their neighbors, they do not even attack the homes of their persecutors though they have plenty of provocation. And when the Eron snatch one of them, they do not seek revenge. The People consider the loss to be simply the will of an unnamed deity.

They laugh often, though they have little to laugh about, and while their songs are sad, their folklore is heroic.

Yet these People have no place in an ordered world. They disgust those more fortunate. If the Arcana were to return order to this world, would they survive?

So many questions . . . so few answers.

Why me?

Why did it have to be me?

At Baddalaur we were discouraged from placing our faith in ephemeral gods who might arbitrarily grant our wishes. Instead we were taught to seek answers for ourselves, and to rely upon our own abilities to achieve our desires. Blind faith was dismissed as superstition. Only the evidence of our five senses was given credence.

But my five senses are not as other men's. I have always had a certain ability to hear colors and taste shapes. When I first met Sioraf she smelled like ivory and moonlight to me. That peculiarity of mine has been heightened since I began using the Arcana.

Yet I tried very hard to conform to the pattern my teachers set for me. I convinced myself that their teachings encompassed all truth, and I condemned all those things which they condemned.

If I did believe in those gods they denied, however, I would pray that I had never found any of the Arcana. These ancient artefacts of a bygone race are causing me to ask questions for which there are no answers. Worse; they are forcing me to make decisions no mortal man should make.

From the Journal of Caeled Silverhand

CHAPTER THIRTY-ONE

CHAPTER THIRTY-ONE

In six days he had grown full-sized, going from blind and helpless to mature and lethal in a fraction of the time it would have taken either of his parents. And although he had never known his human mother or his saurian father, he was instinctively aware that he was related to both species. Human and saurian alike were kept in cages in the offices and dungeons below the palace; he felt kinship with both.

He knew what he looked like, having seen his reflection in bowls of drinking water. He had seen others similar, but not identical, in other cages. He had watched with interest the comings and goings of the small creature who ruled this dark world. And he had seen the Shining One, she whose face and odor permeated the chapel which had been his nursery. He had often awakened to find her standing outside his cage, staring intently through the bars. There were times when he thought he had a special connection to the Shining One. He would have called her mother, if he had known the word.

✧   ✧   ✧

"They are developing very quickly now. This one can be considered full grown." The man once known as Pelotas nam Crucas, but who was now called simply the Breeder, stepped up to the cage and squinted in at the creature sleeping on a pallet of straw.

Heavily wrapped in a hooded black cloak, Sarel stared into the cell. The mature New Bred creature was almost human, more flesh than scales. Only the serpentine cast to its features and its protruding, poisonous fangs betrayed its origins. Venom from the fangs had eaten away much of the flesh of the lower jaw.

"This male was the most human of the current crop of New Bred. Although we soon discovered it was unsuitable for our purposes, we allowed it to live to observe its reactions," the Breeder was explaining as he consulted a scroll of kenaf. "It is intelligent, fast and deadly. A woman on her way to give birth walked too close to the cage. This specimen reached out, grabbed her and bit her before anyone could react. Its poison is so virulent the woman was dead by the time she hit the floor. We managed to cut her infant out of her alive, though, so all was not lost."

The New Bred twitched in his sleep and rolled over. Sarel stared. The creature's spine was clearly visible just below the surface of the skin.

"It is useless as a warrior," said the Breeder regretfully. "The bones are far too brittle and one blow to the back would shatter the spine."

"What will you do with him?" Sarel asked, unconsciously using the pronoun as she observed the creature's massive genitals.

"Kill it and feed its flesh to the others. Nothing goes to waste here."

"The New Bred twins. What stage are they at now?"

"They are obedient and have rudimentary speech."

"Will they know me?" Sarel wondered.

The Breeder's sycophantic smile oozed oil. "Everyone here knows and worships Blessed Sarel."

"Even you, Breeder," she replied in a throaty whisper, drawing her hand down the man's sallow cheek. Her fingernails scored his flesh.

"Especially me."

"Bring me the twins."

The voices disturbed the creature, dragging him out of a deep and dreamless sleep. Rolling over, wincing in pain as the bone in his back grated against the hard stone, he came slowly to his feet. Beyond the cage the Shining One was waiting. Within the hood of her cloak he could glimpse her eyes, violet against her pale skin. Shambling close to the bars, he suddenly struck out at them. His hand smashed against unyielding metal, but he turned it sideways and thrust it through the bars.

As Sarel glanced toward him the creature in the cage held out his hand to her in a gesture of entreaty.

The small man with the dead eyes appeared, followed by two other beings. Unlike many of the creatures in the cavern these were clothed, attired in black garments that resembled wet flesh. One of the pair was male and resembled the Shining One aside from a reptilian tail barely visible below its tunic, while the female was very scaly and had a shock of white hair. When they saw the Shining One they crouched, not daring to raise their heads to look at her.

"Have you named them yet?" Sarel inquired. The twins had grown since she last saw them. Their bodies were filling out, their bones lengthening, their teeth and claws ever sharper.

"No, Majesty. I leave that to you."

Sarel nodded. She would have had the Breeder whipped if he dared to name her children. These were the first New Bred twins to be born, and though many women had conceived twins, always before the saurian babe had devoured the other in the womb.

"Let them be called Abhel and Ebhena."

The Breeder nodded and noted the names on his scroll. Initially, they had not bothered with names, but it was now policy for all the New Bred. He had discovered it gave them a sense of pride and even though the social structure was still primitive, units were forming. Those whose names were similar tended to band together.

"You say they are obedient?"

"To your every word, my lady."

"They do understand what we say, then?"

"They understand simple commands."

"Stand!" Sarel ordered. The New Bred twins rose from their crouching posture and stood erect, eyes fixed on her face now. She turned to the cage and pointed to the creature with the malformed spine, then wrenched back the heavy bolt and opened the door. Immediately, the creature came shambling forward, arms outstretched . . .

The Shining One had come for him! As he knew she would. Perhaps she had given birth to him and was at last ready to claim him. She would take him away from this terrible place where every day brought only pain and more pain. She would lift him in her white arms and carry him far, far away, to some brighter world where the two of them would be together and she would cuddle him and stroke him and he would not hurt any more.

His jaws worked as he struggled to reproduce human sounds in order to please her.

When the Shining One spoke, the damaged New Bred carefully repeated the word.

"Kill."

Sarel and the Breeder stood back and watched the New Bred twins rip the damaged body apart. "It was going to kill you," the Breeder said, still shaken.

Sarel shook her head. In the final moment before the twins leaped upon it, she had seen something in the creature's eyes. Something which struck a vague chord in her memory, the injured look in a child's eyes when it is being beaten for something it did not do. Hurt and pain and a terrible sense of betrayal.

For the first time she realized that the New Bred might have feelings too.

She turned to the Breeder. "Discourage any emotion in these creatures," she ordered. "Totally—aside from worship of me."

CHAPTER THIRTY-TWO

When Gwynne was a child of only six or seven cycles she was solemnly informed that there were gods and goddesses who demanded blood sacrifices, and demons who stalked the night to steal ka. Ka were spirits ripped from sleeping bodies or captured as they emerged from the newly dead. The demons carried away these spirits to suffer eternal tortures in the Circle of Helan. Gwynne's nurse, Mother Gema, a toothless Amorican slave, sent her to bed with these terrible tales ringing in her ears. When the little girl awoke screaming in the night her parents could not imagine why.

Then one morning Gwynne discovered that the nurse was gone. "I decided to sell her," her father had said without elaborating. Considerable time passed before Gwynne learned that actually Mother Gema had been executed for attempting to convert the little girl to the Amorican Heresies.

Now, more than thirty cycles later, the images the bitter old woman had instilled in Gwynne's head returned. She smiled stiffly; old Gema would have thought herself in the Circle of Helan if she could see this.

Gwynne was seated with her back to the wall in an enormous cavern in the cliffs, the central chamber of the People. From this cavern, narrow tunnels led away in various directions, giving interior access to other caves and other levels. The cliffs were all but hollow, providing a veritable fortress for their inhabitants.

A huge fire blazed up from a pit in the middle of the chamber, sending twisted shadows dancing along the walls. Smaller fires were scattered around the perimeter, so the air was thick with the smell of cooking fish and burning driftwood.

And monsters moved in the shadows.

None of the People were normal as the rest of the humankind defined normality. Many were without limbs, or possessed deformed arms or twisted legs. Crooked spines were commonplace. Some walked with the aid of sticks or propelled themselves in wooden carts. There were others whose afflictions made Gwynne's stony skin seem a minor annoyance. She saw flesh bubbling with open sores, skins encrusted with flapping wattles, and one unfortunate whose entire hide was peeling off his body in long, thin strips.

There were some whose damage was in their heads, so they screamed and shouted and mouthed obscenities. Yet all were equal here, the mad and the maimed, the crazed and the crippled. They were the People, and gentle with one another.

They circulated through the vast cave, gathering around the fires, eating and laughing. From a dim recess came the skirl of a pipe accompanied by a singing voice that trembled and wailed.

In another area, children cavorted through the steps of a dance, though some danced on one leg and a stick and several others maintained their balance with the aid of rudimentary tails.

Gwynne, accustomed to receiving stares of pity and disgust, found to her relief that no one was paying her any attention at all. As she continued to observe the People she realized she was no longer looking at their deformities, but at their tattoos. The wildly imaginative designs drew and held her eyes, forcing her to judge them as she would judge works of art, with objectivity and appreciation.

The Stone Warrior felt curiously at ease. She could not recall the last time she was so relaxed. Perhaps when . . . her thoughts skittered away from memories of a happier time, when she had a family of her own, a future . . .

That was before the Void had taken everything from her. She had been left with only one object in life: to find the twins and force them to reverse the process that was slowly killing her—and then to destroy them.

But sitting here, surrounded by those who were worse off than herself, the driving urgency faded. The Stone Warrior was at peace.

A shape moved at the edge of her vision and Gwynne turned her whole body to look into the shadows. She could just glimpse the edge of a bare-toed foot, a child's foot.

"Come out into the light. Let me see you," she said, using the same tone she once used with her own children.

A boy stepped out of the shadows. A skinny little creature with a pointed chin, he looked to be about twelve cycles, the same age as Collum, her own son. But Collum had been taller, stronger, like his father.

When the boy moved forward, Gwynne saw that he was dragging his left leg. The limb was withered and twisted, its pale flesh traced with a few blue lines where the boy had begun tattooing himself. As he came closer he looked unflinchingly into her eyes. "I saw you earlier," he said. "I saw the sand eels attack you."

"They could not penetrate my thick skin." Gwynne attempted a smile.

"I wish I had skin like that," replied the boy. "Can you feel hot and cold, or is it truly like stone?"

"It is very like stone." Gwynne rapped her left arm with her right knuckles. "This surface of mine will turn a knife or a sword—or a sand eel bite—but if heated by the sun it takes a long time to cool down. And if chilled by the rain, it remains cold until the sun comes out again."

"Will you tattoo it?" he said, coming closer.

"I doubt if I could."

The boy came close, his eyes fixed in fascination on her bare forearm. Gwynne breathed deeply of the unmistakable fragrance of childhood, young flesh and clean sweat and wind-tousled hair. Memories flooded through her; she briefly closed her eyes in pain.

"You could draw on your skin instead of tattooing," suggested the boy. "I know herbs that take forever to fade if you crush them in fish oil. You could paint brilliant designs and then you'd be *beautiful*."

The Stone Warrior opened her eyes. "Do you really think so?"

"I'm certain," he assured her.

Sitting down beside her, the boy used both hands to drag his left leg forward. "I've started working on this myself," he said proudly, indicating tattooed spirals of black and ochre. "I use dye from the manylegs we catch in the sea, and stone scrapings. I'd thought about doing a picture of a seabird, but when I traced it on the sand first I couldn't get the wings right. So I decided to draw a design instead. Circles within circles; see? What do you think?" He peered anxiously into her face, eager for approval.

"It will look spectacular," Gwynne said huskily. There was a burning sensation at the back of her throat. For once she was glad she had no tears to cry. "I am Gwynne," she told the boy.

The boy's eyes—sky blue—opened wide in alarm. "Oh, but you should not give me your name!"

"Why not?"

"There's magic in names. A sorcerer can make you

do all sorts of things, or can do all sorts of things to you if he knows your name. You should only give your name to someone you really, truly trust."

"I'm not a sorcerer. Are you?" Gwynne asked.

"No."

"What will you be? Will you follow your father's trade?"

"My father is dead now," the boy replied. He stared down at the ground. His thin shoulders trembled.

"Your mother?"

"I never knew her." He began furiously massaging his withered leg. Gwynne pretended not to notice the tears that splashed onto the skin.

"Mock," he announced abruptly. "My name is Mock."

"I thought you said you could only give your name to someone you trusted."

"Yes." When he looked up at her his eyes were swimming. He drew a deep breath. "I trust you."

Gwynne reached out and touched the boy's shoulder. She dare not squeeze for fear her insensitive fingers might cause him pain. "Thank you, Mock, I am honored. And I trust you." They sat in silence; the boy resumed rubbing his leg, only more gently now. At last Gwynne inquired, "If your parents are no longer alive, who takes care of you?"

"The People."

"Are there many children without parents?"

"More and more," Mock told her. "So many that we have a cave of our own now. Would you like to see it?" He stood up, pivoting on his good leg with the skill of long practice, and held out his hand to her. Gwynne took it as gently as she could. More than ever she regretted the numbness of her flesh. She ached to feel that soft, warm little hand.

Mock led her through a warren of caves, down long winding tunnels etched with pictograms of unguessable antiquity, past a cave piled with skulls, another littered with scraps of Old Metal. "We find bits and pieces in some of the lower caves," Mock explained as she peered inside. Gwynne caught her breath. With the proper equipment and a skilled engraver, one could mint a fortune in coins from the contents of the cave.

They went on, entering another tunnel randomly illumined with fish-oil lamps set in niches in the walls. Something scurried as they approached; one of the tiny cave lizards, no doubt. Gwynne could hardly see in the dim light but Mock had no difficulties.

She heard the children before she saw them, heard the unmistakable sound of youngsters playing, that high-pitched, merry, sometimes raucous music. As she approached the chamber at the end of the tunnel she remembered the times she had shouted at her own children to make less noise . . . what she would give now to hear them shout once more!

Mock disappeared into the chamber hewn in the rock, leaving Gwynne lingering at the entrance. The noise died down. She peered forward, trying to pick out figures in the lamplight, only to discover they were already gathering around her. A semicircle of big-eyed youngsters gazed up at her from a safe distance, though with neither fear nor disgust in their faces.

If they had deformities Gwynne did not notice. She saw only their shy, welcoming smiles and their exuberant self-inscribed tattoos, which employed every color of the natural palette.

Mock came back to her and confidently slipped his hand into hers. "This is Gwynne," he announced to the others. "She gave me her name. And I gave her mine," he added.

A silence followed as the orphans digested this information. Then a tiny girl with clubbed feet and a cloud of golden hair edged closer to Gwynne. "I am Star," she lisped.

Gwynne felt something turn over inside her. Bending, she scooped up the little girl and gathered her against her bosom. Star squealed with delight and threw her arms around the neck of the Stone Warrior.

Then suddenly they were all pressing against her, trying to wrap their arms around her, clamoring for her attention, shouting their names. "I am Nulum! . . . Crystal! . . . Tive! . . . Rishi! . . . Amburr!" But Gwynne did not hear the names, all she heard was happy laughter.

CHAPTER THIRTY-THREE

Crouched in the mouth of one of the smaller caves, Sioraf gazed down at the island below. At first she saw only darkness. But when she willed, a clear membrane slid over her eyes that turned the view a sulphurous yellow against which living bodies glowed dull red. With this enhanced vision, a legacy from her vampir half, she observed the People abroad in the night.

Some were sentries, necessitated by the ever-present dangers of living in the Island Sea. Others were gathering a last few leaves from the stunted bushes and herbs to be found at the base of the cliffs, taking them to supplement the next day's meal. Still others were hapless beings too far gone in madness to realize that night had fallen. They wandered aimlessly over the dunes and along the beach, making disturbing sounds that sent a shiver up the vampir's spine.

Sioraf was hungry. Like the Islanders, her companions could survive on the fruits of the sea and a few greens, but she needed something warmer. The scent of living blood rising to her eyrie from the People below was a powerful temptation. She knew she could strike down any of them with ease, even a sentry, and drink deep of the fluid her body craved. If she chose, she could attack with such stealth that her victim would lapse into unconsciousness without having time to be frightened. There was something deliciously erotic about feeding thus, like a secret tryst . . .

Raising her hand to her mouth, Sioraf bit deeply into the soft pad of flesh at the base of her thumb. The pain cleared the dangerous fantasies from her brain. She dare not feed on such folk. What if their blood was as mismade as their flesh?

Jocylyn, her father, a human who had fallen in love with a vampir—and had that love returned—had always warned her to seek only the purest blood. "Blood is life," he would say, his gold teeth flashing above his bushy beard, "but blood that carries any form of taint will poison you. You are more susceptible to such things than an ordinary human, never forget it."

Sioraf's mother had died when she was born, leaving a grief-stricken Jocylyn to bring up their cross-bred daughter. He had tried to be even-handed in her education, making sure to teach her all he could discover of the history and habits of her mother's race. "I fear that someday the vampir in you may overcome the human," he had warned his child. "Should this happen, you must be fully prepared to live a vampir life."

Even as he spoke those words he grieved, and she knew it; grieved for the human life she might never experience. But he was firm in his resolve to prepare her as best he could, while protecting her from the worst aspects of her heritage. When he had found to his horror that his infant daughter would not touch milk or other human food, he had tried to sustain her on the blood of animals. As the cycles passed, however, he had been forced to admit this was not providing proper nourishment. She was thin, weak, often ill, slow to grow. Obviously she required different fare.

Driven by a father's devotion, Jocylyn had then offered his daughter his own blood. At last she started to thrive. But soon she began demanding more and more and it was he who grew weaker. He realized he would die if he continued.

If he died, who would care for his daughter?

Then he heard somewhere that virgin blood was best. The untapped energy it contained provided highly concentrated nutrients for vampiri. A single sip would do a vampir more good than three draughts of any other human blood.

Sioraf never discovered how her father had acquired the blood of a virgin the first time he gave her some, but she never forgot the result. Fire raced through her veins. She sparkled; she glowed. She felt strong enough to run all day and dance all night, and three moons passed before she grew hungry again.

When she was old enough to hunt on her own, she always looked for virgins first.

Remembering, she ran her tongue over her teeth. How hungry she was! But the only blood she could drink now was Caeled's. After tasting his, all others lost their savor. As the bond between them grew she had become more restrained, sipping delicately for fear of taking too much and harming him.

And when they made love—and they had made love, once—she did not allow him to go so far as to lose his virginity. Taking that final step would mean she could no longer exist on small quantities of his blood, but must demand an amount that would soon put his life in jeopardy.

Sioraf did not want to kill Caeled. Even to keep herself alive she would not harm him. At the same time, she had to admit to herself that her sexual desire for him was growing. He was as frustrated as she was, she knew. It was only a matter of time before they could hold back no longer.

There was another problem. Once Caeled began using the Arcana, his blood had changed. It was growing thinner, bitter. When she fed from his veins, Sioraf could taste . . . age. And magic.

But at least he was human, she thought. Unlike those monsters who called themselves the People.

Down on the beach, one of the People suddenly burst into an insane cackle and the vampir recoiled with disgust.

"You know nothing about him," protested the tattooed woman as her fingers fumbled with the leather straps.

"I know more than you think," Tenjiku grunted. He sighed in relief as the last strap was unfastened and he was freed from the wooden supports. They enabled him to stand and walk in spite of bones as weak as reeds, but the wood dug into him and the leather chafed him. By the end of each day he was acutely uncomfortable, cursing the contrivance he would bless anew in the morning.

The tattooed woman caught the frail man in her arms and gently lowered him onto his bed. There she stripped him like a child. Using a sponge wrung out in herb-scented water, she bathed his desiccated body, paying particular attention to the deeply indented marks left by the wooden supports. Over many cycles the cage had caused scars that would never fade.

Tenjiku sighed with pleasure at the touch of the warm water. "Ah, dear Kyrie, why do you distrust that lad so?" he inquired.

The woman automatically glanced over her shoulder to ensure that no one had heard the old man use her name. "I have no gift for prophecy, Tenjiku, but I can recognize danger. The one called Caeled has an aura like summer thunder."

"Do not fear him . . . rather pity him."

"I do not fear him," she replied. "I fear *for* you."

Tenjiku was genuinely surprised. "What harm can he do me?"

"You are old. The excitement of his presence alone might kill you. Just look at you—merely talking with him has exhausted you."

"Talking with anyone exhausts me," Tenjiku said, knowing she would never dream he included her. "But is death the worst that could happen to me? I have lived my span and beyond; I have lived so long that even death has forgotten about me. What other fears should I have? Pain? I have lived with pain for a thousand cycles, I know pain better than I know you.

"You cannot imagine what it is like, Kyrie, to grow older and older and still not die. To see everyone you know into their graves, and yet remain behind. There was a time I thought loneliness was the worst that could befall me, but now I have no fears of that." He smiled toothlessly. "I have my family around me, my People. So you see? I have nothing at all to fear."

Kyrie drew a linen robe over Tenjiku's head and gently worked it down around his wasted body. His limbs were like brittle canes to which shreds of blue flesh clung. Tendons as insubstantial as cobwebs spanned his skeleton. He did not look like a living being; he did not look like a being who had ever lived.

"What will happen to us if you ever do die?" she asked him as she smoothed his bedding. "What would become of the People without you?"

"No one person is the People. We are the People, and the People will survive. If I die there will be others to take my place. There will always be others." The old man reached up with a hand like a bundle of sticks and rested his dry palm against Kyrie's cheek. "If I were only a hundred cycles younger, I would invite you into this bed."

"It would kill you," said the tattooed woman, secretly pleased.

Tenjiku chuckled. "Thus making me doubly happy."

❖　　❖　　❖

He waited until he heard Kyrie's footsteps fading away down the tunnel before he maneuvered himself up in the bed. Awkwardly, he adjusted the seaweed-filled pillow that supported his back. His head wobbled on his scrawny neck. He had reached such a great age that even sudden movement could snap a bone. The last time he cracked a rib—laughing too hard at a lewd story—the bone had not mended, but merely slowly disintegrated within his body.

Kyrie was right, of course. The newcomers were dangerous and Caeled the most dangerous of all, though in a way she could never comprehend. The newcomers represented *change*. The People had only survived by not changing. For many generations they had remained hidden away in their warren of caves, living a life of habit and repetition, avoiding contact with the outside world and those who considered themselves normal.

But Tenjiku had always known this day was coming.

Change was inevitable.

Two thousand five hundred cycles taught him much. As deathless aeons passed, those barriers of time which only a few could peer through dissolved. Eventually, past and present and myriad futures lay revealed to him. A thousand cycles ago, Tenjiku had discovered how to control such visions. He learned to pick a strand of time and follow it and live within it. And he learned the wisdom of not looking too far into the future.

Twice he had broken his own rule; once to plot the course of the Stone of Heaven which the stargazers predicted would fall on the Islands. The People had wanted to flee, but Tenjiku had assured them that they would not be harmed. As he had known it would, the Stone when it crashed to earth devastated much of the land beyond the western seas instead.

Tenjiku had looked at the countless possible futures again when his last-born child lay dying of Eron-scale poisoning. He could have saved him, but should he? He had seen a time in which his son survived and rose to command a terrible army that swept across the Islands, only to be wiped out by the army of the despot Los-Lorcan. In that future his son was captured, tortured, dreadfully mutilated. And he had also seen a future in which that same son—beautiful, beloved, unblemished—had betrayed the People to their enemies.

In another future his son did not figure at all. But a man he had never seen before appeared out of nowhere to lead the People from their long, self-imposed exile to a new land and a brighter future.

A man with a silver hand.

And so he had let his son die . . . and waited for the Silverhand.

Was this the man? Tenjiku was acutely aware of the eddies of power and possibility that surged around Caeled. Could he safely entrust his People to him?

There was only one way to find out.

Closing his eyes, Tenjiku surrendered himself to visions of the future for the third time in a thousand cycles.

CHAPTER THIRTY-FOUR

The boy seemed to take forever to die.

And Rasriel had relished every moment of his suffering.

Toward the end, before the relief of death, the boy had not resembled anything human. It was a tribute to Rasriel's skill that his victim had remained alive for so long despite the tortures the Hieromonach of the Seekers Reborn had inflicted upon him.

There had been such life in the boy's body, so much energy and will to survive . . . and Rasriel had leeched every bit of it. He had felt his own muscles swell and his flesh grow youthfully elastic. Even the hair on his shaven head had begun to grow with almost visible speed. When he rubbed his hand across his chin he felt bristles rasp, though he had scraped his face clean a short time earlier. Perhaps, he thought, he should abandon the Baddalaur custom of ritual hairlessness for those above the rank of Scholar.

He and his followers were a long way from Baddalaur now. And the Seekers Reborn was a very different organization from the original Order of the Seekers of the Way.

His organization. His creation to use as he willed.

Exulting in his newly replenished strength, Rasriel soared high into the Aethyra . . .

. . . and screamed aloud as the light of a vast sun seared his consciousness, momentarily blinding his persona.

He lost all control. Disoriented, he tumbled back to the lower levels, trying desperately to stabilize himself and organize his thoughts.

Suddenly he knew what must be responsible for the turmoil.

A Presence.

Presences were rare in the Aethyra, though not entirely unknown. The most adept of the Seekers occasionally had sensed them, reporting amorphous but incredibly powerful entities who entered the Aethyra, drifted like a pall of smoke through the upper levels, then finally disappeared. Their origins were a mystery, their motives were obscure.

In Baddalaur, a Scholar had once likened a Presence to a whale passing through a shoal of minnows. How would the minnows perceive the giant? Would it even be aware of them?

Scholars spent generations debating similar questions and arguing about the existence of Presences themselves. Perhaps, some had suggested, they were no more than natural disturbances in the atmosphere.

But those few Seekers who encountered them believed.

Rasriel felt his new energy unravelling, stripped from him in one titanic blast. He had encountered a Presence once before—or at least been aware of it as an enormous shadow thrown across the Aethyra. He was much younger on that occasion, and newly initiated as a Seeker. The Presence had leached him of strength then too. Only the swift action of Maseriel, who was Hieromonach of the Order at the time, had saved him.

As the young Rasriel's Aethyra form was drained to transparency and about to be extinguished altogether,

Maseriel had pulled him out of the Aethyra and restored him to his physical body. A great amount of Maseriel's power had been expended on the effort; he was exhausted for days afterward. "Beware," he had warned Rasriel when he recovered. "There are some forces greater than you or I."

Rasriel had obeyed that warning throughout the rest of his career at Baddalaur. He was a self-protective man; survival was uppermost in his thoughts.

But now the powerful infusion of new young life had made him reckless. Without thinking, he had penetrated the Aethyra on the same level where he had sensed a Presence so long ago. It was just his bad luck that the same Presence—or perhaps another—was there again.

Having come to rest in a lower level where he felt no trace of the overwhelming entity, Rasriel pondered his situation.

Had this incident occurred when he was still at Baddalaur, he felt sure he would have been destroyed. What was different now? Could it be because he had put Baddalaur behind him and no longer followed the cringing, debased rituals of the old Order? He had rediscovered more ancient rituals.

The blood was the life, Rasriel reminded himself. And the power. The boy's virgin blood with its additional pain-maddened strength had been what saved him.

Of course! That was the obvious answer! Rasriel felt his confidence returning. While he contained the virgin energy he need not fear a Presence . . . so long as he did not venture too close.

Adopting a leather-winged man-shape, Rasriel soared back into the upper levels. Soon enough he located the Presence, looming to the north and east and apparently oblivious to him. He approached warily, ready to retreat at the first diminution of his strength.

The great amorphous shape seemed to be moving away at some speed. It would be wiser, Rasriel told himself, to let it go. As far as he knew there was nothing to be gained by going any closer. But he was also curious, and curiosity had always been both his greatest asset and liability.

Rasriel hesitated only briefly, then flapped his leathery wings and set off toward the northeast.

In the Imperial Palace in Barrow, Lares came awake suddenly. His violet eyes opened wide, staring. In the sweat-damp bed beside him, Sarel moaned in her sleep.

He had been dreaming, something he very rarely did. Dreams, he told himself, were only unrequited desires, and as Emperor of the Seven Nations he could have anything he wanted, there was nothing left to dream about.

But he had just come back from a nightmare which disturbed him greatly. It contained an ominous atmosphere that had nothing to do with desire and pleasure.

Lares had survived the Imperial court of his despotic father and the machinations of his own court because he had learned to listen to premonitions. Even more than his sister, he was sensitive to subtle nuances. She was the stronger of the two, but he was the more finely attuned.

He was reaching for Sarel when his sister came awake. At once she wrapped her arms tightly around him.

"A dream . . ." she murmured, vaguely uneasy.

"A nightmare," he corrected. "Something serious."

"I thought I saw shadows . . ."

". . . and menacing shapes, yes," he elaborated. He looked up at the painted ceiling as if he would stare through it into the night sky above the palace. "A giant figure or figures coming closer to us."

"In the Aethyra?"

Lares nodded. He shuddered as he recalled what had happened to them the last time they entered the Aethyra.

Sarel rolled onto her back, dragging her brother's body

on top of hers. As if his thoughts were her thoughts, she said, "That won't happen again. This time we will be prepared. Now give me your love, your lust. Join with me, my brother, into one that is stronger than two."

The Aethyra form that subsequently rose from the bed was neither male nor female, but in between. Neither Sarel nor Lares, but both.

Warily, the dual being ascended through various levels of the Aethyra. At last it located the Presence by following waves of energy that radiated from the entity like a net, drawing other amorphous forms to be extinguished as a candle flame extinguishes moths.

The two who were one fled the Aethyra in haste, desperate to return to solid bodies of flesh and bone.

"What was it?" Lares spoke, but with Sarel's voice.

"What the ancients called a Presence," Sarel's lips moved, but the voice was her brother's.

The twins had experienced this transferral of personalities before when creating a single Aethyra form. They were so melded that parts of their physical selves were interchanged.

Wearily, one climbed astride the other. They joined the two bodies mouth to mouth, breast to breast, groin to groin. Their movements were mechanical, their passion joyless, but when they broke apart their *selves* had returned to occupy their proper bodies.

They lay for a while, panting. For once they had no desire to touch one another.

"That . . . *thing* . . . wasn't coming toward us at all," Lares murmured at last, with obvious relief in his voice. His own voice. "It was heading northeast."

"Such Presences are incredibly rare," replied Sarel. "What summoned it in the first place?"

Neither needed to answer.

CHAPTER THIRTY-FIVE

Caeled had never been very comfortable in the Aethyra. From his earliest travels in the world of spirits when Maseriel had shown him the wonders that lay beyond the physical plane, the boy had found the Dreamscape disturbing and sometimes terrifying. He awoke from nightmares unsure whether he had dreamed the creatures that stalked him . . . or they had actually followed him back from the Aethyra.

He had studied many of the writings about the Aethyra in Baddalaur's Great Library, and learned that every race in every era acknowledged the existence of a realm beyond the physical. Some called it the Ghost World, others the Spirit World, the Ethereal Realm, the Otherworld . . . the names it was given were as varied as the people who bestowed them.

In the College, Scholars had devoted their lives to examining the phenomenon of the Aethyra. They had produced maps of the lowest of the thirty levels, those which most clearly approximated the physical world, and had speculated upon the uppermost, unattainable heights. The more adept of the Seekers visited the Aethyra themselves and brought back fascinating but sometimes contradictory information.

Whatever secrets the Aethyra held, not all of them were knowable.

While he was in Baddalaur Caeled's experience of the Aethyra had been limited. Because he was a Scholar who had not yet been initiated into the ranks of the Seekers, he was restricted to the lowest levels. This in itself was an honor, for the other Scholars never entered the Aethyra at all. But from the beginning Caeled had been special, as Maseriel freely acknowledged.

Maseriel had claimed he was the Spoken One.

Caeled had found the lower levels of the Aethyra to resemble vast grey plains partially obscured by rolling banks of mist. Occasionally, he caught glimpses of the levels above, seen as bands of radiant light or spinning fiery globes, but he had little desire to explore them even if he had been allowed.

The Aethyra by its very nature was disquieting. It could neither be fully understood nor fully explored, and its boundaries—if it had boundaries—were without definition. It changed from moment to moment and day to day, brooding above and impinging upon the physical world and yet somehow remaining apart, indifferent.

And there were too many stories of creatures which lurked within the higher levels of the Dreamscape, preying upon the unwary, destroying their journeying spirits. Without its spirit, or ka, a body was an empty shell, vulnerable to invasion by all sorts of mischievous or evil entities.

After he had spent three cycles in Baddalaur, Caeled had been invited to accompany Armadiel to one of the small mountain villages nearby. There a series of particularly brutal and obscene murders had taken place. Women and girls were taken from their homes in the dead of night. In the morning their bodies, literally torn limb from limb, were discovered beyond the village walls.

Eventually the villagers trapped the killer—and were appalled to discover he was the son of their chieftain.

They had in their custody a pale, feeble youth who shambled when he walked and was unable to reply to their questions. It seemed incredible he could have perpetrated crimes which required so much strength. The perplexed villagers had sent to the College to ask for the services of a Lawgiver and Armadiel responded, taking Caeled with him as part of his education.

After one look at the "killer," Armadiel had unsheathed his sword and struck the lad's head from his body.

In the shocked silence that followed, Caeled had watched the severed head tumble through the air, had seen the mouth move, the eyes blink. When it struck the ground with a sickening thud, he clearly heard the thing curse and rave in a voice that was neither human nor animal.

Armadiel then questioned the grief-stricken chieftain at length about his son's activities. He was told the boy had always been fascinated by the Dreamscape, and recently had begun visiting a wise woman who lived in a hut in the forest. He took her food and drink and, his father hinted, performed other, more personal services in return for being instructed in forbidden lore.

Wearing an increasingly grave expression, Armadiel had listened to the evidence. Then he put a sympathetic arm around the bereaved father's shoulders. "There is nothing I could do but what I did," he said. "I am very sorry. His own actions cost your son his life; it was not my sword blow that killed him. He may already have been dead when some evil spirit from the Aethyra entered his body. That was your murderer. Dispossessed now, it will return from whence it came. But let this be a lesson to you all."

"The boy was greedy," Armadiel had commented to Caeled as they rode back up the mountain to Baddalaur. "Obviously he had some sort of gift, and with the wise woman's help he gained access to the Aethyra. But he was unwilling to content himself with its lowest levels, which are relatively safe and form a gradual preparation for the higher reaches. He wanted to fly higher immediately.

"Remember, Caeled, knowledge is only acquired over a long period of time. Experience is gained step by slow step. There are no short cuts. Totally unprepared, that foolish boy met an evil entity in the levels where such beings reside, and it followed him back to the World Below and took over his body."

But Armadiel had been wrong, as Caeled now knew. There were short cuts.

Reaching for his knapsack, Caeled removed the two Arcana. He ran his fleshly fingers along the shaft of the Spear, stroked the contours of the hollow Stone. When he had first joined these two together, his entire being was flooded with knowledge.

With the aid of the Arcana, in one blinding flash he had known . . . everything.

In the days that followed, however, much of that knowledge had faded beyond recall. What remained was complex, almost incomprehensible. Was that because it had come so rapidly? Pondering, Caeled sat cross-legged on the floor of a small, disused cave and stared off into space. He had made up a pallet for himself in the cave and claimed it for his private space. He liked to be alone for thinking, and this dark recess reminded him in a way of his cell back at Baddalaur.

"So you *are* the Spoken One."

He scrambled hastily to his feet, holding the Spear before him.

Something moved; a shadow among shadows.

"Come out!" he commanded. "Let me see you."

The figure solidified. Tall—taller than Caeled—with strongly defined features, the young man was not unhandsome, though much of his face and neck were covered in swirling blue tattoos. The hair on his head was pulled back into a tight topknot. Unlike others of the People, this man was dressed in a moulded breastplate and finely woven trousers. His high boots were ornamented with strips of blue and yellow leather that matched the ornamentation on the hilt of the two-handed sword he carried.

"Who are you?" Caeled demanded to know. He held himself at the ready. This was a warrior; it showed in the way he moved.

The man replied evenly, "You know me, Caeled Silverhand."

"I do not."

"Look again. What do you see?"

"A tall young man with black hair."

The stranger smiled, revealing white teeth. "Interesting that I should have returned in that image," he remarked, sounding bemused. Then his features softened and seemed to flow into one another, changing his face dramatically. Nose lengthened, hooked. Jaw shrunk. Mouth collapsed . . . and Caeled found himself confronting Tenjiku.

At the same moment he realized that the old man was floating above the floor and there was no light in the cave. Caeled should not have been able to see him at all.

"I haven't been a *young* man for more than two thousand cycles," Tenjiku remarked.

Caeled rubbed his metal hand across his face to be sure he was awake.

"You are not dreaming," said Tenjiku as if reading his thoughts. His form shifted again, returning to that of the warrior but older this time, mature. Arrogant. He stretched out his hand. "I am in the Aethyra."

Caeled looked at the hand extended toward him. The image was so perfect he could see the throbbing veins on the back of hand and tiny black hairs above the knuckles.

What power it must be taking for Tenjiku to maintain that image and project it so strongly into the physical world!

"Leave those objects behind and come with me, boy. There is much I must tell you, and show you."

Caeled hesitated, but Tenjiku fixed him with a compelling stare that made him carefully set the Arcana on his straw pallet and reach out in spite of himself. The old man had more than one kind of power, it seemed.

Although he had always been told he could not touch an Aethyra image, Caeled touched the extended hand. Instantly his muscles convulsed as raw energy burned through his body. He squeezed his eyes shut reflexively. When he opened them again he was in the Aethyra . . . but high, far higher than he had ever been before. And he was not in his physical body, which now lay as if asleep on the straw pallet beside the two Arcana. The Caeled who accompanied Tenjiku was his Aethyra persona, identical to his body in every detail—including the silver hand.

He and Tenjiku were enclosed in an immense golden ball floating through limitless black space. What appeared to be fireflies continually batted themselves against the exterior of the globe in a vain attempt to gain entry. Tiny explosions of light marked their failures.

Within the confines of the ball the air was moist, redolent of flowers, and Caeled thought he heard the sound of running water.

Even as he formulated the thought the sound grew nearer. He turned to discover a pastoral landscape materializing behind him, then swiftly encircling him. Flower-starred grass grew luxuriantly beneath high-arching branches laden with fruit. A cloudless azure sky was reflected in a meandering stream.

"Where am I?" he whispered.

"In a landscape of your own devising," replied the warrior Tenjiku, looking around with interest. "Is this some scene you recalled from your childhood, perhaps?"

"I have never seen this place before. I merely imagined running water, and . . ."

"In the Aethyra, imagination has substance," Tenjiku said. "Thoughts can be given life, words can become flesh."

"I know that much."

"The higher you go, the more power thought has." Tenjiku's lips curled, but it was a smile of unutterable sadness. "With a single thought from here—unplanned, inadvertent—one could wreak havoc on the physical world." The smiled faded. "I bade you come with me to show you these things." He stretched out his hands and the golden globe vanished. After a moment of disconcerting dizziness, Caeled found himself and Tenjiku floating high over the Island Sea.

"You now possess two of the Arcana," the warrior was saying as if nothing had happened. "Soon you will seek and perhaps find the remaining two. What will you do with them?"

"I am to remake the world," Caeled replied soberly. "Replace chaos with order. It is my destiny."

"I could make those barren islands down there lush and fertile," said Tenjiku. "Or I could heal the People and endow them with normal bodies that would render them acceptable in any society."

"Why don't you?"

"The effort would be too much for me . . . now. But that is not the reason. Long ago, I *chose* not to use the powers available to me. It was the hardest decision I ever made. Was it the right one? I do not know; I will never know." Tenjiku fixed a penetrating look on his companion. "Now you possess power, Caeled Silverhand, in the form of the Arcana. But do you have the wisdom to use the power?"

"I don't understand."

The sad smile returned to Tenjiku's face. "You will."

CHAPTER THIRTY-SIX

"They like you." The woman with the blue tattoos stood in the mouth of the children's cave, shaking her head in wonder. "I've never seen them take to anyone else before. It is almost as if they recognize you."

"Perhaps they do," Gwynne replied as she paced ponderously through the cave, taking great care not to step on any of the sleeping bodies. Only a few of the children were awake, lying quietly on straw pallets beneath ragged blankets of Eron hide. One or two of them reached out to brush the edge of her leather trousers with their fingertips as she passed by. "I was a mother before . . ."

". . . before the disease took you?" the other interrupted.

"I have no disease. The Duet caused this." Gwynne was surprised to hear how calm her own voice sounded, as if all bitterness had been washed away. She paused at the entrance to the cavern and looked around the chamber one last time. "Good night, children," she said softly. "Sleep well."

There were three or four drowsy replies, then silence.

"What happened to your children?" the tattooed woman asked as they walked down the echoing passageway leading from the cavern.

"The twins killed them. And my husband."

"I'm sorry. I did not mean to cause any offence . . ."

"You didn't."

The two women walked on without speaking again until they neared the end of the passageway. Then the tattooed woman said, "My name is Kyrie."

Gwynne glanced at her in surprise. "I understand it is a great honor to be told a person's name. Why are you giving me yours?"

Kyrie shrugged. "Does there have to be a reason?"

"You know nothing about me."

"The children trust you, that is enough for me."

Gwynne acknowledged this with a stiff nod. "Have you children of your own, Kyrie?"

"No. I thought it would be wrong to bring them into a place like this, to conceive them knowing there was a very good chance they would be born deformed."

"I don't think that any of the children I've seen here are deformed," Gwynne said honestly. "Each is different, yes. Unique. But not deformed."

"I understand that now. And my mate . . . well, he would have agreed with you. We were together nearly ten cycles and in that time we argued about everything, but especially children. He wanted children. He wanted them so badly." Kyrie could not keep the pain and regret out of her voice. Gwynne wished she could think of something comforting to say, but there was nothing. Pain is borne alone, she reminded herself.

They walked out of the narrow tunnel and into the large central cave. Most of the People were asleep, vague shapes gathered around dying fires. A few still drifted through the cavern aimlessly, however, lost in mind if not in body.

Gwynne felt a sudden wrenching pity for them, too.

"Is your mate . . . no longer with you?" she asked gently, aware she might be treading on a wound.

"He is dead." Kyrie's voice was toneless; hollow. "We quarreled one day and he left in a rage. The weather was wild, but he struck off across the island for some reason and was caught in a Shipkiller that swept in from the sea without warning. I found what was left of him, afterward. Not much, hardly enough to bury."

The tattooed woman drew a deep breath. "Now I take care of Tenjiku," she added. "I have ornamented myself with blue tattoos like his, as you see, to indicate my . . . special relationship with him. My special status. I am the nearest thing the People have to a leader; I suppose. Though in truth Tenjiku is the leader. I merely tell the others what he tells me to say."

"Where is he now?"

"Asleep. And he has given strict instructions that he is not to be disturbed. At his great age the slightest interruption to his sleep pattern leaves him exhausted for days."

A shape loomed up out of the night, stopping only when Gwynne's morningstar touched his chest. Neither Kyrie nor the Stone Warrior had seen the figure approaching, but Gwynne was instantly defensive.

"He is one of our guards," Kyrie told her. "Put down your weapon. And you—report!"

"They're still out there and appear to be coming this way," the man replied.

"Ah. Go back to your post, then. And remain alert."

"What's happening?" Gwynne demanded to know.

Kyrie turned to face her. "You were a warrior?"

"I trained and rode with the Snowscalds."

"Even here we have heard of them. They were much-feared mountain bandits in the Seven Nations."

Gwynne shook her head ponderously. "We were not bandits by choice. We were women trying to survive. Free women," she emphasized.

Kyrie considered this. Then she said, "We could use someone of your experience. Our sentries reported suspicious activity on the island you left this morning. We've long suspected that some of the other Islanders are planning to attack us. They do so every now and then. They swear to exterminate us because we are . . . what was that you said? . . . different?

"We've even heard rumors that the Duet themselves are interested in taking over some of these islands. It is said they want to use the caves for dungeons. When we first caught sight of your group this morning, we thought you were part of an attack force. Obviously we were mistaken—but we were not wrong about the danger. Our sentries tell us unidentified hostiles are approaching."

Gwynne said, "Surely you must have trained warriors, if you have repulsed attacks before."

"The People will fight," Kyrie replied fiercely, "as we have always fought—against the elements, famine, the Eron, other Islanders. But we have no battle leader, no commander. Tenjiku has grown far too old and feeble, and I have no gift for such things.

"Long ago, Tenjiku taught us to use what we have: what this island provides and what the sea brings to us. Today the sea has brought us you. A trained warrior." Kyrie paused, flustered. "I am sorry. I did not mean that to sound so callous, so cold."

Gwynne attempted a smile, but her stiffened face muscles would not cooperate. "Oh, I've been used before. Never quite so blatantly, but I appreciate your honesty. Usually I am lied to or made promises that will never be kept."

"We have nothing to offer you," said Kyrie.

A warm light glowed in the Stone Warrior's green eyes. "You have more than you think."

Fingal felt his stomach churn and swallowed bile. He willed himself to absolute stillness, knowing that any movement would alert the figures moving toward him in the dark. Suddenly the coral knife clutched in his withered hand seemed useless. Who knew what was creeping across the causeway? Imperial troops, Island fanatics, slavers, Eron? The People always lived in anticipation of attack, either from the sea or along one of the causeways that linked Home Isle to one of the countless other islands.

It was just Fingal's bad luck to be guarding the causeway tonight.

He was not even supposed to be on duty, but he had lost a game of bones to one-eyed Ramus. He sometimes suspected that the oldster saw far more than he admitted; maybe he had seen him swap the bones. Fingal was usually more deft at substituting his specially weighted playing piece—but perhaps the crafty old man substituted another bone. In any case, Fingal had lost and the forfeit was to stand guard in Ramus's place.

He had barely taken up his post when he saw the first furtive movement on the island across the causeway. He had instinctively crouched down, then crept behind a tumble of rocks for concealment. After a few moments he had raised his head just enough to take a quick look.

There was someone over there, all right, though too far away for him to make out details. But he was certain it was someone or something who had no business being on that island. It could only mean an attack on Home Isle was imminent.

Reaching into his pouch, he had pulled out a peist wrapped in kenaf. The flying worm wriggled as he carefully removed it from its covering. Two transparent wings unfolded, revealing the hues of the rainbow. The peist buzzed in his hand, its large antennae rotating nervously. Then it shot straight up, circled briefly, and flew off in the direction of the cliffs.

Daubed with yellow ochre which identified the position from whence it was released, the peist carried a silent message of danger back to the People.

In time a second guard had come on the run, bent double to avoid detection, although by then dusk had set in. He asked Fingal what he had seen.

"I'm not sure," was the reply. "I've never got a good look at them. But they're there, and they seem to be moving this way."

"I'll go back and tell *her*," said the second guard. "You wait here and keep watch."

As he trotted away Fingal hissed after him, "Yes indeed, you do that. And don't hurry back. Don't bother to send reinforcements. I'm fine out here alone in the dark, you know; just fine!"

Cursing quietly to himself, he settled down to wait.

"The first warning came in just before dusk," Kyrie was explaining to Gwynne. "Now, as you heard, it has been confirmed."

The two women were standing in the mouth of one of the highest caves in the cliff face, a vantage point overlooking half of Home Isle as well as the causeway. Though the night was clear, Gwynne could not make out anything but a dark blur below. It pained her to admit to herself that her vision was failing.

Apparently Kyrie could not see much better, however. "They have the advantage of us," the tattooed woman said, "attacking at night." She stood close enough for her bare arm to brush that of the Stone Warrior. She did not flinch from the contact, Gwynne noticed.

Gwynne closed her eyes and recalled the Siege of Dunloch Pass, when fifteen Snowscalds had held the high mountain pass for ten days against an entire army. Bricu had lead the Scalds then; Gwynne's first commander, the woman who had taught her so much.

The enemy had tried to attack at night in Dunloch Pass, too.

"Light," Gwynne said decisively, echoing Bricu's words twenty cycles earlier. "Let us see who we have to kill."

Kyrie shot her an alarmed glance. "But if we build up the fires they can see us, too. We'll be easier targets for them!"

"We aren't going to build up the fires," replied Gwynne. "Listen to me carefully . . ."

Kyrie listened; gave the order. Soon members of the People took up positions in every cavemouth. As the signal was passed flaming arrows lanced into the sky. At the pinnacle of their arc they exploded, sending out streamers of flaming fish whose light illuminated the causeway.

Two startled figures were trapped in its baleful glow.

Fingal flinched when the light blossomed overhead. Fiery rain splashed down around him, hissing as it struck the sand. Peering over the rocks, he found himself staring into a savage face right in front of him.

With an incoherent scream of terror he launched himself at the figure.

"What's happening?" Gwynne cried.

"One of our guards has attacked them," Kyrie said breathlessly. "Oh! He's down. No he isn't. He's getting up again. . . ."

"He was a fool to attack them alone."

"He was a boy!"

"He certainly acted like one." The Stone Warrior leaned forward, making a futile effort to see for herself. "Are there reinforcements going to his aid?"

"Eighteen now. Another twenty are on the way. There will be a hundred soon."

"And how many of the enemy did you see?"

"Two," Kyrie admitted.

"Just two?" They could be survivors from the shanti, Gwynne thought; some of the Duet's warriors who had somehow followed them. It might well be a trap with others waiting out of sight. "Signal your warriors to make no move yet. . . ." she began.

"Too late."

More flaming arrows exploded over the causeway and the People attacked.

CHAPTER THIRTY-SEVEN

Kichal scrambled to keep his balance as the unexpected brilliance flared overhead. Stones polished round and smooth by the sea slithered under his feet. He flailed his arms but it was no use; with a tremendous splash he fell headlong into the shallows beside the causeway. Meanwhile flaming arrows were tearing holes in the night. Streamers of fire plunged, hissing, into the sea. A tiny geyser of steam erupted beside Kichal's head as he struggled to get his feet under him and crawl back onto the land. Soaked and shaken, he was totally disoriented for a few moments.

But he had trained as a warrior. Those reflexes stood him in good stead now, commanding his body to action while his brain was still recovering its equilibrium.

No sooner had he set foot on the causeway again than a coral throwing stick shattered on the stones, missing him by a hand's breadth. He whirled, seeking the enemy who had thrown the weapon. As he was turning he was drawing his sword from the scabbard affixed to his belt. By the time he had the weapon in his hands he felt strong again, and confident.

A menacing form materialized from the surrounding darkness.

Kichal grunted with the effort of a mighty blow and the sword sang through the air. There was the sound of splintering bone and a scream of pain.

Fire flared to his left, revealing a second attacker approaching at the run. With an expert twist of his wrist, Kichal redirected his blade. It bit deep into flesh; the assailant staggered, then fled howling into the darkness.

Another sound, not a howl but a sinister whirring noise, filled the night.

Kichal dared a quick glance in its direction. Anadyr was standing in the center of the causeway with feet wide-braced as he whirled a length of chain in roaring arcs. As Kichal watched, a strangely hunched figure hurled itself at Anadyr. The links of the chain tore away what passed for its face.

More and more flaming arrows lit up the night sky. Kichal took advantage of their light to join Anadyr, taking up a defensive position at an angle to the scarred giant. Their attackers briefly hesitated, as if unwilling to take on the two together.

"Who are they?" Kichal panted.

The bloody remains lying before them on the causeway had human form, but each was heavily tattooed. One had arms as twisted and gnarled as the branches of a stunted tree. Another appeared normal at first glance, until a second look revealed features that had flowed into one another like melted wax.

Kichal was reminded of the pitiful creatures he had seen in the dungeons the twins kept below Barrow.

"They are Island Trash," replied Anadyr, grateful for the brief respite from attack. When he lowered his arm to rest it, the chain clattered on the stones. "They are the People. They are like me."

"These are *your* people?"

"No! *Not* my people!" came the indignant reply.

Anadyr's voice was harsh with old anger. "They banished my parents shortly after I was born. They dumped the lot of us on a barren island without caring if we lived or died. And we were surely no worse than any of these," he added with contempt, nudging one of the bodies with his foot.

In the silence that followed his bitter speech they heard something scuttling through the night, trying to creep toward them at knee level. Anadyr's thick wrist snapped upward and the chain lashed out like a serpent with a mind of its own.

A body fell heavily into the water beside the causeway.

In the light of yet another blazing arrow Kichal saw Anadyr's face. The giant was too scarred for normal expression, but his one functioning eye glinted with satisfaction.

"We can go on . . . or we can go back," said Kichal. In spite of the combined fighting ability of himself and Anadyr, he realized they were hopelessly outnumbered. To judge by the sounds of shuffling feet and heavy breathing and the glimpses he caught in the spasmodic flares of light, an entire company of the People was making its way toward them along the causeway.

Once Kichal would have found such an experience terrifying. But he had lived and worked with the Bred, the mutant army the twins had created for themselves. Nothing on the island causeway could be any more horrible, he felt sure, than that terrible force. These People were at least human after their own fashion. He was not afraid of them.

He just did not want to die now that he had rediscovered life.

"I bow to the decision of the Bred commander," Anadyr was saying. "Your courage is legendary. Lead and I will follow."

Kichal glanced sidelong at the Islander. "The Bred commander is dead. I think we should save our skins."

Anadyr said quickly, "There is no shame in retreat."

"None," agreed Kichal. He had taken the first step back when the People attacked.

Along the narrow causeway, the People could only attack in groups of three. Those in the front were pushed along by those behind them. As they sensed their prey withdrawing, they redoubled their attack . . . only to walk into Kichal's slashing sword and Anadyr's whirling chain. The pair covered their retreat with a savage defense that soon left more of the People dead or dying on the causeway.

Then, as if they were unwilling to lose any more of their number, the People ceased their attack. No more burning arrows were fired from the cliffs above. Taking advantage of the dark, the People seemed to be withdrawing, dragging their injured with them.

Kichal and Anadyr found themselves alone on the causeway.

They looked around, trying to pierce the gloom. "Are you hurt?" Kichal asked.

"Unmarked . . ." Anadyr began. A coral throwing stick spun out of the night and struck him in the center of the forehead, making a sickening noise. The Islander collapsed without a mumur.

Fresh fire seared across the sky, turning it the color of blood.

New screams of rage and fury tore the night.

The People returned to the attack with redoubled vigor.

Kichal straddled the body of Anadyr and faced the howling mob. He would sell his life dearly. He knew he had first died a long time ago, when Sarel stole his mind and turned him into a *thing*. Then the creature who had been Sarel's puppet had died in the tunnel and he was himself again.

Although he desperately wanted to live, at least when he died this time it would be clean and final.

CHAPTER THIRTY-EIGHT

"Look down," commanded Tenjiku. "What do you see?" Tenjiku was lying on his back on an emerald-green sward, staring up into an azure sky. His eyes were closed against the glare of a beaming sun. Lushly blossoming undergrowth was everywhere, in striking contrast to the near-desert landscape of Home Isle. Leaves rustled in a gentle breeze. Unseen insects hummed. Tiny birds, brilliant as jewels, darted from flower to flower.

Caeled walked to the edge of the tiny worldlet floating in the Aethyra and looked down. His stomach turned over; he swallowed hard. Tenjiku had created—or conjured— a miniature paradise suspended in what appeared to be a transparent ovoid shell, hanging in empty space.

Directly overhead was sky, but at the periphery of paradise the azure bled into the formless grey of the Aethyra. One pace beyond Caeled's feet, the apparently solid ground upon which he stood ended as sharply as if it had been sliced with a knife.

Far, far below, glimpsed through a tatter of gauzy cloud, lay the islands of the People; merely dark shadows on a silver sea.

But tiny lights winked like little red eyes on one of the islands. "Fires?" Caeled guessed. "Campfires? Forest fires?" He glanced over his shoulder. Tenjiku, still lying at his ease on the grass, said nothing. Caeled looked down again, squinting. He understood that this was a test; he simply did not know what he was being tested upon, nor why.

From this height he could at last appreciate the extent of the Island Sea. The vast body of water was white and frozen where it touched the Northlands, discolored and foul around the port cities of the Seven Nations. In the east the ocean was wild with storm, a Shipkiller by its ferocity. In the land beyond the storm, desert sands spun and whirled in sympathy.

To the far west Caeled could make out the line of the Spine, the mountain range that was the backbone of the Nations. He could almost locate the College of the Way at Baddalaur—or the place where the College had been. Further south he recognized the glow that always hung in the sky over the city of Barrow, the Duet's capitol. The streetlamps of Barrow were considered one of the wonders of the modern age, but from a childhood visit he recalled only their smell, an ugly yellow-green stench.

"What do you see?" Tenjiku asked again.

"The world," Caeled replied.

Tenjiku laughed as he came to his feet in one lithe movement with a grace he possessed only in the Aethyra, never in life. "You must hold that image; always hold that image." He put an arm around Caeled's shoulder and squeezed with what might have been affection—or warning. "I had to be sure that when you looked down, you could see more than the ground beneath your feet. When you use the Arcana—and I don't mean the petty uses; I am talking about the final use, the grand use—I want you to remember this vision of the world spread out below you. What you do with the Arcana will affect not only you, but that entire world."

Caeled stared down, suddenly feeling very small and very awed. "What are you trying to tell me? Are you predicting my future?"

"No."

"But you do know what will happen, don't you?"

"I know one version of what might happen. One version only," Tenjiku conceded. "There are many possible futures."

"Are you going to tell me about the one you saw?"

With neither man paying attention to the island of greenery, it began to fray at the edges. Portions of apparently solid earth simply winked out of existence.

Tenjiku was saying, "No, Caeled, I am not, because what I saw may not be what happens. I have wandered for a little way down one of the future roads, looked along a few others, caught hints of still more. I cannot tell you what to expect simply because there are so many." Although the face that turned toward Caeled appeared young, Tenjiku's incredibly weary smile betrayed his great age. "Lines of time which had remained unaltered for generations," he went on, "have been twisted and snarled because you now command two of the Arcana. New possibilities are constantly appearing."

Caeled suddenly discovered that the ground beneath him had vanished. With realization came a moment of shock; then he was falling, plummeting toward the earth far below. His trained mind recognized that his Aethyra persona was simply dropping down through the layers and was quite safe, having no physical body. But he also knew that these realms had a powerful influence on the imagination. If he believed he was striking solid ground, the shock could stun his mind sufficiently to kill him. Swiftly he gathered himself, preparing to . . .

Tenjiku stopped his fall with a single word, a word like a crystal clarion that cut through the nothingness.

A moment later, Caeled had used his own skills to

rise through the levels until he once more stood before the image of the warrior-priest.

"How much education did they give you at Baddalaur?" Tenjiku asked as calmly as if nothing had happened.

Although shaken, Caeled tried to match the other's composure. "Not enough."

"Good. That is a start."

"What can you teach me?"

"More than you need to know." Tenjiku made the slightest of gestures, then his shape warped and twisted, melting into that of an enormous carrion crow. Broad, jet-black wings spread wide, pinions rattling. With a harsh caw, the bird sped away. Caeled swiftly imagined an avian persona for himself. A grey dove took wing to follow the crow.

The crow led him across into the Aethyra. Twice, wolflike images glared out at them from roiling shadows, but slunk away when the crow turned its head toward them. A third appeared; when it lingered too long, blue flames erupted from the hair around its jaws. With a howl the creature vanished.

The crow flapped on. The grey dove followed. Looking down, refocusing his vision so he could see beyond the physical world as Maseriel had taught him to do, Caeled became aware of countless tiny pinpricks of colored light on the lowest level of the Aethyra. Some of these lights were the auras of people and animals on the earth below, going through their daily existence. Fighting or mating or dying caused the auras to flare briefly with an additional expenditure of energy.

Other lights on the same level moved more erratically. These were the souls of those who slept. While their bodies lay unaware their spirits wandered blindly and at random through the Aethyra. Whatever images or events they took back with them to their waking world would be remembered as dreams.

One level above these, brighter lights burned with a

steadier glow. Here were those who had gained a little knowledge. They knew enough to be able to direct their spirits in the Aethyra, so they could move consciously from place to place, but they did not have the skill to construct Aethyra images for themselves in any desired shape. They moved busily from side to side, driven by curiosity but unable to do more than observe. Their actions had no permanent effect on the Aethrya.

Looking up, Caeled saw malevolent shadows and radiant luminosities moving through the highest levels of the Aethyra. These were the spirits of the most powerful, the Adept.

He realized with a start that they were keeping pace with him.

"I know," Tenjiku answered the unspoken question. "But you are safe with me. They can sense the power you radiate, it draws them." The carrion crow folded its wings and flickered into a human shape again, Tenjiku as he must have been in the early autumn of his life: a still-muscular man with grey hair and a plaited beard. One socket gaped empty where the eye had been ripped out by an enemy, but the wound was long since healed. He leaned heavily on a carved stick, ebon in color, with a serpent's image twisted the length of the staff. The stick was necessitated by the fact that one of Tenjiku's feet was missing. Instead he wore a leather contrivance like a toeless boot.

As an act of courtesy Caeled promptly assumed his own human image, complete with artificial silver hand.

The warrior gave a nod of acknowledgement. "Come, Silverhand. Observe." Tenjiku floated upward, drawing Caeled with him. As they rose into higher levels of the Aethyra, shadows fled before them. A handful of amorphous, misty shapes remained, however, making no effort to move away. Peering at them intently, Caeled detected a solid form in the heart of each misty cloud.

"Presences," he whispered. He glanced at Tenjiku for

affirmation. "But no one in the Aethyra can approach a Presence . . . unless . . ."

Tenjiku smiled his ancient smile. "I too am a Presence, Silverhand." As Caeled stared at him, trying to absorb this, he went on, "Now you know the secret of the Presences. We are all human." He ceased moving and hung unsupported by wings, only by will, as he considered his last statement. "Perhaps I should say we were once human," he amended.

"*Are you gods?*" Caeled asked in an awestruck whisper.

The other chuckled. "You do not believe in gods. Or has the Order of the Seekers of the Way changed its teachings?"

"The Order discouraged any belief in gods," said Caeled. "At Baddalaur I was taught that life is controlled by order and organization, by rational thought and will." He paused. "But since leaving Baddalaur I have discovered that not everything I was taught was true."

Tenjiku's full-bellied laughter boomed across the Aethyra, causing shock waves that tumbled the dreaming spirits and sent them scurrying back to their bodies in panic. "So the Seekers did not entirely blind you! Perhaps you got out just in time." Still laughing, he allowed himself to drop as effortlessly as a raindrop through the Dreamscape.

With the same maneuver, Caeled followed him.

"What do you mean, they didn't entirely blind me?" he asked as they sank downward. "The Seekers encouraged research and investigation."

"Only into those areas which suited them," Tenjiku replied. His form blurred as he began to move faster. Caeled hurried to keep up with him. They were travelling at an angle now, not only downward but toward the west. Looking ahead, Caeled saw they were approaching the Spine.

Tenjiku's Aethyra form became a fantastical creature, neither man nor dragon but something in between: a human body with leathery wings, and portions of the feet and legs covered with crystalline scales.

Caeled promptly replicated the persona for himself. The strange wings, he was surprised to discover, gave greater purchase in the currents of the Aethyra. But before he had time to query this apparently physical influence in the non-physical realm, Tenjiku was saying angrily, "The Order of the Way had an overriding obligation: the brothers, Seekers and Scholars alike, were avowed to recover the knowledge of the Elder Times, to preserve and further develop that wisdom. But instead . . ."

With a great flapping of its leathery wings, the persona of Tenjiku guided itself into the heart of the extinct volcano that had been known as Baddalaur and descended to alight in the Central Courtyard.

Caeled followed with a certain reluctance. When he last saw Baddalaur it had been under attack from the Bred. The bleeding, dying bodies of the brothers were piled everywhere, while the Voids the Duet had unleashed were reducing all man-made components of the College to rubble. He half expected to find the courtyard filled with the rotting remains of men he had known, or at the least see jumbled, broken skeletons scattered across the mosaic paving.

But there was nothing, no bones, no corpses. He guessed the mountain scavengers must have feasted well.

Tenjiku folded his wings for an instant. When he opened them again he was himself, or the warrior version of himself. He spread his human-seeming arms to encompass the tumbled ruins of the College. "But instead," he continued, "they betrayed their trust. The Order of the Way betrayed the intention of its founders."

"No!" Caeled shook his head in denial and reached reflexively for Tenjiku, intending to silence his heresies.

Green-white fire blazed around the warrior-priest, bathing his features in a ghastly glow. Tendrils of emerald flame licked out to devour Caeled.

But when one touched his metal hand, the fire exploded and vanished in a puff of green dust.

Tenjiku's face was grim. "Never attempt to touch me in the Aethrya. Never," he warned the erstwhile Scholar. "Do you realize how close you came to complete annihilation?" But even as he spoke, Tenjiku seemed startled by the experience in some way Caeled could not identify—almost as if he was astonished that Caeled had *not* been reduced to ashes.

With a great leap upward, Tenjiku hurled himself into the air. His Aethyra persona was solid enough to send bats skittering from the caves hewn around the inner walls of the hollow mountain.

Caeled followed him. His left arm felt numb where he had absorbed the green fire, but there were no other ill effects. Yet he knew he had come close to death.

To touch an Adept in the Aethyra was to absorb a little of his power. Caeled did not want to think of the consequences of touching a Presence. The power inadvertently drawn from such an entity would have incinerated his spirit; his ka would have been less than the green dust.

"I am sorry," he apologized earnestly as they ascended together. "I was not thinking for a moment, I only knew that you were insulting the brothers to whom I owed my life and all that I am. What you said of them was untrue."

"No, Caeled," Tenjiku told him, "you simply wish it to be untrue." He floated toward one of the larger caves midway up the volcano. Caeled felt himself tense as he followed. This was the Lesser Library, where he had spent much of his youth. Returning to the chamber after all that had happened filled him with dread. Surely ghosts must walk there.

They came to rest just inside the entrance. The Lesser Library, like the rest of the College, was in ruins. Tenjiku gave a quick glance around and then turned to Caeled.

"Remember that I am old, old, old," he said, as if all of this was one continuing lesson. "I was alive in the last of the Elder Times. I survived the Time of Burning. And I was not the only one. The world did not end; there were survivors, surprisingly many, men and women who had sought shelter in deep caves or in the most remote corners of the world.

"The Order of the Way grew out of those survivors. It was founded with the highest ideals, the preservation and passing on of knowledge, so that holocaust would not come again.

"Scholars studied the Elder texts, Seekers sought to recover more of them, and so it continued for several generations. The Order was like a lamp in the darkness. But several generations after the Time of Burning, they begin to realize the power they had. So, rather than share the knowledge for the benefit of all, they hoarded it to sell to new warlords arising from the rubble of the old world."

Caeled was chilled by this speech. It went counter to all he had been taught. The members of the Order had been his idols, men of courage and dedication, law-givers and law-keepers, revered by the common people for their healing and teaching skills. They had given up any chance of personal fulfillment in order to be of service to mankind.

"I cannot believe you," he said flatly. "I cannot. I knew these men. They sacrificed everything."

"Did they? Or did they gain everything? Status, security, respect . . . anything they wanted, the common people gave them as their right because they belonged to the Order.

"Think for yourself, Caeled. Why would I lie to you? The Order is destroyed. You are the last graduate of Baddalaur."

Caeled replied, "If what you say is true—and I'm not saying I believe you—how do you know these things?

Surely they are secrets that would have been closely guarded, known by only the privileged few."

Tenjiku gazed past him into some secret, inner space. The smile that wreathed his thin lips was very bitter. "In the early days following the Time of Burning, the survivors distrusted everything and everyone that was not *normal*. Those who did not conform to their concept of normality were persecuted and exterminated.

"I was, I discovered, not normal. Though I aged, as long as I retained my passion for life I did not die. So I was forced to keep moving. No matter how difficult it became, life was a treasure I did not want to lay down at the hands of a howling mob who thought me a freak.

"I could not afford to stay long in one place for fear my abnormality would attract notice. I did spend a lot of time here in Baddalaur, however. Twice as Hieromonach; I was Tamariel and later Teniel, twelve hundred and then seven hundred cycles ago. On both occasions I was disturbed to discover how far the Order had strayed from its founding principles. Each generation thought more of preserving its own status and privilege than the one before. The simple but noble ideals which inspired the Order originally disappeared under layers of—" Tenjiku interrupted himself with a sound of profound disgust.

Turning to one side, he drifted through a solid wall. Caeled willed himself to follow. On the other side of the wall he found an enormous chamber crammed to the ceiling with books, maps, charts, scrolls, and a veritable avalanche of individual pages fashioned of many materials.

In all the cycles he had spent in Baddalaur he had never heard a hint of this particular chamber's existence, though the College was reputed to contain numerous secret rooms and passages which the younger brothers speculated about endlessly.

"Here you will find the information the Order did not wish anyone else to possess," Tenjiku said. "Plans for cities, individual buildings, transportation, sanitation, docks, bridges, roads, vessels for sea and air. All around you lies the structure of the Elder World, awaiting someone to recreate it in all its splendor. Over the cycles, the hierarchy of the Order doled out tiny nuggets to sell to the highest bidders.

"But they had another reason for keeping this trove secret. To decode fully the information contained herein, they needed very specific tools. Somehow those tools always eluded them. But now you have two of them, two of the four Arcana."

Caeled drifted around the chamber, desperately wishing his physical body was here in Baddalaur. He longed to reach out and touch with fleshly fingers the ancient books, turn the paper pages, stroke the metal and glass sheets and kenaf leaves. To read, to learn, to know . . .

He suddenly turned to Tenjiku. "How *do* you know so much about the Order over such a long span of time?" he demanded. "Is it because you yourself are so old? Or because you were twice Hieromonach?"

The figure of the warrior-priest wavered. Once again the shape altered, unstable as liquid, to reform itself into a younger man, raven-haired, with hawkish features and a fresh eye patch over the left eye. He wore the armor of another age.

In a voice that rang like a bell he replied, "Because before I became Tenjiku, I was Bardal the Lawgiver. I founded the original Order of the Way."

CHAPTER THIRTY-NINE

Blood and pain and suffering drew them.

Sarel and Lares, united in the androgynous persona of an ebon-skinned, smoke-haired, wide-eyed child, hovered in the Aethyra and observed the struggle on the causeway below.

At first the tiny ruptures in the Aethyra caused by violent death in the physical world had attracted them, but then they discovered another reason for interest.

The twins detected a familiar hint, almost a signature, that roused their curiosity.

Not until they were very close to the causeway did they realize they were looking down at Kichal. But it was not the Bred commander, a creature of their own shaping, whom they saw. Kichal had changed drastically. His aura no longer blazed crimson and bloody into the Aethyra. No longer did the shadowy questing beasts of the Dreamscape hover about him, ready to snatch at the quivering spirits he sent screaming into death. Instead he was doing battle with a company of curiously misshapen humans.

"He is a normal man!" the watching child lisped in a girlish soprano.

"He is not what we made of him," the child's male aspect affirmed in a clear, pure voice.

"I destroyed all traces of humanity in Kichal many cycles ago," said Sarel. "How could he have reverted in this way?"

Lares replied, "After what you did to his brain when you introduced that miniature Void, it would have taken awesome power to repair the damage."

"Awesome power," echoed the childish voice of Sarel. Then it deepened into mature anger. "The Silverhand must have healed him!"

The single form that now embodied the Duet soared higher into the Aethyra until it could overlook the entire island. Swiftly, it read in turn each aura that appeared below, each pulsing light emitted by a living creature.

None of them were the blaze of brilliance that identified Caeled Silverhand.

The child shook its head in bafflement as Lares spoke. "Where can he be? Has he left these islands?"

Before Sarel could reply, however, a sudden explosion of death with an accompanying flare of auras caught their attention. They drifted lower once more to find Kichal standing above an inert body, his sword weaving a deadly protective barrier around the two of them. The smell of fresh blood was strong on the night wind.

The watching child shivered. "Do you feel it?" the girl asked.

"Like insects . . ."

". . . crawling over my skin."

The child-shape turned its dark face toward the tingling hint of power. Following the trail like a hound tracing a scent, it floated toward the cliffs. Without effort it moved through solid rock, passing into the innermost caverns where it moved from one chamber to another, looking curiously at the sleeping People.

"Observe," remarked Sarel, "how many of these are deformed. There must be generations of inbred humans living together on this one island."

Lares said, "We must bring the Breeder here. Using these creatures for his researches could cut in half the time he needs for fulfilling our requirements."

His sister's voice warmed with enthusiasm. "Of course! I can see exactly how these caves could be utilized. Laboratories, breeding pens, incubators . . . just think, brother—an entire island given over to the creation of the perfect killer. The place is perfect, both isolated and easily defended."

"But occupied."

"Only for the moment," she replied smugly.

They continued their unseen exploration, a single, disembodied image drifting through caverns piled with plunder from shipwrecks, others littered with bones, still others containing stone jars holding Eron scales.

Sometimes as they passed, one of the People would twitch in uneasy sleep, or start from a particularly vivid nightmare. A few awoke completely, convinced that an intruder was in their cave. A nervous search revealed nothing, however; nothing mortal eye could see.

The twins moved on until suddenly Sarel exclaimed, "It's coming from here! I feel it . . ."

". . . very strongly now," her brother finished.

The child glided into a small chamber, only to be blown out again by a mighty backwash of power. The shock was sufficient to separate the androgyne into identical twins, the Aethyra duplicates of their physical forms.

"What was that?" gasped Sarel as she reached for her brother, grappling to recombine his Aethyra image with hers. But the power within the nearby chamber was sapping her energies. She had no choice but to remain in her separate persona.

Beside her, Lares said in a tense voice, "Whatever it is, we cannot stay here, sister."

Sarel ignored him. With an expression of grim determination on her face she reentered the chamber.

When he heard her scream, Lares hurried after her.

Kichal slashed his two-handed sword before him, warding off another attack by the People. One foolhardy youth threw himself forward, thinking he could roll under the swing of the blade.

He never felt the blow that severed his spine.

Another darted in with a curious sideways scuttling, carrying a weapon made of the rib bone of some giant sea animal. Kichal's sword sliced through the arm that held the weapon. With a despairing cry, the Islander tumbled into the water beside the causeway. He thrashed wildly in a bloody foam.

His companions murmured among themselves and shifted their positions.

The murmur became a low, ominous growl.

Kichal took stock of his situation. He was on a narrow causeway, straddling the body of Anadyr while an increasingly large and hostile force gathered for the kill. The rational portion of his mind told him to leave Anadyr and make good his own escape. But he could not forget that the scarred giant had carried him through the terrible moments in the tunnel, when he felt as if his skull were on fire.

The old Kichal, the Bred commander, would have left Anadyr without a thought.

"Tell me what you're going to do when I bring up archers," said an unexpected voice in the night. Harsh, rasping, almost—but not quite—a masculine voice.

Kichal squinted into the gloom. He could make out a bulky figure pushing through the massed natives. As the figure came up to him, it put its hands on its broad hips and repeated challengingly, "What will you do then?"

He recognized her now; the woman known as the Stone Warrior, one of the Silverhand's companions. Descriptions of her and the others had been circulated by the Duet's minions. He frowned, trying to remember her name. Gwynnth? No—Gwynne. That was it.

Kichal knew nothing about her except that the twins had ordered her capture rather than her death. As their creature he had asked no questions and they had given no explanations. He suspected they wanted to study her stone flesh with the intention of incorporating the same invulnerability into the New Bred.

"Answer me," the Stone Warrior demanded. "I know who and what you are and you don't have the power of the Duet to protect you now. What will you do when the archers come?"

"Die," Kichal replied simply.

"That does not frighten you?"

He shrugged. "I have already lost so much—my family, my past, perhaps even any hope for the future. Death might come as a blessing."

Hefting her morningstar, Gwynne stepped to the edge of the causeway. Kichal faced her calmly, letting the sword hang loosely from his fingers. Its blade would be of no use against her petrified skin.

"I too have lost my family," she told him in a less aggressive tone. "My past and . . ." she tapped her stony breast ". . . my future. The Duet did that to me."

"As they did to me," Kichal replied. "But I am no longer what they made me." He stepped forward, tilting his head as a streamer of flame lit up the night sky. "Look into my face—what do you see?"

The Stone Warrior stared at him. "Much pain," she said at last.

Kichal swallowed hard. He was touched by her perception. "And what is the mark of those humans who served as officers in the army of the Bred?"

"Crimson eyes. Blood-colored eyes. But your eyes are light. Blue. Or grey," she added. "I cannot tell for sure."

"They are grey . . . now," Kichal replied. "Something

remarkable has happened to me. We were trapped in a metal tunnel under these islands, this man at my feet and I. When I entered the tunnel I was Commander of the Bred, with crimson eyes and no soul. When I emerged it was as you see me now."

At that moment Kyrie joined them, clutching a crossbow. She levelled the weapon at Kichal. "How can you talk to him?" she demanded of Gwynne. "We must kill this brute! Do you not know who he is?"

"I know who he is . . . or was," the Stone Warrior replied.

"He is inhuman, a monster," the tattooed woman spat. "He razed the Ring Forts to the ground and laughed as the hospital burned. He led his Bredi against the defenseless villagers on the High Marshes and exterminated them just so the Duet could have their land for raising horses." Her finger tightened on the trigger. "He levelled the holy cities at World's Edge, stealing what bits of Old Metal they contained for the Duet's palace at Barrow. Three hundred Allta died that day," she said—and fired.

At the same moment Gwynne struck the crossbow with her fist, shattering the stock as Kyrie pulled the trigger. The bolt hissed harmlessly into the sky.

"I'll not deny I did these things," Kichal said quietly. "All of them and worse. Yes, I destroyed the population of the High Marshes so the Duet would have pastures for their perissodactyls. Five-toed horses were more important to them than humans, and what was important to them was important to me. I put the torch to the holy cities at World's Edge for the sake of a little Old Metal, and felt nothing as the Allta defenders died. I felt nothing," he repeated more softly, as if he could hardly believe it now.

"But I was under the control of the twins," he went on. "Especially Sarel." He turned and spat her name into the bloody sea. "I don't offer that as an excuse, merely an explanation."

Kyrie snarled, "I say we kill him!" Behind her the People howled their approval.

"Then you make yourself no better than he was," Gwynne told her.

"Was? Still is! Look on the ground around you. Those are the People he has killed here tonight."

"He was defending himself." Gwynne glanced at the silent body of Anadyr. "More than that—he stood and fought to protect a fallen comrade when he could have turned and run. I will not harm such a man."

The crowd of the People listened in sullen silence, but they listened. There was something about the Stone Warrior that demanded respect.

"For many of you here," said Gwynne, "those with minor blemishes, it would be possible to leave this isle and find a better life on one of the other islands or on the mainland. Yet you remain here to work and fight beside your friends. Why?" She rounded on the nearest man. He shrugged and backed away. "Why?" she asked again, turning to Kyrie.

"Because we are not animals. We look after our own."

"Then how can you condemn Kichal for doing the same?"

"Because he . . . he was Commander of the Bred!"

"Is that the only reason you have?" Gwynne asked. "It is not good enough. I tell you now—everything changes. Everything. Nothing stays the same." With an effort she hunched her heavy shoulders and strode ponderously into the night. But her voice drifted back to them. "Do what you will. But I promise you I will kill the man or woman who harms him."

As she walked back along the causeway, a shape materialized out of the gloom to lope alongside her. At first it appeared to be a huge blond wolfhound. Then the form became unstable, shifted, flowed . . . into that of Madran.

"And where have you been?" Gwynne asked the Madra Allta.

"Around," he replied casually. "But I'm more interested in you. I saw what you did back there. You're changing, Gwynne. You're not as hard as you were."

"Hard?" The Stone Warrior gave a bitter laugh.

"You know what I mean. Somehow this island is changing you."

"Not the island. The people," she replied.

Sarel's scream of triumph still echoed in the chamber. In her intense excitement she was unable to hold one stable form, but warped through a dozen changes before finally returning to the replication of her physical body.

Lares crouched beside her, staring in wonder at the objects on the straw pallet. He reached out with a trembling hand to point at the Stone, the Spear.

"The Arc . . ." Sarel began and then stopped, unwilling to name the objects in the Aethyra in case the very sound of the name called something.

"But where is the Silverhand?" Lares asked.

The body lying on the pallet beside the Stone and Spear gave an anguished cry in its sleep and rolled over, exposing an arm that ended in a silver hand.

Sarel drew back, staring. The Silverhand's body, but without its aura. The essence was elsewhere.

Why had they not detected him in the Aethyra? What power had he to cloak his presence in the Ghost World?

"If we cannot find him, he must be more powerful than we thought," Lares continued his sister's unspoken thoughts.

"But only because of these," said Sarel. "Without these he is nothing." Leaning forward, she brought her face as close as she dared to the Stone and the Spear.

In their Aethyra forms the twins could not touch or take the Arcana, but even so, the raw power emanating from the objects felt like a million insects crawling along their nerves. Sarel gasped.

She caught her brother by the hand and their two

bodies flowed together into androgynous union. The creature thus formed turned and hurled itself into the Aethyra, speeding toward Barrow. Although neither Sarel nor Lares spoke, within the head they shared, thoughts were forming and plans were taking shape. Before sunrise, they would have the largest shanti fleet ever assembled launched into the skies. The New Bred would blood themselves on the islands.

High over the islands, Rasriel watched the shapes that were Sarel and Lares move through the caves. His curiosity piqued, he drifted lower, using ancient techniques to blanket himself from their Aethyra sight. He was aware—though obviously they were not—of certain objects in one of the caves. The objects radiated power, but they were quiescent . . . for now.

And as he sped back towards his lair, he wondered how long it would take him to lead the Seekers Reborn to the islands and claim the Arcana.

CHAPTER FORTY

Caeled came awake very slowly, as if climbing out of some dark pit. Fragments of his Aethyra journey with Tenjiku spun around him like windblown leaves. Tenjiku the warrior—Bardal the Lawgiver—who were one and the same; the hidden library in Baddalaur . . . the books, the charts, the maps . . . the dreadful waste of knowledge.

With awareness came pain.

All he had been taught, everything he had believed, had been premised on a lie.

The members of the Order had not been the dedicated benefactors of humankind they purported to be. They were no better than the mountain bandits they loathed. But at least the bandits took what they wanted honestly, with sword or knife; they did not steal with lies and half-truths. The bandits committed their robberies in order to survive; the Seekers hoarded intellectual treasures that could have benefited everyone simply to make themselves more powerful.

And these were the tyrants who had sought to make him into one of themselves.

That terrible realization had wrung a cry of pure

anguish from Caeled. He had sought to recover his emotional equilibrium but could not. Despairing, he had fled the Aethyra and crept back into his body of flesh and metal.

Now he awoke to find the realization, and the pain, were still with him.

"I thought you were dead."

Caeled struggled to sit up. The cave was very dark, but he heard the rasp of cloth nearby and felt the disturbance in the air caused by a living being. When he reached out, his hands encountered a soft and rounded breast. "Sioraf?"

"Why—who else were you expecting? I came looking for you." The vampir lay down beside him on the pallet. Her body felt cool and polished against him; she was naked. Her lips touched his face, her breath was moist against his cheek.

"I was afraid you were dead," she repeated. "I've been waiting for a while, but your body was so still."

"I was . . . sleeping."

When Sioraf pressed her body against his, there was no mistaking his immediate, surging response. "Let me wake you," she whispered. She brushed her lips across his mouth, carefully keeping her needle-sharp incisors sheathed. She needed sustenance; she hungered enough now to ravage this body, to rip and tear at flesh in order to gorge on blood . . . but this was Caeled. She would not do him harm.

Instead, she contented herself with biting his lip in tender, erotic play, drawing just enough blood to taste. A few drops of virgin blood would suffice to keep her alive. But the blood was not as sweet as it had been before he first used the Arcana. The metallic tang of power repelled Sioraf.

Perhaps if she were to fire Caeled's blood with passion, she thought, the sweetness would return?

She must be very careful. Although use of the Arcana was ageing him, he was still a young man with a young man's desires. The virginity that gave his blood its exceptional potency would be easily lost if she went too far.

With a sigh, she nestled against him. Caeled's arms enfolded her and Sioraf felt the cold touch of the silver hand against her back, but did not flinch. It was just a part of him as the fangs were part of herself. She hugged him in return, pressing her breasts against him.

He felt her nipples stiffen. He inserted his right hand between their bodies and began massaging her breast, exploring with never-ending wonder the incredible liquid yielding of female flesh.

"Mmmm," she murmured. One of her own small hands joined his between their bodies, then moved downward across his belly.

Caeled gasped when she touched him.

Sioraf asked softly, "How does that feel?"

"Do you have to ask? Can't you tell?"

She chuckled against his throat. Her fingers encircled him and began a gentle stroking, but even before his hips could take up the rhythm she released him. "No," she whispered.

"I must . . ." The words were a groan. He pressed himself urgently against her.

"No," Sioraf said again. She moved fractionally away. "Perhaps someday, Caeled. But not now."

"Why not? I can't wait until someday! Don't you want to . . ."

"I do!" she replied with total honesty, surprised by the depth of her own feeling. Never before had she felt tenderness for a living being, save for her father. The emotion made her relationship with Caeled all the more complicated. "But you know why we have to control ourselves."

A shudder ran through him. "Help me," he pleaded.

"Then you may feed."

Her hands returned to his body.

✧   ✧   ✧

Later, much later, as Sioraf snuggled close to him, her lips and teeth licked clean, the tiny punctures in the crook of his arm already healing, she said, "While you lay here unaware, there was much excitement."

"What?" Caeled asked drowsily.

"Kichal and another man came across the causeway and were stopped by the People. Kichal and the other killed many, injured more."

"What happened to them?"

"The People were about to shoot them with arrows, but Gwynne saved them."

"Gwynne! Why? She has no love of the Bred."

"She said that Kichal was changed. She said that nothing stays the same."

Opening his eyes, Caeled stared into the darkness. Once he thought that only the future was mutable. But Tenjiku had shown him that the past too could change. And those changes were the most devastating.

Tenjiku had forced him to question everything . . . but there were too many questions and not enough answers. He stretched his body, changing position, and the edge of his metal hand touched the head of the Spear.

A spark briefly illuminated the darkness.

He knew what could give him the answers.

CHAPTER FORTY-ONE

"I discovered this last night," Madran explained as he trotted confidently through the maze of tunnels that riddled the cliffs. With head lowered and nostrils flaring he followed an invisible trail. He was, as always, barefoot, and moved as silently as a wraith.

Caeled followed close behind, holding aloft a fish-oil lamp he had borrowed from Tenjiku's chamber. The burning oil tainted the air and left a smoky wake.

"Be very careful here," advised Madran, coming to an abrupt halt. Caeled almost ran into him. Peering over the shoulder of his comrade, he felt his stomach lurch. The Madra Allta's blunt toes were curled over the edge of an enormous pit.

Caeled gingerly eased forward to stand beside him. The rays from his lamp were not strong enough to reach the opposite wall, so he had no real way of judging the pit's size. "How deep do you think it is?"

Madran reached over and jiggled the lamp, causing a spill of oil that ignited and fell blazing into the cavernous hole. The two watching from the brink were able to follow the tracery of fire until it went out, but it never touched bottom.

Madran turned to Caeled and cocked one shaggy eyebrow. "Does that answer your question?"

"What is this pit? Is it a natural formation?"

"These islands are very old," the Allta replied, "possibly the oldest part of the Nations. It is said they once were part of one great land, but following the Time of Burning that land came apart. Great areas of it just . . . disintegrated. Broke up, were swept away by wind and firestorm. Some mountain peaks became islands and the sea rushed in to drown what was left." He grinned cheerfully at Caeled, displaying an awesome array of teeth. "Your Seekers and Scholars weren't the only historians, you know. The travelling circuses did much more to keep the ancient legends alive for the common people. During the Cold Season there was little demand for circuses, so the performers would gather to talk and sing and tell stories among themselves. They held competitions among themselves, in fact, to see who knew the most about the past. Tales of the islands often featured."

Caeled shook his head. "Not in the histories I studied."

Madran raised both eyebrows. "I *am* surprised. Are you unaware that for generations these islands—or rather, the continent they once belonged to—was known as the cradle of civilization?"

The young man stared at him. "I never heard that before."

Madran barked a laugh. "What a sheltered existence you led in Baddalaur! You claim to have received an education there. Well, it was a most selective education. I'll wager any dog in the streets of Barrow knows more about a lot of things than you do."

Taking a step to his left, Madran pointed down. "Come and look." A narrow stone strip an arm's length wide was chiselled from the inner perimeter of the pit, gradually spiralling down into the darkness below.

Caeled said dubiously, "Do we have to?"

"I think you should."

"Perhaps you should just tell me what you found."

"Perhaps you should see it."

Caeled sighed. "This had better be good."

"It is," Madran promised, leading the way.

Caeled stepped onto the inclined trackway and fixed his gaze on Madran's comfortingly solid back. The traumatic events of the previous day, his night with Sioraf, and a lack of sufficient sleep had left him feeling hollow-headed.

When Madran had pried him out of Sioraf's arms at dawn, he had been unsure whether the Allta was real or an extension of his dreams. Groggy and yawning, he had tried to burrow back into the pallet. But Madran had demanded most urgently that Caeled come with him, and at last the young man gave in.

"What led you here in the first place?" he now asked, making conversation to keep from thinking about the chasm that yawned to his right. As if it exerted a magnetic influence, the pit kept tugging him toward the edge of the narrow trackway.

"The smell." The acoustics of the pit made Madran's voice sonorous, sepulchral.

Caeled replied, "I can't smell anything but this lamp."

"Can you not? Usually your nose is almost as good as mine. Take another sniff, Caeled. The odor of metal, Old Metal, is very strong here."

"Does this lead to another underground city, then?"

"No."

The young man sighed. "I'm really too tired for these games."

"Perhaps you should not have spent the night disporting with a vampire."

"I wasn't . . ." Caeled began, then added quickly, "What I do with Sioraf isn't any of your concern, Madran."

"You're right; it's not my concern. But if she drains your human life from you and turns you into a rapacious beast, it will be up to me to rescue you by killing you."

The echoes in the pit distorted the tone of his voice so that Caeled could not tell if he was joking or not. "And you have your destiny—remember?"

This time Caeled did recognize the sarcasm. "What destiny is that?" he asked.

"To recover the Arcana, destroy the Duet, restore order to the world." Madran shrugged his heavy shoulders, then half-turned and smiled back at Caeled. "Simple things like that."

"Once I would have agreed with you. Now I'm not so sure."

"Good," Madran said, surprising him. "You're too young to have a fixed fate. You should live first; experience will lead you to your destiny."

"We may not have time to wait," Caeled replied ruefully. "What I have to do now is recover the remaining two Arcana. They will take care of the rest."

They continued in silence. Once Caeled glanced up, but could see nothing; his world had shrunk to the circle of flickering yellow light thrown by the fish-oil lamp. He had a sudden moment of panic when he realized there might not be enough oil to get them back to the surface. "Is it much further?"

"No." Madran stopped and caught Caeled's sleeve and pulled him into a tall, narrow tunnel opening off the trackway. "The others were empty . . ."

Until that moment, Caeled had not realized there were other openings in the wall of the pit.

"But this one . . ."

Caeled blinked as a wash of cold air struck his face. At the same moment he became aware of another source of light, a watery opalescence just ahead. He followed Madran around a curve of the narrow tunnel, then stopped, mouth agape.

They stood at the entrance to an enormous circular chamber sheathed in panels of a dull grey material. The ceiling was so high it disappeared in shadow. Scores of round windows set in the walls lent a greenish hue to the chamber, as if they opened onto daylight but were overgrown by vines.

Caeled ran his hand along the wall, tracing a line of rivets bigger than his palm. Tall metal constructions vaguely resembling huge animal skeletons stood at intervals around the floor, which was carved into great squares. Wooden boxes, metal cases, tubes and containers of a slick substance he had never seen before were stacked everywhere.

In the exact center of the chamber was a long metal carriage. An oval framework atop the carriage was draped with masses of silvery cloth that hung in limp folds.

Caeled's footsteps echoed across the floor as he approached the ancient artefact cautiously and with reverence. He had seen remnants of the Elder Times before. In Baddalaur there had even been an immense mirror, a flat slab of polished glass taller and broader than he was, but never anything like this. Even the underground city had held nothing comparable, being given over to structures designed for everyday life.

But this . . . this was . . . He ran his hands across the tapered walls of the carriage, touching curious fingertips to thick glass circles, ducking his head to peer into a peculiarly shaped door. Within he saw seats and tables and a bewildering array of pipes and tubes.

Taking a step backward, Caeled craned his neck to look up at the framework above the carriage. When he raised his fleshly hand to touch the metallic-looking fabric, it felt like silk. "What is this?" he asked in wonder.

Madran caught him by the arm and pulled him back. "I asked myself the same questions," he said. "But only as I was leaving did I realize the answer." He stabbed a forefinger in the direction of the carriage, then instructed Caeled, "Think of the shanti the Duet sent after us. It had a basket of wood and bamboo and a balloon supported on a wooden frame . . . but the Elders knew the secrets of materials we cannot even guess at."

"A shanti?" Caeled looked from the carriage to Madran and back again, seeing the object with new eyes. It might be the oldest artefact in the world, possibly even older than the Arcana. "If only we could fly it!"

"There are doors over against the far wall," replied Madran. "They're huge and thoroughly jammed, but I think we could find a way to force them open. They would allow this . . . this air-ship to get to the outside world if we knew how to operate it. Or even more important, if we knew how to fill the balloon with gas that rises."

"We don't," Caeled cried excitedly, "but Tenjiku does!"

Even as they came up out of the pit, they knew something was wrong. A low moaning drone echoed and reechoed through the hollowed-out interior of the cliffs. The sound was punctuated by high-pitched yelps and screeches. At first Caeled thought the islands were under attack; then he realized these were not the sounds of battle.

They raced through a seemingly endless succession of tunnels until they came at last to the central chamber, where they found the People gathered. Madran used his bulk to push through the milling, weeping throng until he caught sight of Gwynne. She was at the far side of the chamber, beside the tunnel that led to the inner caverns. "What's wrong?" he demanded to know.

The Stone Warrior turned to look at him. Even though her face was incapable of displaying emotion he and Caeled could see the sorrow in her eyes. Through lips that barely moved her words came in a husky whisper.

"Tenjiku is dead."

CHAPTER FORTY-TWO

"This is all your fault," the woman with the blue tattoos snarled as Caeled elbowed his way through the crowd. "We welcomed you, and this is how you have served us!" As she started toward him she dropped her hand to the hilt of the coral knife in her belt. With a movement faster than the eye could follow, Caeled's silver hand shot out and crushed the coral to powder.

Brushing past her, he made his way to the narrow tunnel which, he knew from having observed Kyrie, provided a back entrance to Tenjiku's private chamber. Soon he was kneeling by Tenjiku's bed. His silver hand hovered above the sunken face as if in benediction. Tiny, glittering sparks rose from the corpse to curl around the metal fingers; the last tendrils of the old man's life energy.

Caeled heard angry breathing at his back. "You exhausted Tenjiku enough to kill him," Kyrie accused as she came up behind him. "When I came in here this morning to wash and dress him, he was sitting up in bed with his eyes wide and fixed. I thought then that he was dead, but when I bent over him he whispered a few words, then died in my arms."

"What did he say?" Caeled wanted to know, glancing over his shoulder at the woman.

She folded her arms and glared back at him in angry silence.

Caeled turned to face her. "What did Tenjiku say?" he repeated in a level voice that was all the more commanding for its lack of emotion.

Kyrie bit her lip.

"Please, it could be important," he told her. "It could be vitally important."

Ignoring his request, she said bitterly, "He was fine until yesterday. Then you and the others came, and you spent more time with him in one afternoon than anyone else in the last ten cycles. He was overtired when he lay down last night; I could feel it. I knew him. I knew him better than anyone.

"I told him then not to waste any more time with you. I told him you were nothing more than shipwrecked wanderers. But he would not listen to me. He had been waiting for you, he claimed, for a thousand cycles. But he just said that because he was so tired, his mind was wandering."

"And what did he say to you this morning?" Caeled patiently reiterated.

Her cheeks burned with anger beneath their tattoos. "The great Tenjiku's last words to me are none of your concern!"

Caeled took one swift step forward. In an eyeblink his silver fingers were wrapped around the woman's throat, applying enough pressure to convey menace without— yet—doing damage. "I will be the judge of that. Tell me."

When she looked into the young man's eyes, Kyrie saw no emotion there, no grief, no anger. They were dark mirrors reflecting only her own face. In that moment she knew the Silverhand was capable of killing her without hesitation.

This was not the young man she had led into Tenjiku's

chamber the previous day. What could have happened to change him so? She swallowed hard against the pressing silver fingers, and moistened her lips with her tongue so she could speak. At once the pressure eased.

"Tenjiku said . . . said his ka would be waiting," she whispered.

Caeled released the woman so suddenly that she lost her balance and staggered backward, coughing. She touched her fingers to her bruised throat, then spat in Caeled's wake as he turned and strode back toward the central chamber. She called after him a curse she had heard Tenjiku use, words that were older than the Nations themselves. "May the rain burn you and the fire freeze you; may the air be too thick to breathe and too thin to keep you alive!"

Caeled blinked rapidly, trying to convince himself his eyes were watering as a result of the smoky fires in the central chamber. He had seen plenty of death; surely one more could not make him cry. Searching out Gwynne and Madran among the milling, keening People, he summoned them with a nod and led them off to one side.

"Tenjiku is dead, all right," he informed them. "But before he died he told that tattooed woman who took care of him that his spirit would be waiting."

Gwynne's green eyes were puzzled. "What does that mean?"

"His spirit, his ka, will linger in the Aethyra for a while; that was his final message for me. I shall have to go into the Aethyra to talk to him, but I will need you both to stand guard over me while I do. His woman is blaming me for his death. It may just be grief talking, but she seems pretty adamant about it. If she convinces enough of the others, there might be trouble."

Madran swivelled his shaggy head to look back at the crowd. He observed Tenjiku's woman on the far side of the big cavern, talking excitedly and waving her arms.

People were beginning to gather around her. Others were turning to look curiously in the direction of Caeled and his companions. Madran growled under his breath. The hackles began to rise on the back of his neck as they always did when he sensed threat. "We do seem to have a problem," the Madra Allta affirmed. "Is it so important you contact that old man's spirit, Caeled? Can we not simply leave now, before . . ."

"It's very important," Caeled insisted. "He knows so much, there are so many questions he could still answer for me. . . ."

Gwynne's response was instantaneous. "Don't worry, we'll watch over you. Let's go back to that small cave you were in earlier, it's more private there." She bent her gaze on the crowd, skillfully separating those who would lead from those who would follow. If it came to a fight, she would incapacitate the leaders first. The Stone Warrior was curiously reluctant to actually hurt any of the People—but her first duty was to Caeled.

Perhaps it would not come to blows, she thought hopefully.

Sioraf was still asleep on the pallet she had shared with Caeled. Leaving Gwynne and Madran on guard at the entrance to the small cave, the young man went in. He stood over Sioraf for a long moment, gazing down.

Curled up on the straw pallet with her dark curls clinging in damp tendrils to her forehead and her tiny fangs covered by her soft lips, the vampir looked like a trusting child. She was partially covered by a badly-cured Eron hide whose few remaining strands of coarse hair contrasted sharply with her bare flesh.

Caeled knelt beside her, unable to resist touching her shoulder with his fingertips. At once Sioraf came totally, ferociously awake. In one swift bound she was off the pallet and crouched ready to spring. Her lips were drawn back from her teeth, her fingers hooked into talons.

"It's me," Caeled said hastily, holding up his hands in surrender.

Vividly blue eyes stared at him for a moment, then refocused. Recognition softened Sioraf's features. Where a moment before she had been total vampir, now she became a woman.

"Caeled." Her voice was low and sweet. She caught his right hand and pressed her lips to the palm in apology. "You startled me."

He replied with a shaky laugh, "And you startled me! I just wanted to lie down on the pallet for a moment and compose myself . . ."

Sioraf pouted, though her eyes sparkled with laughter. "You meant to lie beside me and seek composure? Should I be offended?" Then, looking at him more closely, she sobered. "What's wrong?"

"Tenjiku is dead," interjected Gwynne from the mouth of the cave. She unslung her morningstar and leaned it against the wall, keeping it close to hand. She had already assessed their tactical situation. The cave would be easy to defend, the entrance was small and the approach narrow.

On the downside, as long as they stayed there they were trapped. The People could easily smoke or burn them out. Looking to Madran, she knew he was thinking the same thing. "Why don't you . . . and Sioraf . . . station yourselves outside?" she suggested in a low voice pitched for his keen ears only. "One of you on either side of the cavemouth and some ten or fifteen paces away. Don't let anyone get closer than that."

The Allta nodded agreement.

Although within the chamber Caeled did not hear what Gwynne said, he was aware that something had passed between them. "What's wrong?" he called out.

Madran replied calmly, "Nothing's wrong, be easy in your mind. But you might send Sioraf out to keep me company while you do what you have to do." His deep voice was reassuring. Not for the first time, Caeled felt a surge of warmth toward the big Allta. In their time together Madran had taken on an almost paternal image in his eyes. Caeled had never known his father, but he would like to think the man might have been like Madran: gruff but kindly, brave, resourceful . . . loyal.

Then Gwynne's voice said in a much sharper tone, "Just hurry up, Caeled, will you?"

He lay down on the pallet and settled himself comfortably in the warm place vacated by Sioraf. He could still smell her, a fragrance of moonlight subtly mingled with a saltier, fleshier scent.

Struggling to clear his mind of recent memories, Caeled closed his eyes.

The Aethyra was vast and amorphous, as grey and insubstantial as smoke yet swarming with countless images. Menace and splendor lurked within its layers, huge entities brooded along its ever-shifting borders. The alive, the not alive and the never alive all influenced the Dreamscape, playing their parts in that much larger realm beyond the limited five senses of humankind.

But Tenjiku was nowhere to be found. Though Caeled searched diligently for the slightest hint of Tenjiku's spirit, he found no trace. Perhaps, he thought, he was too late, and the essence of the ancient man had already been carried away on the Ghost Winds that blew through the Aethyra. Or perhaps Tenjiku had been unable to control his ka, to keep it relatively close to his body after death.

Aching with disappointment, Caeled let himself float back toward his fleshly body. As he sank he looked down upon the glow of colors emanating from the living in the World Below. He noticed that the colors seemed exceptionally agitated, their hues heightened as if the auras were being stimulated from some outside force. Vivid green and intense purple were shot through with bars of gold and amber. Scarlet blazed, burned orange and then yellow and ultimately white-hot with rage.

Caeled redirected himself toward Tenjiku's chamber. The room was empty of all but the corpse. Outlined by the dim light from a single lamp, the figure lying on its bed looked tiny and pathetic. As he gazed at the sheet-covered body, unconsciously Caeled's Aethyra form warped through a number of shapes, finally assuming the image of a young boy—the boy he had been before he went into Baddalaur. The boy whose curiosity was almost larger than his wiry body.

Had Tenjiku really been Bardal the Lawgiver, Caeled was asking himself. Was he one of the Elders? There were so many questions only Tenjiku could have answered. A man that old, with that much knowledge, was a resource beyond price. He could have ruled the world, could have brought back the magic of the Elder Days. But instead he had chosen to live out the last five hundred cycles of his life hidden away among the exiles of the Island Sea. Why? And what could have been sufficient, after such a long life, to bring about his death at last?

"When you have lived as long as I have, when you have done all that I have done, there is little left to live for and little left to do."

Startled, Caeled spun around. His form changed again, metal armor flowing out of his left hand to encase his entire image.

The voice was Tenjiku's, but the being which had silently materialized behind Caeled had no shape. It might have been a roiling cloud. Then the suggestion of a face, or faces, briefly appeared, only to vanish with the next change in configuration.

The cloud became more dense. Within its heart Caeled glimpsed something almost solid, yet it too kept changing, assuming one form after another. At last it resolved itself into the features of the old man.

"If you are truly Tenjiku," Caeled challenged, "tell me what we did last night."

The face in the cloud smiled. "I took you back to Baddalaur, Caeled Silverhand. You and I went home." The shape blurred, then condensed like smoke sucked inward. When it cleared, Tenjiku the Warrior stood erect and proud, looking as tangible as in life. "I always knew that I would return to Baddalaur one last time," he said. "I was simply waiting for the right reason."

"Was I the right reason?"

"Probably the only reason."

"And when you were dying you left a message . . . for me?"

Tenjiku responded with a grave nod. "I did."

"What have you to tell me?"

"I have little time left, so I must be brief. If I do not manage to answer all your questions, forgive me. In time you will have the answers, that much I can promise you.

"I know you are curious about many things. Much of what I could tell you would be worthless, however; indeed, much of what I know has been worthless since the Time of Burning. I was a master of the magic then, but when the world fell I became nothing more than a wanderer, living on the same skills that had kept my ancestors alive. It was a brute existence but valuable in its own way. The basic skills of survival are always worth learning and practicing. They ensure the future.

"As the cycles passed I acquired more knowledge—knowledge relevant to a new age. But much of that too is worthless now. The training and knowledge I carried within me for two-and-a-half thousand cycles mean nothing today. They apply to a way of life long gone. Many of them I could not even begin to describe in language you would understand."

As he heard these words, Caeled felt his heart sink. Tenjiku was telling him that it was all for nothing, the wisdom he sought was of no more use than grains of sand.

"Likewise," Tenjiku went on, making it even worse, "many of the abilities I acquired in my seasons of wandering are now superfluous. Crafts mastered even fifty cycles ago are outdated, of no value to anyone. Some of them are too sophisticated for the current age, while others are too crude. The world is changing, Caeled, and the rate of change is ever faster. That is what always happens before . . . a fall."

Tenjiku laid his hand on Caeled's arm. The young man felt a warmth suffuse him, as if his Aethyra form were a physical body. At the moment of connection the two soared into the Dreamscape until the islands lay far below them like chips of ice on a blue cloth.

Tenjiku's warrior image wavered and expanded to become a crystal globe, with Caeled locked inside. The sphere dipped, dropping dizzyingly toward the sea, then spun off to the south and west, moving so fast that the water below was a sheet of metal, and the distant stars became streaks of silver.

The crystal ball came to a halt in the Aethyra several layers above Barrow. From this vantage point Caeled's vision encompassed the sprawling area from the City of the Dead on the north to the ancient, long-abandoned mines that still scarred the earth to the south.

"Have you never wondered why we do not progress; why civilization does not advance to a higher level?" inquired Tenjiku's voice, resonating from the transparent spherical walls. "In this age humankind relies primarily on crude tools of stone and wood, and few buildings rise above two stories. Do you not question this?"

Caeled gave the only answer he knew. "We lost the Elder lore in the cycles following the Time of Burning."

"That is not a sufficient answer. There were disasters in the Elder Times, fires and floods, plagues and stone storms, and wars more terrible than you could comprehend. I began as a warrior, but eventually even I was sickened to the core by what I saw people do to one another. Although I had to go on fighting, for various reasons I learned to hate war. Always at the back of my mind was the hope that things might be different someday, somewhere. I longed for a place where people would befriend one another no matter what their differences . . ." His voice faded away, then returned, its tone changed.

"Sometimes, Caeled Silverhand, humankind sank into an abyss of darkness and ignorance. But before that final Time of Burning it always recovered, coming back stronger than before, adding to its store of wisdom, finding new ways of doing things when the old ways had been lost. Why has there been no recovery this time, can you tell me?"

Caeled said slowly, "In Baddalaur, Scholars debated that very question. Some believed it was because we had lost the skill of working metal during the Time of Burning, so that what little we made was soft and debased, practically useless. Others claimed that the Elders had used up all the good ore and nothing worthwhile remained. But whatever the reason, the achievements of the Elders could hardly be reproduced without tools the equivalent of theirs, so . . ."

"Not entirely true," interrupted Tenjiku. "Humankind has failed to progress because the Order of the Way curtailed the dissemination of knowledge. They sent Seekers to locate any intelligent youth and bring him to Baddalaur for training. Those who would not come, they killed, in order to prevent progress from taking place independently."

Caeled could feel Tenjiku's anger not only in his tone of voice, but in the rigidity of the sphere around him. Its crystal walls were brittle with suppressed rage.

The voice continued, "The policy I just described did not take place during those periods when I served as Hieromonach. Under my rule the Order was a source of enlightenment. But when I had to move on, others with different aims took my place. Some were good people whose ideals I could not fault. The majority, however, sought power within the Order for their own gratification. The Seekers were corrupted to their purpose!"

Caeled noted with some dismay that Tenjiku was repeating himself. These accusations were not new; he had made them before in Baddalaur. Many old people lapsed into tedious repetition; was it possible Tenjiku was wasting these last precious moments?

"But despite the abuses the Order perpetrated," the warrior continued, "the world moved on. Inevitably, there were changes. The number willing to train as Seekers and Scholars gradually diminished while men and women of intelligence were being born in increasing numbers elsewhere. In time, new schools and colleges were founded which accepted women, something the Order had begun refusing to do. Although actually, the first three Hieromonachs after my initial founding had been women. Two of them were very fine, very . . ." Tenjiku paused as if some personal memory was gouging too deeply into his thoughts.

Caeled waited, increasingly concerned that he would learn nothing further. The old man was rambling.

After a moment, however, Tenjiku began talking again. "As you know, the brothers of the Order dedicated themselves to finding the Arcana. It came to represent the ultimate power—or abuse of power—to them. With the ancient artefacts designed by the Elders they could alter the world forever, wiping away everything they disapproved of, killing individuals or exterminating whole nations for any reason or none. If they chose, they would be able to alter the configuration of the land, raise continents from the seabed, change the weather, shape men from beasts and beasts from men."

"As the Duet is doing now," Caeled interrupted impatiently. Was it possible Tenjiku had nothing of value to impart?

"Just so. But the Arcana could do it in the blink of an eye. With the four symbols of power in their control, the hierarchy of the Order would have been . . . as gods."

Tenjiku fell silent. Within the crystal sphere his last words still resonated. Then all at once the glassy ball dissolved into glittering dust motes and Caeled found himself floating in the grey Aethyra once more beside the persona of Tenjiku.

Pointing down toward Barrow, the warrior asked, "What do you see?"

"Barrow, the capital of the Empire of the Duet."

"Once the Empire of Los-Lorcan," mused Tenjiku. "And before that . . . look deeper, Silverhand. What else do you see?"

"A vast city, sprawling, dirty . . . containing both great wealth and considerable poverty," Caeled concluded.

"What are the emotions of the inhabitants?"

Caeled concentrated on the colors of the countless auras rising into the Aethyra. As he identified the dominant emotional threads he reported, "Contentment. Greed. Love. Jealousy. Ambition. And a great deal of . . . respect."

"Respect for the Duet," Tenjiku interpolated. "Now describe Baddalaur through your memory of the auras it cast."

"Baddalaur was huge too," Caeled recalled. "But it was vertical rather than horizontal because it was built inside an extinct volcano. There was always a lot of tension in the auras at Baddalaur. Scholars worrying about their work, Seekers worrying about their assignments, everyone desperately concerned about pleasing the Hieromonach. Everyone . . . anxious. To be honest, I don't recall much contentment. I remember fear though."

Tenjiku's voice was gentle; persuasive. "Why fear?"

"I don't know. Something in the very atmosphere, perhaps. For one thing, we were encouraged to mistrust everyone but the Order. And we all felt under tremendous pressure. We feared failure; we feared falling below the standard set for us by the Hieromonach."

"What happened when one of the brothers did fail?" the soft voice urged.

"I don't know," Caeled repeated. "I guess I never really thought about it until now. But I seem to recall that some of them . . . just disappeared . . ."

"Just disappeared. Yes. So many . . . disappeared." Tenjiku's voice took on a bitter edge. "You remember Baddalaur as a place filled with anxiety and fear. Fear of outsiders, of failure, of the Hieromonach. That is how the Order would have recreated the world, Caeled: as a world of fear. Bear that in mind when . . ."

"When what?"

"When you look at the world as it is now."

"Are you telling me things are better under the Duet?"

"No. Simply different. But their aims are similar; they want to conquer. The Order sought conquest through the control of knowledge; the twins mean to do it with their Bred armies. Now look," he commanded, pulling Caeled lower.

In the docklands south of the city a vast shanti fleet had gathered. Two hundred brightly colored balloons floated like children's toys, tethered to undercarriages. Long snaking trails of beings that were neither human nor Bredi, but combined the worst features of both, were making their way into these carriages.

"They will go to the islands, looking for you," said Tenjiku. "Their mission is twofold: destroy you and capture all four of the Arcana. My People can hold them off long enough to give you time to escape. You must survive and secure the two remaining Arcana before the Duet's minions can. Travel fast and light, Caeled Silverhand."

"Travel where? *What am I to do?*" He could sense Tenjiku fading, withdrawing. His imminent loss filled Caeled with a rising panic.

"Head north and east to the holy well at Tonne,"

whispered Tenjiku's voice, growing fainter with each syllable. "The site of the Elder city of Lowstone. You will find the other two Arcana there."

"The other two . . . and then what?" Caeled demanded. "What do I *do* with them?"

"Anything you desire," said the voice just before it faded away altogether. "When you possess the Arcana, *you* become a god."

CHAPTER FORTY-THREE

Abhel twisted his neck, his forked tongue flickering between his parted lips as he looked up into the clear blue sky. His muscular tail thrashed the dirt behind him in an agitation which he quickly restrained. The round pupils of his eyes abruptly narrowed to saurian slits.

Overhead, the sky seemed empty save for a pair of long-billed gulls. To his altered vision they were outlined with pale green light as they swooped and screeched. But there was nothing else, nothing to alert him to trouble. Giving a negative shake of his head, Abhel turned and met his twin's eyes. Though no words were spoken, he heard Ebhena's question clearly.

I thought I saw something. Did you?

I felt something, Abhel replied. *It is gone now.*

Although they were born of the same ruptured womb, they were almost totally dissimilar. At a casual glance Abhel appeared human—until one noticed the vaguely reptilian cast to his face and a faint patina of scales that began at the back of his head and flowed down his spine to thicken into a powerful tail.

Ebhena's torso was firmly cast in the Bredi mold,

covered with scales and plates of body armor inherited
from her saurian antecedents. Mammalian breasts, though
rigid and without nipples, identified her sex, while her
face further betrayed her human origins. Her cheekbones
were high and finely modelled, her nose straight, her
lips curved. These pleasingly symmetrical features were
crowned by a startling mane of white hair that matched
her eyebrows.

In common with her twin, Ebhena also possessed
savage talons and double rows of spiky teeth.

Early in their development the pair had discovered
that they could converse without words. At first they had
assumed that all Bredi and humans could do the same.
When they eventually realized their ability was unique
they kept it from the Breeder, instinctively knowing he
would find some way to use it to his own advantage, not
theirs.

Abhel and Ebhena stood impassively waiting their
turn to be loaded into the shanti with others of the New
Bred. Their brief lives had been spent in the pen and
the training schools, where any emotions were
assiduously discouraged. Emotions would be a handicap,
they were told, for the lives they were meant to lead.

Instead they were taught to use knife and sword, spear
and mace. When they closed on a victim, in addition to
their weapons they employed teeth and claws to
devastating effect. What they killed they could eat, unless
instructed otherwise. And they were always hungry; that
too was bred into them.

Their inbred speed and savagery served them well.

Victims for the New Bred to practice upon were
selected from the petty criminals in the dungeons at
Barrow; criminals held to serve as reluctant gladiators
for games in the arena recently built by the twins.

Now Abhel and Ebhena, together with others of the
New Bred, were heading north to put their training to
practical use. They were going to do battle with a terrible

traitor, a man with a silver hand who had threatened their beloved Sarel and Lares. They had been shown what appeared to be magical images, but were actually glimpses of Caeled in the Aethyra, caught in a revolving mirror of Lares' devising. These images were displayed while their trainers chanted, "Here is the enemy, kill him, kill him!" over and over again, until the blood of the New Bred was heated to frenzy.

Then they were loaded into the shanti.

Their orders were simple: "When you arrive, destroy every living creature on the island. No one is to remain alive."

"How do we know the Silverhand won't destroy them with the two Arcana he already has?" Lares asked, watching as the first of the shanti rose into the sky.

Sarel pressed herself close to her brother, breasts flattening against his arm. "That is a risk we must take. However, I am relatively certain he does not know how to make proper use of them. He is not hairless like those initiated into the ranks of the Seekers, so we must assume he rose no higher than Scholar. Therefore much of the esoteric lore hoarded within the College was not made known to him—no doubt including full information about the Arcana. Perhaps he would have become a Seeker in time, but we destroyed Baddalaur before that happened. So now, with only partial knowledge, he is struggling to use something he does not fully understand."

"I hope you're right, sister." Lares turned and wrapped his arms around his twin, drawing her close, finding comfort in her nearness. Although he was older by a couple of heartbeats, Sarel had always been the dominant half and he preferred it that way. "But how can we be certain?"

"He has but one hand and is travelling with a woman afflicted with some dreadful skin disease. If he had mastered even a fraction of the Arcana's power, he would have grown himself a new hand and healed his comrade's flesh," Sarel replied sensibly. She slipped one hand inside her brother's tunic and stroked his bare chest, knowing that her touch would distract him from his fears more than all her words. She did not want Lares to be anxious. His fears and pains hurt her more than her own.

More of the shanti took off, floating like brilliantly-colored bubbles into the clear air. The sight would have been very beautiful had it not been marred by the stench of burning fuel that followed the craft.

Lares pinched his nostrils closed with his fingers. "Excrement and rotten eggs," he muttered. "Do they have to stink like that?"

His sister laughed. "That is a sweeter fragrance than perfume, if it signals the destruction of our enemy!"

"It will also warn him," said Lares. "There is no element of surprise if even in the dark he can smell them coming and prepare himself. He may not know precisely how to use the Arcana, but any attempt he makes could disrupt our plans." He paused, then suggested, "Why not arrange some form of distraction, sister?"

Narrowing her eyes as she always did when thinking, Sarel swiftly reviewed their campaign. The shanti would be travelling to Seamount, where they would take on guides who knew every part of the Island Sea. She had already sent instructions by peist to Lamar in Rock to make the arrangements. With good weather it was half a day's flight to Seamount, which meant the shanti, gathered into attack formation, should reach the Silverhand's island by dusk. They would fly low over the water, coming at the island from all sides.

The shanti captains, red-eyed humans commanding companies of the New Bred, had been given instructions not to feed the Bredi for the last leg of the journey. By the time they reached the island the hybrid warriors would be very hungry.

Unlike previous generations of Bredi whose saurian

blood made it difficult for them to fight in the cold, the New Bred had been developed to perform in all weathers and all conditions of visibility. Even if they should land in total darkness, they would be able to function at peak performance. With their warrior skills and their ravenous appetites, the occupants of the island would have no chance.

If everything went according to plan, the island would be secured during the night. The twins meant to set out at dawn in the imperial shanti to view the scene of the triumph. But all of this was contingent upon the Silverhand being unable to mount a defense with the Arcana.

Obviously, a distraction would be an added safeguard.

Sarel gave her brother an appreciative hug. "Your suggestion has merit," she told him. "Give me your strength." She gently disengaged herself from his embrace and took a step backward, pulling her diaphanous gown off over her head. "I think I shall pay one of those Islanders a visit."

Lares grinned as he stripped off his own clothing. He knew and enjoyed the look in his sister's eyes; they held, for someone, the promise of pain.

CHAPTER FORTY-FOUR

"Tenjiku's woman has whipped some of the People into a frenzy," Gwynne remarked as she stepped from the cave. She held her morningstar aloft like a torch leading the way. Caeled shouldered his pack, then he and his companions fell in behind her. A sullen cluster of Islanders stared at them, but she returned their stare with a challenging gaze until one by one they dropped their eyes.

Gwynne laughed, a harsh explosion of sound. "That lot marched up here while you were, ah, away, demanding Tenjiku's killer—that's you, Caeled—and it looked ugly for a while, but then the children appeared."

"The children?" Caeled suddenly realized that a number of children had gathered about them, keeping pace as they advanced. Some moved with difficulty. They gave Madran and Sioraf a wide berth, but kept their eyes fixed almost worshipfully on the Stone Warrior.

"The children swarmed around the entrance to your chamber, laughing and playing until the adults had no choice but to retreat. They would never do anything to harm the children."

Caeled reached out and touched Gwynne's arm. "Thank you for staying."

The big woman blinked. "I have to keep you alive," she said briskly. "One of these days you're going to cure me of this stone flesh."

"I will," he promised.

They were following a narrow trackway leading down to the main group of caves. At the end of the trackway another group of the People had gathered. Caeled could see the spears they brandished, heads chipped from stone and shell, and the knives of coral. Primitive weapons.

"Where are you taking us, Gwynne?"

"Kyrie—that's the name of Tenjiku's woman, but don't let her know you know it—has taken on his role as leader here. I think you'll want to talk to her, Caeled. She's announced that the two who came across the causeway last night are to be tried for killing some of the People.

"And as it happens, one of them is Kichal, Commander of the Bred," Gwynne added.

Caeled halted in his tracks. Following close behind, Madran almost bumped into him. "Kichal Red-Eye led the army that destroyed Baddalaur." He was surprised to find he spoke without rancor. Since meeting Tenjiku, he had come to look on Baddalaur in a different light. Perhaps by destroying the brotherhood the Duet had done the Seven Nations a service.

But no sooner did this thought cross his mind than he shook his head furiously, feeling as if it were a betrayal of his friends. His first friends, brave Armadiel, Scholar Nanri who had taught him so much, Nasariel who had crafted his metal hand. Surely they had not been evil men?

Yet . . . yet they had belonged to the Order and willingly obeyed its precepts. Had they done so out of ignorance of its true purpose? Or had they known and simply chosen to ignore that knowledge, being as guilty of greed and ambition as all the rest? Was that why Scholar Nanri, when he discovered the location of the Arcana, had never told anyone else?

Caeled resumed walking again, lost in thought. The children pressed closer, trying to touch or be touched by Gwynne. From time to time she gently lowered her insensate hand to rest it upon a childish head. A little girl with clubbed feet and golden hair even caught hold of the edge of the Stone Warrior's leather tunic and gave it a tug. When Gwynne glanced down, the toddler laughed up into her face. "Star," murmured the Stone Warrior lovingly.

Meanwhile, the second group of hostile People spread out across the track, spears and knives levelled. One, a big woman whose naked chest was tattooed with a snarling sea monster that coiled around her breasts, stepped forward. "You can go no further!"

Gwynne hefted the morningstar and planted her feet. If they attacked, she would take out the big woman first. She felt, rather than saw, Caeled take up a position on one side of her and Madran on the other. From past experience she knew how well Caeled could fight with no weapons at all, and as for Madran, although he habitually carried a sickle, nature had armed the Madra Allta.

"You should let us through," said Gwynne calmly. "We mean no harm."

The other woman replied between clenched teeth, "Not one more step. I'm warning you."

Gwynne promptly strode forward.

There was a flicker of movement as Sioraf interposed her body between the Stone Warrior and the other woman. She did not bother to draw her ripple-edged knife from its scabbard, but raked her long fingernails across soft breasts where a sea monster coiled, drawing blood. Simultaneously Sioraf's tiny fangs pressed against the woman's shoulder. "You too can be vampir," she hissed.

Meanwhile Madran warped through a score of minute

alterations until the precise moment when he ceased to
be a man and became a huge wolfhound was lost. He
hurled himself at the nearest Islander with such force
that the man's spear went spinning away. Then Madran
was ravening at his throat, closing his jaws on terrified
flesh.

The other Islanders hastily backed back away, though
Sioraf and Madran held their individual victims fast.
"Don't kill them," said Caeled. "Just don't let them go.
Keep them as hostages for our safety."

Madran responded with a soft growl.

With her troop of children following in her wake,
Gwynne led Caeled past them and on to the enormous
central cavern. In spite of the fires and the fish-oil lamps
burning inside, it took a moment for their eyes to adjust
to the smoky gloom. Silence fell over the People gathered
within as the pair entered. Walking shoulder to shoulder
now, they crossed the floor. The crowd made way for
them with a sullen, sibilant murmur.

The day before, the atmosphere had been one of
welcome. The feeling today was very different. Only the
children seemed relaxed, those who still clustered around
Gwynne. The adults were tense, eyes flickering nervously
from Caeled's face to that of the Stone Warrior and back
again. The most able-bodied of the People had moved
to the front rank of the crowd, shielding the weaker and
more deformed.

Gwynne looked neither to the left nor the right. The
rigidity of her muscles made it difficult to turn her head
anyway, but she wanted to make no move that would
betray fear. Following her example, Caeled kept his chin
up and his face impassive as they advanced.

He tried not to notice that the People closed in behind
them.

When they reached the rear of the cave they found
Kyrie seated on a primitive throne, a bench made of the
bones of sea mammals and driftwood, lashed together with

strips of Eron skin. The throne stood upon a dais of hard-packed earth. Before her, held at spear-point by some of the People, were Kichal and the semi-conscious Anadyr.

Caeled's eyes swiftly scanned them both, identifying and assessing.

"How dare you!" Kyrie was shouting at him. "You are not welcome here any more!"

"How dare you," Caeled retorted, putting a hard edge on his voice until it echoed through the vast chamber. "This shames the very name of Tenjiku."

Color flushed Kyrie's skin, a dark stain beneath the blue tattoos.

While she was trying to think of a suitable reply, Caeled continued to study Kichal. To his surprise he was looking at a man not unlike himself. Within the brown-flecked grey eyes was an almost palpable sadness.

"I thought you were some sort of monster," Caeled said to him, wonderingly.

"I was," replied Kichal. The sadness in his eyes deepened.

"Gwynne says the Duet made you what you were."

"They did. It was not my choice. I was never a brutal being until . . ." Kichal paused, obviously struggling for words. "But what they did to me is in the past now. The curse is lifted."

"Does the Duet still claim your allegiance?"

Kichal's mouth hardened into a grim line. "I have sworn to avenge myself on them in any way I can, for what they did to me and my family. And what they made me do to others," he added, wincing at the memory.

"Don't listen to any of this!" Kyrie ordered the assembled People. "It is a plot, a trick of the Duet. I can see it now. The Silverhand was sent by them to slay our beloved Tenjiku and now the red-eyed monster himself is here, preparing the way for their arrival!"

Caeled told her, "I doubt if the twins have any desire to visit this barren piece of rock."

Glancing at his silver hand, Kichal said, "Don't be so sure. You're here; that's all the reason they need."

Caeled motioned to Gwynne and the children to stay behind him, then turned to face the massed Islanders. Raising his arms, he commanded, "Listen to me!" His voice rang through the cave. In Baddalaur he had been trained to control not only the muscles of his body, but his breathing; he could make his words resonate in a way that forced attention. Even Kyrie listened.

"I was the last person to speak with Tenjiku," he announced with pardonable pride. "I knew him in person only briefly, but I have known about him and those like him for a very long time. He was one of the Elders and a survivor from before the Time of Burning. He attempted to bring law and order to a disordered world. Sometimes he succeeded, other times he failed.

"But when he came to these islands, he believed he had finally found a place where he could establish and maintain a rule of peace and tolerance. That was very important to him. He had seen so much of war, of destruction. He wanted things to be different here.

"He united your tribes and taught you there are no strangers. The only strangeness comes from within, he said. Look around you—and then look at us. None of you are normal by the standards of the Nations—but are we? A one-handed Scholar, a vampire, a woman of stone, a Madra Allta. And now these two: one of your own by the looks of him, an Islander who has suffered terribly. Have any of you worse scars than his? And a man who was perverted by the Duet, turned into a monster against his will. Are we any different from you? If Tenjiku were here, would he blame us for our flaws, or would he find beauty in us as he did in you?"

An approving murmur ran through the crowd. Men and women nodded agreement as their eyes met. The tense atmosphere in the cavern eased perceptibly.

"Don't listen to him!" cried Kyrie, shaking off the spell

cast by Caeled's voice. "Remember your friends who died on the causeway last night!"

Caeled countered, "These two fought to defend themselves from an attack on their lives. An attack, as they perceived it, by . . . by what?" His smile was deliberately broad, inviting his listeners to supply the missing word. "Put yourselves in their position. They were exhausted, battered, hungry, alone in a strange place . . . and then they were suddenly attacked . . . by what?" he asked again.

"By monsters," someone in the crowd conceded. A ripple of self-conscious laughter ran through the cavern.

"We would fight back too," volunteered someone else.

"You told me yourselves," Caeled went on, "that you do not take revenge on the Eron for killing to eat, and thus survive. Those of your number who died last night were killed so these two might survive."

Kyrie clenched her fists. The Silverhand was winning; she could see it in the faces of the People. If she did not act now she would lose them. To take Tenjiku's place as their leader she must be strong and forceful; the trial of the two from the causeway had been meant to demonstrate her leadership abilities. Now Caeled was making a persuasive argument against any trial, undermining her authority before it was even established.

She clenched her fists more tightly until her fingernails cut deep into her palms. Her head was beginning to pound; black spots were dancing before her eyes. The last two days had been very difficult. It was the Silverhand's fault, the Silverhand . . . he had killed Tenjiku . . . probably smothered him . . . and now he was going to deny her rightful place as leader of the People . . . did he want to lead them himself? Was that it? Did this usurper dare to think he could take the place of the great Tenjiku?

"Why should you force these two to endure a trial?" Caeled was asking the crowd. "Have they not suffered enough already in their lives? Can you not give them the benefit of the doubt, as Tenjiku would have done?" He turned to Kyrie and asked her directly, "What are you trying to prove?"

Slowly, the tattooed woman rose to her feet. She knew she must control her anger if she were to have any chance against him. He was too plausible, too persuasive; she must be cold and calculating. Leaving her bench—formerly Tenjiku's bench, the Seat of High Honor—she walked toward Caeled with her hands folded and her head bowed, as if she accepted all he said. Her attitude remained totally submissive until she stood right in front of him.

The knife flashed out of her sleeve before anyone saw her move. Only the speed of Caeled's reflexes saved him. He threw out his left hand and the knife screamed across the metal palm.

Almost simultaneously, the cavern echoed to a loud crack like the breaking of a branch.

Kyrie slumped sideways. Her body fell toward Kichal and he caught her instinctively, though from the first touch he knew she was dead. Kichal had felt much death in his time. He cast a swift glance around the cavern, trying to discover who had attacked her.

Kyrie was dead, her neck at an unnatural angle, yet her mouth moved. Lips and tongue writhed, shaping a sound that turned into the laughter of a much younger woman.

Cruel, triumphant laughter.

"You cannot run forever, Silverhand!" exulted the voice of Sarel. "I am coming for you now!"

CHAPTER FORTY-FIVE

When the woman known only as Vesta first established the convent school on the rim of the Eastern Ocean, there had been only three students, one of them her own daughter. The idea of anyone daring such an enterprise in that location was considered madness.

But as the cycles turned, more and more young men and women came out of the dark, wild Steppes, drawn by the promise of a place of enlightenment where knowledge was freely given in exchange for work in the convent's fields and gardens. Even this work was a form of education; the Steppe nomads had no concept of planting grain and vegetables and staying in one place long enough to enjoy the harvest.

When the sons and daughters of the nomads returned to their tribes filled with these new ideas and undertook to implement them, the elders had protested that their ancient way of life was being threatened. Shankar the Warlord had ridden south to the Convent of the Lady with one hundred of his pony soldiers, determined to bring the children away from such corrupting influences. His army arrived brandishing spears decorated with

307

human skulls, and howling like wolves for blood.

Their departure was more subdued. Shankar's confrontation with ebon-skinned Vesta had become the stuff of Steppe legend. Subsequently, twenty of Shankar's own children had studied in the convent, and now their children in turn were receiving an education in the sprawling complex.

Asiz had come to the convent school as a boy. His father, a minor warlord, had been a progressive thinker who realized that if the nomads were to survive as a people, they had to move with the times. So he had encouraged his son to make the journey to the school and devote himself to the study of reading and writing and calculating.

But when Asiz completed his education, he had disappointed his father by choosing to remain to teach others. It was a decision he had never regretted. Over the cycles he had introduced many innovations, including the study of other languages and cultures and the collecting of a vast body of regional folklore. The school had begun drawing children not only from the Steppe tribes, but from the nearby mountain mining towns and the marsh villages as well.

Asiz liked to think that Vesta, who had disappeared as mysteriously as she had once appeared, would have approved.

During the cycles he had spent learning, then teaching, and finally administering the convent school, he had encountered many unusual situations and dealt with many peculiar beings. In a fluid and unstable world where forms were in a constant state of flux, the region was more unstable than most. Second only to the Island Sea, the area seemed to attract the disaffected and the bizarre. Weird rituals celebrated deities unknown elsewhere, and in the swirling purple mists of autumn phantoms lured the unsuspecting to unimaginable fates. Everyone knew the Steppes were haunted; creatures that were little more than myth elsewhere in the Nations roamed freely there.

But Asiz had never encountered anyone like the narrow-headed, sharp-featured man who stood before him now, radiating arrogance. "Your offer is . . . generous," he assured his visitor.

"More than generous." Thin lips pressed tightly together, thin fingers drummed impatiently on folded arms.

"And I can see where your knowledge and learning would be of immense use to us here in the convent. Indeed," Asiz continued, dropping his eyes to avoid the man's unnerving, unblinking stare, "we are honored that one of the legendary Seekers should consider us."

"We are dedicated to introducing wisdom and order into this chaotic world," Rasriel said smoothly. "When we learned of this convent, it seemed a natural extension of our own work."

Asiz forced himself to meet Rasriel's eyes once more. The Hieromonach of the Seekers Reborn was an impressive figure. He dressed entirely in white: stark, coarse, heavy cloth that somehow seemed more majestic than bright colors and fine fabrics. His gaunt face with its deep set eyes was both implacable and compelling.

"Let me be certain I understand your offer," said Asiz. "You wish to take one hundred young men and women from our school for training by the Seekers?"

"That is correct."

"And you want nothing in return?"

The other man's voice was cold. "What price can be put on education?"

"None," Asiz agreed. "And it seems extraordinarily generous. I would have to consult with their parents and the tribal elders first, however, as a matter of . . ."

Rasriel whirled away and picked up the staff which he had propped against the smooth sandstone wall. "I expected a little more foresight from a man in your position, Asiz," he said over his shoulder. "By the time you seek out all the parents and tribal elders, and they question and fret and debate among themselves, you will have wasted more time than we are able to give you. Decide now," he demanded as he strode toward the door. "There are other schools, other masters who will be less hesitant about securing new advantages for their students."

Asiz raised a hand, blinked, licked his lips nervously, made a desperate, instantaneous decision and hoped it was the right one. "I shall have them ready by noon today," he promised.

Rasriel turned back with a new light in his eyes, a dark and somber glow like that of candles seen through black water. "They must be . . . pure," he specified. "Do you understand? A candidate for the Order must be virgin. There are no exceptions."

"These are children of the Steppe," said Asiz, relieved now that the decision was made. "Their people prize their virginity above all else. Marriages are arranged, and male and female alike must be proven unsullied before the wedding gifts are exchanged between their families."

"So I had heard." Rasriel tucked his chin into the cowl of his robe before the other man could see the smile on his face. "So I had heard. I think it a most commendable custom."

CHAPTER FORTY-SIX

High in the cliffs, the stronghold of the People was all but empty. Beams of early afternoon sunlight slanting through cavemouths highlighted spiralling dust motes. Voices could be heard drifting up from the beach, making a strange, funereal music as they bewailed the deaths of friends and family. Their keening was accompanied by the muted roar of the sea.

The small group gathered in the mouth of one of the caves watched the ceremonies below with interest. The People were methodical in their rituals, doing what must be done while their melodious mourning never faltered.

It reminded Caeled of the song of the Eron.

When the last goodbyes had been said, the dead bodies were launched onto the breast of the sea like so many small boats, with wooden stakes driven into them to support sails crafted of Eron hide. The People understood the building of small boats; fishing was their principle livelihood. The sails caught the breeze and carried the bodies away, riding the white-crested waves.

"What happens now?" Gwynne wondered.

Kichal replied, "I would advise you to flee." He was

311

standing well inside the cave so that his voice echoed hollowly. A grim and silent Anadyr reclined in pain nearby, back braced against a stone wall. The giant's scarred head was swathed in a bandage of fronds and mud.

"I have never run from anything in my life," Gwynne said, glaring at Kichal.

Madran spoke up. "Perhaps not, but Kichal makes sense. There is a time to fight and a time to run." Noticing that Anadyr was shivering, the Madra Allta went to the center of the chamber and hunched over the smouldering fire. Crouching low, he blew it to fresh life, sending a shower of sparks freewheeling toward the blackened ceiling.

"The twins know you're here," Kichal told Caeled. "They have already sent me to capture you. One failure won't stop them, they never accept a failure, it only makes them angry and urges them to greater effort. I suspect their whole shanti fleet is on the way here even as we speak. They want you very badly, you know."

"You said, 'they sent me to capture you,'" Caeled pointed out. "Why not, 'they sent me to kill you'?"

"I was under orders to take you alive. Originally they wanted you dead; Sarel in particular hates you. But then they changed their minds. I don't know why; they never explain the orders they give."

Caeled's dark eyes brooded. "I suspect they only want me alive long enough to lead them to all four of the Arcana. But the Duet must never have the Arcana. With such power they could cause terrible destruction, worse than anything that has gone before."

"Then flee!" Kichal reiterated. "Before they can find you, disappear! It shouldn't be that difficult. There are a thousand uncharted islands in this sea, and great expanses of wilderness in places like the Steppes where you could vanish without a trace."

At that moment an agonized shriek cut through the afternoon air; a mother screaming in pain as she mourned her son. Caeled shrank from the sound, flinching at its intensity. He was suddenly reminded of a time when his own mother Myriam had cried out like that, though for a very different reason.

She had been attacked by a Gallowan sailor, one of the "clients" she serviced in order to support herself and her son. The man had broken her wrist rather than pay her the few miserable coins she requested, then had set about beating Myriam's face to a pulp for good measure. While he was thus engaged Caeled had stabbed the sailor in the back with a fork from the table, putting all his puny, childish strength into the thrust.

Whirling around with a bellow of outrage, the man had flung the little boy against the wall of the filthy rented hovel. Caeled's skull struck the wall with such force that lights exploded behind his eyes and he slid to the floor. The sailor pulled a vicious-looking skinning knife from his belt and bent over him.

Caeled's mother had promptly smashed a stone bottle of cooking oil over the sailor's head, then as he lay unconscious, she sawed his throat open with his own knife and relieved him of a purse full of New Coin. When Caeled came to, in spite of a terrible headache and recurring waves of nausea, he had helped his mother conceal the body beneath the midden heap behind the house. Then, and not for the first time, the two fled in the middle of the night, leaving their pitiful belongings behind in their never-ending, never-successful search for a safe haven and a better life.

Funny, he had not thought about his mother in a long time now. But being with Tenjiku had brought back many memories of the past, in addition to making him question everything—including his reasons for this foolhardy quest.

Perhaps it was time to give it up, Caeled told himself. He could take the Spear and the Stone and toss them into the sea, then disappear as Kichal suggested. Sioraf would go with him, he need not be alone, even if Madran

and Gwynne opted to go their own ways. At last, with
Sioraf, he might find that safe haven, that better life . . .

But it would change nothing.

Choosing safety for himself would not stop the despotic
reign of the twins. It would not heal Gwynne's petrifying
body or bring the dead back to life. The Duet had been
responsible for so many deaths, including that of Myriam.
Caeled had a sudden, painfully vivid memory of the last
time he had seen her, or what remained of her: a puddle
of some noxious, greasy substance dripping from a foul-
smelling bed. That was what the twins and their Voids
had made of his mother.

His right hand, the hand of flesh, automatically sought
the battered, stoneless ring he wore on a thin cord around
his neck, the only token he retained of hers. If he walked
away now, it would change nothing. But if he stayed . . .

If he stayed there would be more deaths, more mothers
bewailing their slain sons, more children orphaned, more
blood on the twins' hands. But this time the blood would
be on his hands also. Inadvertently, he had drawn the
twins here. Anyone unfortunate enough to get in their
way would suffer. If he chose to fight them, there would
be immediate pain for a greater number than if he took
Kichal's advice and fled.

Caeled narrowed his eyes, trying to reconstruct the
recent past in the light of new knowledge. Kichal said
Sarel in particular hated him. Originally the Duet had
wanted him dead. Originally—when? Had the twins sent
the Bred into Baddalaur in search of him? Were the deaths
of the brothers and the ultimate destruction of the College
also to be laid at his feet? Cold settled in his belly.

"Caeled?"

Sioraf's soft, whispery voice pulled him back to the
here and now. He turned to find the others looking at
him. Madran's forehead was deeply furrowed, his shaggy
eyebrows drawn together over his liquid brown eyes. He
wore the expression of a father observing a son on the

brink of manhood, anticipating all the pain he might have to endure and wishing there was a way to spare him.

Gwynne's features were as rigid as ever, yet managed to convey an impression of conflicting emotions. She had no fear for herself, but she wanted Caeled to remain alive to help her exact her own vengeance on the twins. At the same time, she had new reasons for living, reasons that would make flight a painful option for the Stone Warrior.

Inhumanly lovely Sioraf was searching Caeled's face with an expression of anxiety that touched him deeply. She seemed to have no thought for herself at the moment; she extended a slender hand as if her only desire was to comfort him.

Then there were the two newcomers: the scarred giant, Anadyr, obviously in great pain but choosing to ignore it, and Kichal, tired and world-weary and somehow touchingly human after all. They were all looking at Caeled, watching him. Waiting for him to make the decision upon which their very lives might depend.

The necessity for choice hammered at the young man like nails being driven into his flesh. He spoke aloud to the others, seeking guidance.

"Last night Tenjiku took me into the Aethyra and showed me many . . . wonders," he told them. "He was a great man who had borne many names down through the ages. In his way he had helped shape the Nations as they are today."

The others listened, not sure where this was leading. Silence had fallen outside. Only the high-pitched cries of the gulls echoed the earlier laments of the People.

Sweating, Caeled brushed his hair off his forehead with his metal hand. "There are many things Tenjiku only hinted at, many things he almost, but not quite, revealed to me." He looked from one face to another, willing them to understand. "I could not force him to answer my questions, he was much more powerful than I. I could only listen to whatever he wanted to say.

"But at last he told me where the other two Arcana are."

Sioraf gasped. Madran's jaw dropped. Gwynne's green eyes blazed.

Caeled went on, "Tenjiku—or rather his spirit—also told me that these Islanders, his People, would hold the Duet at bay while I go to find the Arcana." The young man's lips twisted sardonically. "Then once I possess all four artefacts, the twins and all their evil can be blotted out of the Nations. When I have the Arcana I can do anything." Dropping his voice, he added as if to himself, "Anything at all."

"You might sound a little happier about it," Madran suggested.

"Happy? What happiness is there to be found in this?" Caeled turned wide, pleading eyes toward him. "Why me, Madran; can you tell me? What gives me the right to make life-and-death decisions for others? Why should I have this power I never asked for, never sought?" The young man's voice sank to a near sob. "Why me?"

Madran stepped forward and caught Caeled's shoulders, holding him at arm's length to stare into his troubled eyes. Even the big Allta sometimes forgot that the Silverhand was little more than two and twenty summers.

While Caeled never spoke of his early life, Madran had the impression that it had been very hard indeed. After a terrible childhood, the boy had spent many cycles in Baddalaur as an acolyte to the Order. He had risen to the rank of Scholar and acquired much book learning, But Madran doubted if the brothers of the Order, despite their conviction that the Silverhand was the long-prophesied Spoken One, had prepared him for life outside the walls of Baddalaur. If they had done so, he would not be so troubled and uncertain now—would he?

The Madra Allta felt a lash of anger against the men who had tried to force Caeled into their own mold. They had taught him only what would support their own authoritarianism; they had sought to deny him faith in anything other than the Order. All this they had justified as being for the greater good.

Madran growled deep in his throat. He had little patience with the greater good. He could only see the pain in Caeled's eyes.

He said, "For whatever reason, you do have this power. You have been chosen. By someone, something. It is as simple as that. Now you must chose whether to accept and use the power, or reject it. Remember, Caeled, there is always choice. Choice is both blessing and bane. We Allta believe that when the gods shaped us, the demon lord crept in and introduced the concept of free will. It was his curse upon us, his way of torturing us with doubt and guilt and anxiety. But these are balanced by the possibility of improving our lot.

"Whether we like it or not, the world turns upon choices, Caeled. Think how fixed and boring life would be otherwise. It would have the sameness as . . . as rock," Madran concluded, then cut his eyes toward Gwynne, hoping she would not take offense.

"What are you telling me?"

"I'm saying that if you do not want to do this, if you do not want to go and recover the two remaining Arcana, you can simply walk away now. None of us will blame you. We respect your right to choose." ·

"But if I turn my back on the Arcana, Madran, what happens to the Nations, the Islands, the People . . . what will happen to all of you?"

Madran's grin was a flash of white fangs and a lolling pink tongue. "We will make our own decisions about what happens to us," he assured the young man. "That, you understand, is our privilege."

Kichal sat down on a rounded stone and cleared his

throat. "Whether you go or stay, Silverhand, people are going to die. The twins have already set their plans in motion. The troops I led were supposed to bring you back alive and reasonably intact if possible. And we would have done, if things had turned out differently. But the next warriors who arrive to do the Duet's bidding will be merciless killers, I assure you." As he spoke he flicked a glance over Caeled and his companions, wondering how he could have been so indifferent to their fate. In a short space of time each had become real to him. Living, as he was living.

"I think you should ask yourself," he told Caeled, "whether the deaths that will follow are to have any deeper significance. Are these people to die just because your presence brought the twins here? Or will they die to buy you time to recover the two remaining Arcana and defeat the Duet? If that is the reason, at least those who give up their lives will know they are doing so for a worthy cause. I have observed," he added cynically, "that men prefer to believe they are dying for a worthy cause."

Caeled turned to Gwynne. "What would you advise? You were my first ally; I respect your judgement."

For once the Stone Warrior was glad of the relative impassivity of her face. "True friends will not tell you what to do," she told Caeled. "They will merely support whatever decision you make."

"But no matter what you choose, the world will go on," Kichal interjected.

"No!" Anadyr's voice was harsh, rasping. "Look at him! Can you not see the shadows that gather around him?" Grunting with pain, the giant Islander rose stiffly to his feet. There he stood swaying, supporting himself with a hand on Kichal's shoulder. "On the Islands we call people like this Silverhand accursed, because they are fated to bear others on their shoulders. Life is hard enough for one, it is terrible indeed to be responsible for more than your own self. Yet this unfortunate man," he jabbed a finger in Caeled's direction, "carries the destiny of the world. What he does or does not do will make a huge difference."

Caeled closed his eyes and lowered his head, employing the techniques he had been taught in Baddalaur to calm his thundering heart. He felt as if the world were fragmenting around him. He longed to sleep, to lie down and close his eyes so that when he opened them again, he would discover this had been nothing more than a dream, and he would be back in his familiar cell at the College, surrounded by known and trusted Scholars and Seekers, with everything laid out before him and a straight, certain path to follow. . . .

But this was no dream.

When he raised his head, his eyes were bright with unshed tears. "Sioraf. What do you say?"

"Make your decision," she replied. "But whatever you do, wherever you go, I will be with you." Her voice and her startlingly blue eyes were very calm. She had made her choice. Everything fell into place for her after that.

Surprisingly, Caeled turned to Anadyr. "Do you really believe I can make a difference?"

"The people of these islands have lived thus for hundreds of cycles without change. Yet you have altered their lives in a single day and a night. Your presence has affected these others, changing their destinies, entwining them with yours, and now you have ensnared Kichal and myself. If you had not been here, then Kichal would not have been sent to capture you, and I would not have been assigned to guide him. Without you, Kichal would not have recovered his humanity and I would not have found a friend." The Islander's broken-toothed smile was strangely gentle, at odds with his horrific appearance. "As that shaggy fellow says, you are cursed to bring change. Learn to live with the curse and call it a blessing."

Slowly, gravely, Caeled Silverhand nodded.

Turning away, he walked outside the cave and gazed

down toward the beach. The others followed silently behind.

The People were lining the shore, staring out to sea while the bodies of their dead sailed away. They had done what they must do. There was not enough wood for funeral pyres, and the waterlogged, stony soil was unsuitable for burying.

Above the cries of the gulls, Caeled thought he could hear a child's laughter.

He had brought chaos—change, Anadyr would have said—to the islands. Whether he stayed or went, there would be suffering.

He watched the Islanders come streaming up the beach toward their caves, people of every tribe and description, united as the People because they had once been outcast by circumstance or deformity.

They were going to die.

The thought chilled him. He gazed down at the children, many of whom would now never reach adulthood, never know the joys and sorrows that life had to offer. A pack of little ones ran ahead of the main group. When they saw Caeled looking down at them they pointed up at him. Then, as they recognized Gwynne at his shoulder, they started to make the climb to join them.

Soon they came shouting and laughing along the trackway to the cavemouth. A little girl reached out timidly to touch Caeled's silver hand. A boy, bolder than the rest, rapped it with his knuckles and laughed at the sound it made as he hobbled past to form part of the circle gathering around the Stone Warrior.

"Mock!" she cried warmly, reaching out to him.

The children pushed and shoved one another in their eagerness to be close to her. Her green eyes glowed with joy. She had known them for less than a day, yet she knew all their names as she brushed hair from a boy's eyes, kissed another's skinned hand, congratulated a third on finding a peculiarly shaped stone, admired a girl's first tentative efforts at self-tattooing.

The Stone Warrior looked up suddenly, her eyes catching and holding Caeled's over the heads of the children. Her lips moved and though he was sure she did not speak, he heard her as clearly as if she had shouted.

"You can make a difference."

CHAPTER FORTY-SEVEN

Sullen and silent, the People gathered in the central chamber. They were stunned by the death of Tenjiku the Everliving and then Kyrie's extraordinary death. Few would have admitted to liking the dead woman. She had tried to keep anyone else from getting close to Tenjiku, and for that she was resented. There had been a grudging gratitude, however, for the tireless care she had given the old man.

When she openly declared herself their leader after his death a few of the People had complained, but none had opposed her. She carried a certain aura of authority as a result of her proximity to Tenjiku for so many cycles, and besides, it was well known that she had once killed an Eron with her bare hands.

At least Kyrie had been a leader. Now she too was gone and the isle and its People were defenseless, drifting like a rudderless ship. There was some talk of slaying the outsiders because they had brought so much trouble with them. Cooler heads pointed out that Tenjiku had welcomed the Silverhand. Perhaps it might be best, they said, to treat him and his companions with wary respect.

Just look what happened to Kyrie when she attacked him!

Mention of Kyrie's death sent shudders through the People. Many of them had heard her speak with the voice of a young woman, though it should have been impossible with a crushed throat and broken neck.

"Listen to me." Caeled used his trained voice, projecting it over the heads of the crowd, pitching it at the very back of the chamber. The murmuring People fell silent. Those who could not control themselves were sternly shushed by the others.

Caeled had taken a position in front of the bench which had once served as Tenjiku's royal seat. He was careful not to sit on the throne itself, aware that his every action would be scrutinized and judged. The slightest wrong note could turn them irrevocably against him.

Madran and Gwynne stood at the foot of the dais, keeping an eye on the crowd. They knew how quickly a mob could turn. Gwynne was concerned because the children had gathered around her feet and if it came to a fight, she would not be able to use her morningstar without fear of hurting them.

Kichal and Anadyr stood on the opposite side, also watching the crowd. Kichal was hungry and thirsty, and obscurely pleased by both very human sensations. In spite of his injury, Anadyr stayed close beside him, making every effort to look intimidating.

Half hidden by the dais and the bench, Sioraf crouched in the shadows. She was aware that her appearance disturbed the People, who like most of humankind were repelled by vampiri.

"Hear me!" Caeled gazed at the crowd, making eye contact with as many people as possible, drawing them in. The compelling Rasriel himself had been his teacher at Baddalaur in the art of speechmaking. That training stood him in good stead now as his mind swiftly sorted the phrases he might use, selecting some and rejecting others. He must capture their interest, command their respect, and earn their sympathy, if he was to gain their support.

"I am Caeled . . ." he lifted his metal hand, ". . . sometimes called Silverhand. I have also been referred to as the Spoken One . . . elsewhere. And I am cursed," he added, deliberately employing the Anadyr's term.

A murmur rippled through the crowd. A few closed their fists into balls, extending first and little fingers to ward off evil.

"My curse led me to this isle to meet with the man you knew as Tenjiku," Caeled continued. "Legend has given him other names. He was a great man who long outlived his allotted span because he was waiting, waiting for me. For the Spoken One. Our spirits have wandered together in the Dreamscape. So great was his power that his spirit could survive death and meet with me thus, to communicate. He had much to show me and tell me.

"Because I had arrived at last and he needed wait no longer, he chose to allow his outworn body the rest it deserved. But even though the flesh died, his spirit remained lively. From the Aethyra he showed me the future. The future of the People, of this island . . . and of all the lands and seas beyond.

"You, the People whom Tenjiku loved, are at the heart of this future. He assured me that you would stand and fight, that I could rely upon you to hold the army of the Duet at bay while I go in search of . . . of tools that will bring an end to the twins forever. Ancient artefacts of great power known as the Arcana. I have two of them already, but I must have the other two."

"Why should we help you?" someone shouted.

"I'll not force you to do anything against your will. You make your own decisions. But even on this remote isle you must be aware of the cruelties inflicted by the rulers of the Seven Nations. Should they wish, the Duet would come here and crush you as casually as they would crush a nest of insects. While such tyrants live no one is safe.

"The price of stopping them will be high, and it will be extracted in blood and pain. But in return, I can promise you . . . I can promise you this."

Stooping to reach into the bag at his feet he pulled out the Spear and held it aloft in his metal hand. Thin, glowing tendrils twisted around the shaft, shocking the crowd to silence. Then from his bag Caeled removed the Stone and held it up in his other hand. He let them all take a long look at the strange object with its indecipherable carvings.

Lowering the point of the Spear, he inserted it into the hole in the center of the Stone. Next he raised the Spear so that the Stone slid along the shaft. At a given point there was an audible click.

The coiling tendrils were transformed into a pulsing ribbon of radiance from which sparks flew like tiny stars. A shimmering ball gradually took shape. Slowly, almost delicately, the ball detached itself from the head of the Spear and floated upward towards the ceiling. When it touched the soot-blackened roof of the cave, it exploded in a great wash of silver light that flooded the large chamber.

Suddenly the cave was filled with the scent of new mown hay. Beneath that fragrance were hints of spice and exotic blossoms whose sweetness bloomed like summer in the chamber. All the while the silver light blazed overhead, chasing away every shadow, bathing everyone in its beneficent glow.

One by one, the People began to laugh—or cry—and reach out to touch one another with trembling fingers.

They could not believe their eyes. But they had to accept their sense of touch as they explored a mystery beyond comprehension.

In the healing blaze of silver light, they were no longer deformed.

The People were whole.

❖   ❖   ❖

Gwynne was weeping. The children clustered around her were perfect in every respect. Missing limbs were restored, spines straightened, skins were unblemished, features unwarped. Mock stood on two sturdy legs; Star danced on high-arched, elegant feet.

Gwynne bent down and spread her arms wide, gathering them to her with a cry of delight.

Only when she felt their throbbing warmth against her own body did she realize that she too was changed.

She could feel them touching her sensitive, human skin. When Star pressed a silken cheek to hers, Gwynne kissed the tiny girl with tender lips.

Then Caeled staggered and the silver light faded.

At once the bodies of the People resumed their former shapes.

Tears of happiness turned to sobs of heartbreak. The loss was almost too much to bear.

"Do it again!" someone—a child—called plaintively. "Make the good come back!"

"I cannot," Caeled admitted sadly. His voice was leaden with exhaustion; the hair at his temples had gone very grey. He looked ten cycles older than he had moments before, and there was a quaver in his voice when he spoke. "As you see I only have two of the objects I need, those tools I mentioned before. The Arcana. I need the other two to effect permanent change. With them I could use the silver light to paint a better world for you."

"If we stand and fight for you, can you get the other two?" someone demanded to know. "Will you use them to repay us?"

"This I swear," Caeled said. "But you will not be fighting for me only; you will be fighting for yourselves, you will be fighting as Tenjiku wished."

The objections Caeled had been expecting were surprisingly few. "We have no experience . . . we are not warriors . . . we have no one to lead us."

Gwynne was speaking even before she realized she

had stepped forward. "If you will have me, I will lead you." She opened her arms to the crowd of adults as she had to the children, stony arms, heavy arms, arms that ached with loss.

"I am like you," she said. Then she carefully lowered her hands to rest on the heads of the children. "And I have a reason to stand and fight."

Kichal coughed, drawing attention to himself. "No one knows the Duet or the Bred better than I. Let me help. Let me make amends for the harm I once did . . . when I was a monster."

Caeled waited, aware that the moment was held in the balance. A single dissenter could destroy the mood by pointing out the certainty of defeat, the guaranteed agony of death and dying. Many would die in the attempt to keep the twins occupied until Caeled could get to the other Arcana and return . . . if indeed he ever returned.

Suddenly the little girl clinging to Gwynne's arm gave a shrill cry and pointed toward the cavemouth. All heads turned to look in the direction of her outstretched finger.

A shape moved in the opening, silhouetted against the light. It looked like one of the People, old and crippled, advancing awkwardly. But as it entered the chamber the form flickered and altered and then, as they watched open-mouthed, became a dead man slumped in a wooden cage; became Tenjiku the Warrior, tall and proud; became a radiant youth attired in a shimmering white cloth that covered him from neck to feet.

The image shifted again, revealing in swift succession a myriad of forms—warrior, priest, merchant, bard, Hieromonach, prince, brigand, and finally Tenjiku the Everliving, the old man who had ruled the isle for as long as legend.

He looked towards Caeled and raised his hand in salute.

Then he simply vanished.

Someone toward the rear of the chamber gave a cry of despair.

Caeled took a deep breath, steadying himself. "What say you then?" he challenged, overriding his exhaustion by sheer force of will. "Can I rely on you to stand for me, for Tenjiku, for yourselves?"

For a moment there was a silence so absolute he thought he could hear the beating of their hearts.

Then the reply rocked the cavern.

"We will stand!"

CHAPTER FORTY-EIGHT

Lamar stood on the dock, tilting his head back and shading his eyes with his hand. In wavering lines like the patterns of migrating Serif geese, the shanti passed overhead. Sunlight washing over the colored balloons revealed only beauty. An observer on the ground had no intimation of the horrors that rode in the carriages underneath.

The innkeeper turned away from the water's edge and pushed his way through the crowd lining the dock. They were all staring into the northern sky, nudging one another, questioning, pointing. The island was rife with speculation, but no one with the exception of Lamar knew the reason for the massive shanti fleet.

Suddenly Lamar exploded with a string of curses. A drunken sailor had lurched into him. If Anadyr had been with him, the sailor would be lying in the gutter with a broken jaw. He was surprised to find that he actually missed the Island Trash. Anadyr had been with him so long that he had become like a faithful hound, appreciated only in his absence.

As Lamar pushed open the door of his tavern he was

wondering how much he could charge the twins for Anadyr's services.

The usual crowd was leaning on the bar or slouching in the rickety chairs beside the splintery tables, drinking from wooden beakers. One of Lamar's whores was filling in for him behind the bar, sipping a drink she hastily set down when her employer entered. She made a great fuss of serving the nearest customer instead. In a corner, three men were arguing over a game of Black Bird. The air smelled of liquor and pipe smoke and unwashed bodies.

"Good times comin'!" one of the older regulars called by way of greeting to Lamar.

The innkeeper went around behind the bar and pulled on his leather apron. "Why do you say that?" he asked as his eyes automatically counted the number of empty beakers.

The paunchy, grizzled man raised his bleary eyes toward the ceiling, indicating the sky above. "Duet's going to war. With the Steppes probably, or the Northlands. Don't matter which. War means soldiers, and soldiers means work. Seamount's the largest isle hereabouts. They'll have to stop here for supplies. Good money to be made from soldiers; they eat and drink and whore. Make us rich."

Through the plates of thin shell that covered the windows, Lamar could make out the shanti dropping toward the northern horizon. Their brilliant hues were distorted by irregularities in the shell pane until the colors ran like blood. Lamar scowled. No one would make anything out of this war—except the Duet. They were using an army now that was not like any army of human or Allta warriors. According to Kichal, the twins had created themselves a force called the New Bred: creatures that were neither human nor beast, but something in between. Warriors who ate their kills and seemed to have no interest in sex, an emotionless, fearless army that could continue to fight despite the most appalling injuries. What could stand against them?

"Good times comin'," the old man chuckled again.

But not for the islands, thought Lamar ruefully. Catching the whore's eye, he jerked a thumb in the direction of upstairs. "Take a customer with you," he advised, "and do some real work for a change." Then he took a clay pipe from his pocket and prepared a comforting smoke. His instinct for survival was screaming a warning at him. He wondered how long it would take him to liquidate his assets and get as far away from the Seven Nations as possible.

The well was ancient, a cylindrical shaft sunk deep into the earth and lined with a curious form of molded stone. The material was white and glossy in spite of its great age, proof if any be needed that it was a relic of the Elder Times. Within the hut surrounding the well, Rasriel and the strongest two of his Seekers Reborn waited as a hundred children were sent in to them, one by one. The youngest was less than six summers, the eldest no more than twelve. They came obediently enough, though their faces were pale and their eyes wide and anxious.

At a signal from their Hieromonach the two Seekers took each child in turn by the arms. "Quiet now," Rasriel would say, gazing sternly at the youngster as he spoke. "You must be quiet and still, that is an important part of the ritual."

His authority was unmistakable. No child dared argue. They were far from home, from friends and family, from anything that might have given them confidence. Meek as lambs they submitted, one by one.

While scouting the area from the Aethyra, Rasriel had noticed an unnatural configuration in one of the oases that bordered the Steppes. When he went down to examine it more closely he found a peculiarly shaped hut, more metal than stone, more rust than metal, and within the hut—the well.

The moment he saw it he knew how to make use of it . . . all he needed was to find the fuel.

And then he had learned of the convent school.

Had Rasriel believed in gods, he would have considered himself blessed.

One by one the children were herded into the hut and the warped metal door slammed shut behind him. They were still alive when Rasriel tossed them into the well.

The ceremony hearkened back to rituals practiced by the Seekers of a bygone era. The great Bardal the Lawgiver was credited with developing a technique for the instantaneous transfer of a physical body from one location to another. Using his method, the original Seekers were able to travel anywhere they liked in the blink of an eye. But as the cycles passed, Bardal's teachings were diluted until many such skills were lost.

However, a later generation of Seekers had discovered that some relics of the Elder Times still possessed a summoning force. By harnessing a giant outpouring of energy, it was possible to travel from one relic to another as if moving along invisible roads. Then eventually even this practice was abandoned as being too difficult, too impractical. The invisible roads became part of forgotten legend buried in the dustiest archives of the Great Library at Baddalaur.

An inveterate researcher in his student days, Rasriel had discovered the ancient tracts, read them, and dismissed them as works of imagination . . . until the time came when he decided to reconstruct the Seekers. Then from the cluttered storehouse of his brain he resurrected rituals like that for using the invisible roads. He employed them anew with variations such as this one, which allowed him to supplement his personal strength with virgin sacrifice.

The Seekers of the Way would never have condoned

such a deed. But for the Seekers Reborn there were no constraints.

When the one hundred innocent children had been tossed into the well, the rest of the Seekers Reborn crowded into the small hut. A few despairing cries could be heard from the bottom of the pit, but they paid no attention. Silently they watched as Rasriel emptied barrels of reeking fish oil into the hole.

The voices echoing within the well grew frantic with terror.

Bowing his head, Rasriel summoned an image of the Island Sea. He narrowed his focus until he was concentrating on one island, one particular headland he had viewed from the Aethyra, impressing it into his thoughts until he could see it as clearly as if he stood there in person.

Simultaneously his followers gathered around him. Their arms wrapped around one another's shoulders so they formed a living ring. Without breaking the circle, Rasriel straightened up and spoke a single word. A yellow spark danced in the air before him, hovered briefly, then tumbled to the ground as a blackened cinder.

Beads of perspiration broke out on his forehead as he repeated the word. This time a scattering of sparks glittered in the shadowy interior, most of them dying as they fell. But one single fiery particle swirled over the rim of the well and tumbled into the blackness below.

A solid cone of flame shot high into the desert air.

The terrible, unnatural fire did not roar or crackle, but horrified observers who saw it from a distance claimed afterward that it sounded like children crying, and swore they could see monstrously distorted human shapes writhing in the flames.

The hut and all it contained vanished in that inferno.

Only four of the Seekers Reborn, including Rasriel, survived the traumatic shifting of their physical selves to the islands. But four was enough, the Hieromonach told himself.

He was shaken by the experience, yet wildly exhilarated. He wanted to throw back his head and scream his triumph aloud. Until the actual moment, he had been only partially convinced the ritual would work. The children could have spoiled everything by refusing to cooperate, causing a struggle that would have weakened him too much to complete his task. Fighting self-doubt had been his greatest challenge.

Now that he had succeeded, Rasriel felt as if he could do anything he chose. As if he was entitled to do anything he chose!

As he ran a hand across his soot-blackened face, he happened to glance toward the south . . . just in time to see the first of the shanti appear over the horizon like a swarm of brilliantly-colored peist.

CHAPTER FORTY-NINE

"I've never seen anything like it." Kichal gazed in wonder at the huge metal shanti. "The twins would kill for something like this." He stopped suddenly, feeling color burn in his cheeks, and glanced over his shoulder to find Caeled grinning at his discomfiture. "I mean, this is what the Duet have been trying to build, but they simply don't have the skills." Kichal ran the palm of his hand across the smooth surface of the ancient craft. "How did they do it?" he wondered aloud. "See how closely joined the plates are; and this metal, so thin yet so strong. Truly, this is the work of the gods."

"This is the work of men," Caeled contradicted him. "Nothing more. But they had godlike powers. And it was those powers which ultimately brought about their destruction."

Kichal shook his head. "I cannot believe that. With such knowledge, such power at their command, how could they have allowed it to destroy themselves?"

"Consider the Duet," Caeled replied. "They are the most powerful beings in the Nations, and yet do they use their power for good? You know the answer as well as I do. Their abilities seem to be dedicated to causing destruction. They have the knowledge to mold living flesh according to any pattern they choose, it seems— so do they develop stronger humans, longer lived, more beautiful and wise? No, they shape monsters, bred only to kill and maim. They have learned how to put something inside men's heads which destroys their higher consciousness, making them worse than beasts— as you know from your own experience, Kichal. They could use this same skill to go into diseased bodies and eliminate the disease . . . but they do not.

"Try and imagine Sarel and Lares with a hundred times the power they now possess . . . and you only begin to approximate the abilities of the Elders. They were not gods, I cannot call them gods." There was an image, brief, flickering, of the Aethyra Presences. "They were not gods," he repeated quickly, "but they were extraordinary people. Yet something went terribly wrong."

Kichal ducked his head and stepped through the doorway into the metal body of the shanti, wiping away a thick matting of gauzy spiderweb. His voice echoed hollowly within the curved walls. "I thought the Elder Times were supposed to be . . . paradise."

Caeled followed him through the low doorway. "Perhaps the Elders would think ours a time of paradise," he began, then stopped suddenly. Kichal was facing him, knife in his hand, grey eyes narrowed, mouth set in a grim line. Before Caeled could speak, Kichal had flipped the knife so that he was holding it by the blade, then threw it at him.

Swifter than thought Caeled dropped to one knee, allowing the knife to sail harmlessly over his head. As it hummed through the air he balled his hands into fists of flesh and metal. He was coming to his feet in one angry, fluid motion when he heard the distinctive crunch of metal into flesh behind him. He whirled in time for a thick pink ichor to spatter onto his clothing. When it touched his metal hand, it sizzled.

A carrion spider was impaled by Kichal's blade just above the door. The hairy legs were still twitching, the hooked jaws thrashing.

With his metal hand, Caeled crushed the creature to pulp.

As he pulled Kichal's knife free, he noticed that it had embedded itself in an engraved plaque above the door. He brushed cobwebs and encrusted insect cases from the plaque until he was able to trace the Elder script with his fingertip. "*Invincible,*" he read aloud, forming the word slowly. The people who had built this ship had probably named it for themselves or their ancient time. But they and their time were long gone. Only time was invincible.

"That's twice you've saved my life," he remarked as he turned to return the knife to Kichal.

"If I were to save it a hundred times, it would still not be enough," Kichal told him. "It's because of you that I have come back from the dead. That's a debt I can never repay."

Caeled's smile was surprisingly boyish on the face of a man who now looked at least thirty-five summers. "You could repay a major portion," he replied, "if you could tell us how to inflate the balloon up there." He jerked his thumb toward the ceiling.

"That's simple," Kichal replied.

"This is an absolute treasure trove!" exclaimed the Stone Warrior. She stood in the center of a chamber that was far too square to be natural. The walls were lined with horizontal sections of Old Metal, wider than a man's hand but no thicker than a finger's thickness. More of the flat metal shelves lay tumbled along the floor, together with other bits of metal in every size and shape. A framework of metal spars arranged to form a large X stood at the far end of the chamber.

Mock, who had led Gwynne to the chamber, laughed at her wonder. "There are many caves like this," he told her. "There are even deeper ones, but we do not go into those for they are supposed to be haunted." He peered earnestly into her face. "Do you think there really are such things as ghosts?"

"Whoever tells you such tales to frighten you should be beaten," Gwynne replied with surprising passion. "Children should never be taught fear. There is enough of that in the world already."

She wrenched one of the horizontal metal sections free from the wall and swung it through the air, judging its weight with professional skill. With a few alterations it would make a good weapon, she decided.

The absence of weapons had been one of the major problems in planning the defense of the island. The People possessed coral knives and spears made of driftwood and shell which, while they could be honed to some degree, were also very brittle and tended to disintegrate with the first blow. There were slingshots aplenty—the children used these on seabirds, with telling effect—and coral throwing sticks, but no crossbows. The ordinary bows that had been used to fire the flaming arrows were not strong enough to send a missile through a solid human body.

If the People were to make a stand against the Duet's army they would need better weapons, Gwynne had been telling herself . . . when she remembered the room piled high with metal which Mock had shown her on the way to the children's cave.

The place the People called Home Isle appeared to contain a number of Elder influences. Even the caves within the cliffs were not totally natural, having been enlarged and enhanced over many cycles. Since she had set out on this odyssey with Caeled, Gwynne had seen more remains of the ancient days than she ever knew existed—and somehow she suspected there were more still to be discovered.

She was certain that the room where she now stood dated from the Elder Times. Although the Stone Warrior liked to think she had little imagination, if she listened hard enough, she thought she could almost hear the footsteps of the retreating Elders as they walked down the corridors and abandoned the place forever.

When her fading hearing detected the thud of heavy footsteps just outside the chamber, her heart leaped. Her hand fell to her morningstar.

Anadyr strode into the room. He was holding a gleaming length of chain in his hand, and his scarred face was twisted into an approximation of a smile. "Look what I found! I think these were storerooms. There's a whole series of them farther on. I work for a man named Lamar on Seamount Isle. He has storerooms like this under his tavern. He never lets anyone but me go down there." He swung the metal chain; it moaned on the air.

Gwynne cast her eyes around the chamber again. It did indeed look like a storeroom, but one where the shelves were made of metal instead of wood; another example of the extravagance of the Elders. Gesturing to the scarred Islander, she called his attention to the metal spars. "Could we put a point on some of those?"

At once he understood. They were of a length to make fine spears. "It's possible. Or we could make separate spearheads and fasten to them. There's material aplenty here." He lifted a narrow, flat sheet of metal from the debris on the floor and attempted to bend it. It bent only slightly. Gwynne took it from his hands and folded it easily, then bent it back and forth until it snapped, leaving two long lengths of metal, each with a ragged edge on one side.

Anadyr was staring at her in amazement and something akin to worship. "That's . . . I never saw a woman as strong as you," he said hoarsely.

"And I pray to the gods you will never see another like me. Here, take one of these. They make a crude sword, but they're better than none."

Anadyr accepted the sword as if she were presenting him with a precious gift.

"In Barrow the shanti are inflated with midden gas. The stench—mercifully, I was hardly able to smell anything—is appalling." Kichal was gazing speculatively at the series of pipes running across the high ceiling of the vast chamber that held the flying craft. He pointed. "See there, where that large tube fits into the end of the bag that lifted the craft?"

Caeled nodded.

"That is roughly the same arrangement the Duet use for fuelling their shanti. We need to follow that tube and see where it goes, Caeled."

The two men walked the length of the chamber with their heads tilted back, tracing the curve of the overhead piping.

"Are the Duet's shanti vulnerable in any way?" Caeled inquired as they walked.

"Yes. They are unstable; if the bag is burst and the gas escapes, they fall out of the sky and nothing can be done to save them. That's how those sea creatures destroyed the shanti that brought me here. They burst the bag." He laughed aloud. "If only the twins knew what happened to their grandiose scheme, how easily savage brutes undid them!"

Then the smile faded from his lips. "However, I don't think you will have much chance to attack the shanti, Caeled. I expect they will send a much larger fleet the second time; they may have as many as a hundred by now. If I was in command of that fleet I would attack from all sides simultaneously, using the warriors in some of the shanti to pour down a covering fire with the crossbows while the others' craft descended. Then those on the ground could lay down covering fire to allow the remainder of the fleet to land.

"Not all of them will attempt landing, however. Some will almost certainly remain in the air to coordinate and control the attack." Kichal stopped walking and pointed. "Here, look."

The tube that ran from the shanti fed into one of the tall cylinders Caeled had noticed when he first entered the chamber. The cylinders, in racks of ten, were fitted with nozzles which attached to a strange, flexible black pipe. The pipe connected the cylinders to the tubes. On top of each tube was a circular wheel.

Curious, Caeled reached out and gave the nearest wheel a spin with his silver hand. Long disused metal shrieked in protest. Then icy, bitter air hissed from the flexible pipe, blowing it to pieces. He swiftly forced the wheel back to its original position. The hissing air was cut off.

"I wonder . . ." Kichal murmured. He pulled his gloves from his belt and stuck one over the end of the tube and nodded at Caeled, who slowly turned the wheel. The fingers of the glove popped open. Kichal's grin was triumphant. "The Elders obviously discovered a way to capture the midden gas. If we can fix this . . ." he touched the ruined tube, "we can inflate this shanti."

Caeled stepped back to survey the rows of cylinders. "There seems an enormous quantity. Does midden gas burn?"

"It certainly does, it . . ." Kichal was gazing hard at the cylinders himself. He stepped close to one, applied his nose to the fitting at the top, inhaled deeply. "But this has no stink of middens."

Caeled was following his own line of thought. "I recall when one of the ovens in the kitchens at Baddalaur exploded. The flue was very old and warped and it must have become clogged with soot and grease, so the fire inside kept building with nowhere to go. Gases got trapped in the oven, we decided later. When it began to roar with a most terrible noise we all ran outside. Within moments the thing exploded; it hurled debris clear into the Central Courtyard."

Kichal turned to look at him with interest. "Did it indeed?"

Sioraf, sitting on the highest peak on the island, adjusted her vision to bring the figures on the beach far below into sharp focus. A group of children were swarming into the sea, laughing and shouting as if it were a game, and then running out again, carrying shells and stones which they deposited in large wicker baskets. Others were weaving slings for slingshots out of strips of leathery seaweed, while still others, under Gwynne's guidance, were pounding the edges of metal strips with rocks to beat them into cutting blades.

Most of the adults were engaged in blocking up the lower approaches and entrances to the caves. They did this swiftly and efficiently, with the familiarity of long practice. An Eron attack or the arrival of brigands on the island had long since taught them how to prepare for defense. Within special chambers deep inside the cliffs they kept enough food and fresh water stored to last through a relatively protracted siege.

But all their precautions would not be enough, Sioraf knew. The New Bred would come and take the isles and kill everyone on them. All they were doing was delaying the inevitable . . . just as she was with Caeled.

If she did not find fresh blood soon, she would be unable to keep from tearing him apart in her hunger. The appetite of a starving vampir was implacable.

A splash of color appeared on the far horizon, still too distant for human eyes. But vampir eyes were drawn to it instantly, pupils contracting, narrowing to slits, seeing the colors far differently than human eyes. Sioraf squinted . . . and discovered that the sky to the south was swarming with shanti.

She hissed, a soft, private sound, the plaintive cry of the vampire. Death was approaching: sure and certain death. Perhaps if she drank all of Caeled's blood now, without waiting, she would have enough strength to save herself. Not even the New Bred would be able to stand against a freshly fed vampire. Standing, she looked down onto the beach, then shook her head pitingly. All their preparations would be for naught.

They were all doomed.

she heard a soft, private sound, the gentle sigh of the wind. Death was a compassionate and certain cure. To spare the death of all of them she had now withdrawn life, so would soon extinguish it.

She tilted until the prow faced the sand. Leaning against a gently piled surface, shutting, she turned down onto the floor, even shedding their piety. All their expirations would then be manual.

They were all done.

CHAPTER FIFTY

With ponderous grace, the shanti floated over the horizon. They were as brilliantly colored as desert orchids against the evening sky, but like the Raqi orchid, whose scent is foul, these blooms exuded a disgusting odor. As they passed over the islands they left a nauseous miasma in their wake. For days afterward the rain would stink of faeces.

Abhel captained the lead shanti with the latest charts of the Island Sea—drawn by Blessed Sarel herself— spread out on the table before him. His forefinger—pale flesh that ended with a hooked black talon—tapped the chart, indicating an island that lay directly ahead. It looked as if it might be the island they sought; the headland was similar as was the curve of beach, and the narrow causeway connecting it to the next isle.

I have found Kichal's shanti!

Ebhena was commanding a shanti on the left wing of the formation; her thoughts instantaneously bridged the distance to her brother's mind. Nodding, Abhel moved his hand across the chart to locate the island which lay below his sister's aircraft.

There has been a battle here, I think, she informed
him. *I see bodies below; red-eyes and some other sort
of creature are scattered everywhere. And the Bred
Commander's shanti lies wrecked on the beach.*

Any sign of Kichal himself?

None.

So, thought Abhel; Blessed Sarel had been right.
Kichal's shanti had gone down. Sarel thought it might
have crashed and sunk due to natural causes, a storm
perhaps, but with the evidence of the battle it became
much more likely that some enemy had attacked the craft.
If so, had the Commander of the Bred survived?

Abhel had only seen Kichal once, on an occasion when
the famous red-eyed leader visited the training pens. One
of the New Bred had lost control and attacked the man.
As Abhel watched impassively, Kichal had torn out its
throat with his bare hands, as easily as he might scoop
the pulp from a fruit.

It was hard to imagine the Bred Commander being
taken prisoner.

Frowning, Abhel summoned a mental image of his
sister's face and sent his thought to her. *Drop down and
investigate.*

At once.

Abhel leaned his arms on the table to make it look as
if he was studying the chart, then closed his eyes.
Instantaneously he was sharing Ebhena's senses, seeing
what she saw, hearing what she heard. He was with her
as her shanti swung in low over the island and vented
its gases with a roar, enabling it to hover.

Then a rope ladder was lowered over the side and
Ebhena started to climb down. Through his sister's eyes,
Abhel watched the land and sea revolve beneath her as
she clambered down the swaying ladder, thick strands
of white hair blowing across her eyes. She was still three
man-heights about the ground when she dropped on all
fours onto the reddish sand of the beach.

Even before she straightened, Abhel knew as well as she did that nothing lived on the island. The stench of death was overpowering, stronger even than the odor from the shanti.

Ebhena picked her way through the scattered remains of the aircraft. The cloth bag was ripped open, the basket beneath was splintered. When she realized it was impossible to determine whether the shanti had crashed or been struck down, Ebhena turned to investigate the nearest body. *I'm looking at one of the red-eyes now.*

The original army of the Bred had been only marginally intelligent; the red-eyes were the human officers with which Blessed Sarel controlled them. They were formidable enough to dominate even the Bred because they no longer responded to pain or fear. The Bred Commander had been one of these.

The man over whom Ebhena now crouched had been speared twice in the chest and again through the back. Even so, he had taken a long time to die. *He continued to fight until the last moment,* Ebhena reported to her twin. *There is blood everywhere. He ignored his mortal agony.*

After he was dead, much of the flesh of his face and neck had been eaten away. Abhel, sharing his sister's thoughts, wondered just what sort of being had inflicted such damage.

Investigating further, Ebhena came upon the rotting remains of a sea creature covered in a mixture of fur and scales. *This is a hideous thing.* Two crossbow bolts still pierced its chest, but these had not caused its death. The neck had been snapped, the head turned almost completely around, yet like the red-eyes it had continued to fight while ichor leaked from its body and splattered the beach around it.

Whatever they are, they managed to bring down a fully armed shanti and kill or capture the crew. They were at least a match for Kichal's band of officers. Standing up, Ebhena dusted off her taloned hands. *And if they did take prisoners, I suspect they've eaten them by now.*

Returning to himself, Abhel opened his eyes and stared through the window of his own shanti at the island he was rapidly approaching. *I wonder, are there more such creatures on this island we're supposed to take? Are they allies of the Silverhand?*

Probably. Ebhena crouched and leapt upward, three times the height of a tall man, to catch the dangling rope ladder. She swarmed up it hand over hand. *But this time, they will not be attacking a solitary shanti.*

Abhel nodded. This time the enemy—whatever they were—would be facing the might of the New Bred, creatures much less human, and even more ruthless, than Kichal and his red-eyes. When Abhel and those like him were finished, no one would remain alive on the island.

"Give the order," he said aloud. "Let the shanti spread out according to the plan, encircle the island and then hold position. We will attack with the dawn."

Why wait? Ebhena wondered, even as she was repeating the order aloud to her own crew. *Why not attack tonight? The humankind do not like to fight in the dark.*

Remember, we may be fighting more than humankind. Perhaps these sea creatures can see at night as well as we do. No, let the humans become aware of us, let them spend a sleepless night worrying and exhaust themselves with their foolish emotions. Then we will attack with the dawn. Abhel walked to the bow of the craft and looked down at the isle: primitive, desolate. *Little wood for weapons, probably only with stone and bone tools, ill-fed, unarmored.* He bared his teeth in a savage grin. *By midday it will be all over,* he added confidently.

Will it even take that long? Ebhena wondered.

CHAPTER FIFTY-ONE

What you never had, you never missed.

Culp had been born with no legs. Although at the time of his birth he should, according to custom, have been put into a sand eel nest, his mother had successfully concealed him until he was two summers old. The People could condone the killing of the newborn because they believed infants were not yet occupied by a spirit when they first entered the world. But they could not countenance the killing of an older child who obviously contained a spirit.

Because of his deformity, Culp had grown to manhood viewing everyone and everything from below. But from an early age he found certain advantages to his reduced size. He could fit into nooks and crannies no one would suspect, enabling him to observe many supposedly private moments and overhear many secrets without being detected. Little happened on the island that Culp did not know about.

Nor were his movements as restricted as one might suppose. By his tenth summer he had explored as much of the island and its warren of caves as could be reached by a boy with abnormally strong arms, propelling his body on a flat trolley made of driftwood. The trolley was a creation of his own. Culp had no legs, but there was nothing wrong with his mind.

When he realized he had a natural skill for looking at a piece of driftwood and seeing the purposes to which it might be put, he had apprenticed himself to a carpenter. At first the other apprentices had made fun of the legless boy, but soon they learned to respect his skill. The wood seemed to tell him its secrets, so that instinctively he knew how to bend and shape it, and how much stress it would bear.

Once he had learned carpentry and surpassed his teacher, Culp went to work with the stonecutters. He soon found he had an equal talent with their material. He employed stone in ways the People had never attempted before. From there he went on to working with Eron leather and bone. Anything that required skill with hand and eye was a showcase for his talent. At six and twenty summers of age he was unanimously declared the master craftsman of the People. His crowning achievement was the creation of Tenjiku's walking frame.

Culp thought he was contented with his lot until the newcomer, Caeled, unleashed the Silverlight. Then for a few unforgettable moments he knew what it was like to have legs, to stand tall, to walk. To look other men in the eye.

When the Silverlight vanished and he was returned to his stunted condition, he was shaken with anger. Anger with the gods for having given him such a body, anger that he had been shown perfection only to lose it again. On a deeper level he was enraged to realize how much he had always longed to be normal, a fact he had successfully hidden from himself.

But Culp had lived with anger and frustration all his life. He had long since learned how to channel them, turning them into energy. The Silverhand had given him a tantalizing glimpse of how things could be if he secured the two missing artefacts. From that moment, Culp was determined to do everything in his power to make Caeled's quest successful.

Culp had long known about the caves in the lowest levels of the cliff face, but never attempted to negotiate his trolley down the steep, torturously twisting passages that led to them. He had seen enough in the upper caves, however, to make an educated guess at what must lie below.

But when Anadyr carried him down the narrow walkway that spiralled around the walls of the strange well and they entered the chamber where the enormous metal shanti waited, even Culp was astonished. He gasped like a child viewing stars for the first time.

"Put me down. Put me down now! I want to see for myself!"

Anadyr deposited him on the ground, then unstrapped Culp's trolley from his broad back and sat its builder upon it. Wooden wheels rumbling, the small man hastily propelled himself across the floor to examine the shanti at close range. Ignoring Caeled, Madran, and Kichal, who watched him with interest, he reached up, stretching himself to his limits to touch the underside of the carriage with reverent fingers. "The workmanship," he whispered. "Imagine the hands that made this."

Caeled crouched down beside him. "I need your help," he said simply.

Culp's smile was sardonic. "Most people do, sooner or later. That's the only time they pay any attention to me."

Caeled's metal fingers pointed. "That bladder atop the shanti was meant to be inflated with gases which travelled from those cylinders through those tubes on the walls and into the bag. But the connections between the cylinders and the tubes have perished. I am told you are a master craftsman; can you fashion something that will enable us to rejoin the two?"

"Lift me!" Culp commanded. "Let me see the connections myself."

At a nod from Caeled, Anadyr picked Culp up again, trolley and all, and carried him to where Kichal was standing beside the cylinders. Squinting in total concentration, Culp examined the situation from all angles. He pursed his lips. He nodded to himself. Several times he muttered, "Mmm."

Then he turned his face toward Caeled. "There are certain sections of Eron backbone that could be fitted to these with a bit of filing and adjustment, I think. Any possible leakage could be sealed off with pitch. The difficult part will be making sure the fitting is as snug as possible."

"How long will all of that take?" Caeled wanted to know.

"How long do we have?"

"The Duet's shanti fleet is on the horizon."

Culp frowned. "I will have to fit the bones, of course, and then apply several layers of pitch, allowing one to cool and grow firm before I put on the next. How much time do I have?"

Caeled looked at Kichal, who gave a negative shake his head. "If I was in command of that fleet I would attack now and not give the defenders of the island an opportunity to gather their forces. Or . . . they might hold off until dawn, knowing we are aware of them and hoping we will exhaust ourselves with sleeplessness."

"We just have to do the best we can," said Caeled. "You must work through the night, Culp. Now—what will you need?"

Culp ran delicate fingers across the metal cylinders. "I must have certain tools from my chamber, and the appropriate bones, of course. There is a supply in one of our storerooms. Backbones, mind you. You'll recognize them when you see them. And pitch, and Eron fat, and wood for a fire . . ."

Anadyr grunted. "I'm on my way. Where do I go to get everything?"

Culp gave him swift instructions. Within moments the scarred giant was running from the chamber, his footsteps echoing thunderously behind him. Culp listened to them for a moment with an unreadable expression on his face. Then he turned back to his task, measuring the openings with a skilled eye and a piece of leather thong he pulled from one of the many pockets in his clothing.

Satisfied, Caeled left him to it. Now that they were taking positive action he was trembling with an excess of nervous energy. The sensation was not unlike that of fear, but he had experienced fear before. This was different, strangely exhilarating.

Knowing he might die in the battle to come, he felt alive in every part of his being.

He joined Madran, who was standing below the huge double doors set high in the wall of the chamber. The Madra Allta gave him a swift, assessing glance. "Calm yourself," he advised. "You're feeling the energy that comes before a battle, but it's a dangerous excitement. It can exhaust you—and it can also make you reckless."

"I am calm," Caeled insisted.

Madran grinned. "If you say so." Jerking his chin in the direction of the doors, he asked, "Have you given any thought to opening these?"

"Not yet. We don't need to open them until we're sure we can fly the shanti."

"Somehow I feel confident that shanti will fly, Caeled. I'll take a look at these doors and see if they can be forced. Maybe our big friend Anadyr can help. In the meantime, you should ask Kichal to teach you what he knows about controlling this sort of craft. Unless, of course, the topic was part of your instruction at Baddalaur," he added mockingly. Madran's contempt for such education was obvious.

"I learned a lot at the College," Caeled replied seriously,

"but now I find that very little of it was of any practical use. I studied the history of shanti, for example, but there was no instruction at all in flying them."

Madran turned back toward the doors, placing his hands on his hips and craning his head to look up. Abruptly he divested himself of the sickle he always carried, crouched, and leaped to a height none of humankind could achieve. His gnarled toes curled around a narrow ledge at the base of the doors, while his fingers clutched the rim of a sunken recess heavily laced with spiderwebs. The doors were of solid metal, set onto a sort of metal track.

When Madran stood upright and gave them closer scrutiny, he found that the doors were untarnished, almost shiny. Objects made of New Metal developed rust within a very few days if not constantly oiled. But these doors were not New Metal.

Three cycles previously, the circus of which he had been a member had travelled south and west beyond Karfondal to the tiny principality of Klare. The country was accessible only through a series of narrow, easily defended mountain passes, and throughout its history had successfully resisted any attempt at conquest by its more powerful neighbors in the Seven Nations. The capital of Klare was exceptionally wealthy, with more metal used in the construction of its buildings than Madran had ever seen before. Some was Old Metal taken from the remnants of a nearby Elder city sunk beneath the waters of Red Lake. Though the metal had lain beneath the surface for generations before being reclaimed by Klarean divers, it was untarnished, almost shiny.

The circus had performed for the prince of Klare, a short, sharp-nosed man who had never once laughed or applauded throughout the performance, but had rewarded them all handsomely afterwards. Behind his royal throne—which consisted of a strange fitted seat covered with cracked leather—there had been a pair of metal

doors similar to those Madran was now examining. When
two ashen-skinned servants slowly turned metal wheels
set into recesses in the center of the doors, they had
slid open on metal tracks, flooding the palace with
sunlight.

Recalling this, Madran tore away more of the matted
webbing in the recess which provided his handhold. A
carrion spider appeared, mandibles clashing in anger at
the desecration of its home. Madran hammered it to pulp
with his fist so swiftly it had no chance to bite him, then
ducked his head and licked his hand clean before he
finished pulling away the last of the cobwebs.

His fingers touched rounded metal. A spoked wheel
was fitted into the recess.

Madran gave a bark of triumph. Once he had cleaned
out the dirt, greased the rails, oiled the wheels . . . the
doors just might open without having to be forced. And
if his sense of direction was as accurate as ever, they should
find themselves looking out into open space. Although
the vast chamber seemed to be deep underground, it was
somewhere near the base of the cliffs but not actually below
the ground level of the island, he felt sure. The vine-
obscured windows dimly revealed outside light.

Glancing over his shoulder, Madran tried to gauge
how big the shanti would become if the balloon was fully
inflated. It should pass through the door with room to
spare. Panting with excitement, he set to work.

When Caeled entered the central chamber Gwynne
hurried toward him. She tried to avoid the milling people,
but so many collided with her unyielding flesh that she
gave up apologizing.

She said to Caeled in an urgent tone, "The sentries
report sighting as many as two hundred shanti. Kichal
has told me there will be a minimum of fifty of the New
Bred to a shanti, though they can hold much more. So
that's . . ."

"I know, I can count," he replied through tight lips. He brushed past her, intent on his own thoughts.

Gwynne reached out and caught hold of the young man's silver hand. The metal sparked, sending green and blue fireflies dancing across the woman's stony fingers. Sighing, Caeled turned to look at her. "I know, Gwynne," he reiterated. "Even if the sentries can't count accurately you're badly outnumbered, you don't need to remind me."

"Outnumbered? There are twelve hundred people on this island, Caeled. A quarter of them are children, another quarter are unfit for any sort of fighting. That leaves at the most six hundred men, women and older children facing perhaps ten thousand!"

"You knew the odds would be high."

"High, yes—but this is impossible."

"Nothing is impossible," Caeled told her with a confidence he did not feel himself.

"We will need a miracle to defend this island."

"That's what I go in search of—a miracle."

"I need more, and I need it now," Gwynne insisted. "You must use the power of the two Arcana you have to kill the New Bred."

"No!" Caeled's voice rose. Heads turned to look. In a slightly quieter tone he said, "I won't use the Arcana to kill. That would . . . that would taint them."

"If you do acquire all four Arcana and attempt to reshape the world then many hundreds of thousands may die anyway. Not to mention the Duet."

"That's something I shall have to face when the time comes. Maybe, with so much power at my disposal, there will be another way . . ." But he knew there would not be.

Gwynne glared at him. "So you're going to do nothing to help us! We are supposed to sacrifice ourselves for you, but you won't help us."

"On the contrary, I'm going to do everything I can to

help you. But first let's go see what the situation is for ourselves." Caeled linked his arm through Gwynne's and drew her away. Surprised by the sudden intimacy, she allowed him to guide her up a narrow, steeply sloping tunnel that led from the central cavern, little more than an airshaft at the rear of the great chamber.

One of the children was lying in the mouth of a tiny cave at the end of the passage. She was gazing out at the sky with her face cupped in her hands, entranced by the spectacle of brightly colored shanti floating in space.

Looking over her head, Caeled began counting them. But he already knew it was a daunting number.

Gwynne knelt stiffly beside the child. "Come away, Zoe, you must rest."

The girl looked up. "But just see them, Nana! They are beautiful, like balloonfish!"

Gwynne put her head beside the child's and peered out. Closer than she had realized, their reflections mirrored on a calm twilight sea, a great fleet of shanti encircled the island. The last lingering light made them glow like dark jewels. Deadly jewels, filled with living poison.

The Stone Warrior lifted the girl to her feet, careful not to put too much pressure on the little one's excessively curved spine. "They are indeed beautiful," she agreed. She did not want to frighten the child unnecessarily, yet she must issue a warning. "But remember—the balloonfish you find washed up on the beach can sting. So can these. Come away now, do not let them see you."

The child nodded obediently, then reached up to pull Gwynne's head down to her own level and plant a kiss on the hard cheek. Smiling, she hurried back down the tunnel toward the cavern. As she watched her go, Gwynne unconsciously touched her fingers to her cheek.

Caeled stood beside her. "I can help that child and all the others too. I can give them, and you, healthy bodies. With the Arcana I can make this a perfect world."

Gwynne spat into the shadows. "This will never be a

perfect world. You are a fool to think otherwise. Repair the children, give them a chance at a life, and I will be content."

"I mean to heal them. And to restore your flesh as I promised you."

Gwynne looked out toward the shanti. "My flesh. Yes, I wanted that very much, as I wanted my husband and my own children back. But they can never return; the Void destroyed them. And if I don't get my true form back . . . I don't know, Caeled; perhaps it doesn't matter any more. Some things can never be as they were. Maybe they aren't supposed to be. We have to go on. I set out on this journey with you to avenge my husband and children, then make the twins undo what they had done to my body, and finally kill them. But things change."

"What are you saying?"

"The dream of revenge is no longer driving me. My family was everything to me, everything I ever had, all I ever wanted. Perhaps if we have time someday, Caeled, I will tell you how I rode with the Snowscalds, fought in the Border Wars, ran contraband to the independent coastal towns. They were good times in some ways, but the cycles were empty, the nights emptier. As I grew older, I felt the emptiness more and more.

"Then I met Silan. Oh, but he was handsome! I knew, almost from the first moment, that this man could take away my loneliness. After we pledged to one another I left the Snowscalds and began a new life. For the first time I was genuinely happy. Then Collum arrived and made it even better. Strong like his father, he would be nearly thirteen summers now. Two cycles later there was Marik, so mischievous and merry. After that came Nole, then Bevan. Silan and I thought our family was complete. Then quite unexpectedly we had one more daughter, our precious Derfyl."

Caeled rested his hand gently on Gwynne's shoulder. He could feel pain radiating from her in a raw wave.

"I had everything, everything. We were not wealthy and we had to work very hard, yet we had riches beyond measure. Until the twins took it all away. And I was alone again."

"You are not alone," Caeled whispered, but he knew the woman did not hear him.

"Then the fates led us here." Gwynne went on. "And suddenly I had something to live for, these children who need me. I don't mind their physical imperfections; to me they are beautiful. I cannot let the Duet take them from me too!" Her green eyes grew wild and pleading. "You have to help us, Silverhand!" the Stone Warrior cried.

"I will. Listen to me, Gwynne. I will. I've been thinking. Before the twins raided Baddalaur, they sent Voids into the heart of the College. When the Voids had done their work, the Bred arrived to finish the destruction." He glanced toward the waiting shanti. "I think that may be what they plan to do here."

"The Voids again?" The Stone Warrior's voice rose with uncharacteristic panic. "What can we do?"

"I am going to try and shield the People. But I need you to stand watch over me while I go into the Aethyra."

"It's too dangerous . . ." she started to say, but then she stopped. He knew the danger better than she did. They both vividly remembered what had happened the last time Caeled faced the twins in the Aethyra.

Caeled set his jaw. "I have learned that some choices we make ourselves; others are made for us. This is one of those."

CHAPTER FIFTY-TWO

Voids occurred naturally, if rarely, in nature. Some believed they dated from the Time of Burning, possibly even being a result of that cataclysm, for there was no mention of them in the surviving literature of the Elder Days. A body of folklore had grown up surrounding the Voiding of Cerce, the last Elder city to be inhabited. In a day and a night the entire city, with a population of fifty thousand humankind and Allta, had been consumed by an immense, ravening Void. The swirling grey storm of nullity had finally collapsed upon itself with a characteristic scream, but by that time every living thing was destroyed.

Now Cerce was a habitat for bitter ghosts. Travellers would willingly add two or three days to their journey rather than pass close to the site, where the air still glowed above a vast pit filled with green glass.

When the twins first began experimenting with Voids they had studied the natural phenomena, particularly a static Void that hung above the marshlands south of Barrow. Old maps showed that the marshes had once been desert, high above sea level. When the Time of

Burning brought an end to the Elder Days, the shape and structure of the world was altered.

The marsh Void, a ball of whirling grey smoke little bigger than a human head, spun endlessly above the broken metal skeleton of an enormous boat half buried in waterlogged earth. Sarel and Lares sent countless slaves to the Void, watching dispassionately the effects the ball wrought on a fleshy body. Some, who were pushed forward until they fell into its center, simply vanished; others had their internal organs sucked out of them until their bodies burst open like wet sacks. And there were those who went insane before they even touched the ball.

The Duet had observed with coldly clinical interest the way a human hand, thrust into the Void, could be sheared off as neatly as if it had been amputated by a skilled surgeon. Better, in fact, because the Void cauterized the wound in the same process.

Often, proximity to a Void was enough to cause massive change. Human flesh would begin to decay on a living body; Allta fur would crisp and sear. In no two instances, however, were the effects identical. There seemed to be some individual quality in each live organism that predetermined its response to the Void.

"Perfume smells different on every woman," Sarel had commented in an effort to explain the phenomenon.

Their first attempts at controlling Voids had been crude and uncertain, the result of random curiosity rather than calculated effort. But as hundreds of slaves died the twins perfected their technique. Within a cycle, the Duet could successfully manipulate natural Voids. Within two, they had mastered the art of developing their own. These creations proved more amenable to their control. By the middle of the third cycle they could bring into being Voids of almost any size. Lares worked with large ones of great destructive power, while Sarel preferred to experiment with minuscule Voids. She learned how to insert these into a man's head and numb or destroy selected parts of his mind while leaving the rest of him unharmed and functional.

The twins' delight in their creations knew no bounds when they discovered that the natural energy of physical passion, properly channelled, fuelled the Voids.

Sarel felt tension in her brother's shoulders and stopped moving. She was acutely conscious of the level of her own arousal, but they needed to climax together.

It was through the explosion of their combined sexual energy that their Voids would be created.

Lares opened his eyes, violet eyes, and looked up into his sister's face, a mirror image of his own. "I'm almost ready," he whispered, licking sweat from his top lip. She smiled and danced her tongue briefly over his.

Then she asked, "Can you see the island?"

Lares closed his eyes again. On the far side of the Seven Nations, Abhel shuddered, feeling the other's presence crawl through his skull. The New Bred captain concentrated on the isle directly ahead, fearing even to think of his sister in case the twins sensed the link between them, and realized they could communicate without sound.

"I see it clearly," Lares replied to her question.

Sarel pressed herself against her brother's body, fitting every swelling and hollow to the corresponding contours of Lares. She did not need to see the island through Abhel's eyes; she could see it through her brother's. Lares wrapped his arms around her smooth flesh, palms pressed to her back, fingertips against her spine, and started her moving atop him again.

Within a handful of heartbeats, their passion took them . . .

. . . wrenching them from their bodies, melding their forms together into a single figure of jet and glass, neither male nor female but something of both. Thus joined, they soared into the Aethyra while a huge wave spread out around them: the roar known as the White Scream.

The Scream was at once total sound and a negation of sound. Its volume was sufficient to burst the eardrums, yet it could not be heard in the normal sense. Instead it vibrated through flesh and bone, setting up an unbearable harmonic.

Tiny tears appeared in the fabric of the Aethyra, grew monstrously, shivered the Dreamscape. The White Scream became the birth cry of the Voids.

The stars moved.

Gwynne, standing in the mouth of Caeled's cave and watching the night sky anxiously as she cursed her stiffening optic nerves, saw the stars flicker. The big woman blinked, looked again. For a moment everything seemed black and she wondered if the blindness she had long feared had overtaken her. The very thought terrified her.

Glancing over her shoulder, she was relieved to discover she could very dimly make out Caeled's body lying prone on his pallet. If he was successful, everything would be all right. She would have her flesh and sight and be whole again. If he failed—the children—she did not want to think of what would happen if he failed.

Planting the head of her morningstar on the ground, folding both hands over the end of the haft and leaning on it like a crutch, the Stone Warrior turned back to the night. She was dismayed to discover that one by one, the stars were winking out of existence, vanishing into strange spherical clouds whose outlines were blurred by mist, though the clouds themselves were shot through with sparkling colors. She counted at least eight of the spheres. At the same time she became aware of a barrage of conflicting odors. Raw meat, flowers, herbs, faeces, spices, urine, rot.

She had smelled something similar once before; memories roiled, anguish surfaced . . . she had smelled similar odors when the Void took her family!

✧　　　✧　　　✧

Slowly, almost gently, the misty Voids dropped toward the island.

He had risen high into the Aethyra, as high as Tenjiku had taken him, until he could feel the pressure of the upper levels beginning to press on him. There were thirty planes in the Aethyra; no one, Caeled knew, even the adept Maseriel, had ever claimed to reach the uppermost levels.

As he climbed through the Dreamscape he mimicked a shape Tenjiku had used, that of an amorphous dark cloud with a hint of widespread wings. He wrapped his silver hand in layers of mist to disguise its true nature. Then he waited. Perhaps the twins would not come to him. For his own sake he hoped they would not, but he felt certain they would.

This time at least he was ready for them. His physical body was below, well guarded, and the two Arcana, the Stone and the Spear were clutched in his hands. When needed, he could draw upon them.

He watched shapes moving in the Aethyra below: the spirits of sleeping humans, drawn in their dreams by the gathering of dangerous energies around the island. There were other forms as well in the grey and featureless landscape, creatures neither man nor Allta. Aethyra dream-shapes, nightmares, sleep-terrors, all were being summoned by the events unfolding in the Island Sea. No one would sleep on Home Isle this night, but perhaps it was just as well.

Caeled noted that the atmosphere above the island was sparking with color. Even the auras of small children and the very old were abnormally agitated. There were cooler, calmer spots of light here and there; he recognized staunch Madran's tell-tale signature, and Gwynne standing solid before the mouth of the cave.

His Aethyra vision found Sioraf, lonely and alone atop

a stone spire. On this evening her aura was the color of blood. Anadyr was prowling through the caves in the cliff, making certain all the external openings were sealed and the defenders armed and in position. Kichal was still in the depths, in the chamber with the metal shanti, working with Culp, who radiated pulsing hues of excitement.

Suddenly Kichal's aura blazed too. Caeled guessed that they had managed to link the cylinders to the shanti.

There was nothing to do but wait, then. Wait until the Duet discovered him, or the shanti fleet attacked, or . . .

What appeared to be a black cinder was caught in the web of the Dreamscape. As Caeled watched, puzzled, a second and then a third materialized. Within moments there were eight of them ripping open the fabric of the Aethyra.

And Caeled realized he was seeing the birth of Voids.

Rasriel felt them and knew at once what they were. A thrill of horror ran through him. Crawling out from the burrow where he and his three surviving followers had passed the day, he rolled over on his back and looked toward the sky, adjusting his vision in the manner of a trained Adept so he could gaze into the Aethyra from the physical world. As he watched in dismay, the tiny sparks grew with frightening speed. He saw them coalesce into spinning spheres, then burst from the Aethyra into the World Below.

Behind them he glimpsed a single androgynous form directing and controlling the Voids like a puppet master. Yet beyond this there was something else, something impossibly vast and . . . but the Voids were expanding faster now, swallowing the stars as they would soon swallow the island.

The irony of the situation was inescapable. He had avoided the destruction of Baddalaur, survived to revitalize the Seekers, sacrificed one hundred virgins to bring him to this place . . . only to arrive just in time to fall victim to the Voids once more.

Rasriel had a sardonic sense of humor that only surfaced on the most unlikely occasions. For the first time since the fall of Baddalaur, he threw back his head and laughed.

His laughter sounded like the howl of a demented beast.

CHAPTER FIFTY-THREE

With the dawn, the Voids dropped toward the World Below, growing larger as they came, inexorably drawn to their prey, to life.

Silver light.

Ice cold, knife sharp, a lance of light as pure as crystal.

Silver light!

An expanding beam of breathtaking beauty, pulsing argent and sterling.

Silverlight!

It came flooding out of the Aethyra to blaze above the island in a flat, spinning disc. The disc seemed to draw the beams of the rising sun unto itself until it glowed with an intolerable radiance. The light hovered, then slowly curved downward at the edges to enclose Home Isle in a translucent dome.

When the first Void struck the dome it clung there, unable to break through. A second and third followed until all eight Voids were transfixed, pinned to the shielding silver light.

The creature that was Sarel and Lares howled with rage, pouring their joint anger into the largest of the

Voids. Ravening nullity roared with their voices. Jagged forks of lightning crackled around the trapped Void, briefly outlining the dome that protected the island. The Void screamed again; the lightning danced. Then there was a sound like some impossibly huge tree splitting down its center. The Void collapsed upon itself, turning from grey nothingness to a constantly shrinking blackness that grew heavier and heavier as it shrank until at last it imploded. A mighty rush of air was sucked through the hole it created in the atmosphere.

The discharge of forces surged through the Aethyra like a tidal wave, flinging Sarel and Lares into the upper reaches of the Ghost World. The single creature which was the Duet split into images of emerald and alabaster, then of goldwood and granite, before finally assuming twin shapes of flesh with violet eyes and amber hair—and faces white with shock.

"It's the Silverhand; he is behind this!" cried Lares, straining to be heard above the wind now howling through the Aethyra.

Sarel's eyes were blazing. "Think what we could do with the power he is wielding!"

Her brother nodded. A single thought flashed between them, an urge to action.

They became hawk and vulture, winging through the Aethyra, following a gossamer thread that flowed from the silver light like an umbilical cord. "I see him!" Sarel's voice was a harsh caw.

Caeled's Aethyra form was almost fully concealed by a roiling purple cloud. But his silver hand was visible. The fingers were spread, and from them flowed the silver light.

The twins struggled to get to him, but the power of the Arcana rolled out in waves, driving everything off the higher levels, pushing the various entities in the Aethyra down to the lower levels.

In order to combine their strength, the Duet forced

themselves back into a single body. Any effort was incredibly difficult. The surging Arcana force was like a mighty headwind buffeting the Dreamscape. As they fought to reach Caeled the twins found themselves surrounded by numerous gelatinous beings, shocked inhabitors of the Aethyra. All were seething, searching, struggling to regain what passed for normalcy in the World Above.

When the Duet were still two levels below the Silverhand, he turned to look down at them. His face was a metallic mask. His eyes were discs of molten silver. Slowly, a mere flexing of his fingers, he closed his left hand into a fist and opened it again . . . and a solid ball of cold silver light exploded into the Duet. The missile's impact tore apart their combined image and knocked them into separate entities once more. Helpless to save themselves, they tumbled all the way down to the lowest level of the Aethyra, the level of dreams.

"He's too strong for us, sister!" Lares gasped in disbelief.

"The Arcana is too strong," Sarel corrected. "But he can't keep it up forever. All we have to do is wait until he tires; he's still human, and using the Arcana must be tremendously exhausting."

"But the Voids won't wait," her brother pointed out. Even as he was speaking, another of the deadly Voids collapsed in on itself. Tiny black cinders, impossibly heavy, spun away and through the Aethyra, tearing minute holes as they went.

"What can we do?" Sarel groaned.

"Nothing." The voice that answered her was harsh, arrogant.

The twins whirled around to find themselves confronting the flickering image of a lean, white-robed man. Although his narrow face was turned in their direction, his eyes were closed. "You can do nothing," he told them coldly, "but I can."

"Begone . . ." Lares began, but Sarel put out her hand and silenced her brother.

"Who are you?" she demanded.

"I am Rasriel. I am the Hieromonach of the Seekers Reborn."

Lares snorted. "You lie. The Seekers are no more, we destroyed them in Baddalaur."

"You destroyed the weak and the foolish. My Seekers are the survivors, and we follow the old ways. Ways you would approve of, I think."

"What do you want?" asked Sarel.

He appeared to smile, but with his eyes closed the expression was strangely chilling. "Only to help you."

"How?"

"The Silverhand's physical body is on the island below."

"We cannot penetrate the silver shield," Lares said.

"My physical body is on the island below . . . beneath the silver shield."

The twins watched him, saying nothing. Waiting.

The Hieromonach went on, "The Silverhand maintains the shield by drawing upon the power of the Arcana. But remove the Arcana . . ."

". . . and the shield collapses." Sarel finished. "I'm aware of that. Can you do it? Can you take the Arcana from him?"

"I can. The defenders will not be expecting an attack from someone already on the island and inside the dome."

"And in return?" Lares asked. "Surely you must want something in return. We are not such fools as to believe you would help us out of the goodness of your heart."

"The goodness of my heart?" Rasriel laughed; the very concept was amusing. His laughter was more terrifying than his smile. "Oh, I will be asking a lot."

"If you are successful, we can give you all that you ask for, and more," Lares said.

"Do it, then," Sarel told him. She swiftly clothed her naked female shape in armor of leather and metal, with a heavy helmet on her amber hair. Beside her, Lares duplicated the image.

"Do it, Rasriel, and your reward will be greater than you think. But do not kill the Silverhand. Tear the Arcana from his grasp, then let our Voids and the army of the New Bred have his followers. We shall enjoy playing with this creature as a cat plays with a . . ."

She broke off abruptly. Rasriel was gone.

On the island below, the Hieromonach opened his eyes. He could taste blood and bile in his mouth and every organ in his body felt bruised. Gazing up into the sky, he could dimly make out the dome of silver light shielding the island. He rolled over and got to his feet, ignoring his discomfort. As he gazed up at the stern face of the cliffs, he could almost feel the cavern where the physical form of the Silverhand lay dreaming.

With his own two hands, he would take the Arcana from Caeled nam Myriam. He might give them to the Duet, or . . .

Or . . .

Once he had been terrified of the Duet. Fleeing the ruins of Baddalaur, Rasriel had wanted nothing more than to forget that the twins and their Voids and armies ever existed. But since then he had acquired power of his own. With success came confidence, and with confidence, ambition.

He realized that anyone possessing even two of the Arcana was a match for Sarel and Lares. If he kept the Arcana for himself, he need never fear the Duet again.

It was a very tempting idea.

But whatever he decided, Rasriel would not let the twins and their minions have the erstwhile Scholar from Baddalaur.

It would give him such pleasure to kill the Spoken One himself.

CHAPTER FIFTY-FOUR

Rasriel killed the man without a second thought. His stiffened fingers crushed the soft tissues of the throat, then he snapped the head to one side in a swift, violent movement that broke the neck. Followed by the three surviving Seekers Reborn, he stepped over the still-shuddering corpse and continued down the narrow defile between towering walls of stone.

Several such fissures ran deep into the striped cliffs. As they reconnoitered the area, this one had seemed the most promising, being wide enough for a person to walk through, the ground worn and smoothed by the passage of many feet. If there was a secret route by which someone could enter the heart of the Islanders' stronghold, Rasriel's intuition told him this must be it.

A crunch of gravel warned there was someone ahead of them in the defile. Rasriel signalled silence. They continued to advance stealthily until they came up behind a hunchbacked woman carrying a large basket of dried fish. She was shuffling along as fast as she could, obviously in a great hurry to get somewhere. Somewhere safe.

When she heard footsteps close behind her the woman

turned around, tattooed lips curling into a smile. Before she could speak, Rasriel lunged forward and struck beneath her nose with the edge of his hand, driving splinters of bone and cartilage into her brain. She dropped her basket as she collapsed; he caught her body and flung it to one side. Her dried fish were trampled beneath his feet.

Reaching the end of the defile, the Hieromonach stopped and raised one hand. His followers understood. Swiftly and silently they concealed themselves within the vertical folds of the fissure and awaited his next order.

A cavemouth loomed directly ahead. Like the other caves they had seen, its entrance was sealed with boulders—but here a small space had been left so a person could squeeze through. Rasriel glimpsed movement beyond the opening. Guards within, no doubt.

As he hesitated, trying to decide the best way to force entry, a trio of children approached carrying baskets filled with rounded stones that would serve the People as missiles.

Rasriel flattened himself against the wall of the crevice. "There is a back door," he whispered over his shoulder to the men behind him. "One entrance left for the last stragglers. How humane. We will have to act quickly, before they seal the opening altogether. Stand aside there, let me pass by you." He eased past his men and went back down the defile to the dead woman. The pathos of her huddled form meant nothing to him. He saw her only as something that could still be useful. Bending, Rasriel stripped the worn and patched cloak from her body and wrapped it around himself. Then he picked up her basket, tossed in the remnants of fish, and lifted it to his shoulder, holding it in such a way as to conceal his face.

Returning to the other three, he told them in a harsh whisper, "Follow my lead. Once we're inside, you know what to do." He started for the cavemouth without bothering to look back, adopting a half-crouching posture that made his back appear hunched, and shuffling like the woman he had just killed.

All his life he had been travelling toward this place and time, he thought as he slouched toward the cave. Less than a cycle ago he had been the Hieromonach at Baddalaur, successor to the revered Maseriel. He believed then that he had reached the epitome of achievement. When Baddalaur was destroyed, he had thought his life was destroyed too.

How wrong one could be!

In the aftermath of that holocaust, despair had been his constant companion, the same despair that had eaten at the soft, well-fed faces of his companions, leaving them haggard, sunken-eyed and desperate. But he had shaped those same men into the Seekers Reborn during their long trek in search of a safe haven. Only his will had kept them going, only his will had pushed them on. His will. His indomitable will.

Yes, thought Rasriel. My will be done.

Now he was on the verge of true greatness. Since he faced the twins in the Aethyra plans had been formulated in his brain almost without need for conscious thought. Like one following his destiny, he had recognized the track laid out for him.

By this time next cycle he would rule the Seven Nations—through the Duet. The twins would be his minions, bowing to him as they had forced others to bow to them.

The prospect made his pulse thunder with excitement.

Holding up his basket to block the guards' view, Rasriel inserted his body into the partially blocked entranceway. At the same time his followers ran forward to take up positions on either side of the cavemouth.

A hand possessing only thumb and forefinger caught Rasriel's arm and pulled him into the cave. "Hurry along, you. Is there anyone else still out there?" The voice was high-pitched, almost feminine, though the speaker was male.

"A few," Rasriel replied. Tossing the basket aside, with one blow he crushed the man's larynx. A second guard, white-faced with terror, fumbled with a makeshift sword, but Rasriel's foot caught the girl in the center of her chest, shattering her breastbone and collapsing her lungs. Blood bubbled onto her lips as she staggered backward.

When he was a Seeker at Baddalaur, Rasriel, like Caeled, had been thoroughly trained in the arts of battle. The Seekers went out into an uneasy world. He had spent all his life in the College and never used his martial arts except in training. Recently, however, he had discovered how much he enjoyed the physical act, the thud of flesh, the crack of bone, the tear of muscle.

Killing was an unexpected source of pleasure.

Grinning to himself, Rasriel hastily flung off the encumbering cloak and stepped back to allow his men to squeeze through the opening into the cave. One snatched the first guard's spear while another took the dying girl's sword, testing its edge on her throat.

When they were satisfied both guards were dead, they took a look at their surroundings.

They found themselves in a long narrow cave that sloped upward toward a circular opening too perfect to be accidental. Beyond that opening, orange firelight glowed. Shadows moved and writhed on the walls and voices, tense with excitement, drifted down. From somewhere came a nervous laugh.

"Do what you have to," Rasriel said. The Seekers nodded. The plan was simple. They would circulate through the caves, creating as much mayhem as possible, while Rasriel made his way to the place where the Silverhand's physical body waited . . . with the Arcana.

The metal shanti shuddered. Then as if a huge beast were drawing breath, filling its lungs, the bladder began to inflate. The long-disused fabric rustled and crackled but did not tear. A cheer rang through the chamber. Those of the People who had come to watch crowded around Culp to congratulate him. The press of bodies threatened to crush the little man until Anadyr lifted him onto his shoulders.

Kichal stepped up to Anadyr, nodded to the man perched atop him and held out his hand. Culp leaned forward and took it.

"You've done a masterly job. When the People sing of the heroes of the isle, your name will be mentioned," Kichal assured him.

Culp felt unaccustomed color burn in his cheeks. "I just did what I could," he said modestly. "What happens now?"

"Now I need a strong man," Madran interjected as he joined them. He was wiping grease from his hairy forearms. Over their heads the balloon swelled and surged, filling steadily. "We better get those doors up there open before the balloon gets too big to pass through them," the Madra Allta said. "Kichal, send someone for Caeled, will you? We could be away from here very soon."

"I'll go," volunteered Anadyr.

Culp patted the Islander's scarred head. "Put me down, I'll go for the Silverhand. Your strength is needed here."

Bending over, Anadyr gently lowered the legless man onto his trolley. He glanced around and caught a squat, powerfully built Islander by the shoulder. "Carry Culp to the upper levels," he ordered.

The man opened his mouth as if to protest, but closed it again when he saw that Anadyr, Kichal and Madran were all looking at him. He picked up Culp and his trolley and pushed his way through the crowd.

Madran told the others, "I've cleaned away a lot of dirt and rust from the doors, but I still haven't been able to open either of them. I'll need help." He leaped up onto the ledge and almost slid off again thanks to the

Eron fat he had used to grease the rail. He caught hold of one of the wheels recessed in the doors to steady himself, then turned to call down to Kichal and Anadyr. He had to shout to be heard over the roar of the inflating balloon. "Come on up here!" Hanging on to the wheel with one hand, he reached out and down with the other.

Kichal hesitated, measuring the height dubiously. But Anadyr reached up and caught Madran's hand. He hauled himself up, grunting and wheezing, his weight almost breaking Madran's hold on the wheel. When the scarred giant stood beside him on the metal track, Madran said, "These wheels open the doors, I know that. But they're very hard to move, and I'm not even certain which way to turn them."

"To the left," replied Anadyr, surprising him. The big Islander grinned, displaying broken teeth. "I lived on Seamount for many cycles. The townspeople in Rock all bar their doors at night. The bars are set onto the left-hand side of the door and drop down to the right. It is an ancient custom," he added, "unchanged for generations."

"Left it is then." Madran gripped one wheel tightly. "You take the other one," he told Anadyr. Then he called down to Kichal, "We'll try to turn them together so the doors open at the same time. I don't think they will open unless we do both at once. One seems fitted into the other in some way."

"Do it on my mark, then," Kichal shouted from below, glad to take a useful part and thankful that it was Anadyr and not himself teetering on the greased ledge above. "Are you ready?"

"Yes."

"Ready."

"Turn!"

Gritting their teeth, Anadyr and Madran strained at the ancient wheels.

Nothing happened.

"Again!" shouted Kichal.

Muscles cracking, veins swelling beneath taut skin, they leaned into the wheels. For a long moment nothing happened. Then slowly, slowly, with a screech like souls in torment, the wheels began to turn.

Rasriel killed fifteen and left another ten dying as he fought his way through the warren of caverns and tunnels, seeking Caeled. It gave him a certain pleasure to use the Islanders' own weapons against them. He now carried two mismatched swords made of pieces of bent and folded metal. As he worked his way upward, he could hear faint screams of terror coming from below and knew the Seekers Reborn were fulfilling his instructions.

A young man loomed up before him. As the youth started in surprise, Rasriel cut him down with a slashing stroke that almost took his head from his body.

He was close now, so close that he could taste power in the atmosphere, feel the energy swirling around him like an invisible current. Yes, he thought. Yes!

He was breathing very hard, though not from exertion, as he hurried one.

The caves were in chaos.

Culp's immediate reaction was that the Bred had managed to land on the island and break into the stronghold. There were bodies of the dead and injured everywhere, and fires were burning out of control in the great central cavern. Somewhere close by a child was sobbing as if its heart would break. Elsewhere the clash of Gwynne's metal weapons could be heard, mingling with shouts and curses and shrieks of pain.

"Put me down!" Culp commanded the man who was carrying him. "Run back and tell the others what's happening!"

But the Islander ignored him, racing off instead to seek his own wife and children. Culp followed the thread of his voice calling for them until it ended in a gurgling scream.

The legless man knew he had to warn the others. On his trolley he scooted back down the tunnel to the pit, then leaned over and peered into its depths. But he would never be able to negotiate the sloping, spiralling trackway that led to the metal shanti's chamber. He would have to go up instead, find and warn the Silverhand and Gwynne.

Pressing his hands flat to the ground he pushed off again, the small wooden wheels squeaking, the trolley rattling over the uneven ground. He moved through the tunnels as fast as a man with legs could walk. At last he came to a large rectangular ornament fitted into a tunnel wall. Sliding his knife blade under the edge of the engraved panel, he levered it off to reveal a square metal tube that disappeared into darkness. Without hesitation Culp caught hold of the lip of the metal tube, hoisted himself off his trolley and into the dark.

His small size kept him from many things, but it also had its advantages. He had discovered these metal passageways during his lonely childhood, when he could not play as the other children did and had learned to entertain himself by exploring. It had taken him four cycles to map all of the tubes that ran inside the walls. When he was finished, he realized they connected many of the island caves. Those which led to the lowest caves ended in a tangle of twisted metal and stone rubble.

Culp's trolley would not fit through the opening. But he could get along quite well by pulling himself along with his elbows and sliding on his belly, for the surface was smooth and seamless. He travelled in unrelieved lightlessness, relying on memory to bring him to the level where he would find Caeled and Gwynne.

As he scooted along he prayed to all the gods of the Island Sea that he would not be too late.

Rasriel rounded a curve in the tunnel and ducked back immediately. There was a woman, another island abomination, standing guard outside a small cave. A studded morningstar leaned against the wall beside her. The vibrations emanating from within the cave told Rasriel he had found Caeled—and the Arcana. No Adept could mistake those waves of raw power.

Now all he had to do was to get past the woman. Leaning the upper part of his body slightly forward, he risked a glance in her direction. She was a freak all right, massive and strangely stiff, with roughened skin that looked almost like stone. She was kneeling, speaking earnestly with a small boy who had a withered left leg. As Rasriel watched, the boy flung his arms around the freak's neck and hugged her, then came limping down the tunnel directly toward the Hieromonach.

Gwynne watched Mock limp away. The boy had brought her something to eat—strips of dried fish and a cup of cool, if brackish, water—and the simple gesture had moved her deeply. When he asked if she wanted to rest she had explained, "I must continue to keep watch. Caeled made the dome of Silverlight that is protecting us all, and I must see that nothing disturbs him or it might weaken the dome."

Suddenly Caeled groaned aloud, a cry of pain and despair. Gwynne turned to peer into the cave. She was shocked by his appearance. In the short space of time since he lay down, he had aged visibly and lost weight. His face was ashen, with deep shadows like bruises beneath his eyes, and there was more silver in his hair. Even as she watched, color leeched from his eyebrows, leaving them white and feathery.

"Caeled," the Stone Warrior called softly. Perhaps it would be dangerous to wake him . . . but if he remained sleeping, and ageing so fast, there was a possibility he might not wake up.

Not for the first time she wondered just what the Arcana did to the user. They made him strong, but at what cost? And how much longer could he maintain the shield in place without destroying himself?

"Nana!"

Gwynne wheeled around, automatically reaching for her morningstar. But she froze when she saw the sharp-featured man holding a blade of her own devising to Mock's throat. As she watched in horror he pressed the weapon against the pale flesh until a thin scarlet line appeared and drops of blood oozed out, dropping onto the little boy's thin chest.

CHAPTER FIFTY-FIVE

"I will kill him," said Rasriel. His voice was flat, matter-of-fact. Gwynne never for a moment doubted that he meant what he said. She had been a warrior for too long; she had learned to recognize the expression she saw on his narrow face, the emptiness in his lightless eyes. It was a malaise which overcame even the most honorable of warriors, that time when human life ceased to have any meaning and any action became acceptable, even excusable.

Shortly after seeing her reflection in a pool with that same emptiness in her own eyes, Gwynne had left the Snowscalds. Silan had come along just in time. When he promised to give her a home and family, he had offered her a way out before the warrior life destroyed the last vestiges of humanity inside her.

But she could not bear to think of Silan . . .

The Hieromonach gestured with the sword. "Step aside. I have no quarrel with you, I want the Silverhand."

"Let the boy go first," Gwynne replied. Her voice was as rock-solid as her body.

Rasriel responded with a chill smile. On his gaunt face

it resembled the rictus of a corpse, a death's head image. Wrapping long fingers in the boy's hair he drew Mock's head back, stretching the young neck to a painful angle. The ragged edge of the metal sawed at his flesh. Mock squirmed desperately but he was no match for Rasriel. The torn skin of his throat parted further. If the cut went any deeper, he would either bleed to death or die of shock and pain.

"You are in no position to make demands," said Rasriel in that same uninflected voice. "I can kill him now and be done with it."

"NO! . . . No," she added, lowering her voice to avoid provoking the man.

The tendons grew taut in Rasriel's arm as he prepared to make the fatal cut. Locking eyes with Gwynne, he commanded, "Move away from your weapon. Step back from the door."

With an effort, the Stone Warrior tore her gaze from Rasriel's face to look at Mock instead. The little boy's cheeks were ashen and tears were brimming in his eyes. Yet he was gazing back at her with absolute trust and confidence. He did not doubt she would protect him.

Then she looked at the sword menacing his life; the weapon she had fashioned. Stained, now, with his blood, as well as clotted hair and gore from the others Rasriel had slain.

Gwynne drew a deep breath. There was no decision to be made. She was not willing to lose another child.

Slowly, deliberately, she stepped out of the cavemouth, moving away from her morningstar. "The Silverhand means nothing to me," she assured Rasriel. "You can have him if you want him. Just release my boy."

"Your boy?" Rasriel echoed sarcastically. "Freaks together, eh?" He momentarily loosened his grip on Mock and the child surged forward. Then on sudden impulse the Hieromonach jerked him back again.

He grinned his death's head smile at the Stone Warrior.

She was different from the other Islanders, he noticed. Her peculiar skin was devoid of tattoos. And though she was uncommonly stiff and awkward, there was something about the way she moved that made him think she could be dangerous. He was unsure if her skin was as hard as it looked, but he suspected killing her would not be easy. "Perhaps I'll keep your boy with me," he told her. "Just to encourage you to behave yourself."

"Who are you?" Gwynne wanted to know. "I don't understand any of this. Can you explain what's going on?" Suddenly it was important to keep his attention fixed on herself. At the very periphery of her gradually failing vision she caught a glimpse of Caeled moving restlessly on his pallet, as if he was trying to awaken. Perhaps if she could keep Mock's assailant talking long enough . . .

"I am Rasriel, once Hieromonach of the Order of the Way," he said haughtily. "But the Order is no more. Now I lead the Seekers Reborn." He smiled at Gwynne's look of surprise. "As for what's happening—there is no need for you to know. Some freak's understanding of the situation is of no benefit to me."

Gwynne throttled a quick surge of anger. Keep him talking, she reminded herself. "Does everything have to be of benefit to you?" she asked innocently.

Rasriel appeared to be astonished that anyone could even ask such a question. To him the answer was obvious. His eyes flashed within their deep sockets. "What I want, I get! And I have come for the Arcana."

"Then let me bring them to you." She made a move towards the door. Rasriel shifted weight in one fluid motion and without loosening his hold on Mock, thrust the sword forward until its point was perilously close to one of Gwynne's eyes.

"Back off," he ordered.

Instead—and without even blinking—Gwynne wrapped her hand around the blade. Rasriel tried to pull the weapon back, but Gwynne moved with him, her weight like an anchor. Her other hand caught Mock by the shoulder and wrenched him from Rasriel's grasp, flinging him away from the pair of them. The child hit the ground hard but did not cry. In a moment he was scuttling on hands and knees into Caeled's cave.

Rasriel realized he had seriously misjudged the woman. He tried to rotate the blade in her hand in order to slice her palm open. But she tightened her grip as if impervious to pain. Thick, honey-colored fluid streaked with blood leaked from between her fingers. "I'm going to kill you," she announced in tones as cold and implacable as those used by Rasriel himself.

He released the sword and lifted his right knee, then drove his foot into the woman's abdomen . . . and rebounded as if he had kicked a wall. Terrible shooting pains ran up his leg.

Still holding the sword by its blade, Gwynne twisted the weapon into a useless ring while Rasriel gaped at her, dumbfounded. Then she tossed it aside. "I think I'll kill you with my bare hands," she told him.

The strain was killing him.

In his Aethyra persona he should not be aware of his mortal heartbeat, his breathing, his cramping muscles. In the Aethyra the traveller could become anything he or she desired, leaving behind the aches and pains of a fleshy body.

But Caeled was in pain now. His metal hand was white with heat, throbbing in time to the pulsing waves of silver light that poured down through the Aethyra to arc over the island. Simultaneously he was aware of the power of the Arcana flowing through his body, burning him like the stinging of a thousand bees. A thousand bees that poured their poison into him until it gathered in pockets in his organs, festering. He could almost feel his tissues disintegrating under their attack.

Still the Voids remained, clinging tenaciously to the

dome of silver light. Two had burst, releasing a sickening wave of negation. But so far the rest seemed stable. If the shield collapsed, they would be free to fall onto the island. Then it would all be over.

Caeled was aware of Sarel and Lares on a lower level of the Aethyra, looking up at him. They warped through various images as they tried to find one capable of penetrating to him, but they were constantly repelled by the backwash of power.

Caeled was aware of another sensation; one much less overwhelming than Arcana power. Irritating rather than painful, it was no more than a touch—like an insect crawling through his hair, or a cobweb brushing across his face. He forced himself to ignore it; he could not afford to be distracted now as he concentrated on sending the last of his strength through the Arcana and into the shield of silver light. But he couldn't hold the shield indefinitely . . . and all that remained now was a last desperate chance.

Mock crouched on his heels and pounded on the sleeping man's chest. It seemed as if Caeled was about to wake up, but then he went rigid and slipped into a deeper sleep. Mock was frightened of the one they called Silverhand, with his hideous metal hand and his dark, intense expression. Mock had noticed that he rarely smiled. He preferred people who smiled.

When the Silverhand had filled the central chamber with silver light and for a few glorious moments healed the People, Mock had thought he was wonderful. Standing proudly on two healthy legs, Mock had been prepared to worship him. But then the silver light faded and they all went back to the way they were before. Mock hated him then.

Now the boy vented his frustration on the sleeping man, striking him in the chest, slapping him across the face, shouting at him, begging him to wake up and save his Nana.

✧   ✧   ✧

For the first time since the stone skin had enveloped her, Gwynne felt physical pain.

Unexpectedly, Rasriel had stepped in close to her and swung his cupped hands to clap either side of her head, driving compressed air into her ears. The pain was indescribable. Agony flooded her brain and she cried out.

While she stood dazed, Rasriel struck again. This time his stiffened fingers sought to gouge out one of her eyes. She struck out blindly, trying to knock his hand away. But Rasriel ducked and her stone hand cracked into the wall, pulverizing the soft stone.

The Hieromonach grunted with satisfaction. She was strong, but limited, unable to turn her head, effectively blind on either side. In Baddalaur, the Seekers had trained to fight armored knights, a throwback to an ancient era when roaming bands of knights in lacquered wooden armor terrorized the countryside. The techniques could still be used against a heavier, better protected assailant.

Leaning back to balance himself, Rasriel again lashed out with one foot, striking high with the sole of his foot, taking her across the bridge of the nose. Tears started to her eyes and she backed away, arms flailing. With an effort, Rasriel hefted the woman's morningstar. He darted sideways, moving crablike out of her field of vision. She was off balance; a blow behind the knees would take her down. Then he would pound her head to bloody pulp.

Weeping with frustration, Mock looked at the Spear in Caeled's hands. Maybe Nana could use it herself to fight the mean man. He reached for it, tiny fingers wrapping around the ancient metal haft . . .

Silver light exploded through the cave. It lifted the boy off his feet as it stripped the flesh from his hands and arms. The force hurled his small body across the cave, where it struck at the edge of the cavemouth with sickening impact, then tumbled out and came to a stop almost at Rasriel's feet.

The Hieromonach stared down.

The Spear of the Arcana was clutched in skeleton hands.

With the last threads of his energy, Caeled set the dome of silver light spinning like a child's top. As it spun it collapsed, disintegrating into a huge silvery whirlpool before slamming out of existence with a sound that echoed to the farthest reaches of the Island Sea. The Voids that clung to it were flung off, hurled away by the sheer momentum. Three fell into the sea, where they boiled the water and destroyed countless aquatic life forms before finally sinking to the seabed. There they continued to gnaw until eventually they broke through the earth's crust, releasing a mighty outpouring of molten lava.

The undersea volcano that roared into life obliterated the very Voids which had given it birth.

The three remaining Voids were flung into the midst of the hovering shanti fleet. There they feasted on the New Bred, trapped in their baskets beneath the gaily colored balloons. When one Void touched a balloon the gas-filled bag exploded, sending long streamers of fire shooting out to set other shanti aflame.

Within a matter of heartbeats, the invincible Imperial Fleet of the Duet was devastated. The few survivors leaped frantically from their flaming shanti before they struck the island or the sea.

Amidst the chaos, Caeled's Aethyra form tumbled back toward the World Below. His scream of despair was lost in the Ghost Winds that howled through the thirty layers of the Dreamscape.

Rasriel dropped the morningstar and plucked the Spear from the dead boy's hands. The finger bones disintegrated into powder at a touch. Rasriel shuddered, not from disgust but from reaction as vestiges of Arcana power trembled through his body.

He had been a boy when he first lay with a woman. The memory of that experience, all-encompassing and unforgettable, had remained with him so vividly that he could still feel the shock of pleasure beyond bearing.

Now he felt something similar—but more, much more. Power crackled like lightning around the head of the Spear. Turning the artefact, he pressed its point against Gwynne's unprotected back. He intended to drive it in, trusting the incredible force of the Spear to penetrate even her stony flesh.

The woman . . . changed.

Stone became flesh; what had been monstrous became human.

And in the same instant, as Rasriel stared in wonder at the transformation, a legless man dragged himself out of a hole in the wall and plunged a dagger into the Hieromonach's groin.

Rasriel reacted instinctively, slashing down with the Spear. His blow broke Culp's outstretched arm, then the Spear's head continued on to tear out his throat.

Howling with pain, Rasriel managed to dislodge the knife from his groin. He spun around, expecting to find the Stone Warrior at his throat, but she was crouched on the ground, cradling the burnt body of the boy.

Her form seemed to flicker between flesh and stone. Tears on her face hardened to crusted salt as she wept for yet another innocent life destroyed. Rasriel drew back his arm to strike. Gwynne looked up. In that instant she yearned to be flesh when he struck, so it would end now and the pain—the terrible pain—would be over.

But her wish was not granted. She felt the stone envelop her even as the weapon swung toward her.

"No!"

A gory globe spun through the air to crash into Rasriel's chest. With a cry of disgust, he flinched away from a severed head. It was barely recognizable as human. Most of the flesh had been torn—bitten—away from the cheeks. The eyes, lips and tongue were missing.

Yet enough remained to allow Rasriel to recognize one of his Seekers Reborn.

Even the Hieromonach could not prevent a shriek of horror at the apparition that came floating toward him next. It was nominally female, naked but covered with blood. In its hands it carried the severed heads of the last two Seekers.

"I fed off your creatures." Locking his eyes with hers, Sioraf delicately licked her lips. "Their blood was bitter," she commented with the disapproval of a connoisseur. "How will yours taste, I wonder?"

Rasriel backed away. Holding the Spear before him, he attempted to ward off the vampire. She tossed the two severed heads at his feet and stretched out her arms.

The Spear rendered her form unstable as it had done for the Stone Warrior. Bone and muscle altered, skin stretched, fingers visibly elongated. Her fingernails grew into black talons, wickedly curved. Then her lips drew back from her teeth to reveal tiny but deadly fangs. As the flesh of her face tautened across her cheekbones, she looked more like a death's head than did the appalled Rasriel.

For a moment, he was looking into the face of a demon.

Then she gave a shudder and the monster vanished. In its place stood a beautiful girl—who was somehow more terrifying.

"Rasriel," breathed a voice behind him.

The Hieromonach whirled around. At first he did not recognize the figure that stood in the cavemouth. Then the figure lifted his left hand and it gleamed silver. The hand was holding the Stone.

"Caeled?" whispered Rasriel. "Caeled nam Myriam?"

The old man, white-haired, withered and gaunt, gave a palsied nod. "I am the Silverhand," he said.

CHAPTER FIFTY-SIX

With agonizing slowness the huge metal doors screeched open. The noise they made was the protest of massive, long-rusted machinery being forced, a sound with incredible carrying power which made everyone who heard it flinch.

As the doors parted a sunbeam slanted into the cavern, filling the vast space with natural light. Kichal's shout of triumph resounded even above the hiss of the inflating balloon.

Madran and Anadyr leaned into the wheels, grunting with effort as they strained to turn them further. The doors moved fractionally faster, sliding on their greased rails as if they finally remembered how. Through the widening opening, the scent of sea air tainted with burned meat, shanti effluvia and the metallic tang of magic entered the chamber.

"The Bred have attacked," Madran announced as he peered out anxiously. Anadyr shouldered in beside him. They found themselves gazing down the far side of the cliffs to a strip of stony beach littered with horror.

Without a word, Madran turned and reached down

for Kichal's hand. The former Bred Commander was about to refuse, but the Madra Allta's alarmed expression and Anadyr's rapt silence convinced him.

Kichal scrambled up onto the ledge. He teetered precariously for a moment, then found secure footing. Squinting down towards the beach, he drew in his breath with a sharp gasp.

Black smoke was curling around the headland to the left, and the air was filled with burning scraps from destroyed shanti. On the reddish sand lay the flaming wreckage of two of the craft; in the water beyond, another bobbed on the tide, folds of burning cloth spread like an obscene blanket over the waves. Beneath the cloth, a writhing figure could be seen trying to extricate itself.

The bodies of the New Bred floating in the water were already being attacked by the gulls.

Only a small portion of the invading army had survived the crash onto Home Isle. Broken corpses were strewn across sand and stone in every conceivable posture. Some looked almost human. Others more nearly resembled the monstrous saurians from which they had been developed. One, who had obviously leaped from a falling shanti, had become jammed in a fissure in the cliff face and hung there, scaly arms outflung as if pleading for mercy. The body was still burning.

"The New Bred haven't attacked," Kichal said in wonder. "They have been attacked." He looked upward so suddenly he lost his balance and swayed backward. Anadyr caught him just in time. "Look there, Anadyr!" Kichal exclaimed, pointing. "What do you see?"

"Nothing. Blue sky."

"But what's happened to the rest of the shanti fleet? There were two hundred in that sky last night."

"Caeled!" Madran cried. "The Silverhand must have destroyed them!"

"Or maybe they have simply landed somewhere," suggested Anadyr.

Kichal shook his head. "I think not. Listen. What do you hear?"

"Nothing," the scarred man replied. "Wind. Sea gulls."

"If the Duet's army had landed anywhere on this island and were alive and able to fight, you would hear them. They sound appallingly bestial."

"Not the New Bred." A muscular figure with an abnormally low forehead rose from below their feet, scrambling up the cliff face. Drawing a sword from his belt, Abhel slashed at Kichal's legs. "We can fight silently— and we kill traitors!"

Anadyr grabbed Kichal and tumbled backwards into the chamber just in time to avoid the swinging sword. Madran, however, leaped upward so the weapon passed harmlessly beneath his feet. When he landed he was balanced on his bare toes. "A weapon!" he shouted, regretting having laid his sickle aside. "Quickly!"

Although he was half-stunned from his fall, Kichal managed to draw his own sword from its scabbard. He hurled it to the Allta, who caught it in time to parry Abhel's next swipe. The two weapons clanged together. Madran broke free first. Taking advantage of his higher position, he hacked downward, the sword scything through the New Bred's white hair.

Abhel's swift reflexes barely saved him. He flinched to one side with pale ichor pouring into his eyes from a deep wound in his forehead.

He was badly disoriented. The destruction of the shanti fleet had come so swiftly. One moment he had been watching the Voids clinging to the silver dome over the island, and the next moment the dome was spinning furiously. When it collapsed, it flung the Voids away like stones from a slingshot.

A heartbeat later the Voids catapulted into the fleet. Abhel had caught a brief glimpse of one of them through his sister's eyes and then he felt it take her, absorbing her into a ravenous howling nothingness. Within another heartbeat a burning shanti had smashed into his own craft, sending both spiralling out of control towards the beach.

Two score of the New Bred survived the crash—none without injury. Abhel was aware of the pain of cracked ribs, but he knew how to ignore pain. It was as nothing compared to his sister's unending scream that echoed and reechoed within his head.

He had thrown back his head and cried out her name, but the sound echoed mockingly off the cliffs, returning to him broken and distorted. Ebhena was gone . . . yet she still existed inside his skull, screaming, always screaming.

Falling to his knees, he had pounded an impotent fist against the ground. The action momentarily lessened the voice in his head so he struck again, deliberately cracking knuckles and tearing his own flesh until Ebhena's scream faded.

But he knew it would never entirely leave him.

With a howl of rage, he had surged to his feet. He needed to kill . . . to hurt and maim . . .

Leading the surviving New Bred, Abhel had attempted to gain entrance to the caves, but all the cavemouths were sealed with stones. Some had been coated with fish oil that the defenders set ablaze. One of the New Bred, a female, tore at the stones blocking an entrance even as the flames ate into her flesh.

Then a singular noise attracted Abhel's attention. A grating, anguished squeal that could not be made by any living thing seemed to be coming from the far side of the cliffs. Leaving a handful of New Bred at the burning entrance to try to force access, Abhel led the remainder around the headland, seeking the source of the sound.

Running ahead of the others, he rounded the headland in time to see the cliff face moving. Rock and shale and crusted earth were sliding down in a miniature avalanche. Earthquake! The Voids had brought on an earthquake!

Then he realized that he was seeing reflected sunlight. Part of the cliff face was metallic . . . and it was moving.

Instinct and pain and the terrible lust to avenge his sister's death drove him upward, knowing instinctively that this was another entrance to the caves. The cliffs on this side of the island were steep but not perpendicular, and studded with stone outcroppings that served as steps and handholds. As he climbed, he realized the grating noise he heard was the sound of huge, ancient doors, slowly opening.

Reaching the aperture, he caught a glimpse of the interior of the cave. Inside—impossible!—was what appeared to be a giant shanti.

Ducking down, Abhel had dropped below the level of the doorway to await events. As the doors slid back even further two men appeared in the opening: a shaggy blond man with the Allta scent strong about him, and an immense, scarred individual. The Allta turned away briefly and seemed to bend down; then a third person stood beside him, someone Abhel knew. Kichal.

The former Bred commander obviously had betrayed them, sold them out to these island savages . . . and been responsible for Ebhena's death. Pressing himself close to the cliff face, the outraged Abhel crept closer.

The base of the door was just above his head. A scramble and a leap and he would be inside.

He could hear the humans talking. Kichal was casually discussing the Bred, no doubt betraying them further. ". . . you would hear them. They sound appallingly bestial."

Abhel had reacted even before he realized, leaping up, slashing at the humans. Kichal and the other one disappeared from the doorway. The Allta avoided his sword, and then somehow there was a weapon in the Allta's hand and Abhel felt a terrible burning sear across his forehead. With an inarticulate cry he turned and slithered back down the slope to join the other New Bred survivors on the beach.

No matter how badly he was wounded, it was his duty to Blessed Sarel to lead them in an attack.

❖   ❖   ❖

With a mighty scramble, Anadyr regained the ledge.
He had his chain in one fist now, and his scarred face
was alight with battle lust. He bent to give Kichal a hand
and soon the other man was beside him, carrying a length
of sharpened metal. Madran silently handed Kichal his
sword in exchange for the metal spar.

Armed, ready, the three watched the New Bred
survivors stream around the headland and race toward
the cliff face. It was not as sheer as on the other side.
Abhel had already proved it was climbable. And the doors
now gaped wide.

"If they get in they will butcher everyone," Kichal
warned.

Anadyr whirled his chain through the air, creating a
sound like the dangerous hum of angry hornets. "We won't
let them get in," he promised grimly.

"There must be thirty or forty of them," Kichal said
as he looked down. "Three of us against so many?"

Shouts and cries filled the chamber behind them. They
turned as a score of the People flooded into the room,
clutching the new weapons Gwynne had made for them.
They swarmed toward the open doors and began pushing
barrels and cylinders against the wall to allow them to
climb up. There was no room for them on the ledge,
but they crowded as close as they could. There were so
many they got in each other's way.

Kichal glanced at Anadyr. "Are you with me, no matter
what happens?"

The Islander nodded.

Kichal said to Madran, "Keep three of the People with
you and hold this entrance."

"And what will you be doing?" the Allta wanted to
know.

Kichal looked down at the rapidly approaching New
Bred, then turned to address the People. "Will you fight
with me for your island?"

Their shout echoed through the chamber.

"Then let's go!" With a wild cry, Kichal dropped from the doorway onto the sloping cliff face and began a frantic scramble toward the beach below.

Anadyr followed him without a moment's hesitation.

And the People streamed out behind them. They stumbled and slithered down the cliff to challenge the invaders, men and women together, a little flood of brave, tattooed people.

In chilling silence, the New Bred ran to meet them.

Abhel was the first to die. He was impaled on Kichal's sword and his skull was crushed by Anadyr's chain. He only had one brief moment in which to be grateful he would not hear Ebhena screaming any more.

From his vantage point in the doorway, Madran watched as the People joined battle with the inhuman invaders. He shook his head in admiration. The Islanders fought as fearlessly as the New Bred, but their courage was born of love, not hate. They loved Home Isle; they would not relinquish it to anyone.

The tide of battle surged back and forth. For a time it seemed as if love would win. The People began to drive their enemy back toward the sea, step by bitterly contested step. In the forefront of the fighting Kichal's sword wove a deadly pattern; Anadyr's chain sang its furious song.

But the New Bred were unremittingly savage. One by one and two by two, the People fell. Madran's large brown eyes mourned each of them in turn, and those who crowded with him in the doorway moaned aloud with every fatality. As they died, the New Bred began to advance once more.

Then, just when it looked as if the battle would be lost, a second band of tattooed men and women came running around the headland.

At the sight of the reinforcements Madran lost all restraint. With a yelp of joy, he scrambled down to join them.

CHAPTER FIFTY-SEVEN

An old man stepped out of the doorway, carrying the Stone in one hand. At the sight of him, Sioraf stifled a scream.

With a creaking of arthritic joints, he knelt on the ground beside Gwynne. The Stone Warrior was still holding the burned and broken body of young Mock. The sound which came from deep inside her belly was neither a sob nor a moan, but a grunt of mortal anguish. Caeled's ancient face twisted in pity.

Reaching out, he touched her shoulder with his metal hand. For a single instant her human form returned. The look on her face was even worse than the sound she was making, an expression beyond the limits of grief. Then, to Caeled's relief, her body returned to stone and her face became a mask once more.

"This boy was trying to warn you," she whispered.

"He was trying to save you," Caeled replied. Leaning his weight on her hard shoulder, he painfully levered himself to his feet. When he turned to look at Rasriel, his old acquaintance was barely recognizable. He did not fully realize how much he too had changed, however.

Through the medium of Caeled, the Arcana had created the Silverlight. And as Caeled ran out of energy to maintain the shield, the two Arcana had begun to feed off his own life essence. When he lay down in the cave he had appeared to be a man of thirty-odd cycles. When he awoke again he had aged forty cycles more.

Even Rasriel, whose bony face was now deeply etched with dissolute lines, looked younger than he.

Caeled attempted to draw a deep breath but his lungs would not expand properly. From deep within them came a phlegmy rattle. His heart fluttered in his chest like a wounded bird, and black spots flickered around the edges of his vision.

He realized then that he was dying.

Rasriel knew it too. His thin lips drew back from his teeth in a vicious smirk. "The Spoken One?" he said mockingly. "I always knew that you were not the Spoken One. Look at you now—withered and broken by the Arcana. The true Spoken One would have wielded them with impunity."

Caeled replied in a cracked and reedy voice, "Everything has a price."

"Even the Arcana?" Rasriel sneered.

"Especially the Arcana."

The Hieromonach gestured with the Spear, drawing tendrils of cold green light on the air. "Yet you used Arcana power for this . . . to protect these miserable people and their wretched island? You wasted the power on them and destroyed yourself in the process. That is a high price to pay for so little. You are a fool, Caeled Silverhand."

"So you say." Caeled's shoulders slumped. His voice could scarcely be heard. Sioraf tried to go to him but he waved her back.

Rasriel said, "You did not make proper use of the Arcana, but I will. I have one, now give me the other."

Caeled shook his head. "I will not . . ." he began, then stopped.

Flickering insubstantially behind the Hieromonach appeared the Duet. Their Aethyra images were twisted and misshapen. Wild-haired Sarel looked like a sapling struck by lightning. Lares was thickened and brutish, more like a Gor Allta than one of humankind.

The old man smiled. "Your masters have come," he told Rasriel.

As the Hieromonach glanced over his shoulder, Gwynne lunged for him. Her stone hands closed on his neck and she smashed him against the wall. Light blazed between them. Then the stone melted from Gwynne's flesh one final time and she slowly sank to her knees. The head of the Spear was buried between her breasts.

Rasriel cruelly twisted the Spear before wrenching it free. With a superhuman effort the woman crawled to the body of the child, shuddered once, and then lay still.

Sioraf dropped to her knees beside Gwynne. She tore open the warrior's leather jerkin and wiped away the surface blood. More gushed forth immediately. Sioraf spat into the palms of her hands and then rubbed the spittle into the wound, watching the vampir saliva bubble as it attempted to coagulate the blood.

She tried again and gave a relieved sigh . . . until she realized the rate of flow was slowing because the Stone Warrior's heart had ceased to beat.

Sioraf raised her chin and looked at Caeled. When their eyes met, she slowly shook her head.

"Give me the Stone," Rasriel commanded, gingerly feeling his bruised throat.

Caeled's heart was racing with a strange, irregular beat. His chest was on fire; his vision blurred.

When Rasriel choked out a painful laugh, the two misshapen images behind him mimicked his mirth. "If I had known that ugly woman was important to you, I would have killed her more slowly," he said. He lowered the Spear until the point was aimed at Sioraf's eyes. "And this one, is she important to you also?"

Caeled tried to remain expressionless, but he was losing control over his body and his face betrayed his concern.

Rasriel grinned his feral grin. "Ah yes, she is; I can see it in your eyes. So I shall kill her too. While you watch. Or perhaps it would be more amusing to scar her and destroy this pretty face . . ." The Spear moved. A thin thread of red appeared on Sioraf's cheek.

Without blinking the vampir ran her finger across the wound, sealing it, then popped her finger into her mouth.

"Aaah, it seems I must kill her," said Rasriel without regret.

"No . . . !" Caeled began, but Rasriel was already thrusting the Spear at Sioraf's throat.

The vampir's speed was startling. Giving a violent swing of her head, she trapped the Spear in the tangle of her dark curls. Then her long-nailed hands wrapped around the shaft of the weapon, holding it with a strength her slender form belied.

"Now, Caeled," she said in her whispery voice.

Torn between wrenching the Spear away from Sioraf or turning toward Caeled, Rasriel hesitated a moment too long. The old man flung himself forward with the Stone clutched in his silver hand. He brought his left arm around in a wide arc, catching the Hieromonach in the ribs. The sound of breaking bone was clearly audible.

For a moment the two men were linked, Caeled to the Stone, Rasriel to the Spear. Then, as the circle of power closed, light blossomed around the two to enclose them in a milky globe.

Sioraf was flung against the wall by the backwash of energy. The dead bodies of Gwynne and little Mock twitched and spasmed with brief, unnatural life.

The dazed vampir saw Caeled and Rasriel locked in mortal combat while massive raw power crackled all around them. Tiny globules of molten silver dripped from the sphere that encased them. When the droplets struck the ground they lost form and collapsed into gleaming puddles.

And then two beasts appeared behind Rasriel, male and female, with human faces but the bodies of monsters. Reaching into the globe, they laid their hands on the shoulders of the Hieromonach. He stiffened. The last vestige of color drained from his face as they nourished him with their malevolence.

Silver light flowed from Caeled, but turned bruise-purple before it touched the Hieromonach and reversed its course in a way no light should do. It flowed back into Caeled's body and he visibly aged in that moment, becoming more frail, still closer to death.

Sioraf was scrambling to her feet when footsteps pounded in the tunnel and Madran in his were-shape, followed by Kichal and Anadyr, came running up. Kichal and Anadyr halted in horror at the scene before them. But Madran never hesitated.

With a howl he launched himself through the air. He left the ground as a giant wolfhound, but by the time he struck the milky globe he wore his human form. He slammed all his weight into the old man who was Caeled, knocking him free from the sphere.

Both men hit the ground hard and lay still.

Within the globe Rasriel, drawing on the twins' dark strength, had already launched his final attack on the Silverhand. A wave of visible hatred, red with rage and yellow with envy, intensified by the Spear, pulsed from the Hieromonach. It was meant to envelop Caeled and suffocate him like a fly caught in amber.

But Caeled was no longer in the sphere.

The tide of hate washed around the interior of the globe, coating its translucent sides, staining them with its own ugliness and then splashing back over the Hieromonach. There was a singular image of a man writhing in agony as he stabbed at the enveloping liquid with the Spear. Then the globe burst like a foul pustule, spraying filth over everything. The smell was nauseating.

Kichal caught Anadyr and pulled him away; Sioraf

dropped to the ground, shielding her head with her arms.

When they dared to look again, Rasriel and the twins had vanished. So too had the Arcana Spear.

As he recovered consciousness, Madran reverted to his were-shape. Within moments he was on his four feet, licking Caeled's face and whining anxiously.

Caeled looked younger, as if he had regained some of his lost youth in the battle with Rasriel. He still appeared far older than his chronological age, however. With his lined face and frosted hair, he might have been a man of fifty cycles. He opened his eyes. He sat bolt upright with a cry of anguish. White light danced on his silver hand, which still clutched the Stone. Ignoring the others, he crawled to where Gwynne's body lay.

"No!" he howled. "No."

Kneeling beside her, Caeled placed the Stone on the wound in her chest, then rested his silver hand atop it. He closed his eyes and turned his face upward, concentrating.

Like a puff of smoke he moved out of his physical body into the lowest level of the Aethyra.

There the twins, with the body of Rasriel between them, were waiting. Somehow they had succeeded in dragging the man and the Spear he held into the Dreamscape with them.

When they saw Caeled approach they struck out at him, lashing him with a whip of fire. But Caeled's grief and anger gave him strength. He assumed a mirror as his Aethyra image, reflecting the Duet's weapon back at them intensified by his own fury.

The blow knocked Rasriel's body from their grasp. Still clutching the Spear, it drifted closer to Caeled.

The twins promptly assumed a single form—an entwined ebon and azure image of crystalline beauty—and flowed toward Caeled.

An unexpected shape interposed itself between them and their prey. They were moving too fast to stop. The brittle crystal shape shattered against the Aethyra spirit of the Stone Warrior.

Standing beside her, clutching her waist, whole and perfect in every way, the spirit of Mock beamed with pride.

"I knew your ka would linger," Caeled managed to say in an exhausted voice. With an effort he dragged Rasriel's body closer. "There is enough life force left in this one to revitalize you, I think."

Gwynne shook her head. "You must give Mock the chance. Restore his living body to him."

The Spear fell from Rasriel's limp fingers. Gwynne reached for it, but her fingers passed through the shaft. At the same moment Caeled realized that her image was fading.

Behind her Mock winked out of existence.

"Let me die in peace, Caeled." Gwynne's voice was a ghostly thread. "Retrieve the Spear and I will go."

The Spear or Rasriel's life force . . . he did not have enough strength left to seize them both . . .

In the physical world, Caeled opened his eyes and made the choice.

The Silverhand glowed, its brilliance seeping into the Stone. Tiny stars of Silverlight began to sparkle in the hole in the center of the Stone.

Minute particles of vivid color danced on the surface of Gwynne's skin, lingering for several moments before they vanished.

Then the Silverlight faded.

And Gwynne opened her eyes. After a moment's confusion, their green depths cleared. "Mock?" she asked hoarsely.

Unable to answer, Caeled merely shook his head.

"Why, Caeled?" she whispered, "why did it have to be me?"

"Because it was the right choice," the weary man replied.

CHAPTER FIFTY-EIGHT

Decisions made.

And what is done, I cannot undo.

Nor would I wish to.

When I called down the Silverlight to protect the island, I knew the risks. I knew it would age me and possibly even destroy the Arcana. But the lives of the People were more important then any ancient artefact.

When I chose to draw the life force from Rasriel's body rather then retrieve the Spear, it was the same choice. As I knelt beside Gwynne's body I could feel her indomitable spirit clinging tenaciously to her flesh, though it was weakening fast. I knew I would find her in the Aethyra. Her love of the boy and the children—aye—and her love for me, would keep her close as long as possible.

But if I hesitated any longer, her ka would have been swept away by the Ghost Wind.

The Spear, however, is lost. Yet in truth, I do not mourn it overmuch. I am aged now past fifty cycles, and to use the Arcana again before I have regained at least a little of my former strength would undoubtedly destroy me.

Briefly I was older, much older. But when I fought Rasriel and the circle was closed—Spear to Stone through Rasriel and me—our life forces mingled. I took a little of his strength, he a little of my age. Then I stole the last of his life force from him to imbue Gwynne's spirit, condemning him to forever wander the lower reaches of the Aethyra as a shade.

I have no pity for him.

Now we will board the metal shanti and head north in search of the remaining Arcana. As we travel I shall try to rest and recover. My beloved Sioraf will accompany me, as will Madran, brave, loyal Madran; I owe him more than I can say. Anadyr wants to come with us too. He claims he knows the location of the Elder city of Lowstone and can guide us there. Gwynne will remain on Home Isle, and Kichal has undertaken to raise and train a truly professional army from among the inhabitants.

The New Bred are destroyed, the last of them wiped out by the People. But Home Isle is not free from threat; there are always dangers for those who live in the Island Sea. And I have little doubt that the Duet will send another army eventually, if only because they cannot bear to be defeated. Should a new invasion come, however, Gwynne and Kichal will see that the People are ready.

They have scavenged some of the New Bred's weapons from the smouldering remains of the shanti fleet, so they will have the nucleus of a real armory. Having defeated the most terrifying of enemies this time, the People know they will be able to do so again.

There is a certain magic in confidence.

As for me, whether I wish it or not I am about to set out on my quest once more. When I have the Sword and the Cup, perhaps they will enable me to retrieve the missing Spear.

Once I would have done this in obedience to my destiny. In Baddalaur I was told that I was fated to change the world by replacing chaos with order. I was assured that total order was desirable—a concept I now question, as I have come to question all my teachings.

Now I am undertaking the quest so that those who struggled and died will not have died in vain.

They longed for a better world.

I will create that world in their memory.

From the Journal of Caeled Silverhand